This is the back of the book.
You wouldn't want to spoil a great ending!

This book is printed "manga-style," in the authentic Japanese right-to-left format. Since none of the artwork has been flipped or altered, readers get to experience the story just as the creator intended. You've been asking for it, so TOKYOPOP® delivered: authentic, hot-off-the-press, and far more fun!

DIRECTIONS

If this is your first time reading manga-style, here's a quick guide to help you understand how it works.

It's easy… just start in the top right panel and follow the numbers. Have fun, and look for more 100% authentic manga from TOKYOPOP®!

The breakout manga that put CLAMP on the map!

RG VEDA
聖伝

At the dawn of creation, the world was a beautiful and tranquil place. When a powerful warlord rebelled against the king, a violent, chaotic age began.... Three hundred years later, a group of noble warriors embarks on a quest to find the prophesied Six Stars before the land is torn apart!

PASSION FRUIT
BY MARI OKAZAKI

Passion Fruit is a unique, unforgettable collection of stylish stories that touch upon our most private inhibitions and examine our deepest desires. This uncompromising blend of realism and raw emotion focuses on women exploring the vulnerability and frailty of the human condition. With uninhibited authenticity and pathos, passion proves to be stranger than fiction.

© Mari Okazaki

PLANET BLOOD
BY TAE-HYUNG KIM

Universal Century 0091. The Mars and Moon colonies fight for repatriation rights over the newly restored Earth. Amidst the bloody battle, one soldier, is rendered unconscious— only to awaken in an entirely different world enmeshed in an entirely different war…

© KIM TAE-HYUNG, DAIWON C.I. Inc.

T TEEN AGE 13+

LILING-PO
BY AKO YUTENJI

Master thief Liling-Po has finally been captured! However, the government offers a chance for Liling-Po to redeem himself. All he has to do is "retrieve" some special items—eight mystic treasures that are fabled to grant their owners any wish!

© Ako Yutenji

T TEEN AGE 13+

D•N•ANGEL

BY YUKIRU SUGISAKI

VOLUME 7

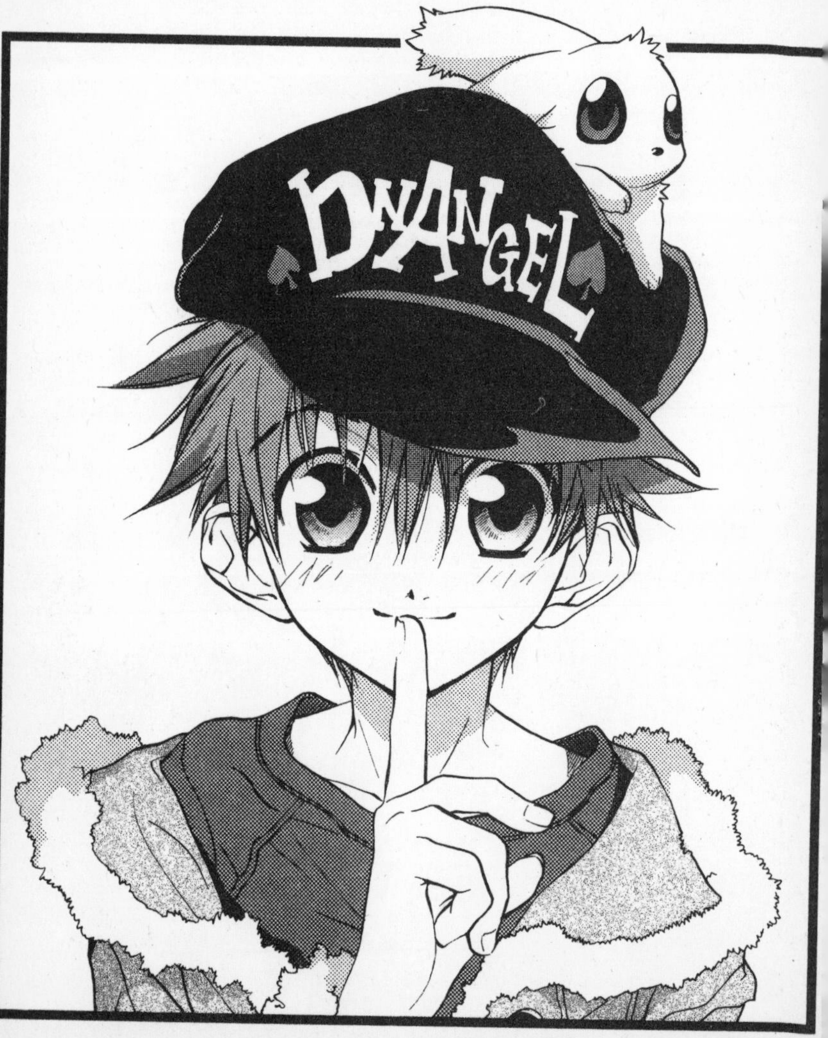

DNANGEL

& STORY

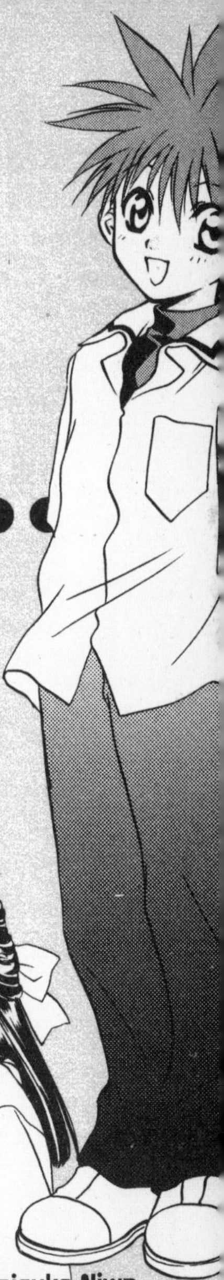

Daisuke and Dark's relationships with Riku and her sister Risa have gotten completely mixed up and complicated—but for now, at least Daisuke and Riku have finally made up and seem to be getting along fine. Things got more complicated however, when Satoshi's "other half" emerged and attacked Daisuke! Dark was able to rescue him, but it's beginning to look as though there's some strange connection between Dark and Satoshi...finally, when Dark and Daisuke went on their latest mission, to steal the "Second Hand of Time," it somehow came back to life and kidnapped Daisuke, pulling him into a mysterious world of snow!

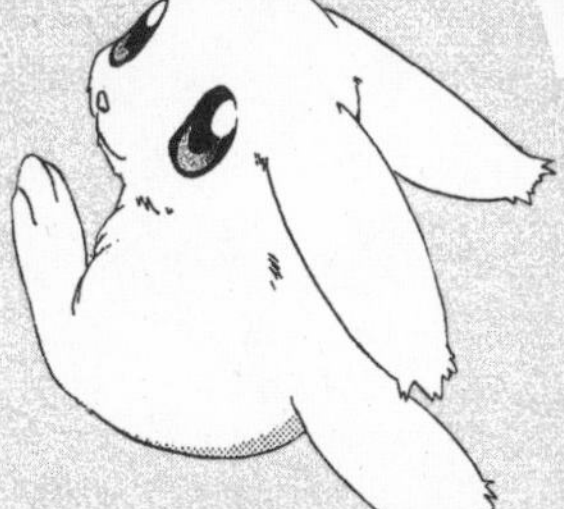

Wiz

A mysterious animal who acts as Dark's familiar and who can transform into many things, including Dark's black wings. He can also transform himself into Dark or Daisuke.

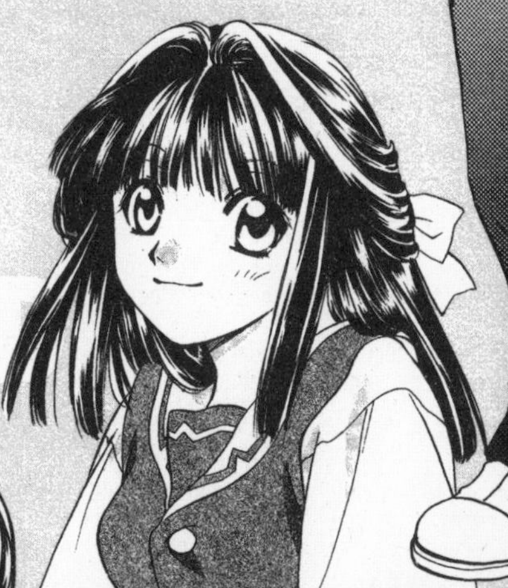

Risa Harada (younger sister)

Daisuke's first crush. Daisuke confessed his love to her...but she rejected him. She's been in love with Dark since the first time she saw him on TV.

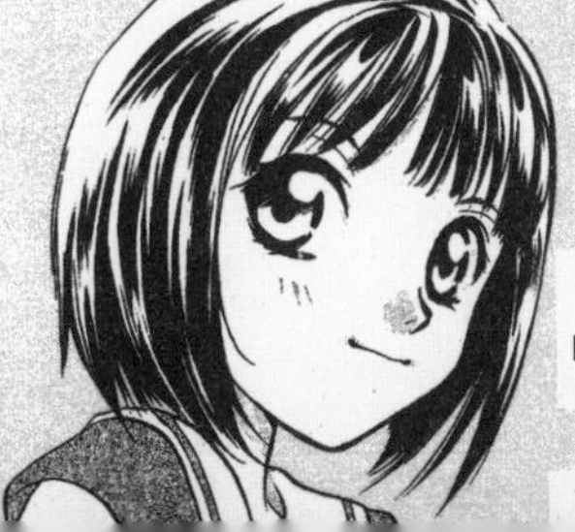

Riku Harada (older sister)

Risa's identical twin sister. She and Daisuke have fallen for each other.

Daisuke Niwa

A 14-year-old student at Azumano Middle School. He has a unique genetic condition that causes him to transform into the infamous Phantom Thief Dark whenever he has romantic feelings.

CHARACTERS

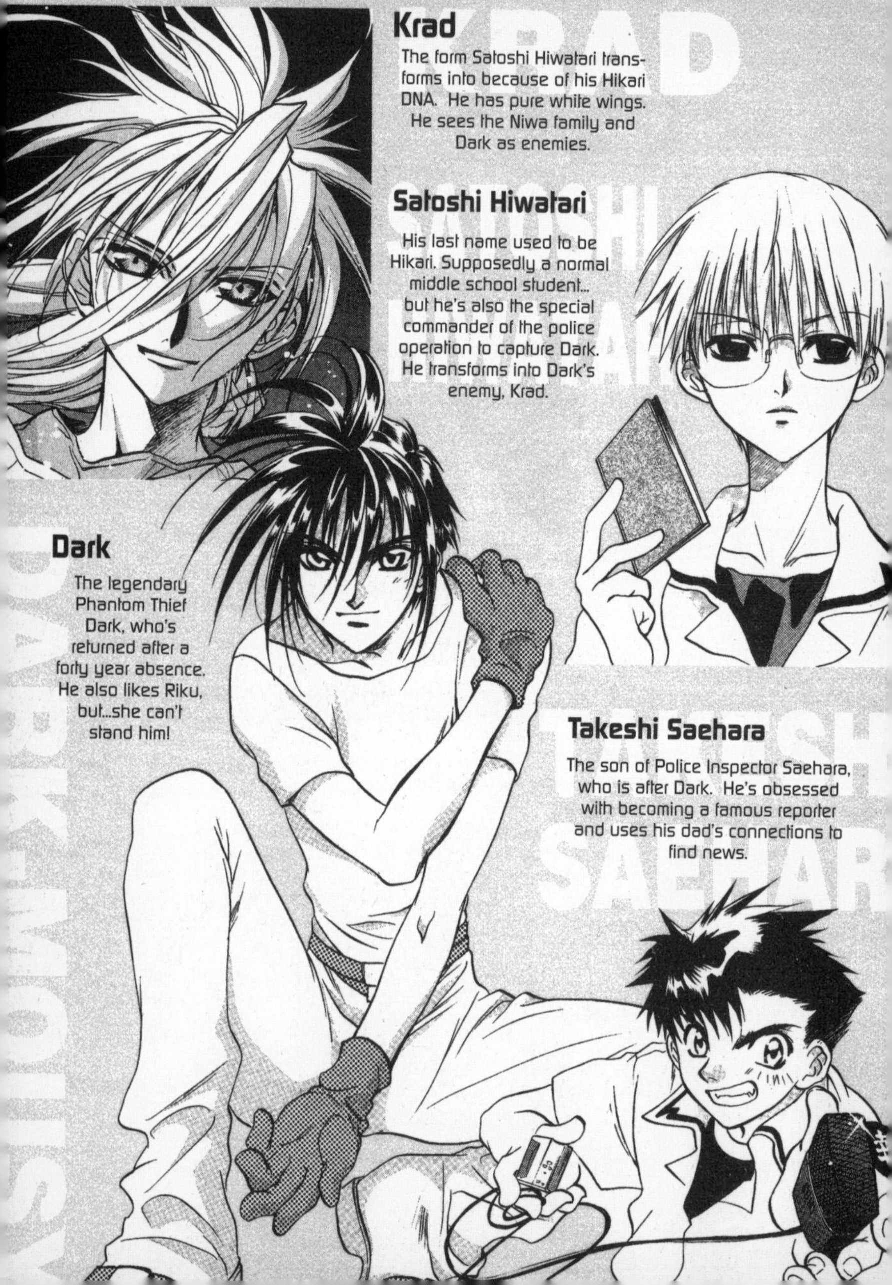

Krad

The form Satoshi Hiwatari transforms into because of his Hikari DNA. He has pure white wings. He sees the Niwa family and Dark as enemies.

Satoshi Hiwatari

His last name used to be Hikari. Supposedly a normal middle school student... but he's also the special commander of the police operation to capture Dark. He transforms into Dark's enemy, Krad.

Dark

The legendary Phantom Thief Dark, who's returned after a forty year absence. He also likes Riku, but...she can't stand him!

Takeshi Saehara

The son of Police Inspector Saehara, who is after Dark. He's obsessed with becoming a famous reporter and uses his dad's connections to find news.

D•N•ANGEL Vol. 7
Created by Yukiru Sugisaki

Translation - Alethea and Athena Nibley
English Adaptation - Sarah Dyer
Copy Editor - Peter Ahlstrom
Retouch and Lettering - Bowen Park
Production Artist - Eric Pineda
Cover Layout - Jennifer Nunn

Editor - Bryce P. Coleman
Digital Imaging Manager - Chris Buford
Pre-Press Manager - Antonio DePietro
Production Managers - Jennifer Miller and Mutsumi Miyazaki
Art Director - Matt Alford
Managing Editor - Jill Freshney
VP of Production - Ron Klamert
Editor-in-Chief - Mike Kiley
President and C.O.O. - John Parker
Publisher and C.E.O. - Stuart Levy

A  Manga

TOKYOPOP Inc.
5900 Wilshire Blvd. Suite 2000
Los Angeles, CA 90036

E-mail: info@TOKYOPOP.com
Come visit us online at www.TOKYOPOP.com

ISBN: 1-59182-956-9

First TOKYOPOP printing: April 2005
10 9 8 7 6 5 4 3 2 1
Printed in the USA

Volume 7

By

Yukiru Sugisaki

HAMBURG // LONDON // LOS ANGELES // TOKYO

CONTENTS

THE SECOND HAND OF TIME PART 3

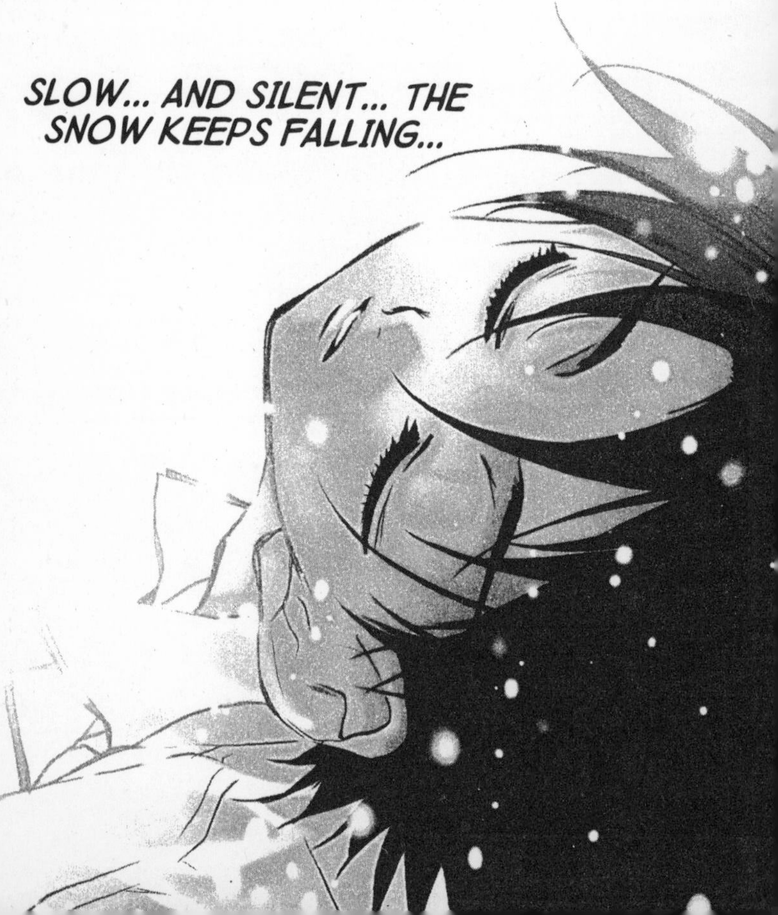
SLOW... AND SILENT... THE SNOW KEEPS FALLING...

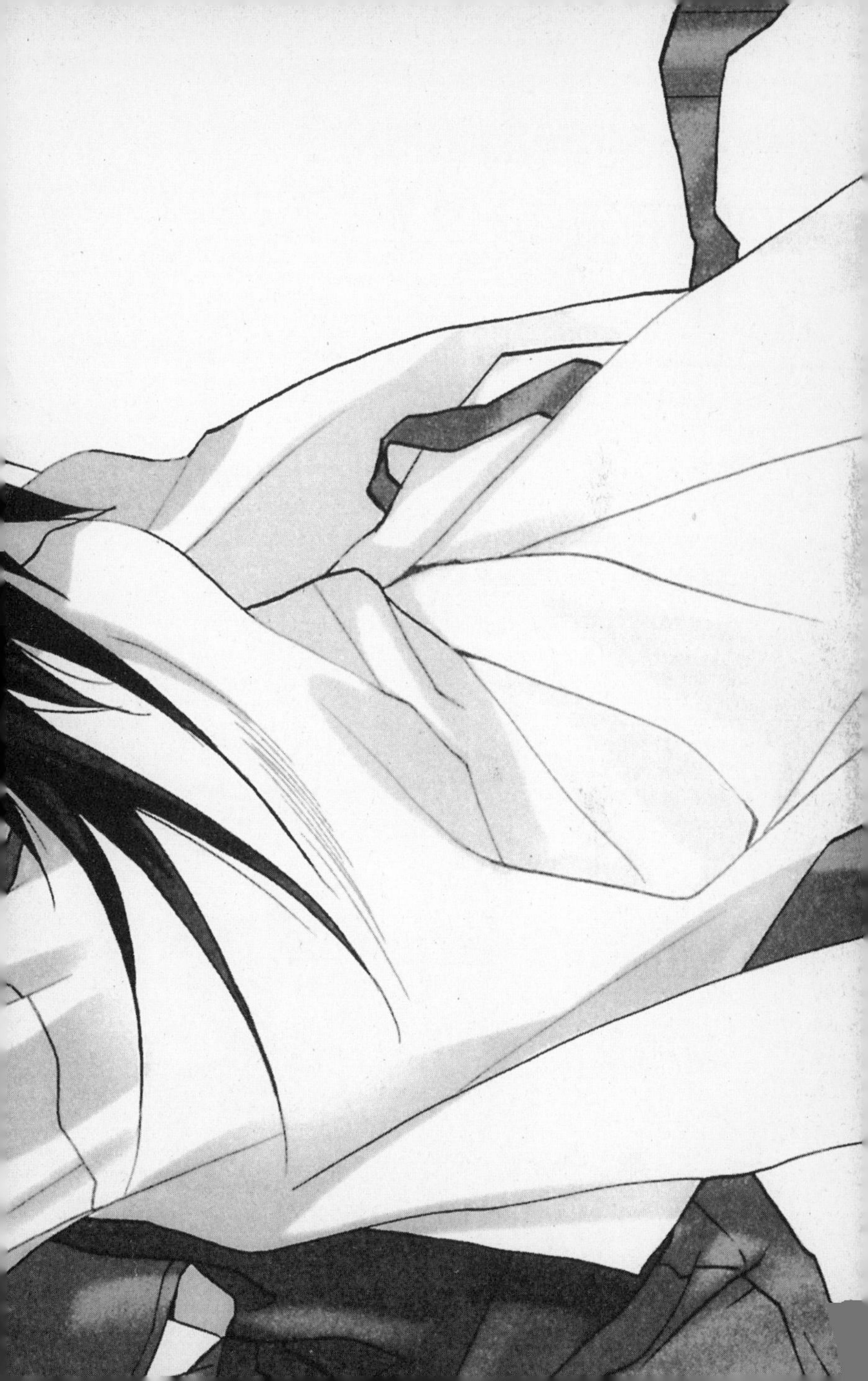

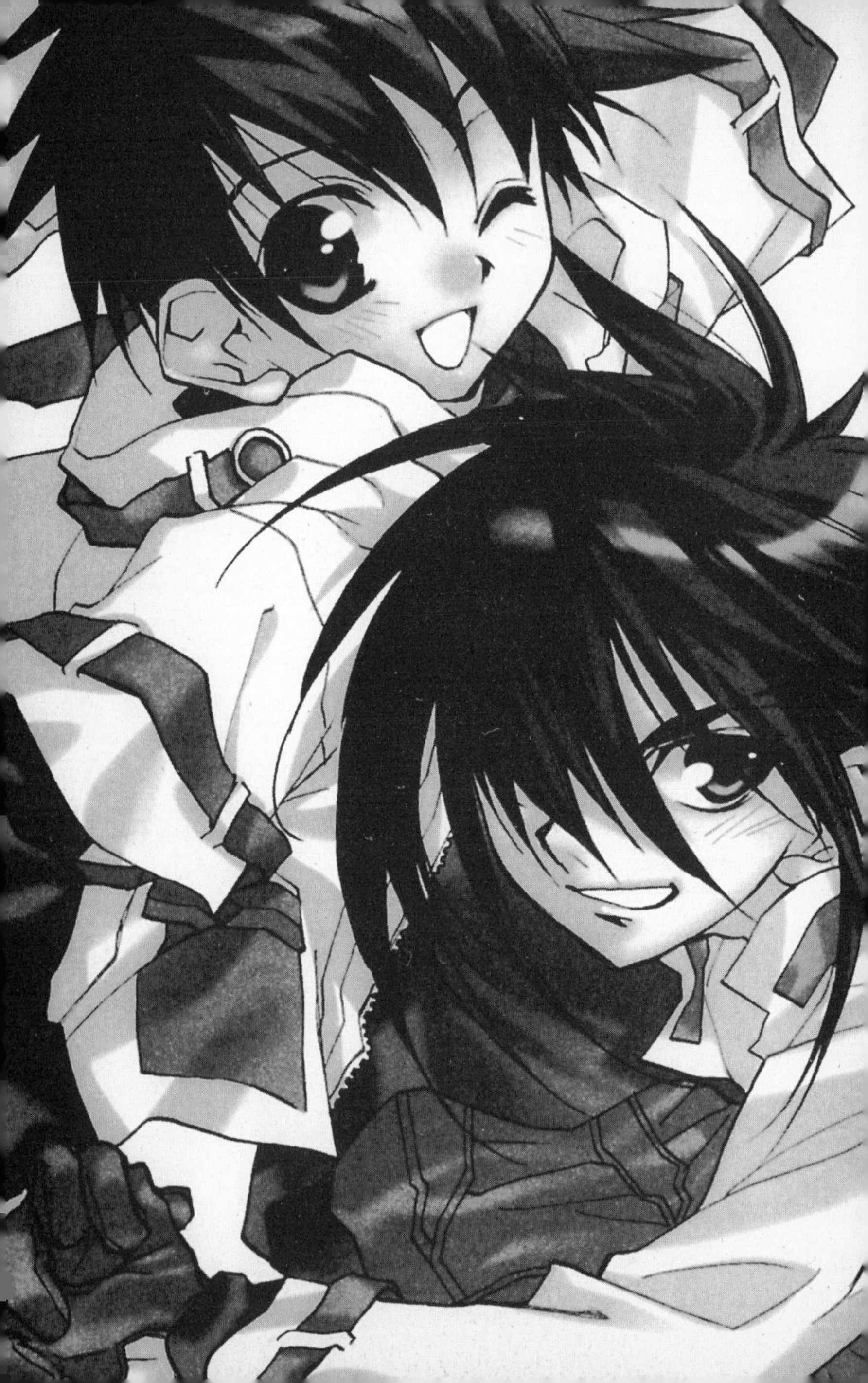

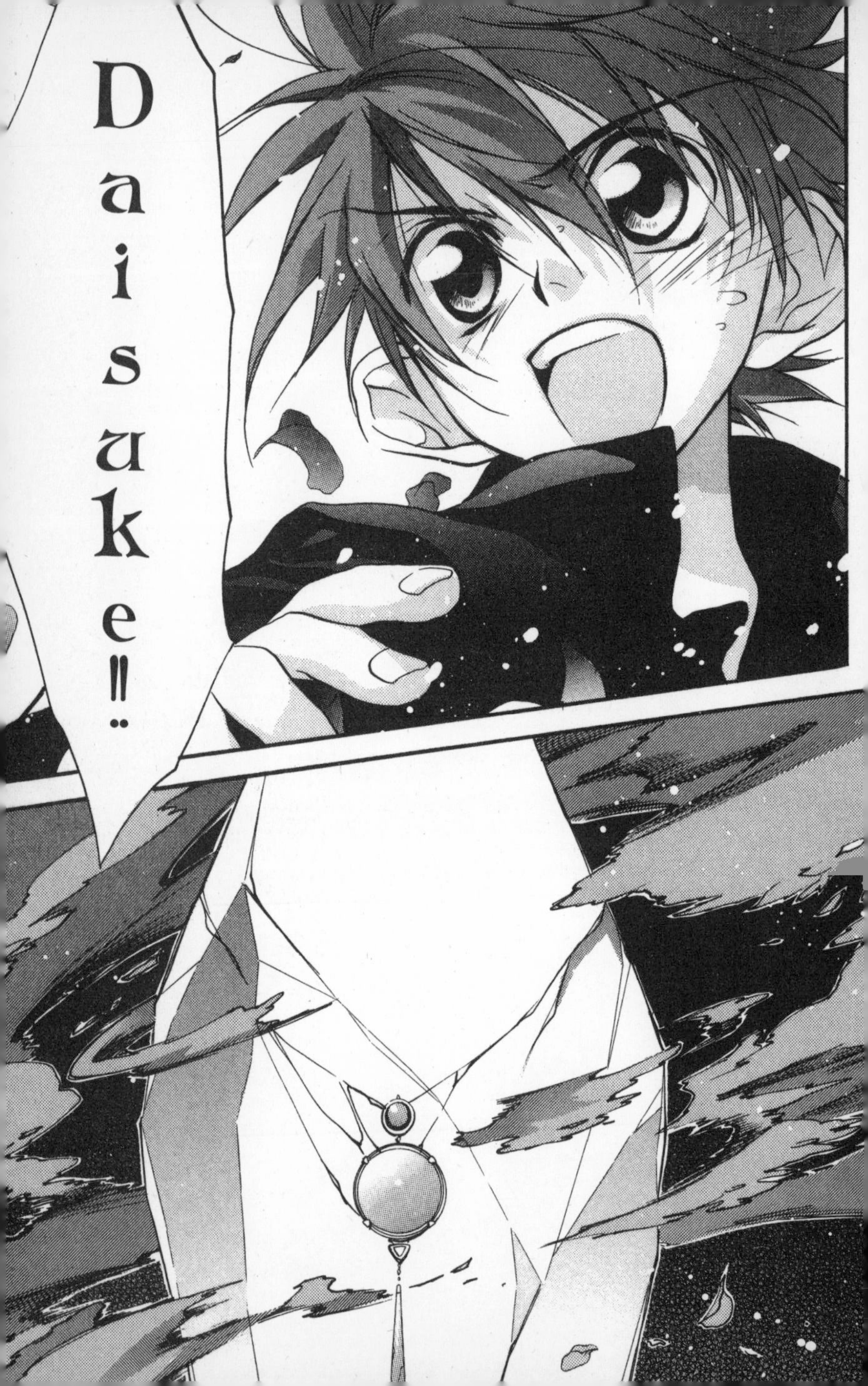
Daisuke!!

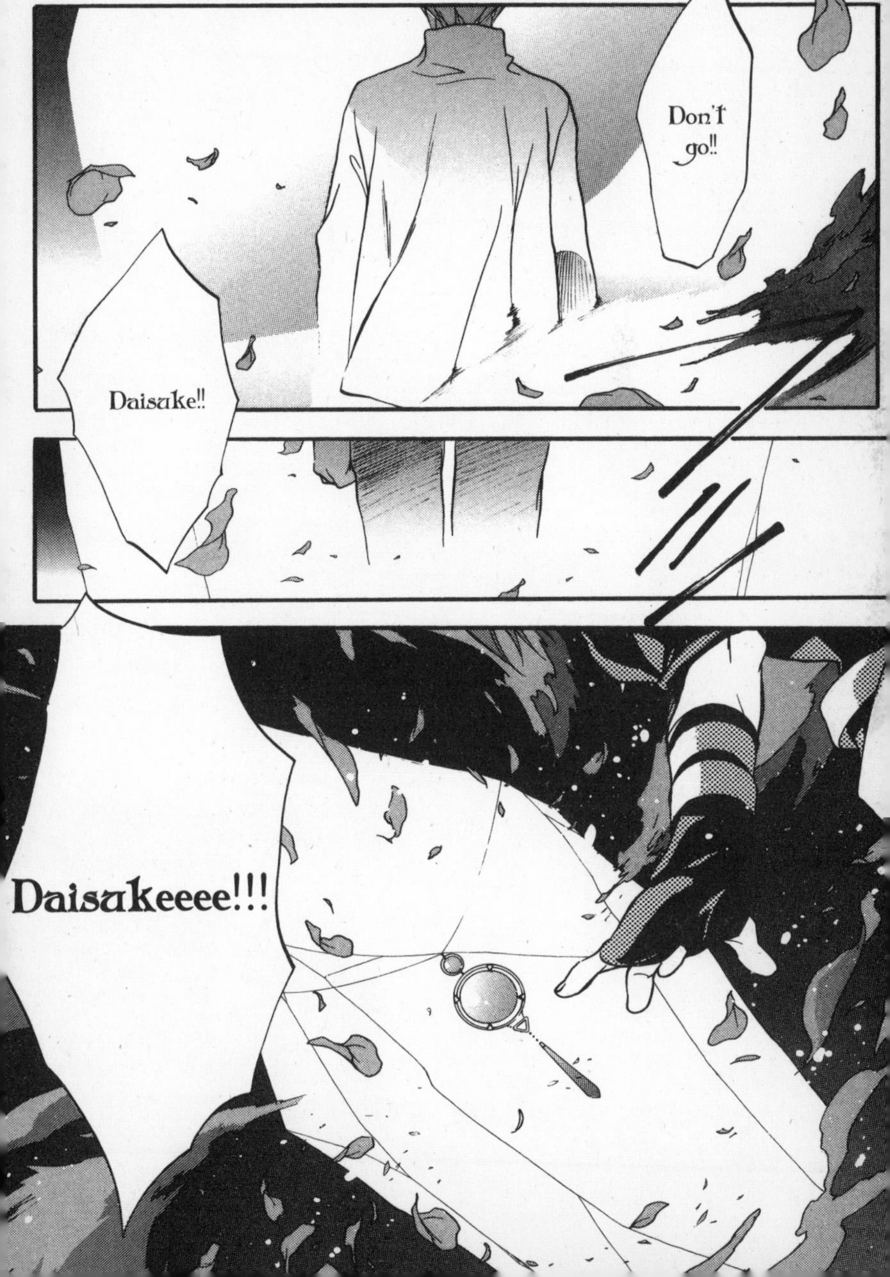
Don't go!!
Daisuke!!
Daisukeeee!!!

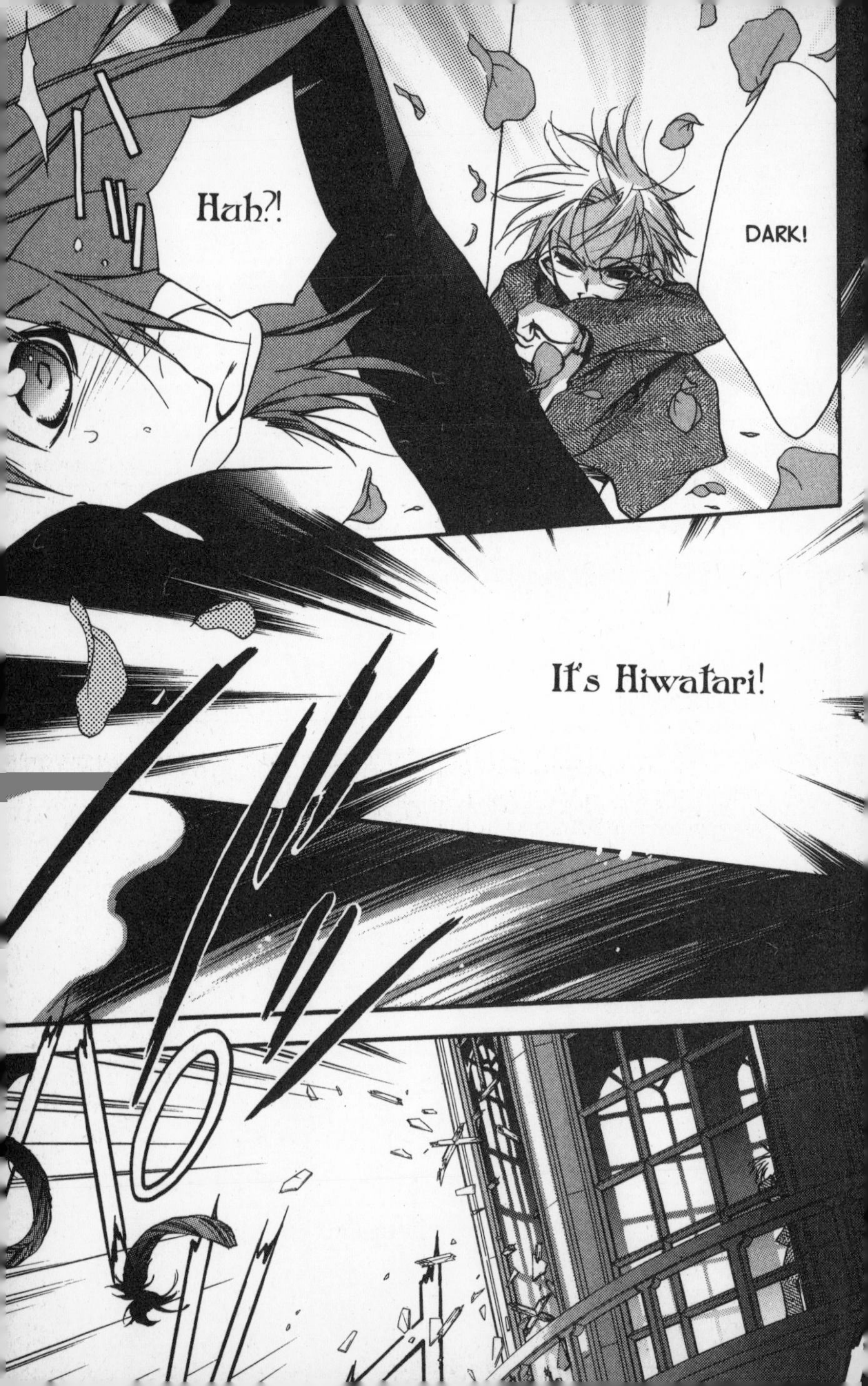
DARK!
Huh?!
It's Hiwatari!

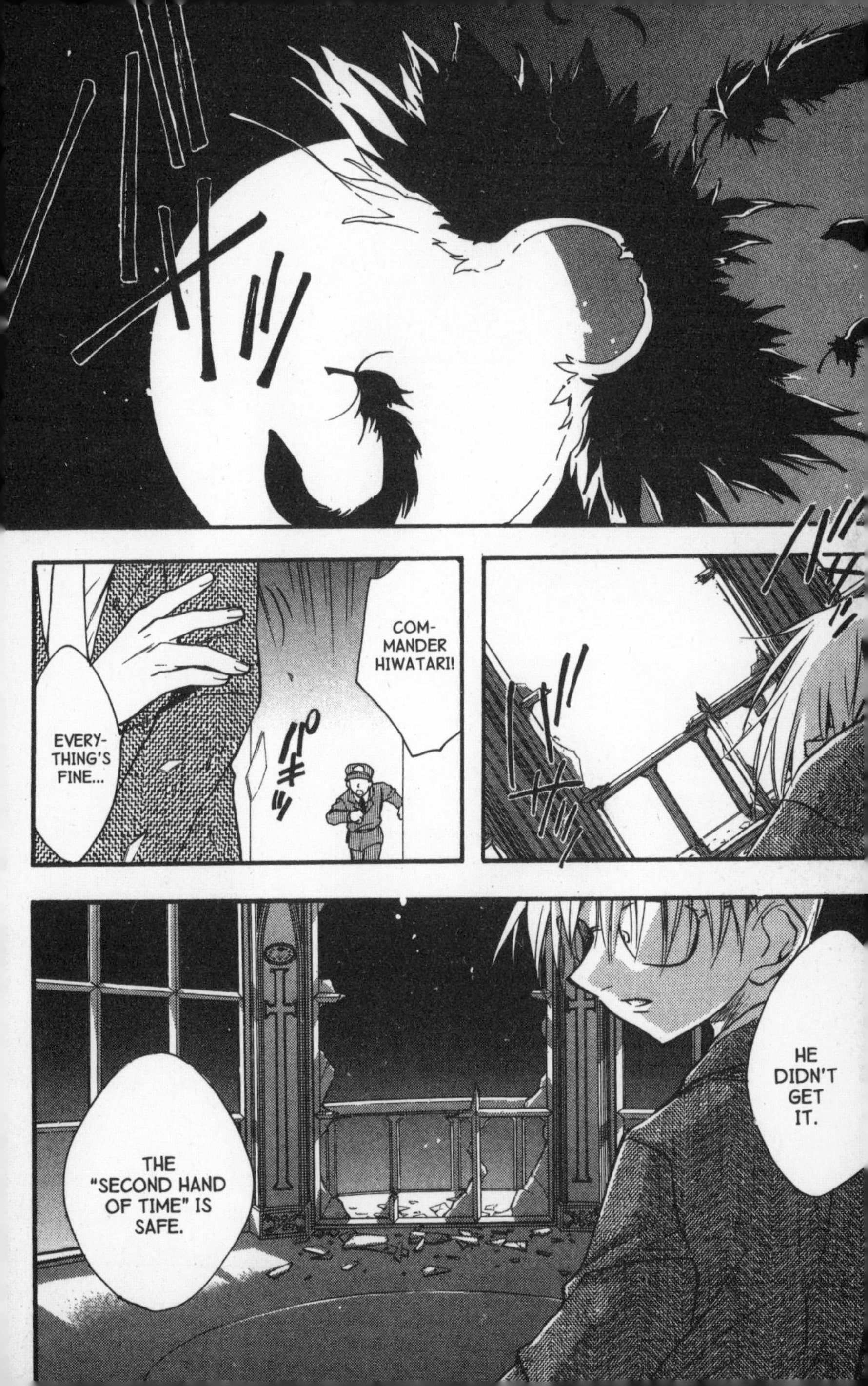
COMMANDER HIWATARI!
パキッ
EVERYTHING'S FINE...
HE DIDN'T GET IT.
THE "SECOND HAND OF TIME" IS SAFE.

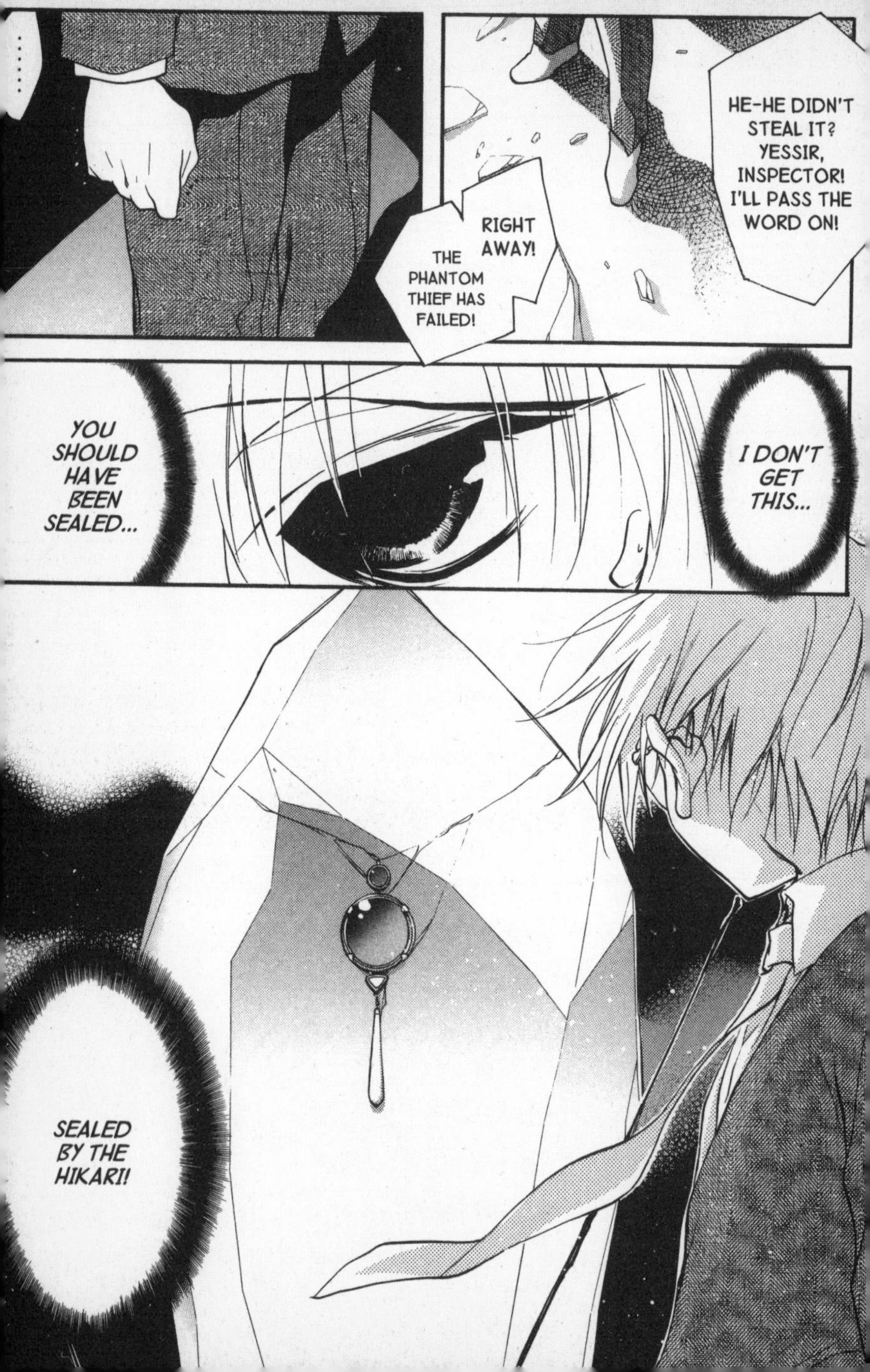
HE-HE DIDN'T STEAL IT? YESSIR, INSPECTOR! I'LL PASS THE WORD ON!
RIGHT AWAY! THE PHANTOM THIEF HAS FAILED!
......
I DON'T GET THIS...
YOU SHOULD HAVE BEEN SEALED...
SEALED BY THE HIKARI!

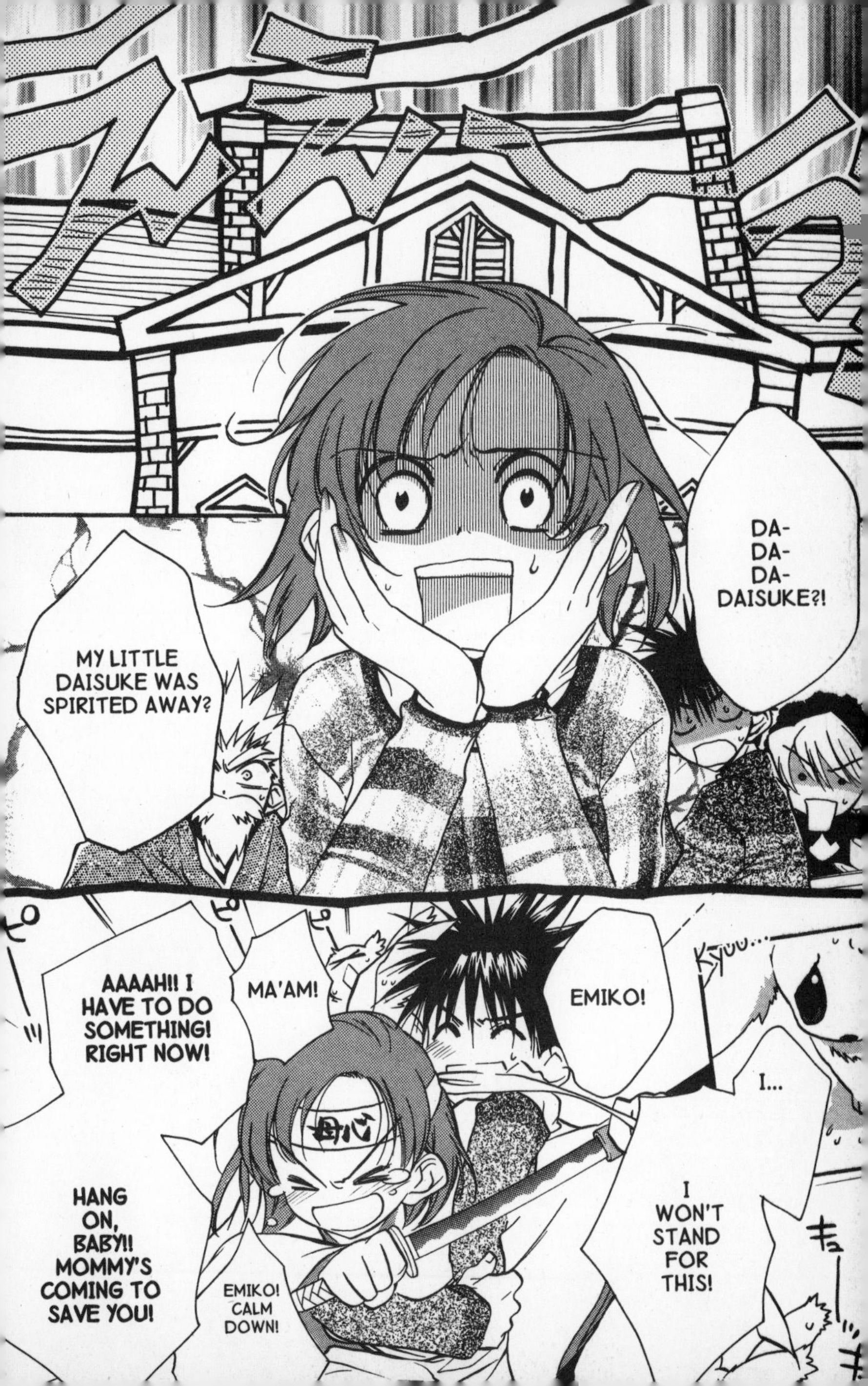
DA-DA-DA-DAISUKE?!
MY LITTLE DAISUKE WAS SPIRITED AWAY?
KYUU...
EMIKO!
I...
MA'AM!
AAAAH!! I HAVE TO DO SOMETHING! RIGHT NOW!
I WON'T STAND FOR THIS!
HANG ON, BABY!! MOMMY'S COMING TO SAVE YOU!
EMIKO! CALM DOWN!

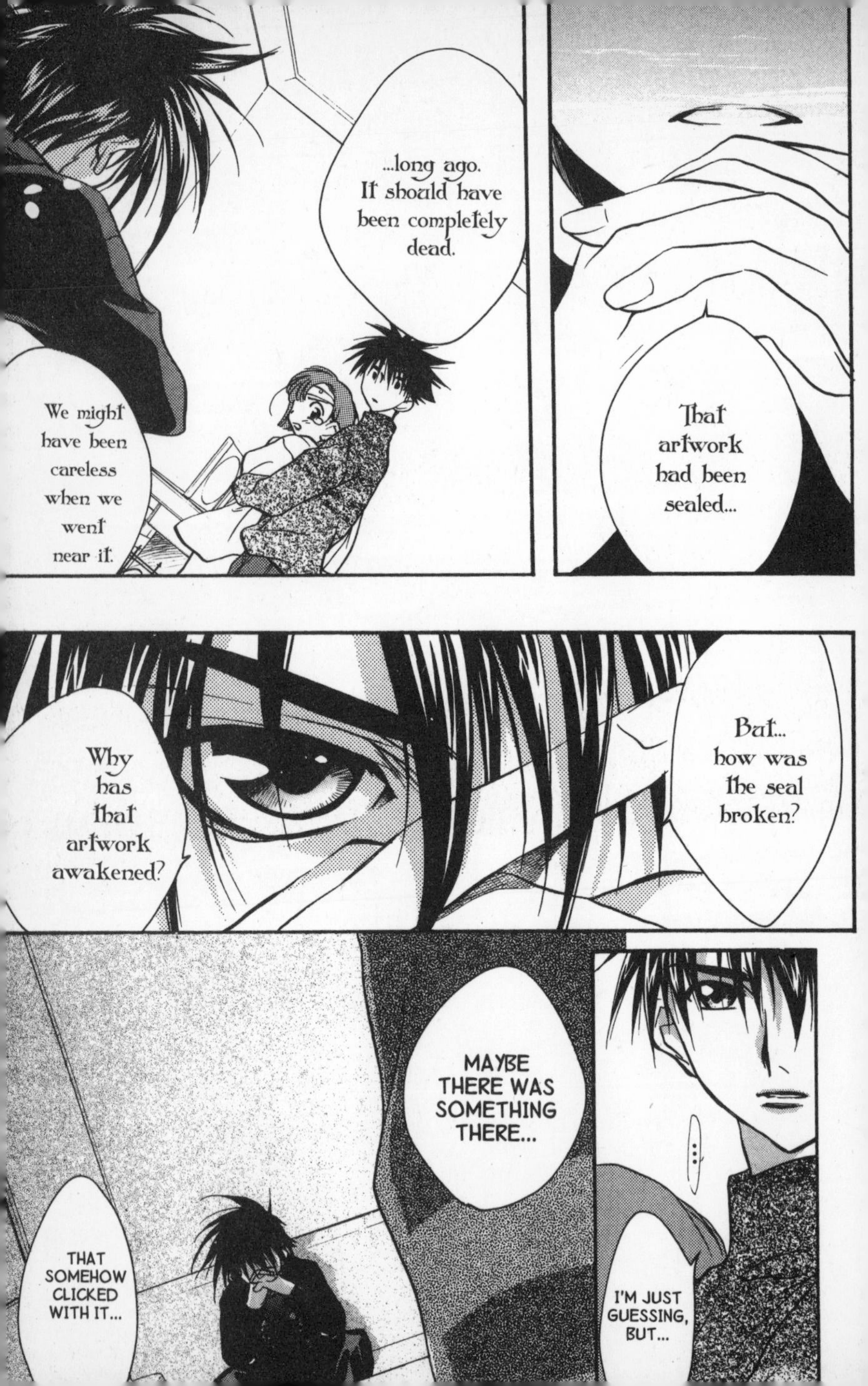
That artwork had been sealed...
...long ago. It should have been completely dead.
We might have been careless when we went near it.
But... how was the seal broken?
Why has that artwork awakened?
...
I'M JUST GUESSING, BUT...
MAYBE THERE WAS SOMETHING THERE...
THAT SOMEHOW CLICKED WITH IT...

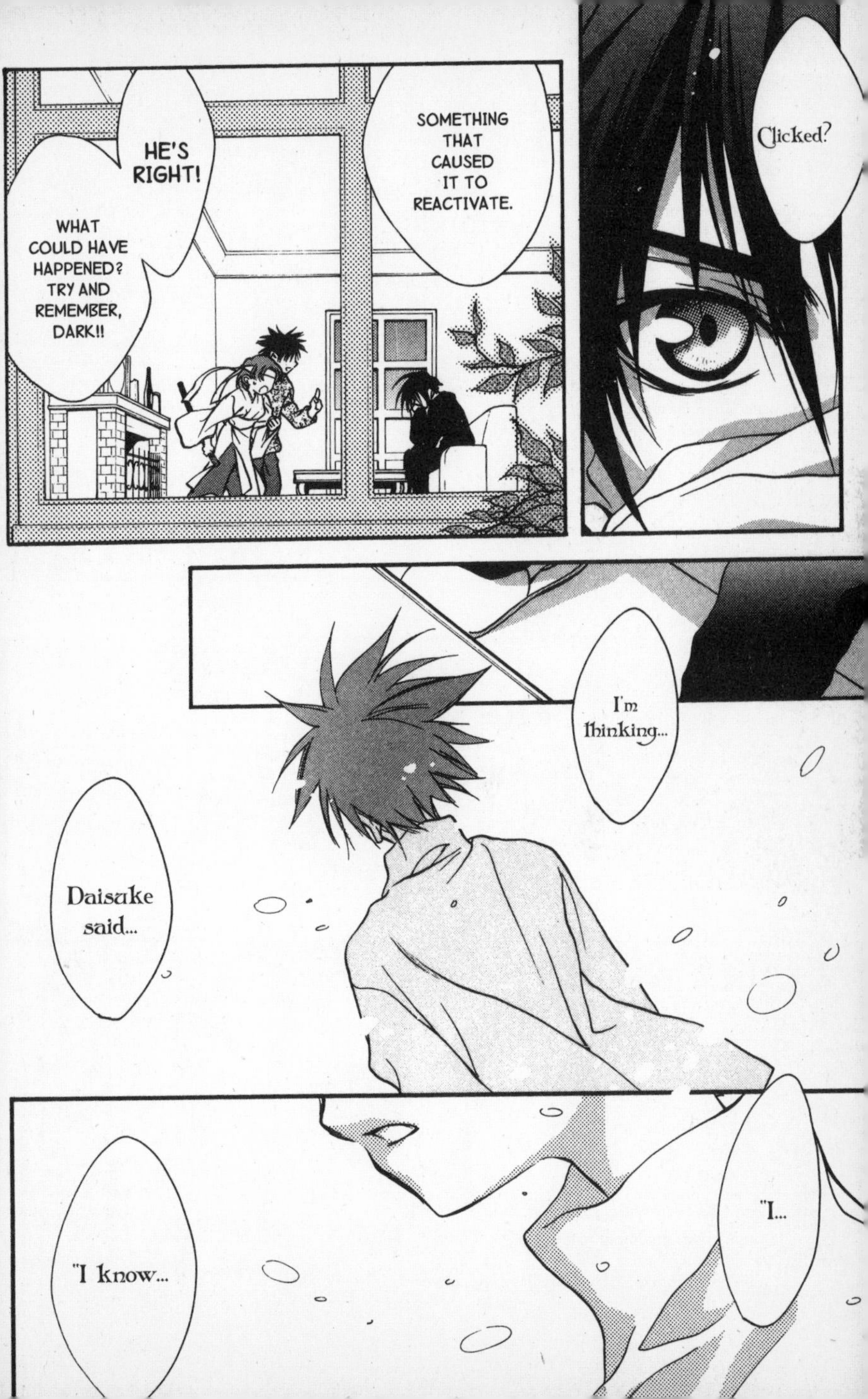
Clicked?
SOMETHING THAT CAUSED IT TO REACTIVATE.
HE'S RIGHT!
WHAT COULD HAVE HAPPENED? TRY AND REMEMBER, DARK!!
I'm thinking...
Daisuke said...
"I...
"I know...

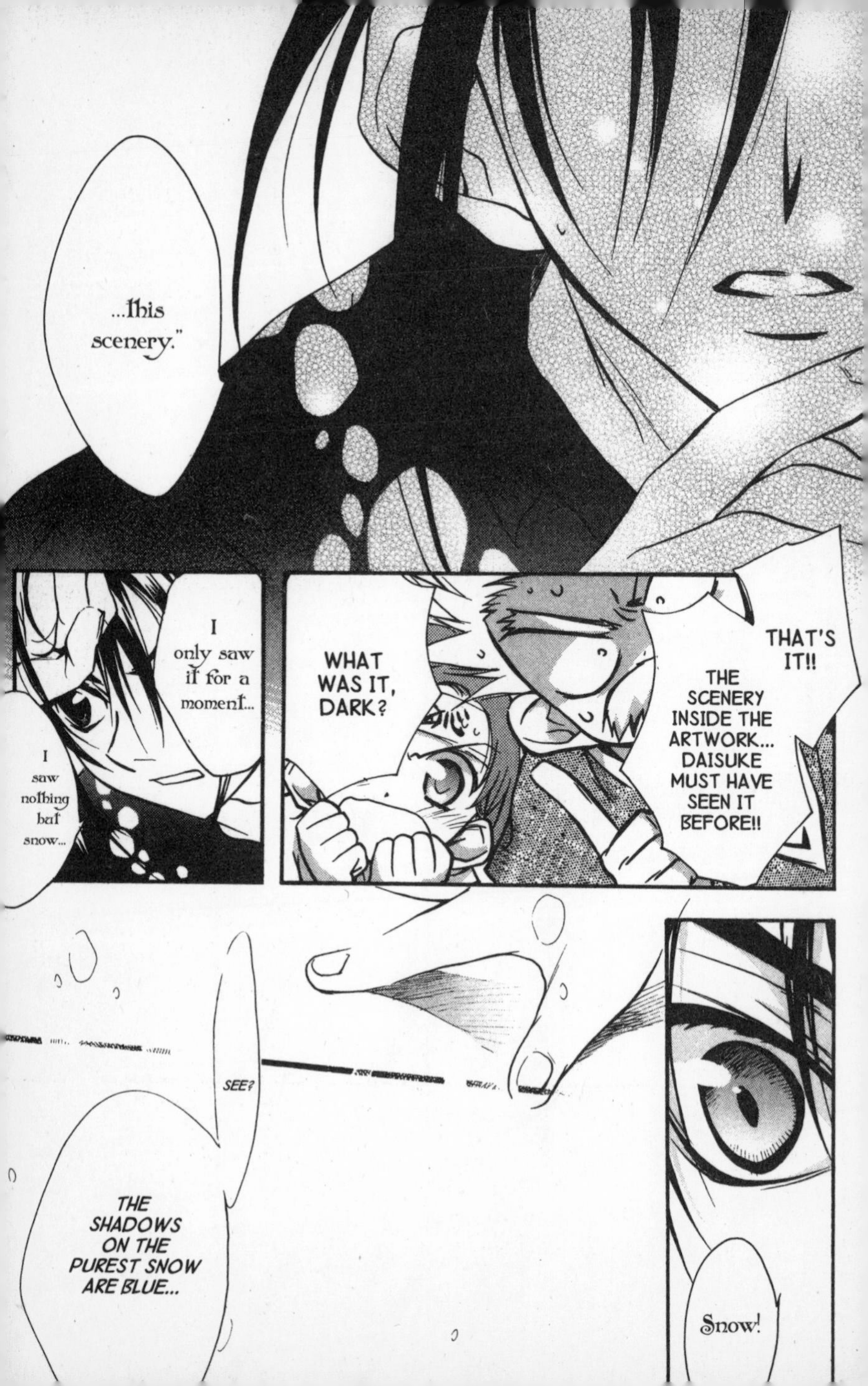

...this scenery."
THAT'S IT!!
THE SCENERY INSIDE THE ARTWORK... DAISUKE MUST HAVE SEEN IT BEFORE!!
WHAT WAS IT, DARK?
I only saw it for a moment...
I saw nothing but snow...
Snow!
SEE?
THE SHADOWS ON THE PUREST SNOW ARE BLUE...

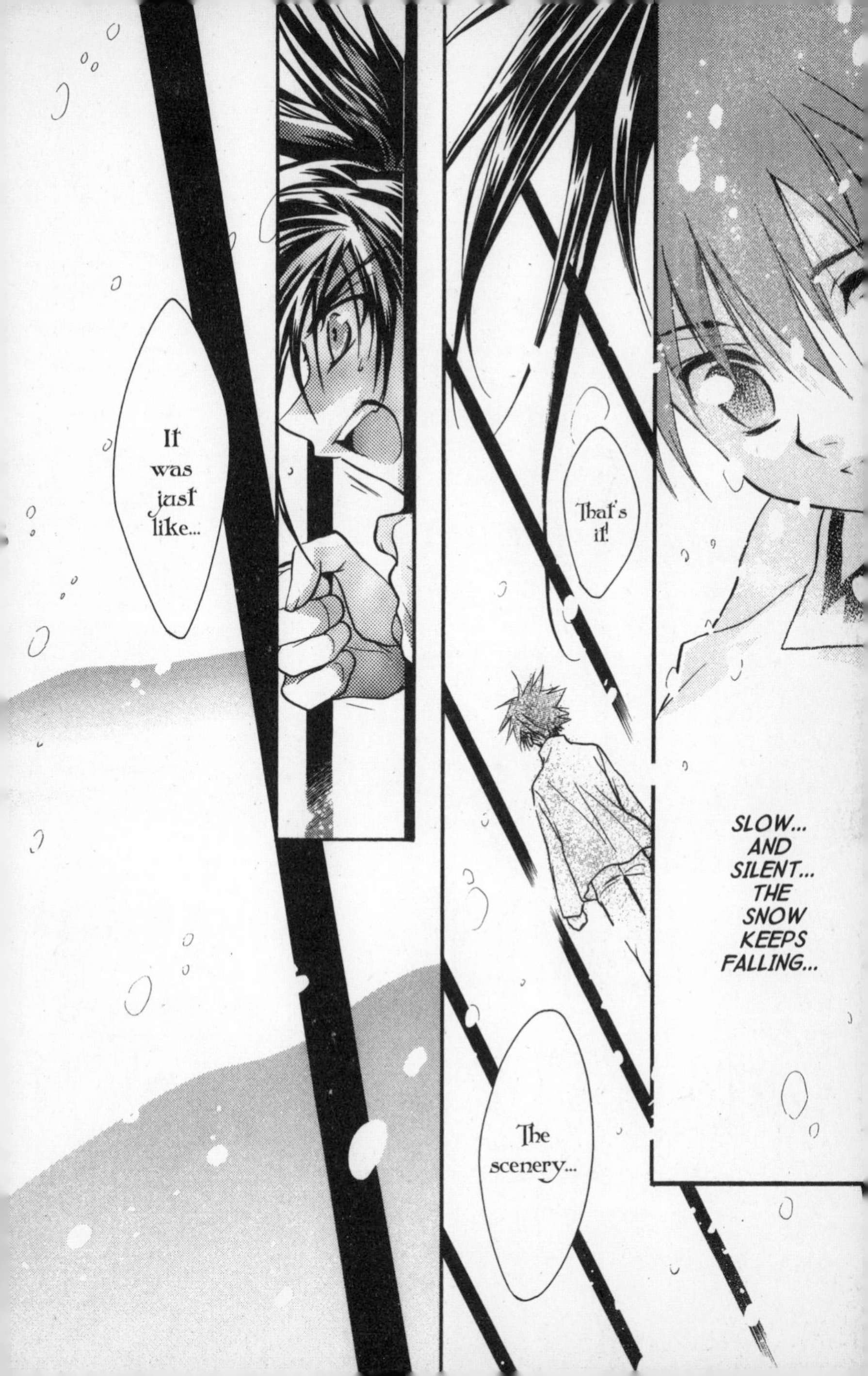
SLOW... AND SILENT... THE SNOW KEEPS FALLING...
That's it!
The scenery...
It was just like...

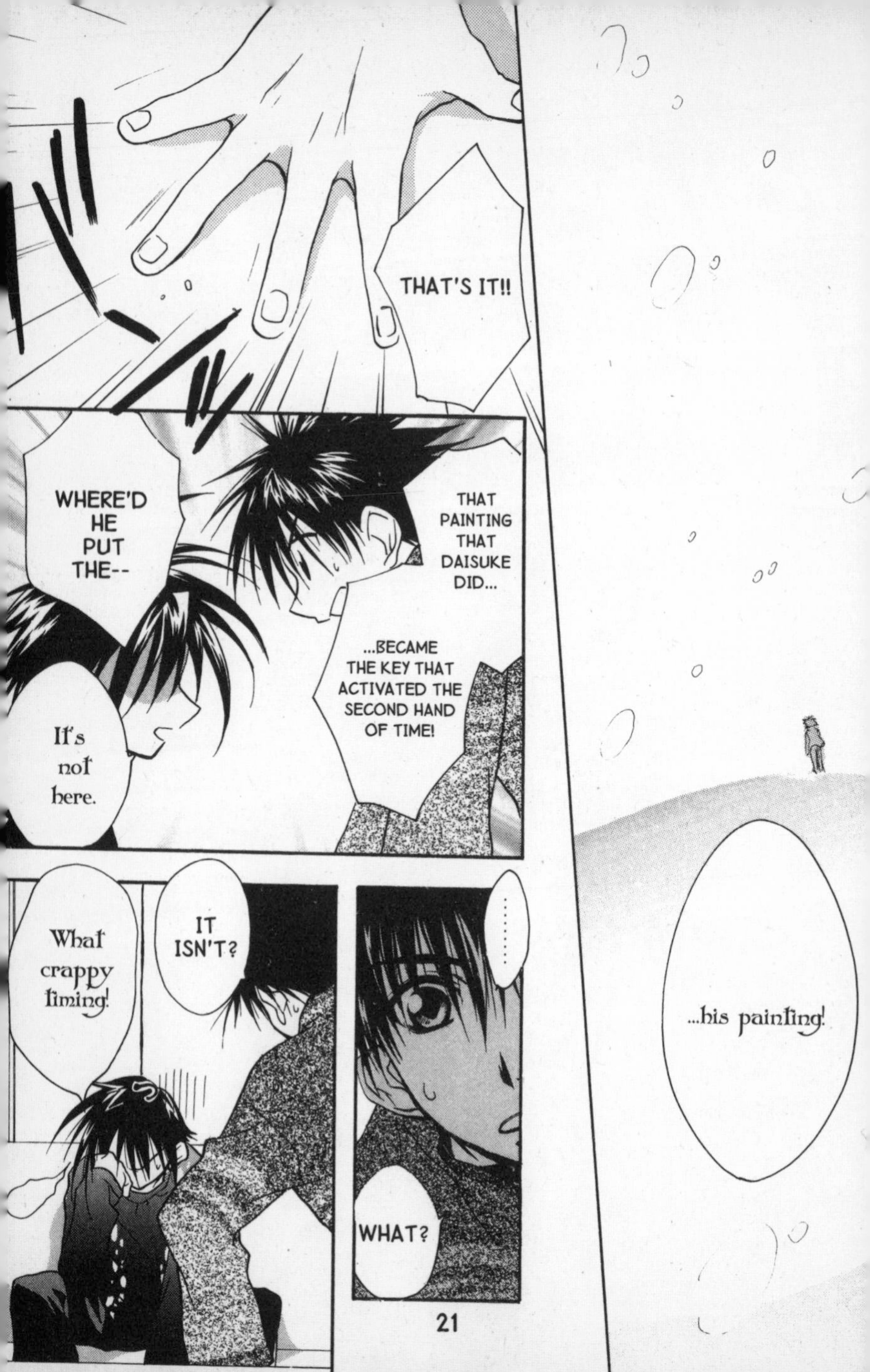
...his painting!
THAT'S IT!!
THAT PAINTING THAT DAISUKE DID...
...BECAME THE KEY THAT ACTIVATED THE SECOND HAND OF TIME!
WHERE'D HE PUT THE--
It's not here.
......
WHAT?
IT ISN'T?
What crappy timing!

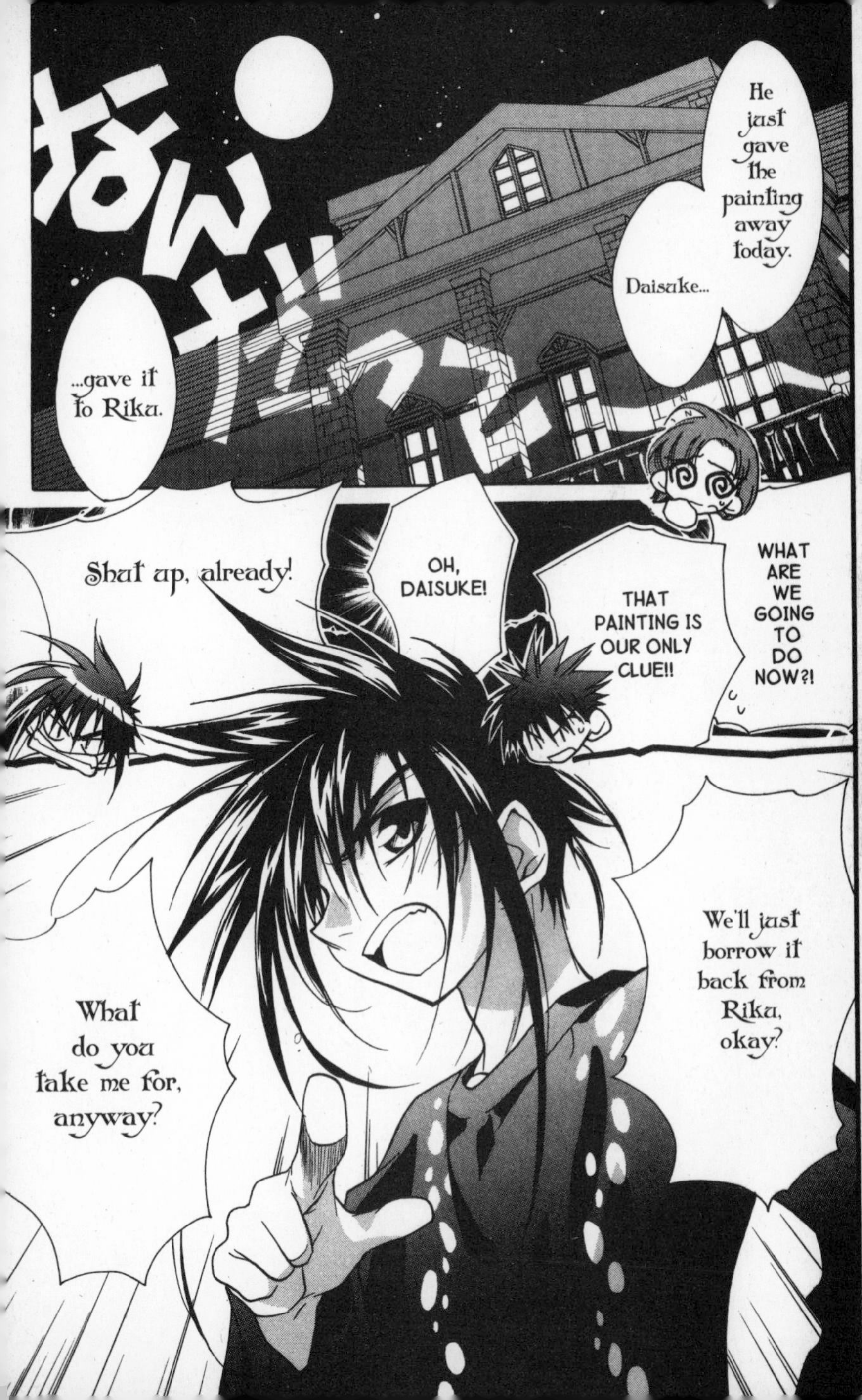
He just gave the painting away today.
Daisuke...
...gave it to Riku.
WHAT ARE WE GOING TO DO NOW?!
THAT PAINTING IS OUR ONLY CLUE!!
OH, DAISUKE!
Shut up, already!
We'll just borrow it back from Riku, okay?
What do you take me for, anyway?

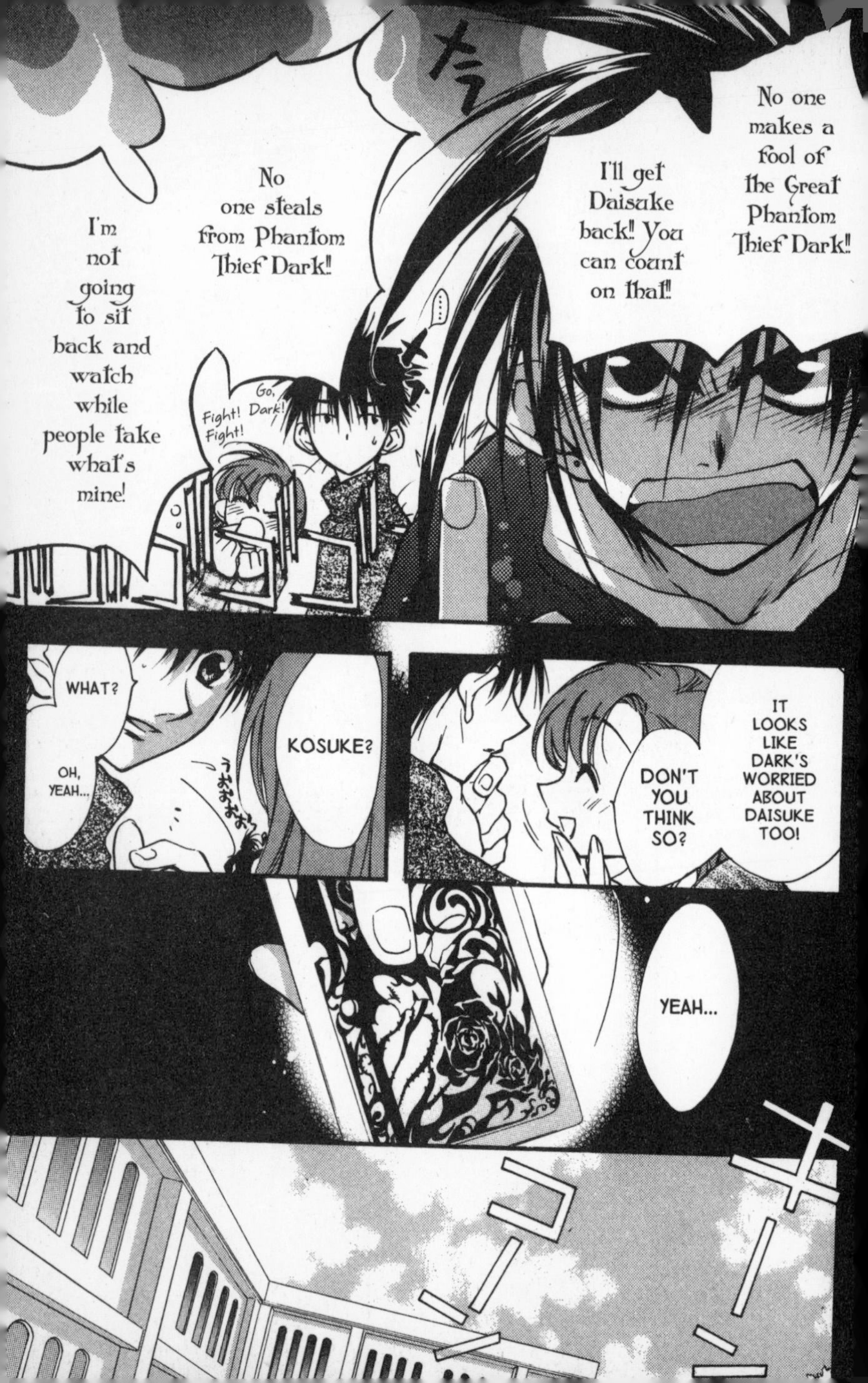
No one makes a fool of the Great Phantom Thief Dark!!
I'll get Daisuke back!! You can count on that!!
No one steals from Phantom Thief Dark!!
I'm not going to sit back and watch while people take what's mine!
Go, Dark!
Fight! Fight!
IT LOOKS LIKE DARK'S WORRIED ABOUT DAISUKE TOO!
DON'T YOU THINK SO?
KOSUKE?
WHAT?
OH, YEAH...
YEAH...

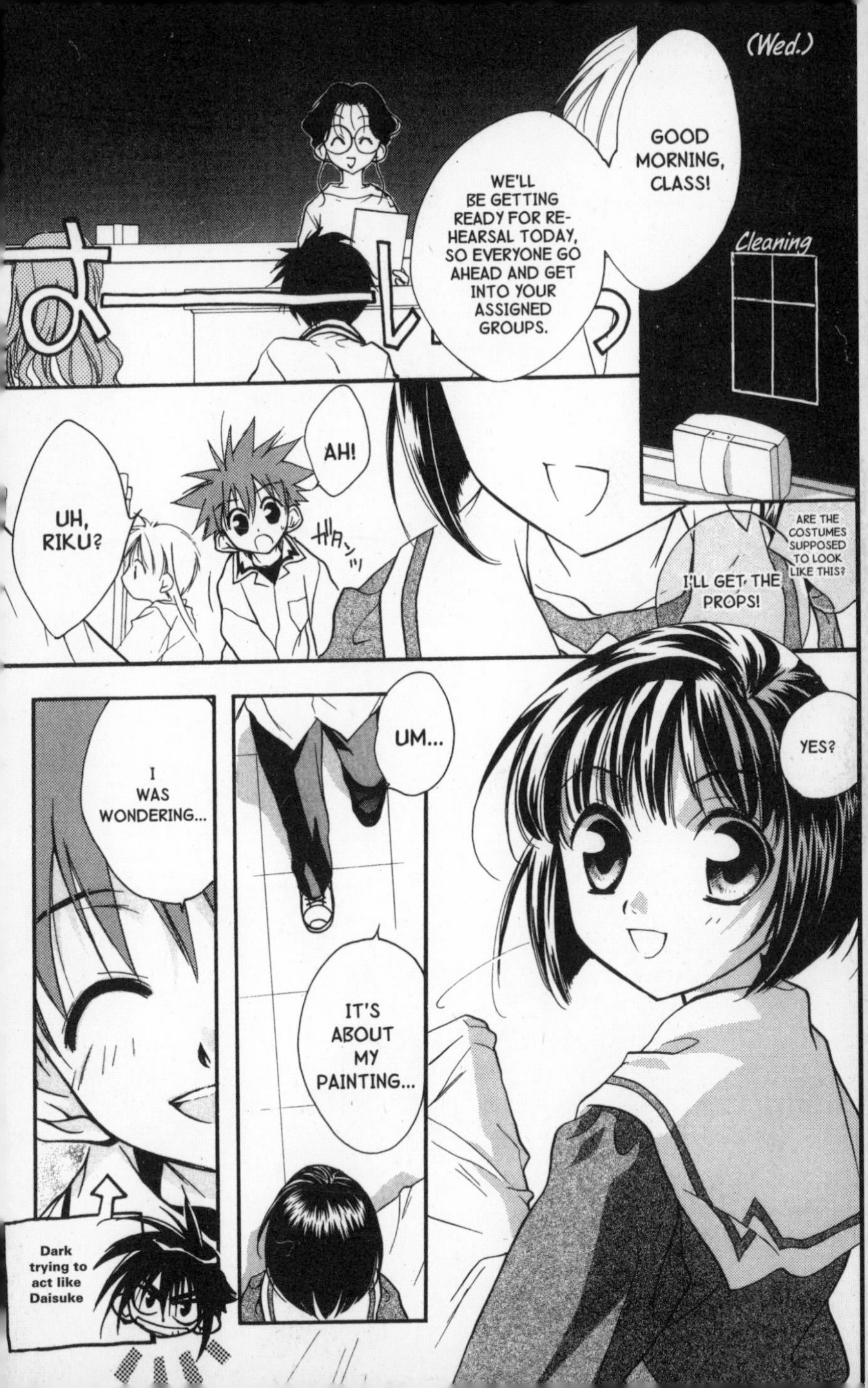
(Wed.)
GOOD MORNING, CLASS!
WE'LL BE GETTING READY FOR RE-HEARSAL TODAY, SO EVERYONE GO AHEAD AND GET INTO YOUR ASSIGNED GROUPS.
Cleaning
ARE THE COSTUMES SUPPOSED TO LOOK LIKE THIS?
I'LL GET THE PROPS!
AH!
UH, RIKU?
YES?
UM...
IT'S ABOUT MY PAINTING...
I WAS WONDERING...
Dark trying to act like Daisuke

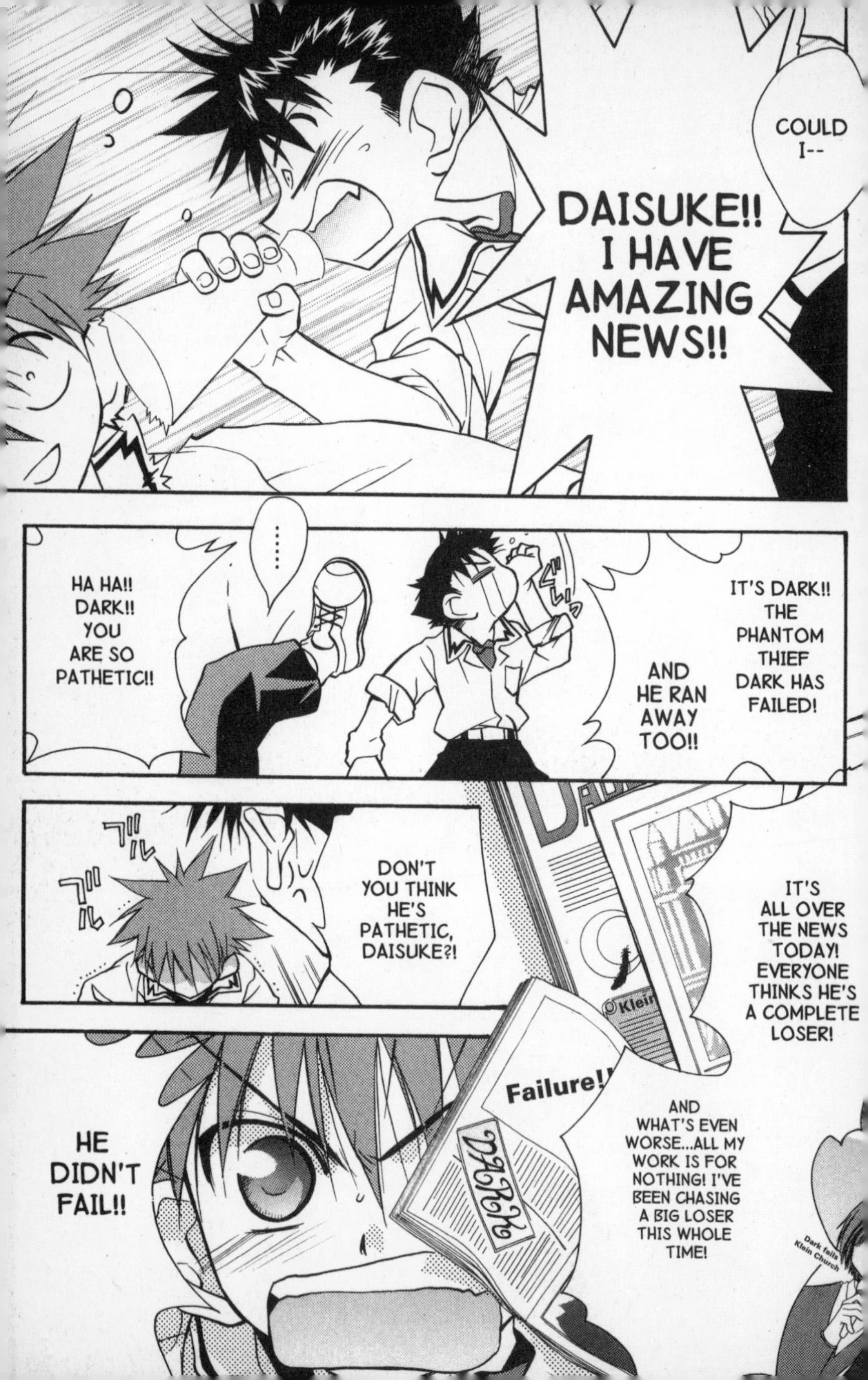

COULD I--
DAISUKE!! I HAVE AMAZING NEWS!!
IT'S DARK!! THE PHANTOM THIEF DARK HAS FAILED!
AND HE RAN AWAY TOO!!
......
HA HA!! DARK!! YOU ARE SO PATHETIC!!
IT'S ALL OVER THE NEWS TODAY! EVERYONE THINKS HE'S A COMPLETE LOSER!
DON'T YOU THINK HE'S PATHETIC, DAISUKE?!
Dark fails Klein Church
AND WHAT'S EVEN WORSE...ALL MY WORK IS FOR NOTHING! I'VE BEEN CHASING A BIG LOSER THIS WHOLE TIME!
Failure!!
HE DIDN'T FAIL!!

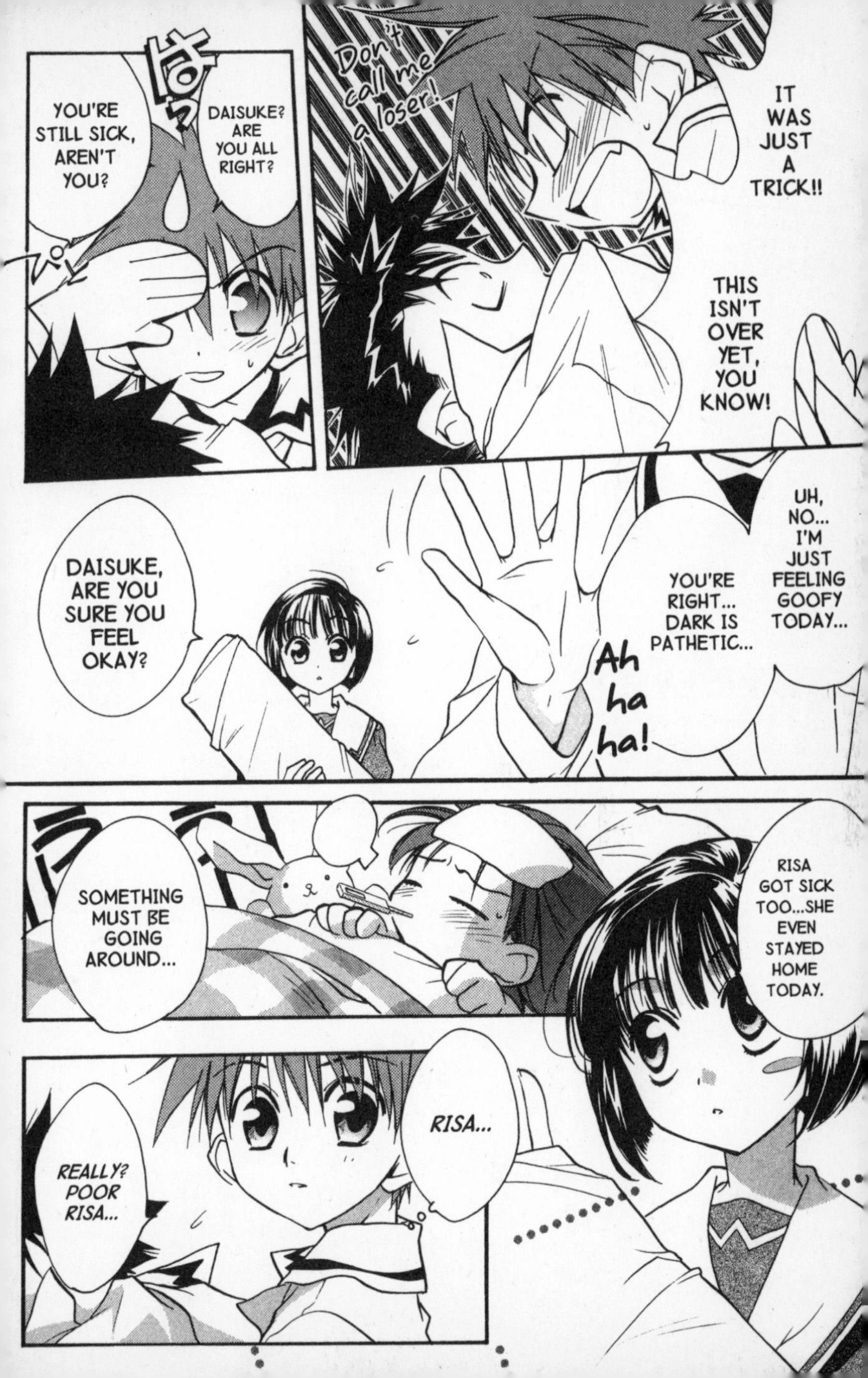
IT WAS JUST A TRICK!!
Don't call me a loser!
THIS ISN'T OVER YET, YOU KNOW!
DAISUKE? ARE YOU ALL RIGHT?
YOU'RE STILL SICK, AREN'T YOU?
UH, NO... I'M JUST FEELING GOOFY TODAY...
YOU'RE RIGHT... DARK IS PATHETIC...
Ah ha ha!
DAISUKE, ARE YOU SURE YOU FEEL OKAY?
RISA GOT SICK TOO...SHE EVEN STAYED HOME TODAY.
SOMETHING MUST BE GOING AROUND...
RISA...
REALLY? POOR RISA...

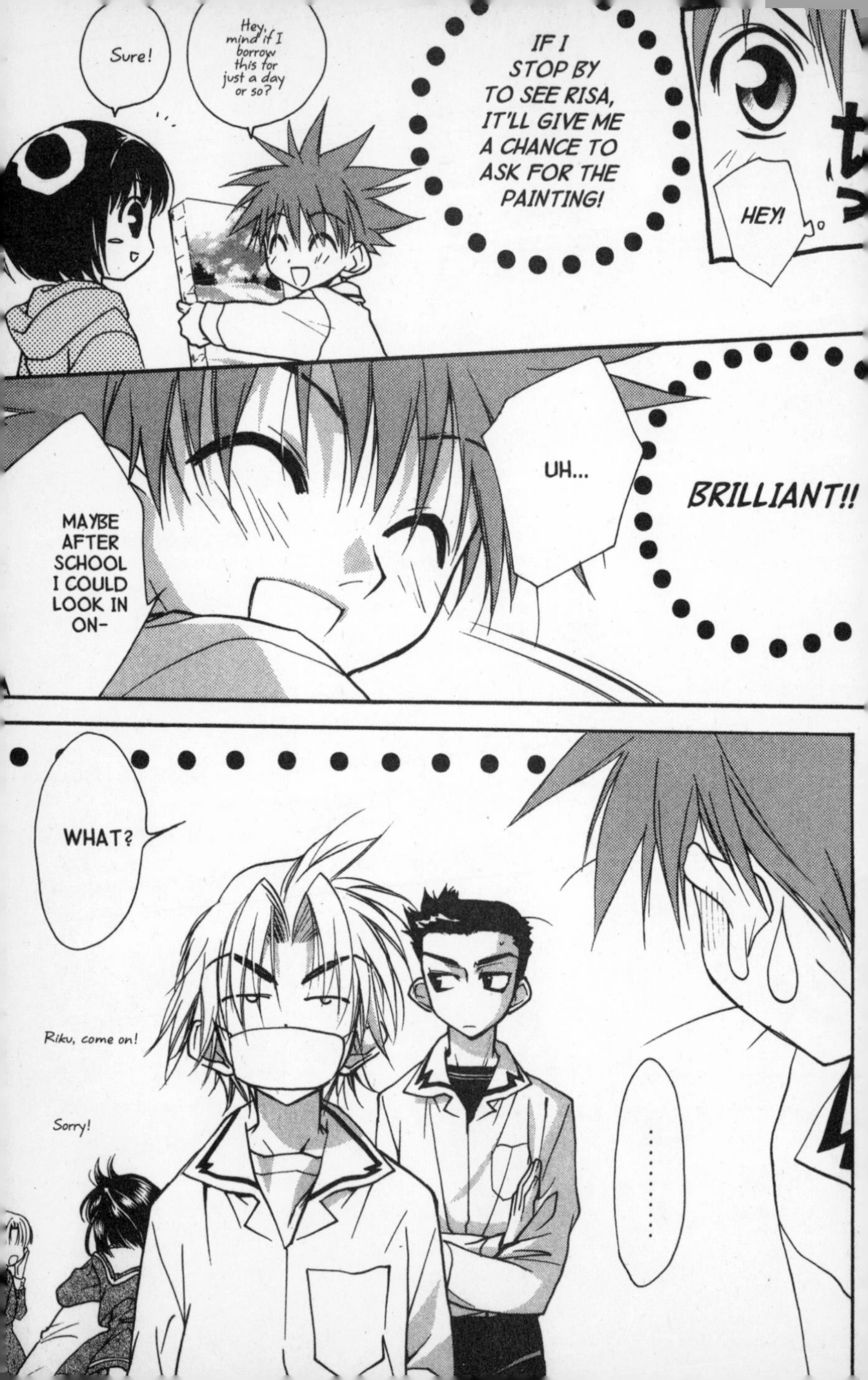
HEY!
IF I STOP BY TO SEE RISA, IT'LL GIVE ME A CHANCE TO ASK FOR THE PAINTING!
Hey, mind if I borrow this for just a day or so?
Sure!
BRILLIANT!!
UH...
MAYBE AFTER SCHOOL I COULD LOOK IN ON-
......
WHAT?
Riku, come on!
Sorry!

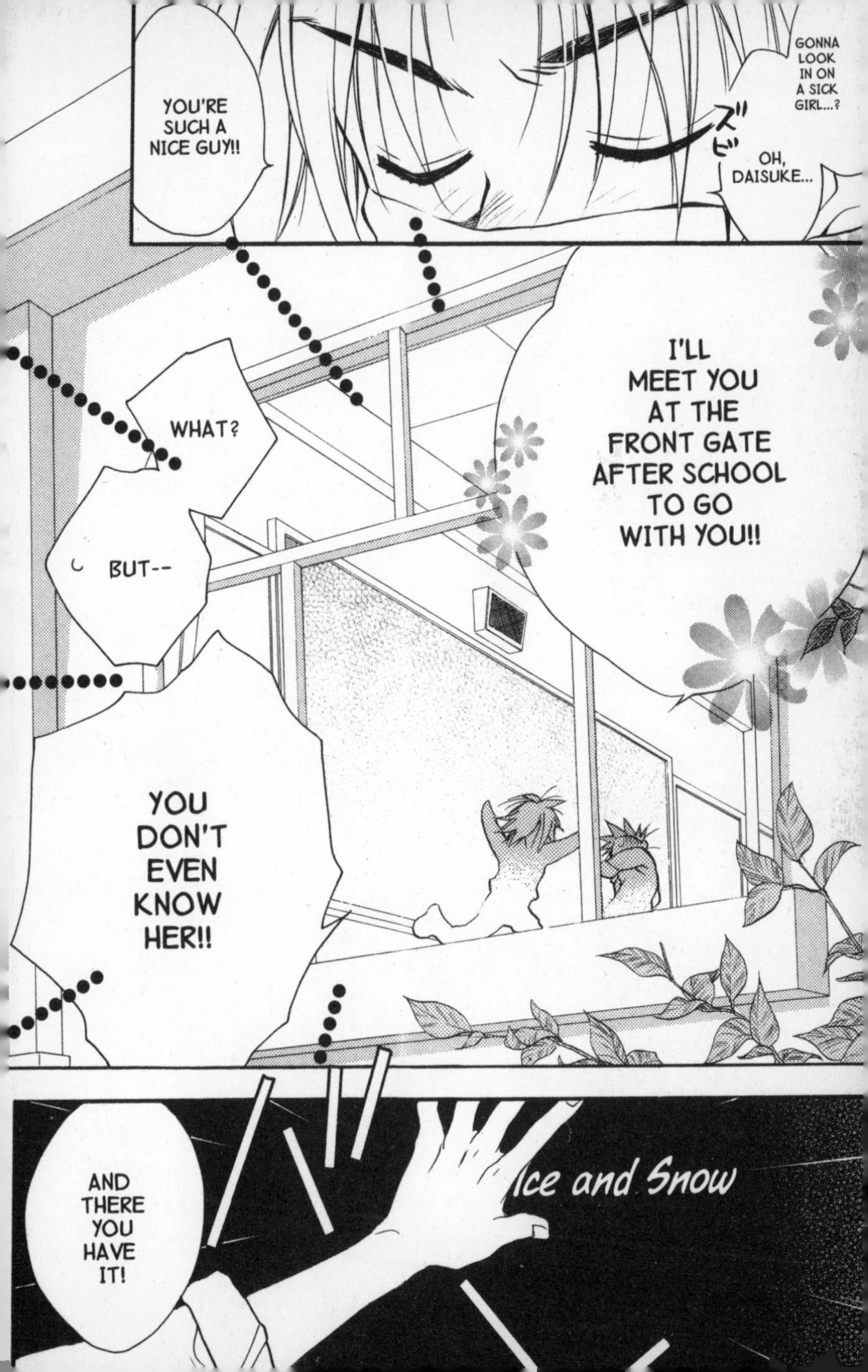
GONNA LOOK IN ON A SICK GIRL...?
ズビ
OH, DAISUKE...
YOU'RE SUCH A NICE GUY!!
I'LL MEET YOU AT THE FRONT GATE AFTER SCHOOL TO GO WITH YOU!!
WHAT?
BUT--
YOU DON'T EVEN KNOW HER!!
Ice and Snow
AND THERE YOU HAVE IT!

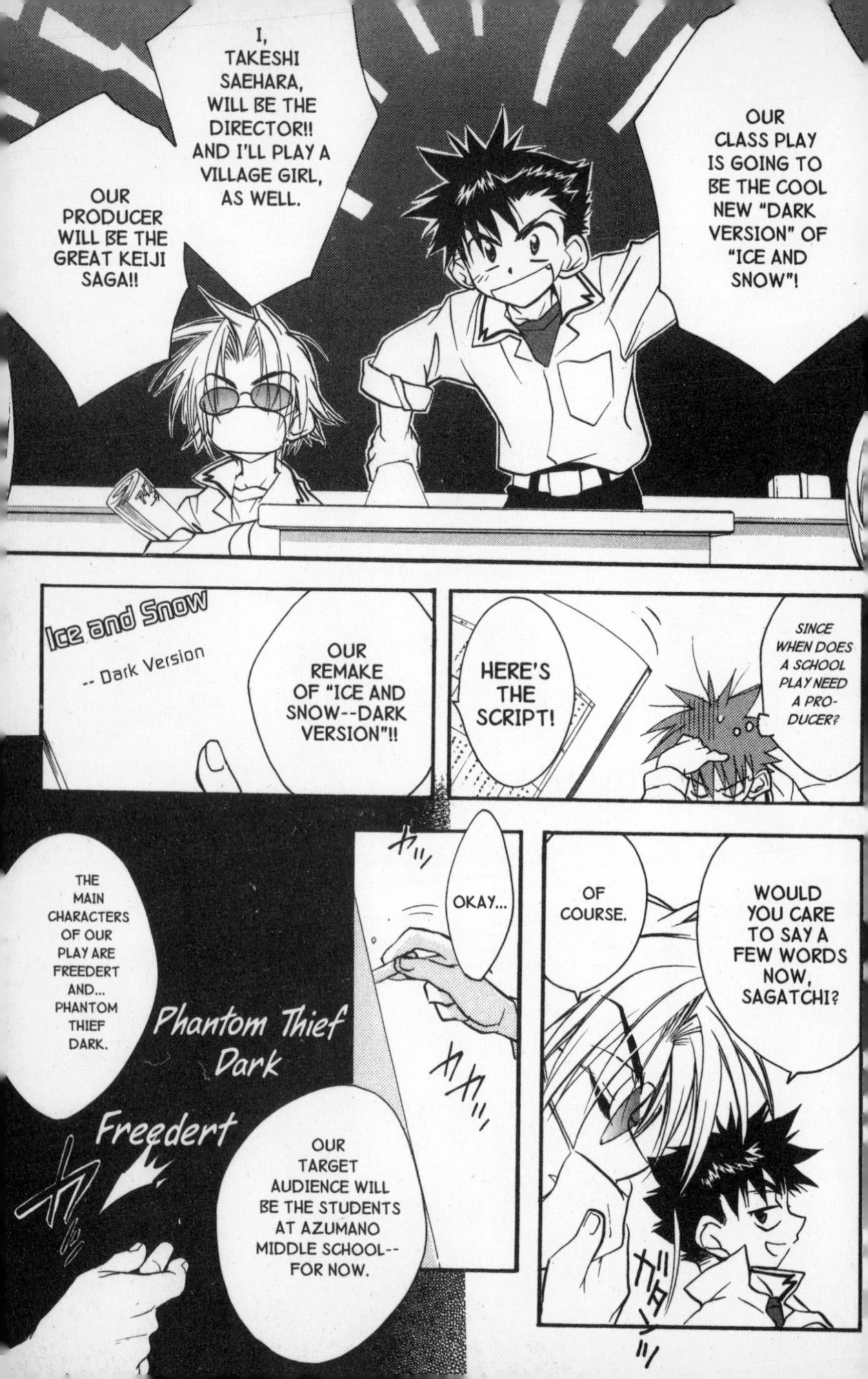
OUR CLASS PLAY IS GOING TO BE THE COOL NEW "DARK VERSION" OF "ICE AND SNOW"!
I, TAKESHI SAEHARA, WILL BE THE DIRECTOR!! AND I'LL PLAY A VILLAGE GIRL, AS WELL.
OUR PRODUCER WILL BE THE GREAT KEIJI SAGA!!
SINCE WHEN DOES A SCHOOL PLAY NEED A PRO-DUCER?
HERE'S THE SCRIPT!
OUR REMAKE OF "ICE AND SNOW--DARK VERSION"!!
Ice and Snow
-- Dark Version
WOULD YOU CARE TO SAY A FEW WORDS NOW, SAGATCHI?
OF COURSE.
OKAY...
THE MAIN CHARACTERS OF OUR PLAY ARE FREEDERT AND... PHANTOM THIEF DARK.
Phantom Thief Dark
Freedert
OUR TARGET AUDIENCE WILL BE THE STUDENTS AT AZUMANO MIDDLE SCHOOL-- FOR NOW.

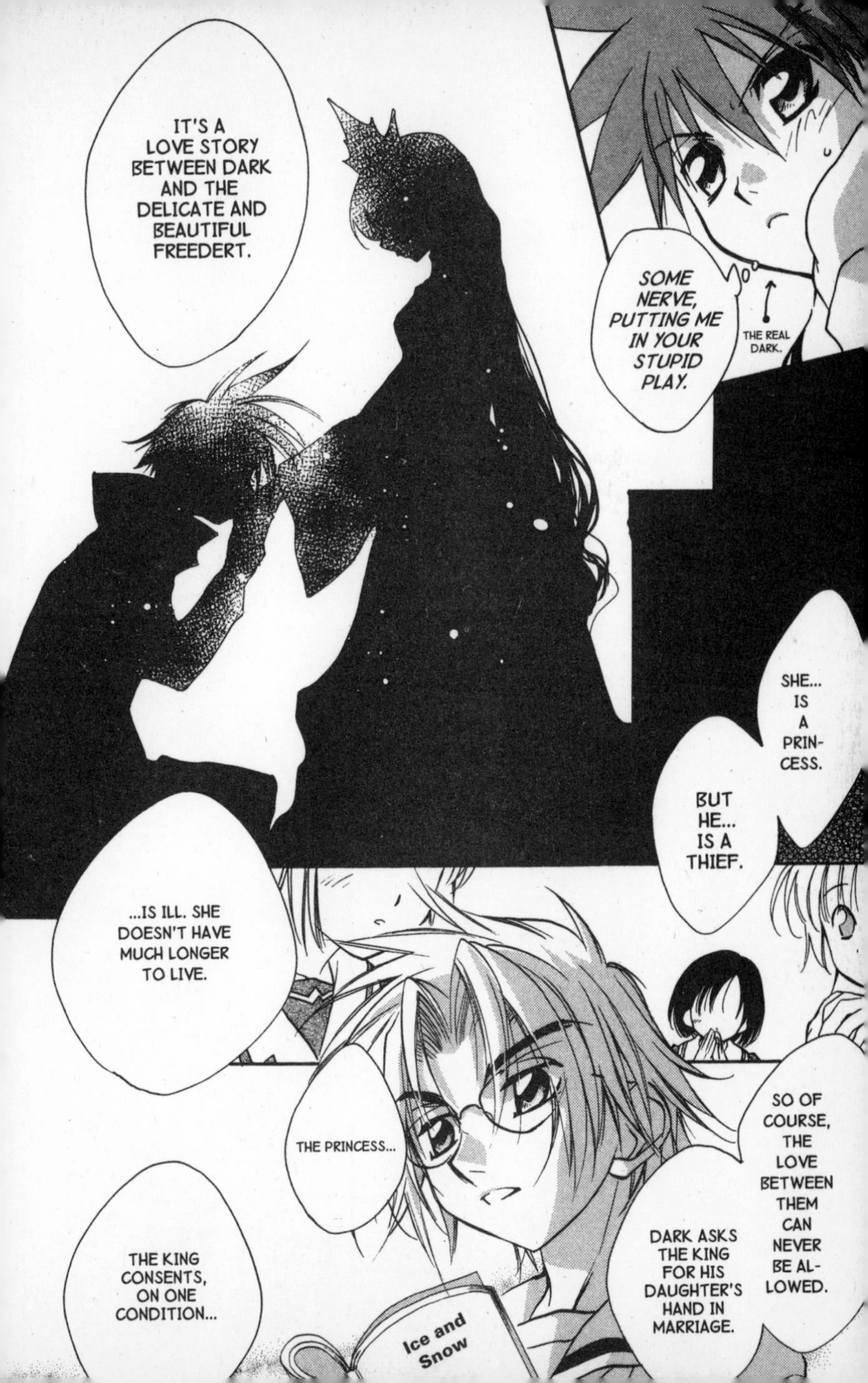
SOME NERVE, PUTTING ME IN YOUR STUPID PLAY.
THE REAL DARK.
IT'S A LOVE STORY BETWEEN DARK AND THE DELICATE AND BEAUTIFUL FREEDERT.
SHE... IS A PRIN-CESS.
BUT HE... IS A THIEF.
SO OF COURSE, THE LOVE BETWEEN THEM CAN NEVER BE AL-LOWED.
DARK ASKS THE KING FOR HIS DAUGHTER'S HAND IN MARRIAGE.
THE PRINCESS...
...IS ILL. SHE DOESN'T HAVE MUCH LONGER TO LIVE.
THE KING CONSENTS, ON ONE CONDITION...
Ice and Snow

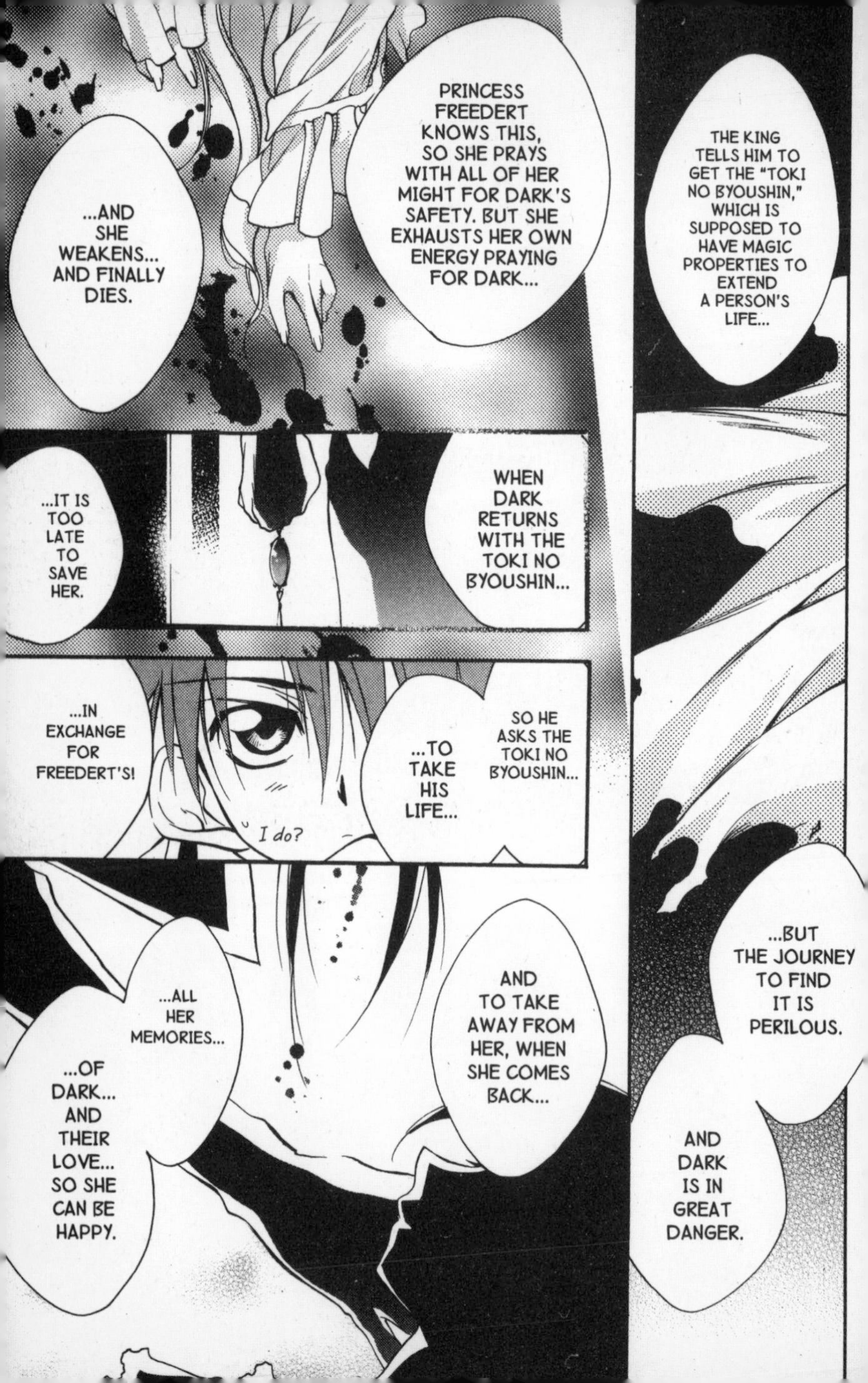
THE KING TELLS HIM TO GET THE "TOKI NO BYOUSHIN," WHICH IS SUPPOSED TO HAVE MAGIC PROPERTIES TO EXTEND A PERSON'S LIFE...
...BUT THE JOURNEY TO FIND IT IS PERILOUS.
AND DARK IS IN GREAT DANGER.
PRINCESS FREEDERT KNOWS THIS, SO SHE PRAYS WITH ALL OF HER MIGHT FOR DARK'S SAFETY. BUT SHE EXHAUSTS HER OWN ENERGY PRAYING FOR DARK...
...AND SHE WEAKENS... AND FINALLY DIES.
WHEN DARK RETURNS WITH THE TOKI NO BYOUSHIN...
...IT IS TOO LATE TO SAVE HER.
SO HE ASKS THE TOKI NO BYOUSHIN...
...TO TAKE HIS LIFE...
I do?
...IN EXCHANGE FOR FREEDERT'S!
AND TO TAKE AWAY FROM HER, WHEN SHE COMES BACK...
...ALL HER MEMORIES...
...OF DARK... AND THEIR LOVE... SO SHE CAN BE HAPPY.

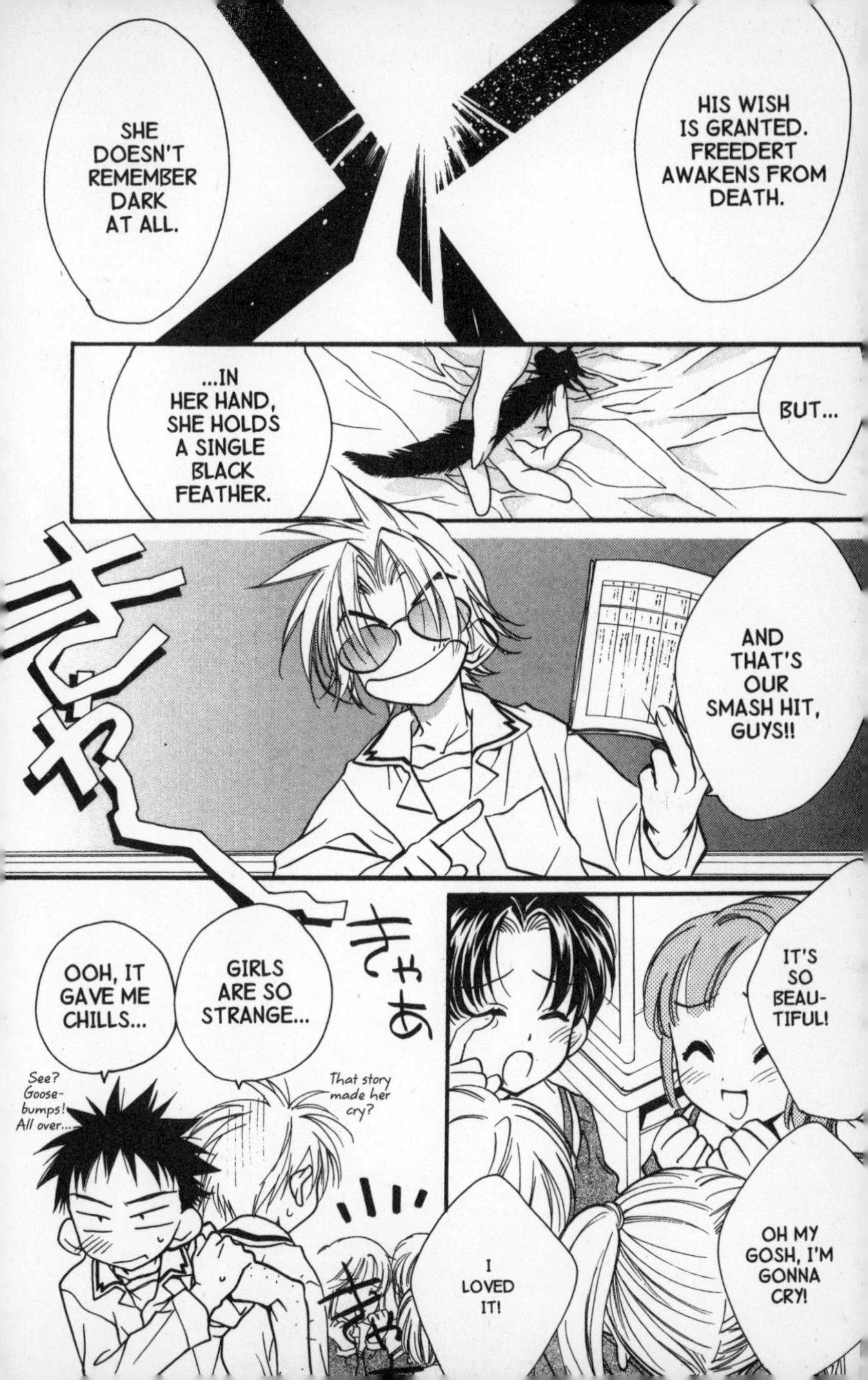
HIS WISH IS GRANTED. FREEDERT AWAKENS FROM DEATH.
SHE DOESN'T REMEMBER DARK AT ALL.
BUT...
...IN HER HAND, SHE HOLDS A SINGLE BLACK FEATHER.
AND THAT'S OUR SMASH HIT, GUYS!!
きゃ
IT'S SO BEAU-TIFUL!
OH MY GOSH, I'M GONNA CRY!
I LOVED IT!
きゃあ
GIRLS ARE SO STRANGE...
That story made her cry?
OOH, IT GAVE ME CHILLS...
See? Goose-bumps! All over...

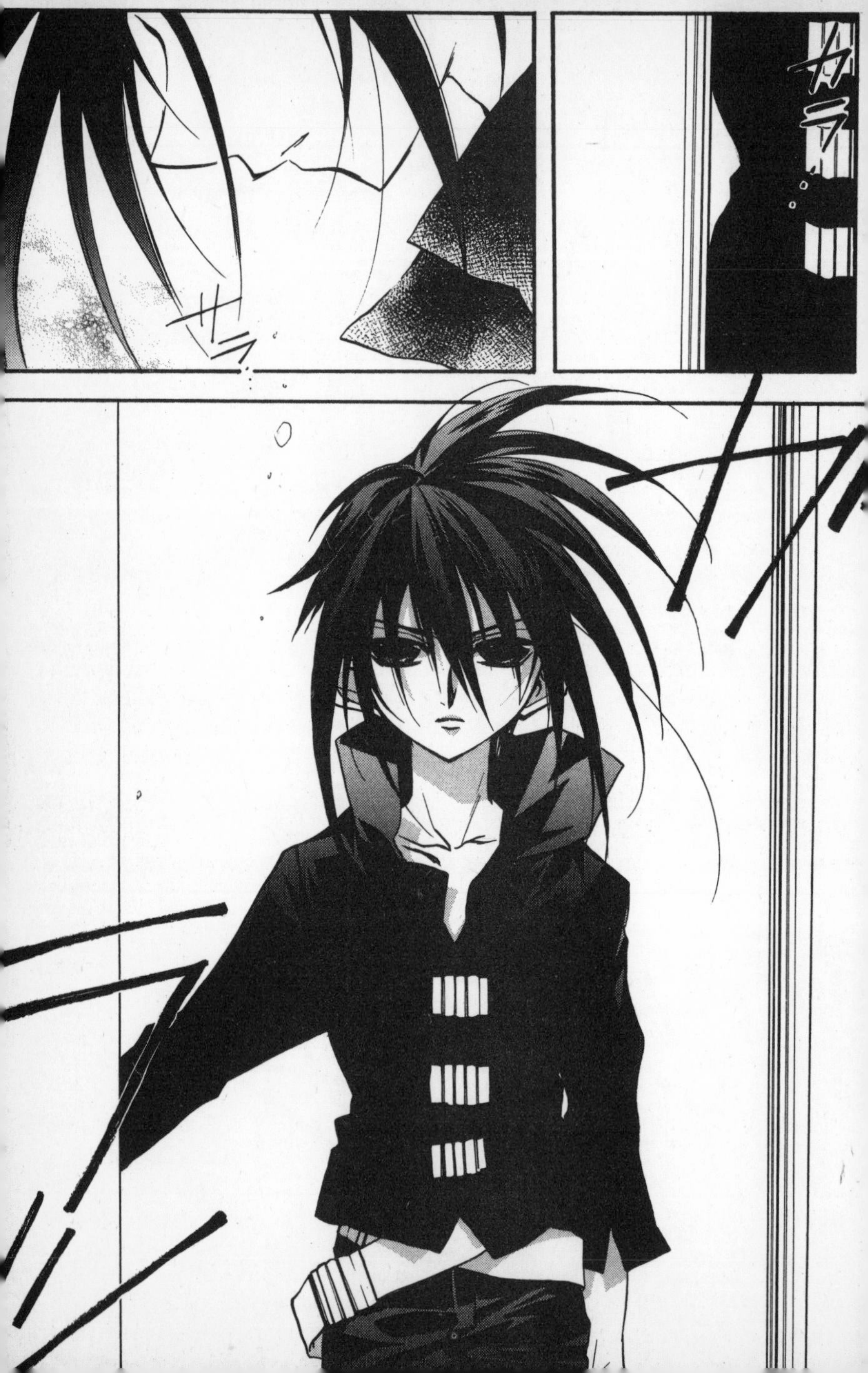
カラ…
サラ…

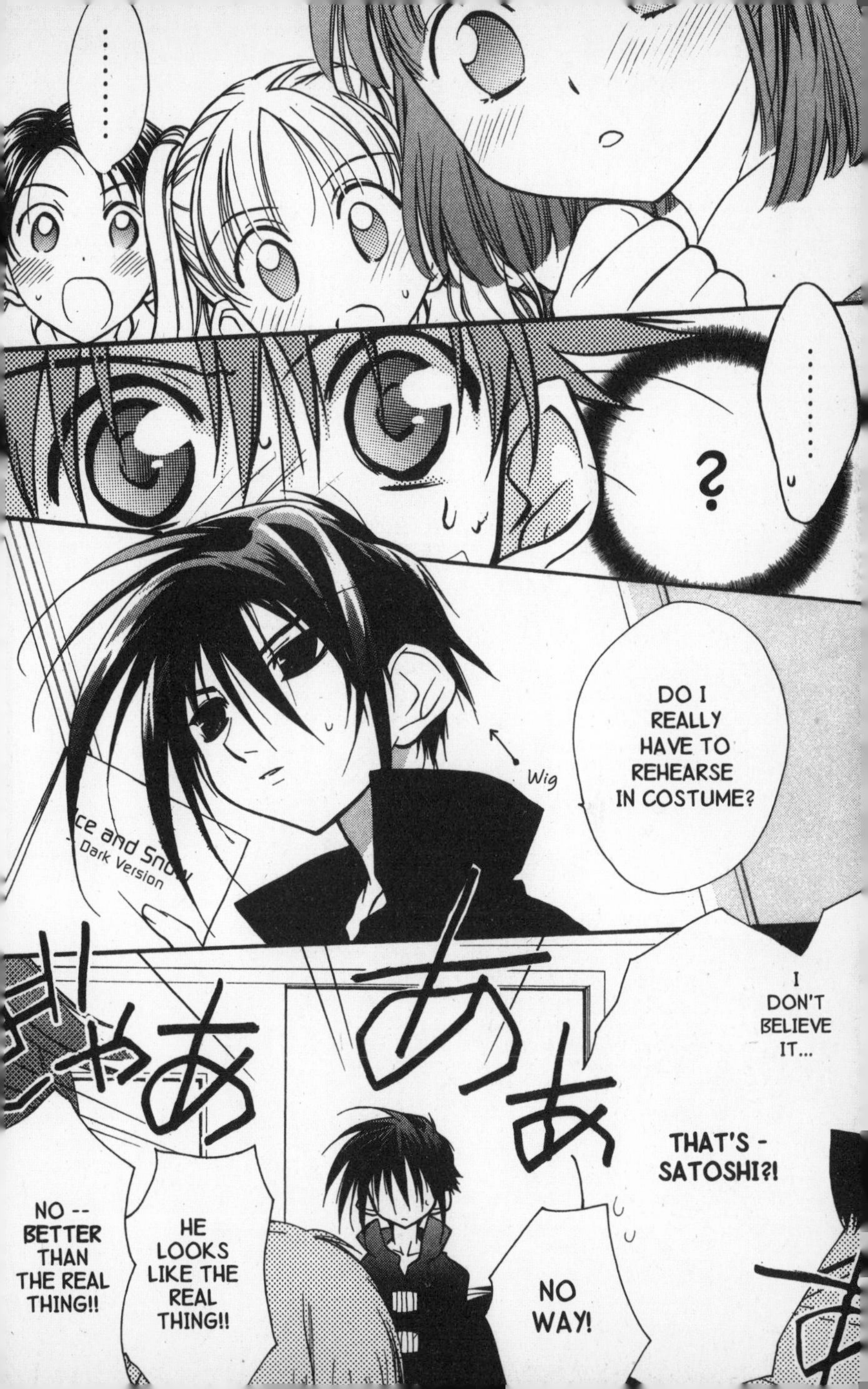
......
......
?
DO I REALLY HAVE TO REHEARSE IN COSTUME?
Wig
ce and Snow
- Dark Version
I DON'T BELIEVE IT...
ああ
THAT'S - SATOSHI?!
NO WAY!
HE LOOKS LIKE THE REAL THING!!
NO -- BETTER THAN THE REAL THING!!

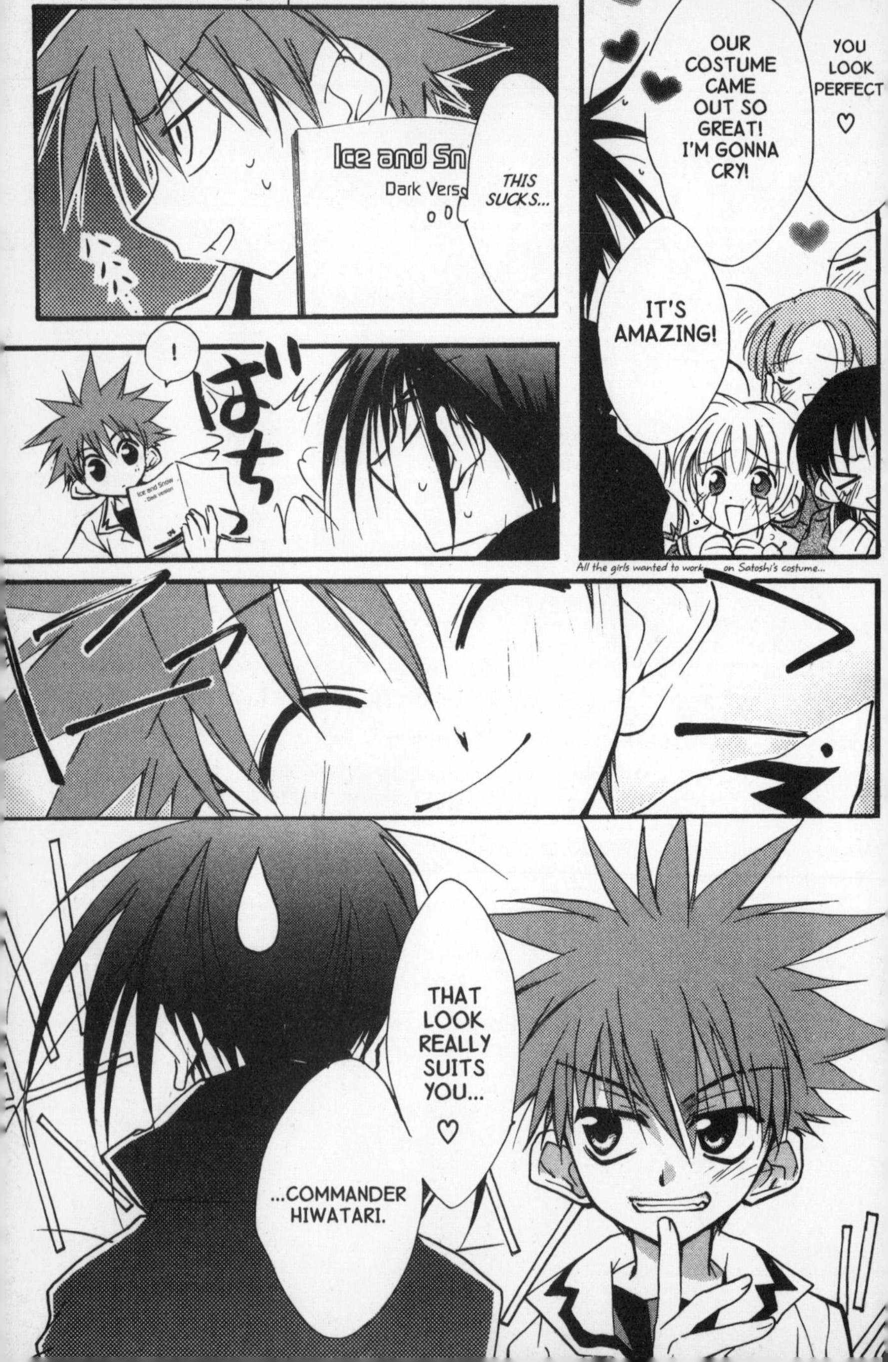
YOU LOOK PERFECT ♡
OUR COSTUME CAME OUT SO GREAT! I'M GONNA CRY!
IT'S AMAZING!
Ice and Sn
Dark Vers
THIS SUCKS...
!
ぱち
All the girls wanted to work on Satoshi's costume...
THAT LOOK REALLY SUITS YOU... ♡
...COMMANDER HIWATARI.

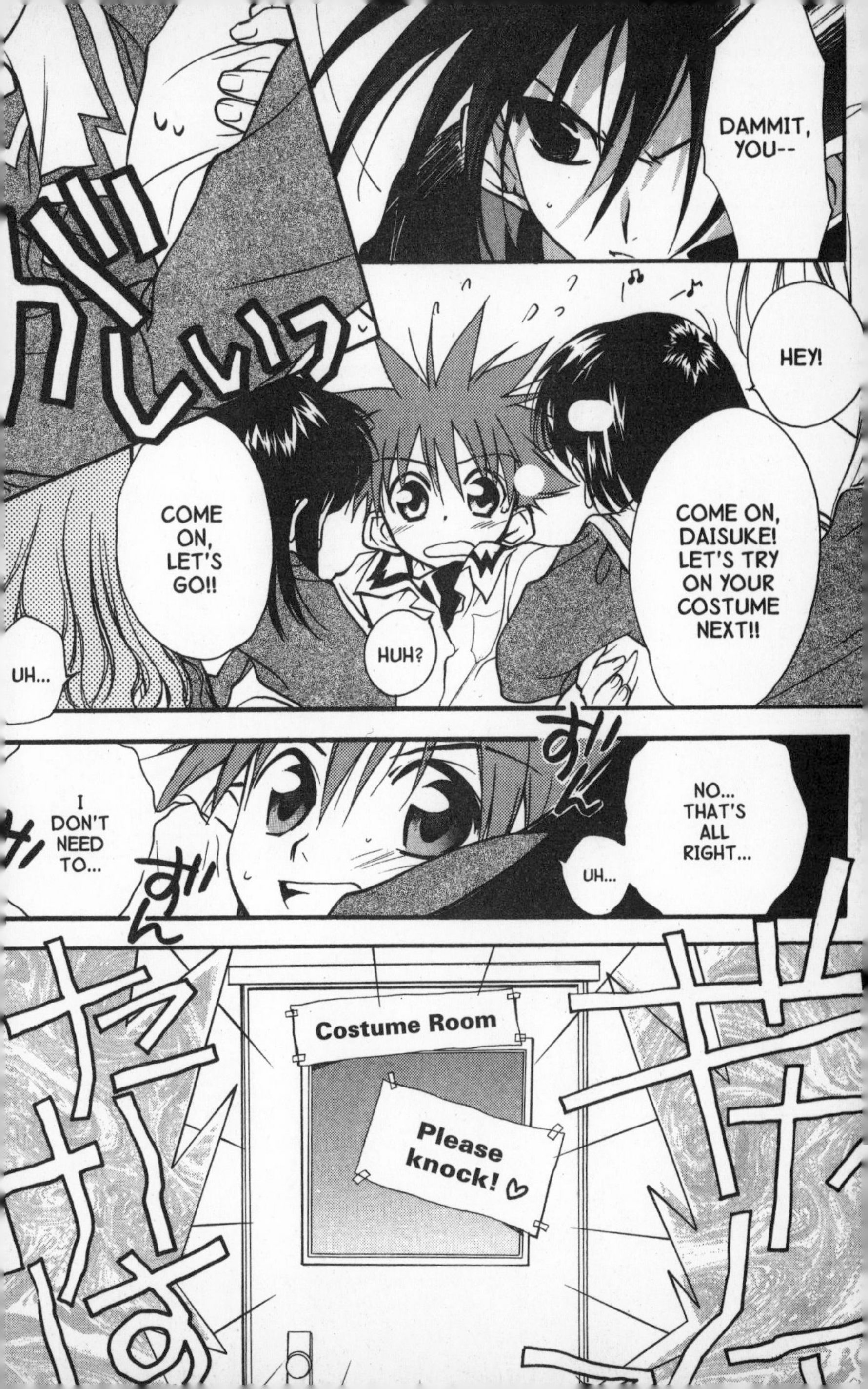
DAMMIT, YOU--
HEY!
COME ON, DAISUKE! LET'S TRY ON YOUR COSTUME NEXT!!
HUH?
COME ON, LET'S GO!!
UH...
NO... THAT'S ALL RIGHT...
UH...
I DON'T NEED TO...
Costume Room
Please knock! ♡

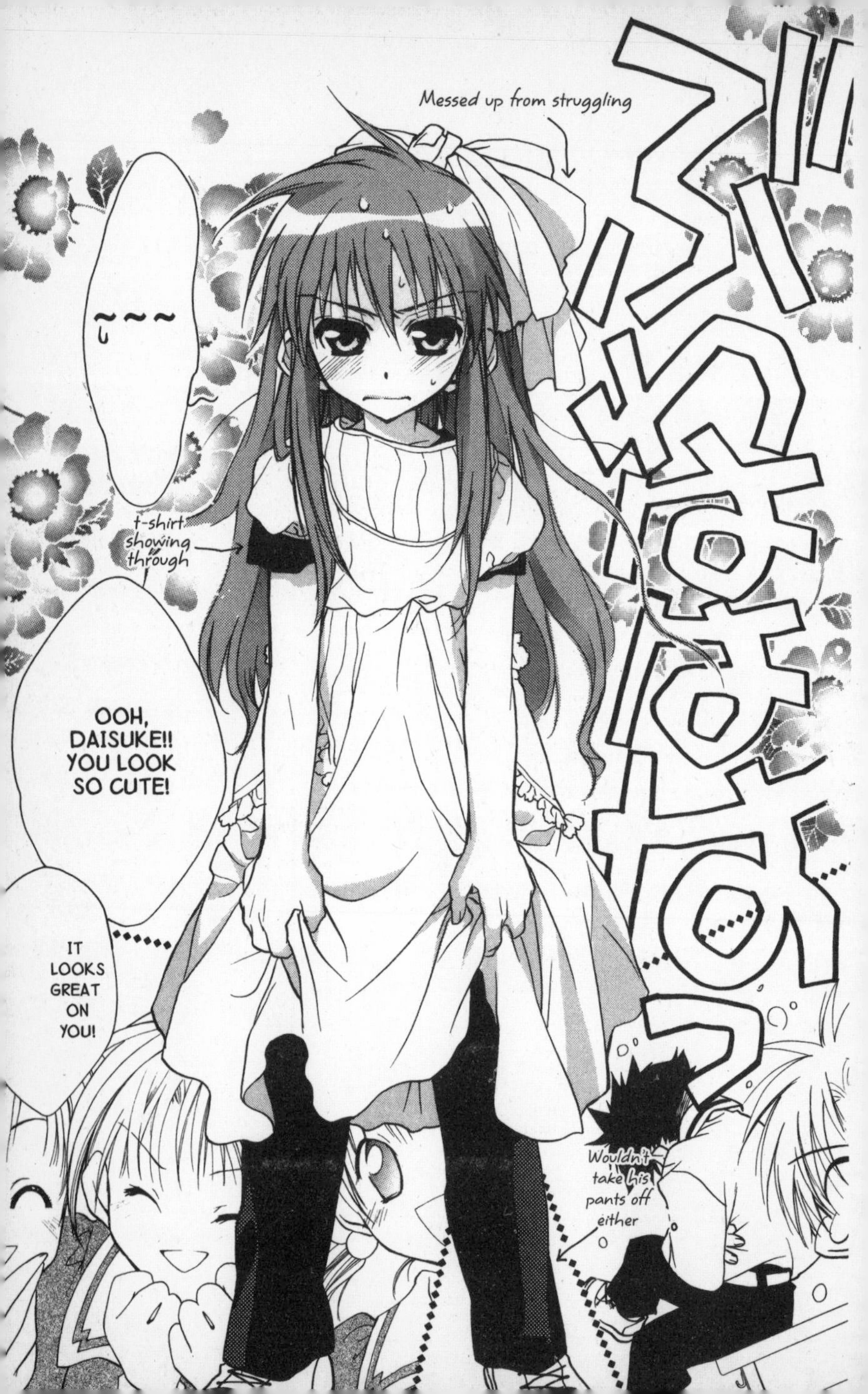
Messed up from struggling
Wouldn't take his pants off either
~~~
t-shirt showing through
OOH, DAISUKE!! YOU LOOK SO CUTE!
IT LOOKS GREAT ON YOU!
~~~

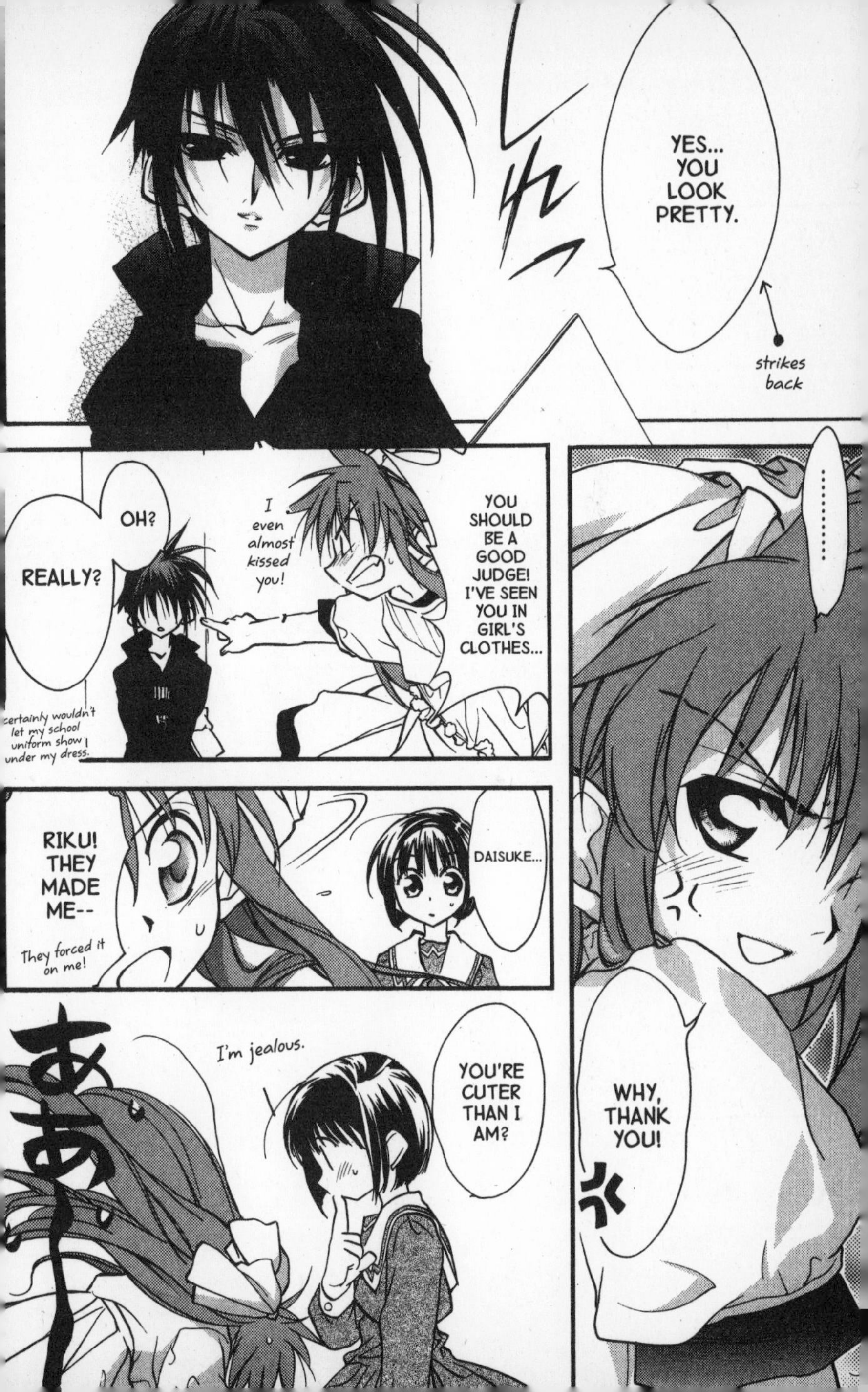

YES... YOU LOOK PRETTY.
strikes back
......
WHY, THANK YOU!
YOU SHOULD BE A GOOD JUDGE! I'VE SEEN YOU IN GIRL'S CLOTHES...
I even almost kissed you!
OH?
REALLY?
certainly wouldn't let my school uniform show under my dress.
DAISUKE...
RIKU! THEY MADE ME--
They forced it on me!
YOU'RE CUTER THAN I AM?
I'm jealous.
ああ

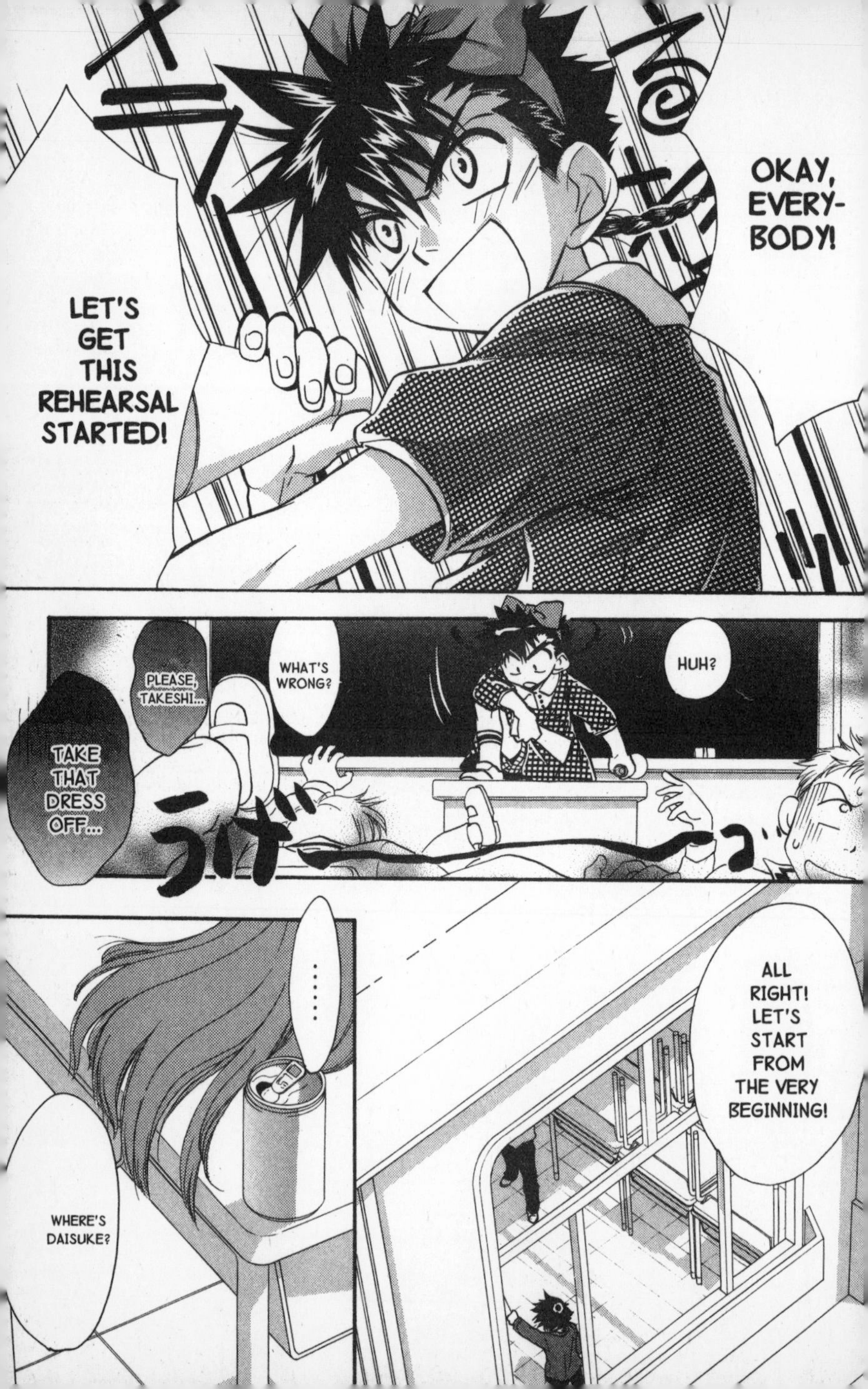
OKAY, EVERY-BODY!
LET'S GET THIS REHEARSAL STARTED!
HUH?
WHAT'S WRONG?
PLEASE, TAKESHI...
TAKE THAT DRESS OFF...
うげーっ
ALL RIGHT! LET'S START FROM THE VERY BEGINNING!
......
WHERE'S DAISUKE?

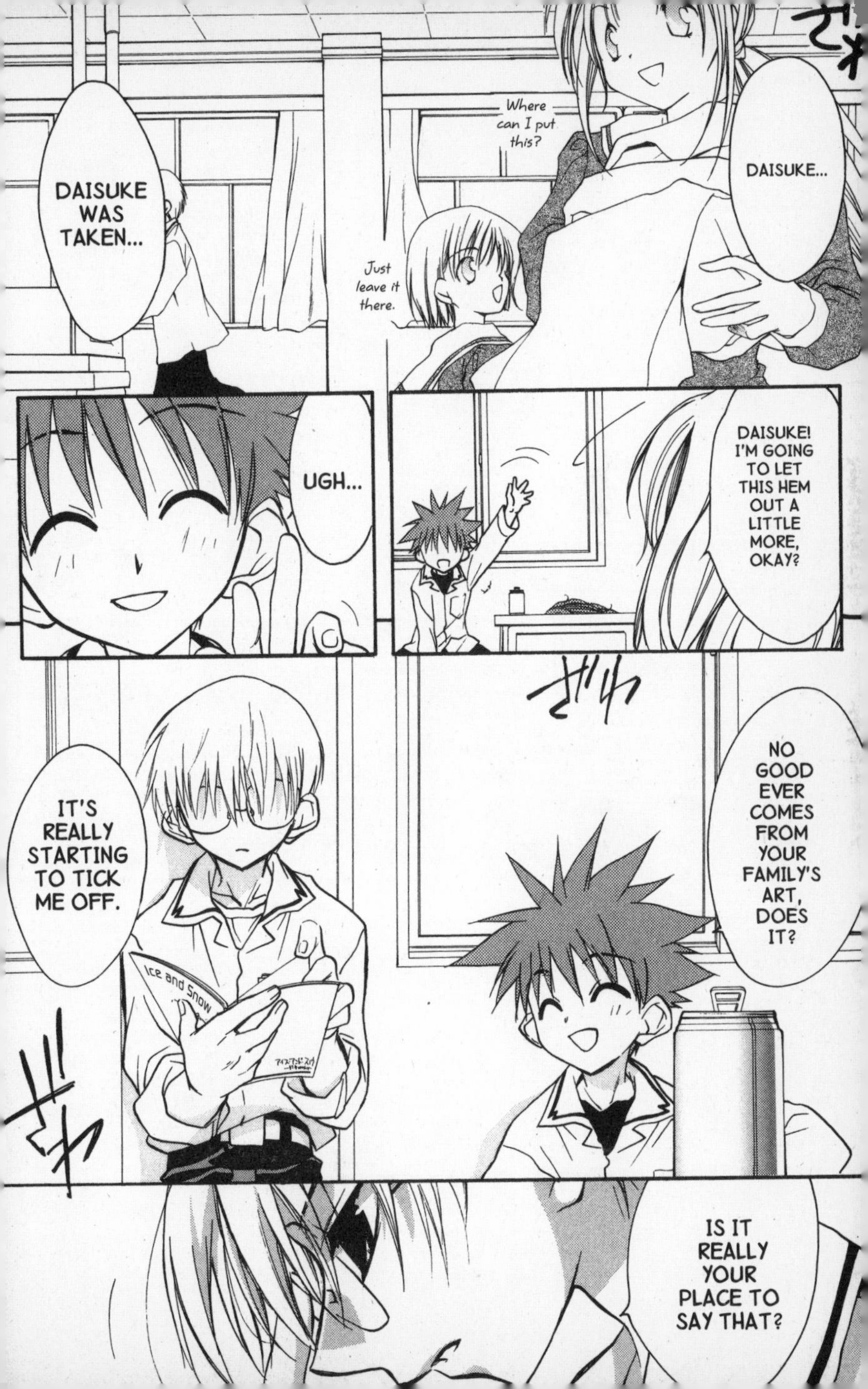
DAISUKE...
Where can I put this?
Just leave it there.
DAISUKE WAS TAKEN...
DAISUKE! I'M GOING TO LET THIS HEM OUT A LITTLE MORE, OKAY?
UGH...
ざわ
NO GOOD EVER COMES FROM YOUR FAMILY'S ART, DOES IT?
IT'S REALLY STARTING TO TICK ME OFF.
Ice and Snow
ざわ
IS IT REALLY YOUR PLACE TO SAY THAT?

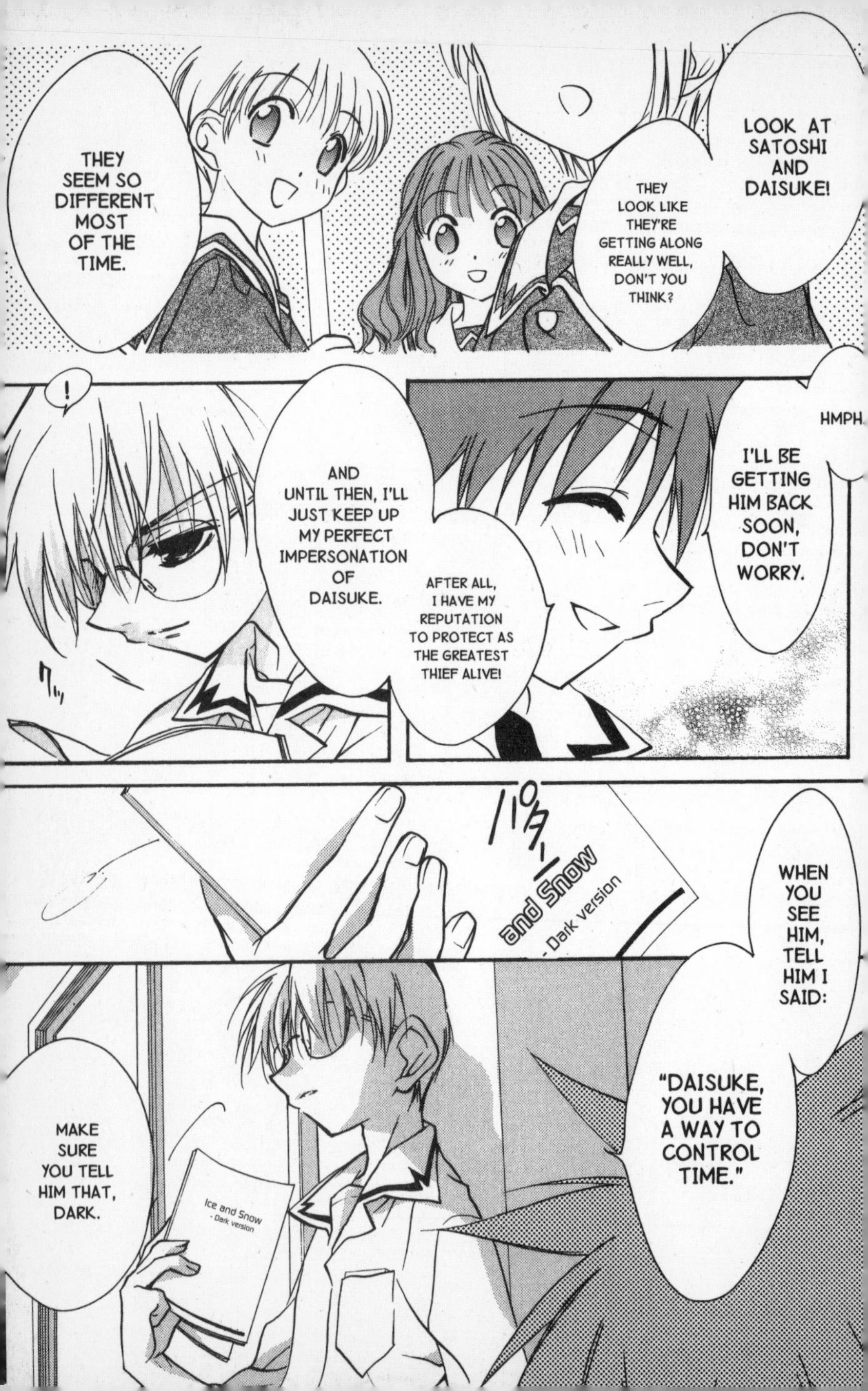
LOOK AT SATOSHI AND DAISUKE!
THEY LOOK LIKE THEY'RE GETTING ALONG REALLY WELL, DON'T YOU THINK?
THEY SEEM SO DIFFERENT MOST OF THE TIME.
HMPH.
I'LL BE GETTING HIM BACK SOON, DON'T WORRY.
AND UNTIL THEN, I'LL JUST KEEP UP MY PERFECT IMPERSONATION OF DAISUKE.
AFTER ALL, I HAVE MY REPUTATION TO PROTECT AS THE GREATEST THIEF ALIVE!
!
WHEN YOU SEE HIM, TELL HIM I SAID:
and Snow
- Dark version
"DAISUKE, YOU HAVE A WAY TO CONTROL TIME."
Ice and Snow
- Dark version
MAKE SURE YOU TELL HIM THAT, DARK.

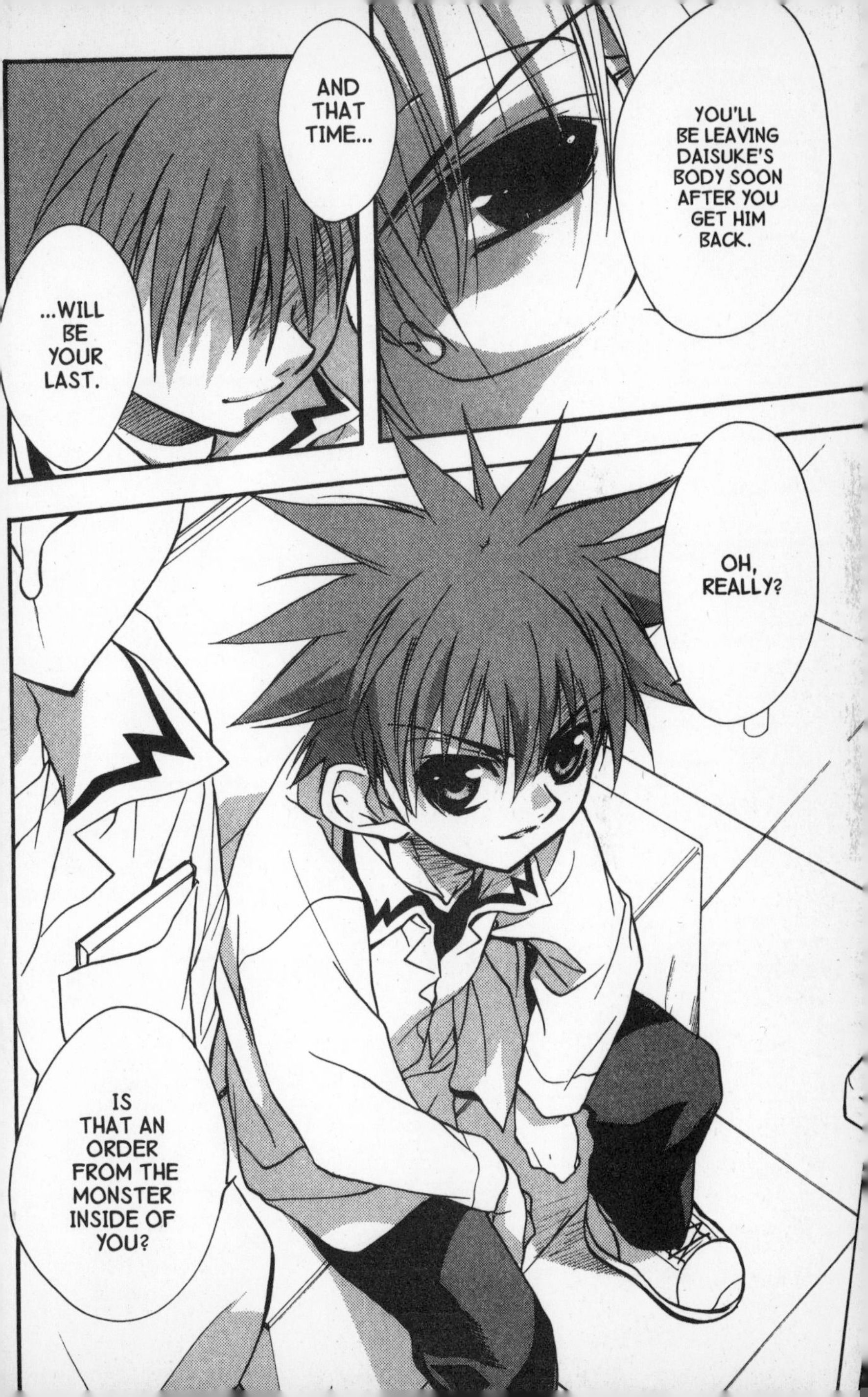
YOU'LL BE LEAVING DAISUKE'S BODY SOON AFTER YOU GET HIM BACK.
AND THAT TIME...
...WILL BE YOUR LAST.
OH, REALLY?
IS THAT AN ORDER FROM THE MONSTER INSIDE OF YOU?

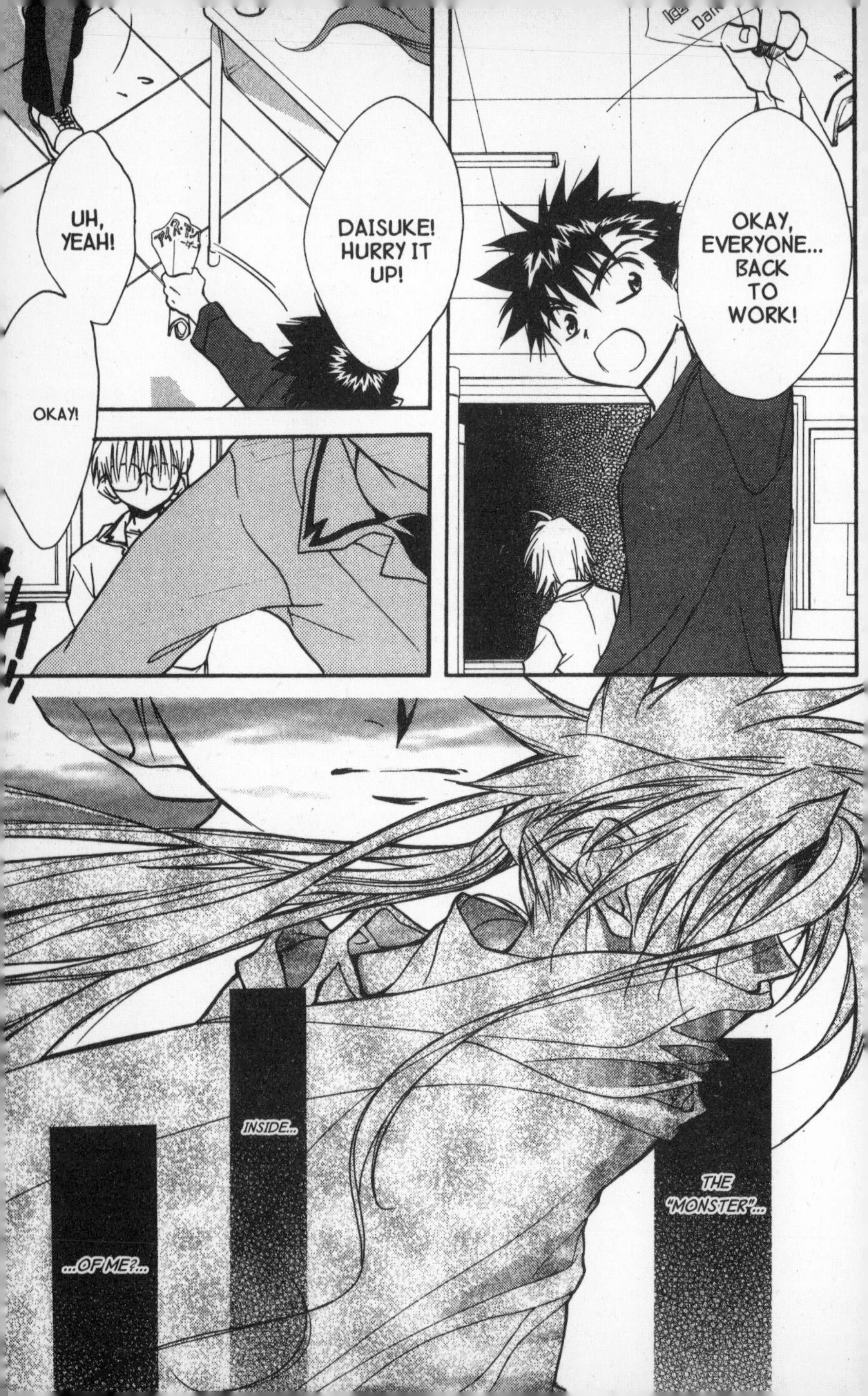
OKAY, EVERYONE... BACK TO WORK!
DAISUKE! HURRY IT UP!
UH, YEAH!
OKAY!
THE "MONSTER"...
INSIDE...
...OF ME?...

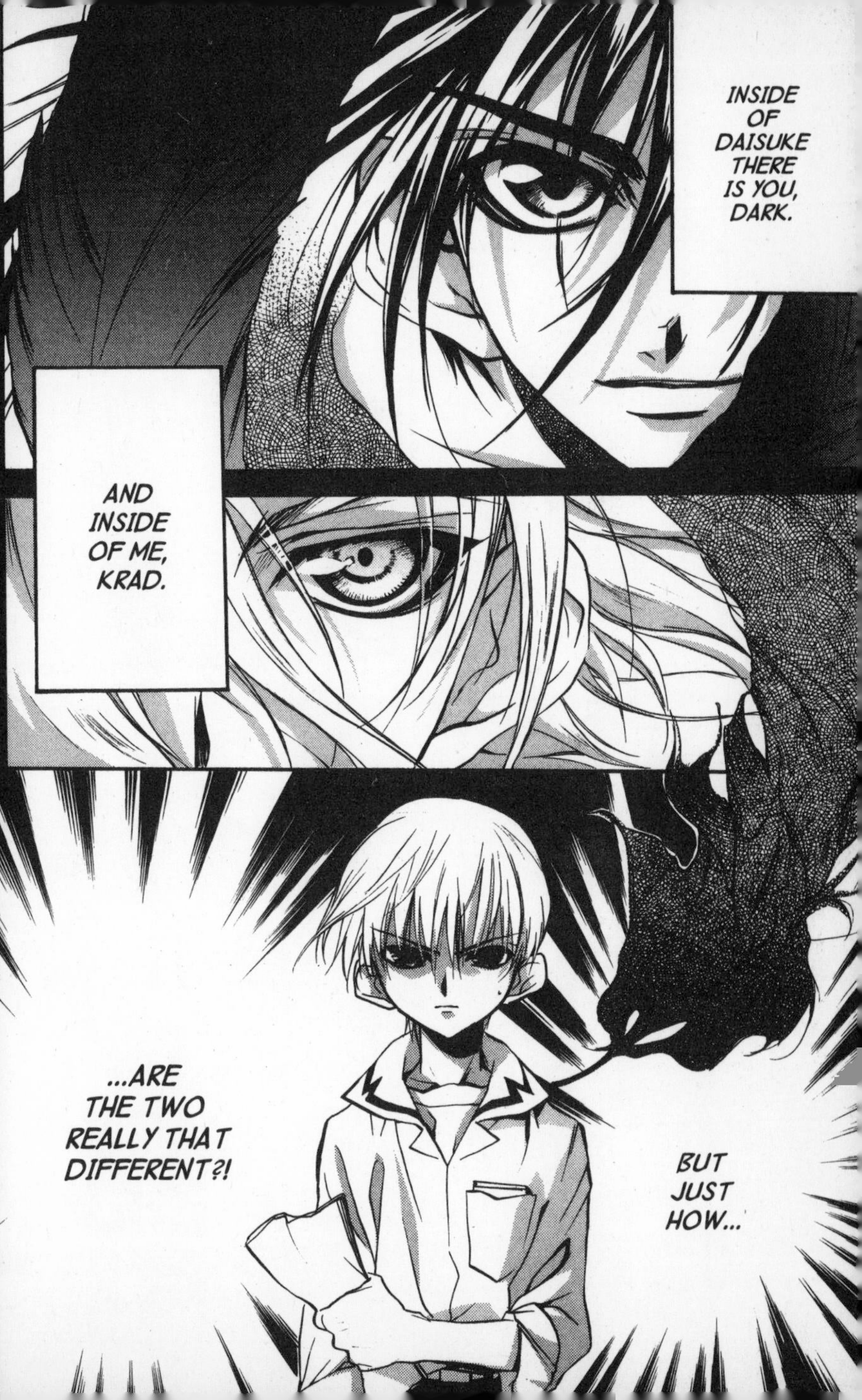
INSIDE OF DAISUKE THERE IS YOU, DARK.
AND INSIDE OF ME, KRAD.
BUT JUST HOW...
...ARE THE TWO REALLY THAT DIFFERENT?!

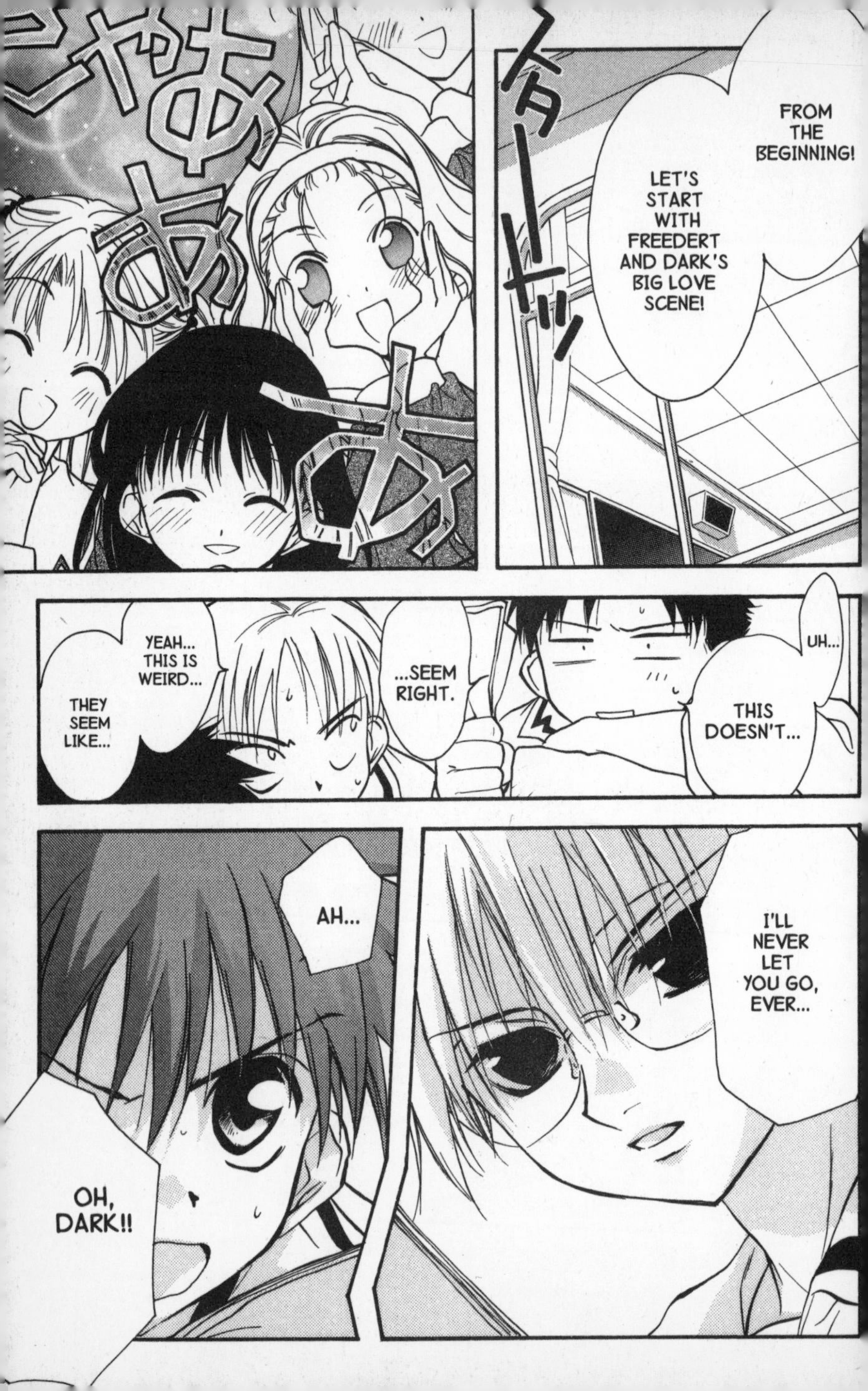
FROM THE BEGINNING!
LET'S START WITH FREEDERT AND DARK'S BIG LOVE SCENE!
UH...
THIS DOESN'T...
...SEEM RIGHT.
YEAH... THIS IS WEIRD...
THEY SEEM LIKE...
I'LL NEVER LET YOU GO, EVER...
AH...
OH, DARK!!

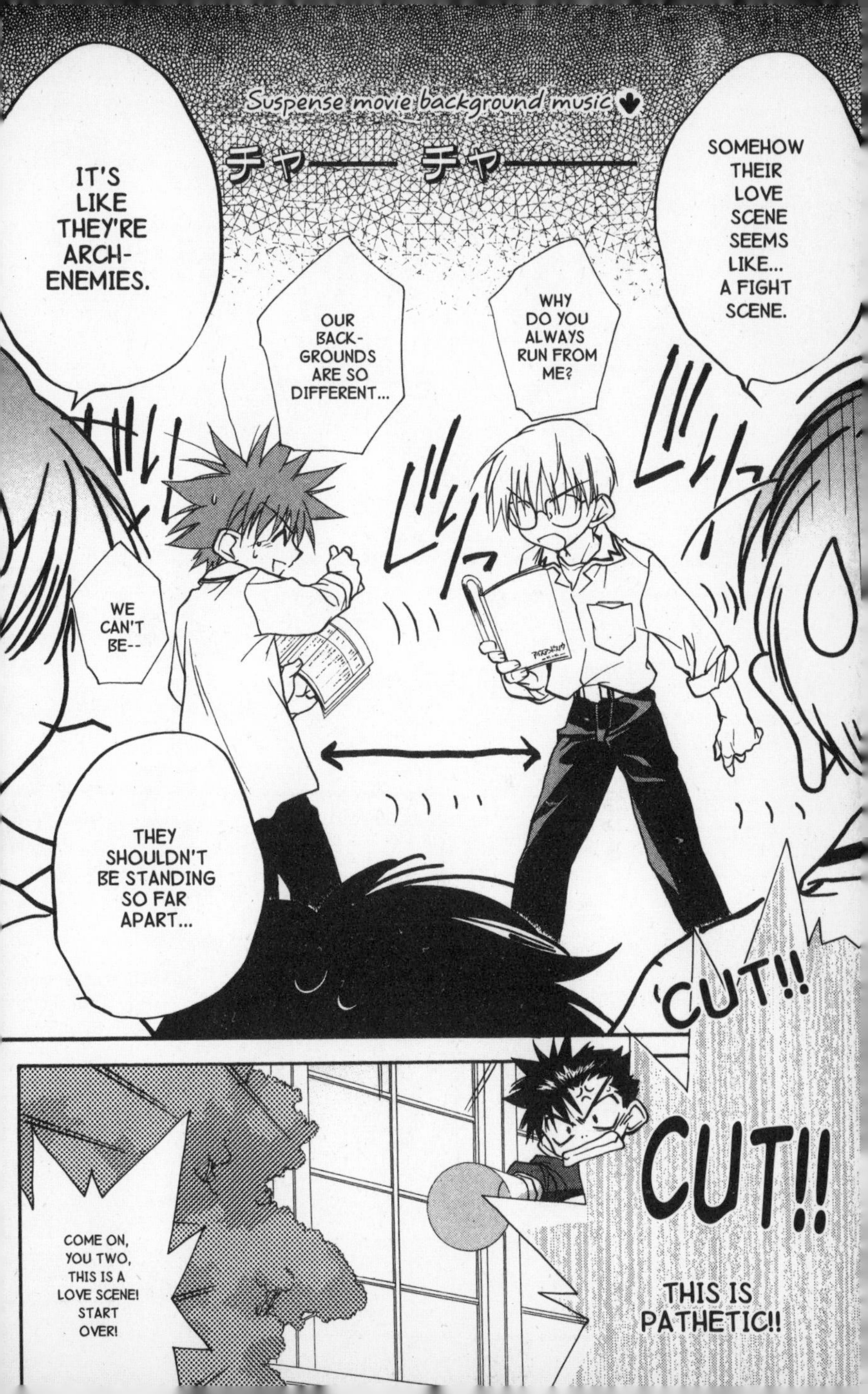
Suspense movie background music
チャー—— チャー——
SOMEHOW THEIR LOVE SCENE SEEMS LIKE... A FIGHT SCENE.
IT'S LIKE THEY'RE ARCH-ENEMIES.
WHY DO YOU ALWAYS RUN FROM ME?
OUR BACK-GROUNDS ARE SO DIFFERENT...
WE CAN'T BE--
THEY SHOULDN'T BE STANDING SO FAR APART...
'CUT!!
CUT!!
THIS IS PATHETIC!!
COME ON, YOU TWO, THIS IS A LOVE SCENE! START OVER!

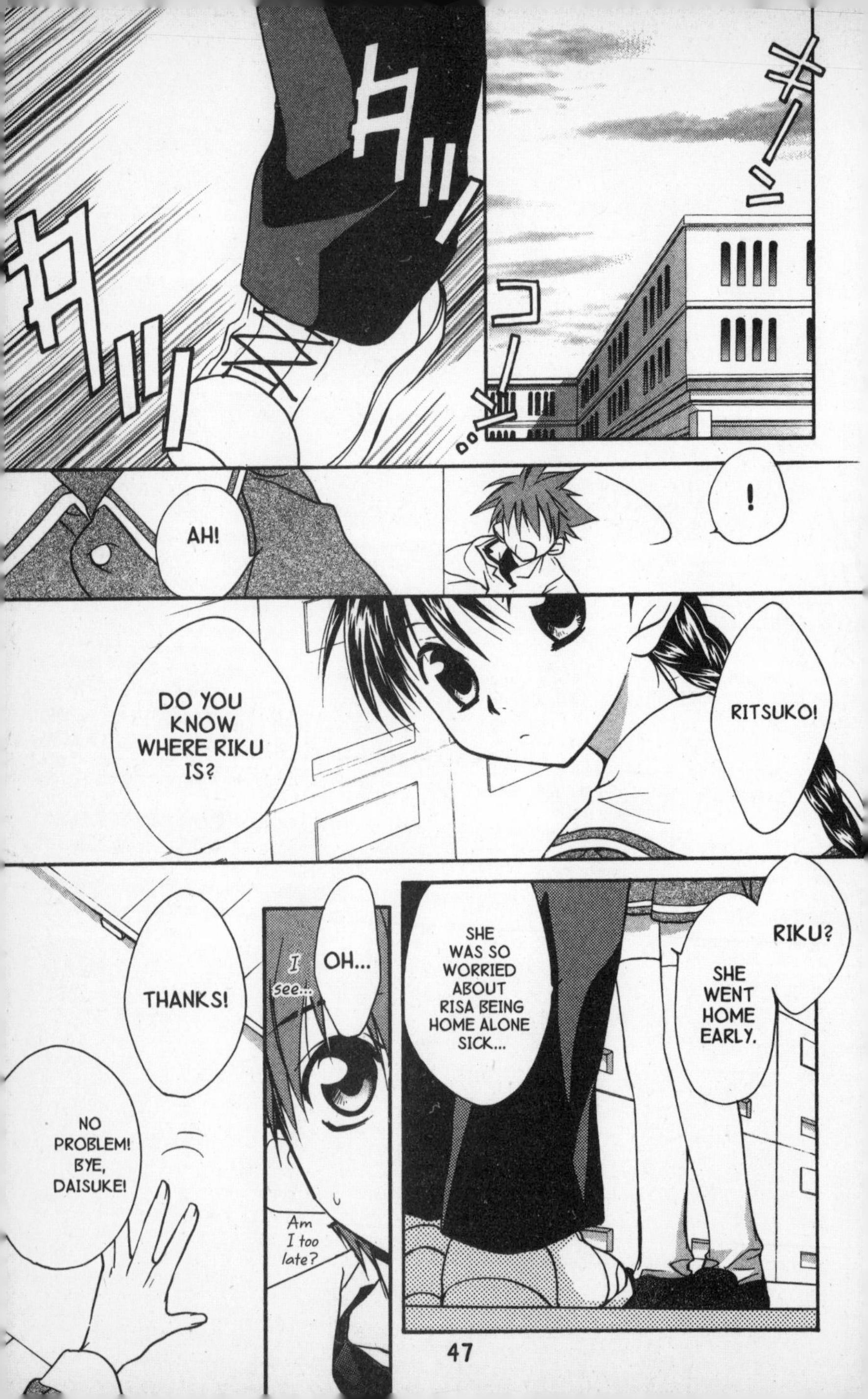
!
AH!
RITSUKO!
DO YOU KNOW WHERE RIKU IS?
RIKU?
SHE WENT HOME EARLY.
SHE WAS SO WORRIED ABOUT RISA BEING HOME ALONE SICK...
OH...
I see...
Am I too late?
THANKS!
NO PROBLEM! BYE, DAISUKE!

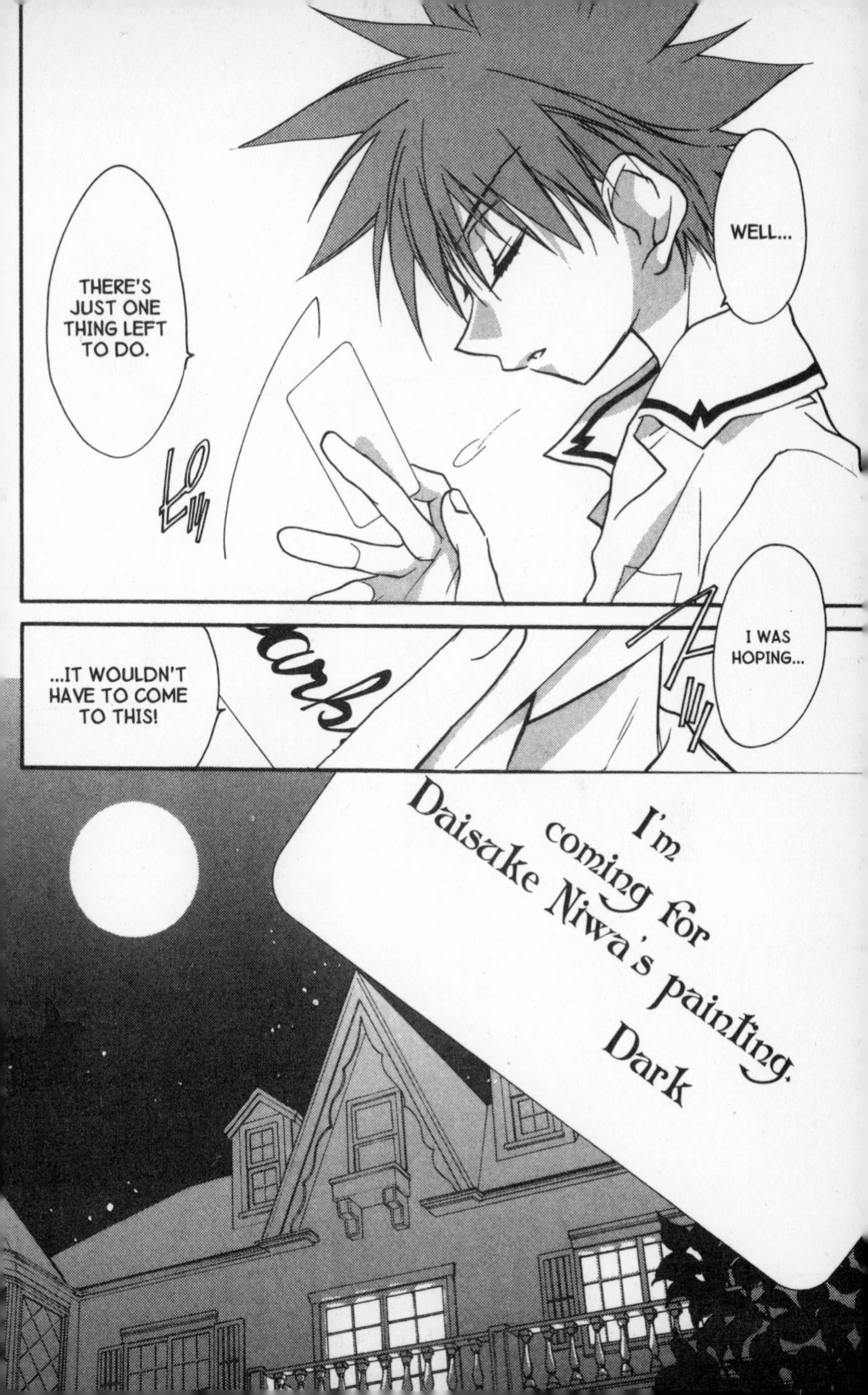
WELL...
THERE'S JUST ONE THING LEFT TO DO.
I WAS HOPING...
...IT WOULDN'T HAVE TO COME TO THIS!
I'm coming for Daisuke Niwa's painting.
Dark

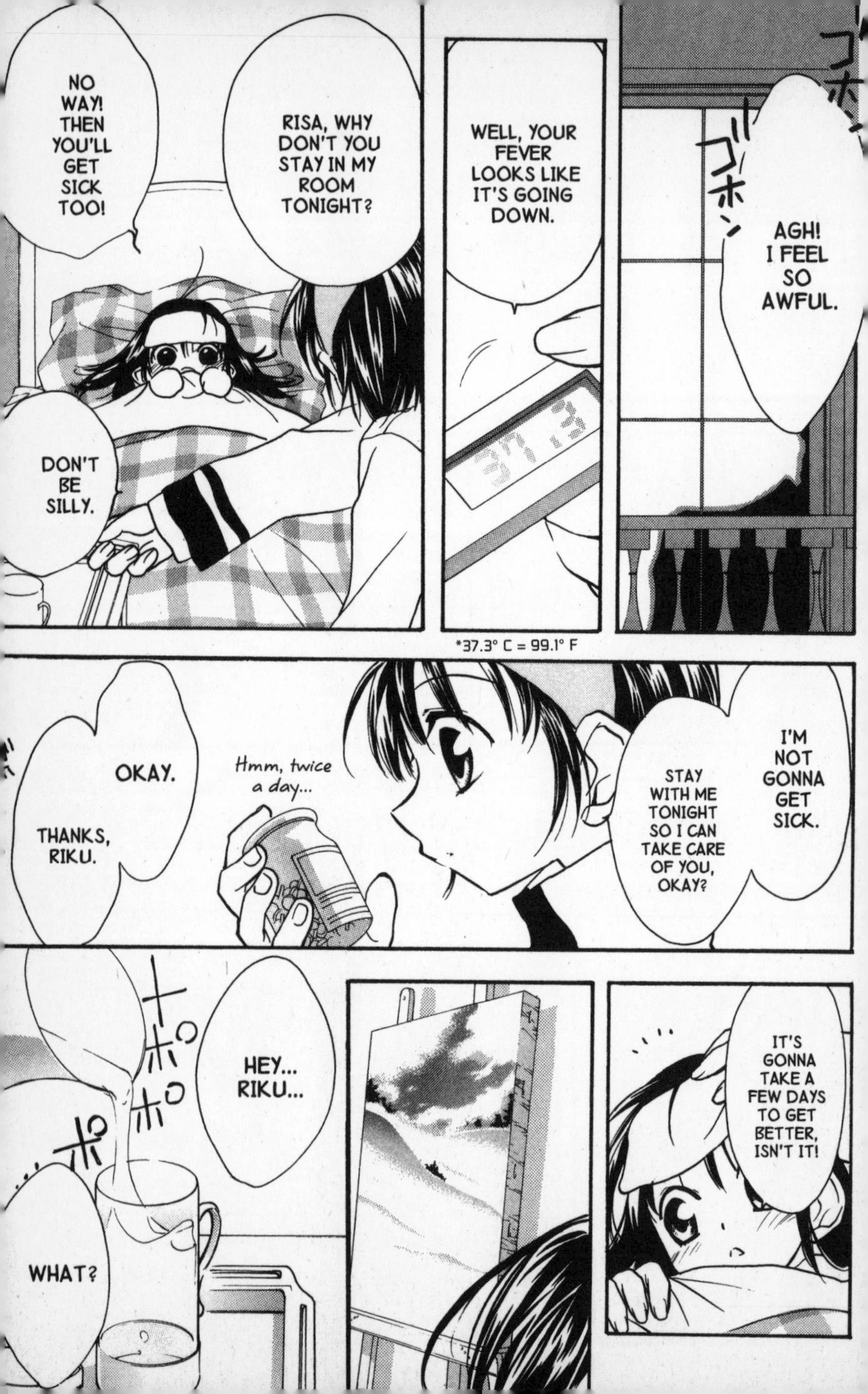
ゴホッ
ゴホン
AGH! I FEEL SO AWFUL.
WELL, YOUR FEVER LOOKS LIKE IT'S GOING DOWN.
37.3
RISA, WHY DON'T YOU STAY IN MY ROOM TONIGHT?
NO WAY! THEN YOU'LL GET SICK TOO!
DON'T BE SILLY.
I'M NOT GONNA GET SICK.
STAY WITH ME TONIGHT SO I CAN TAKE CARE OF YOU, OKAY?
Hmm, twice a day...
OKAY.
THANKS, RIKU.
IT'S GONNA TAKE A FEW DAYS TO GET BETTER, ISN'T IT!
HEY... RIKU...
ホロホロ
ポ
WHAT?
*37.3° C = 99.1° F

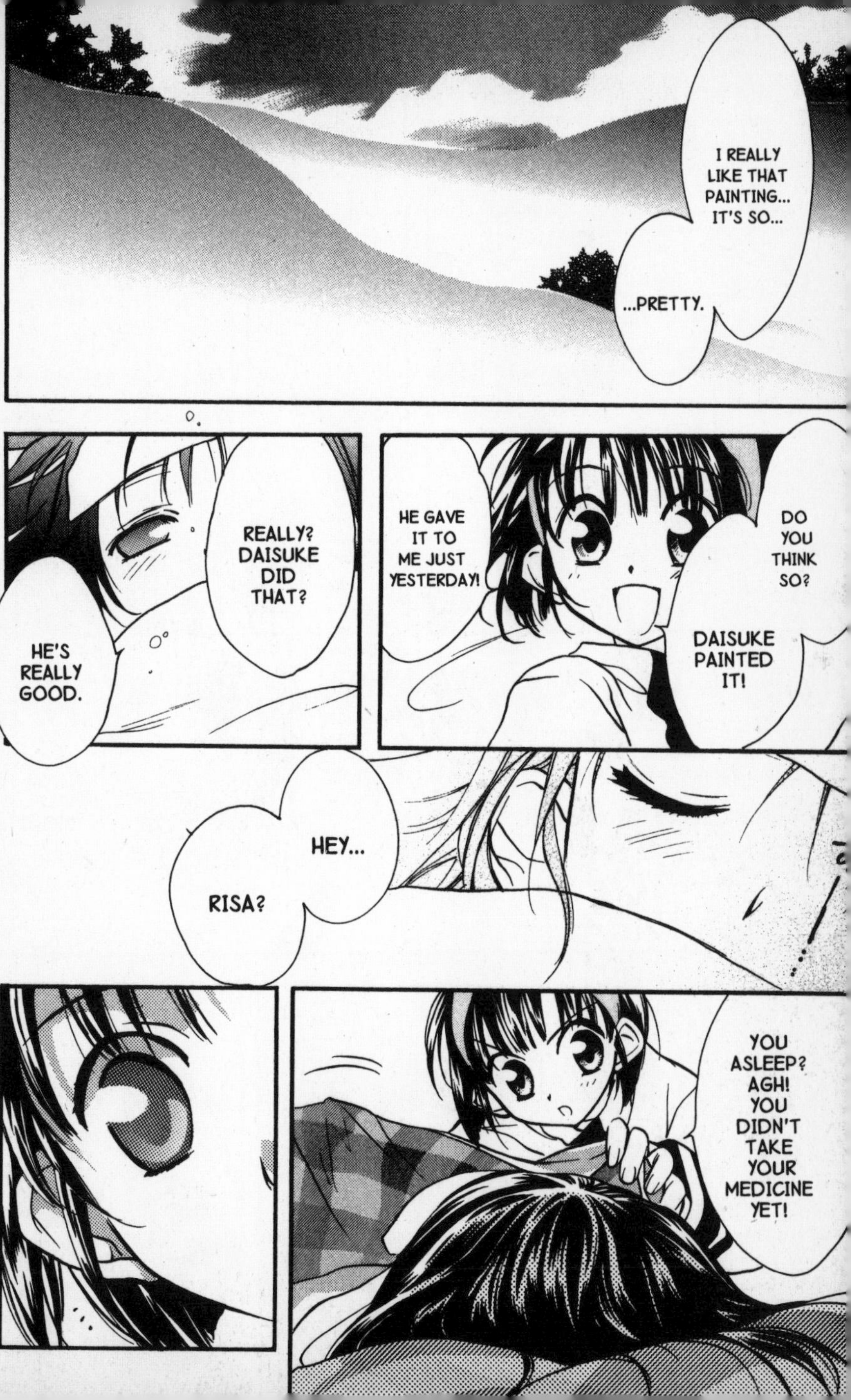
I REALLY LIKE THAT PAINTING... IT'S SO...
...PRETTY.
DO YOU THINK SO?
DAISUKE PAINTED IT!
HE GAVE IT TO ME JUST YESTERDAY!
REALLY? DAISUKE DID THAT?
HE'S REALLY GOOD.
HEY...
RISA?
YOU ASLEEP? AGH! YOU DIDN'T TAKE YOUR MEDICINE YET!

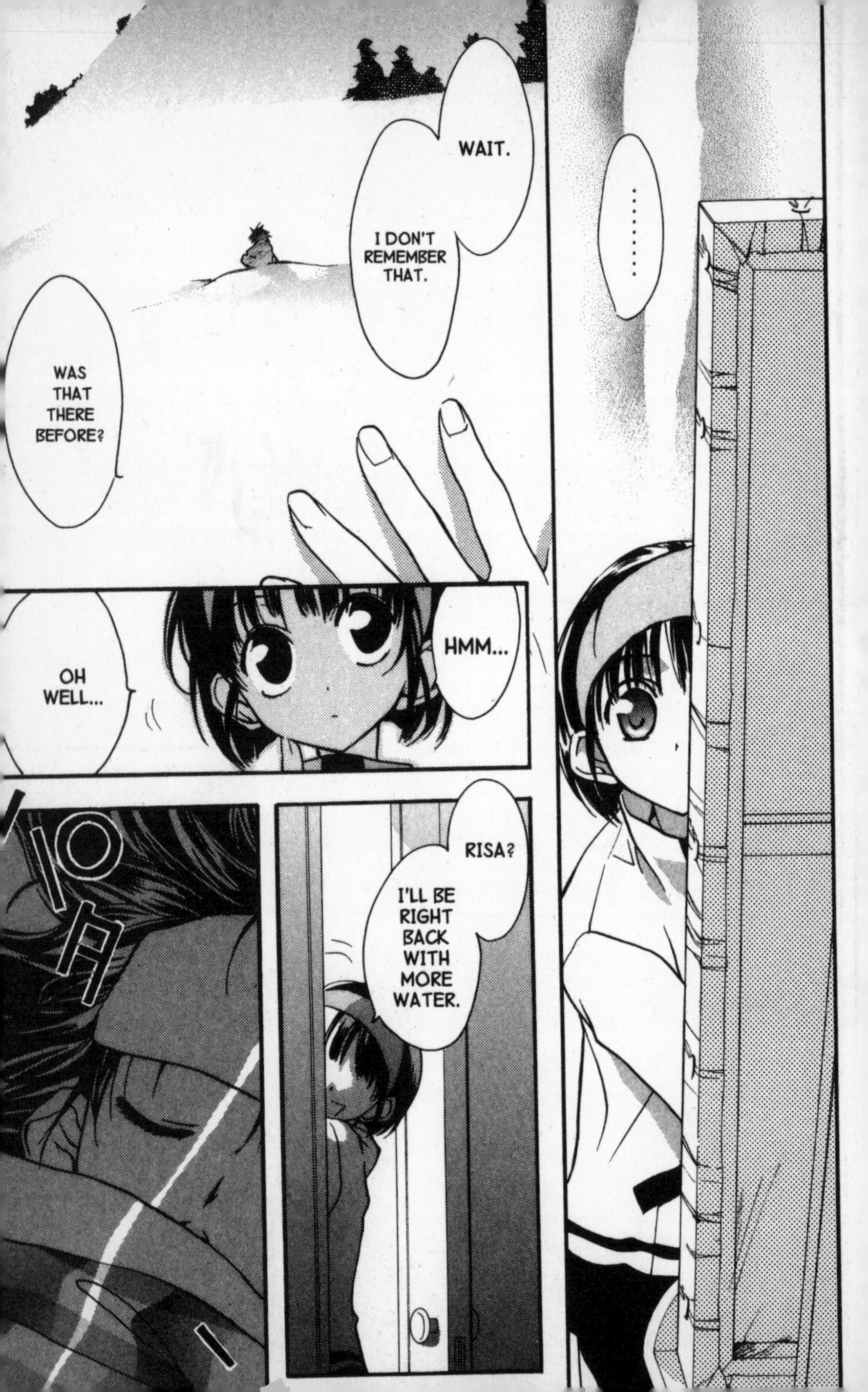
......
WAIT.
I DON'T REMEMBER THAT.
WAS THAT THERE BEFORE?
HMM...
OH WELL...
RISA?
I'LL BE RIGHT BACK WITH MORE WATER.

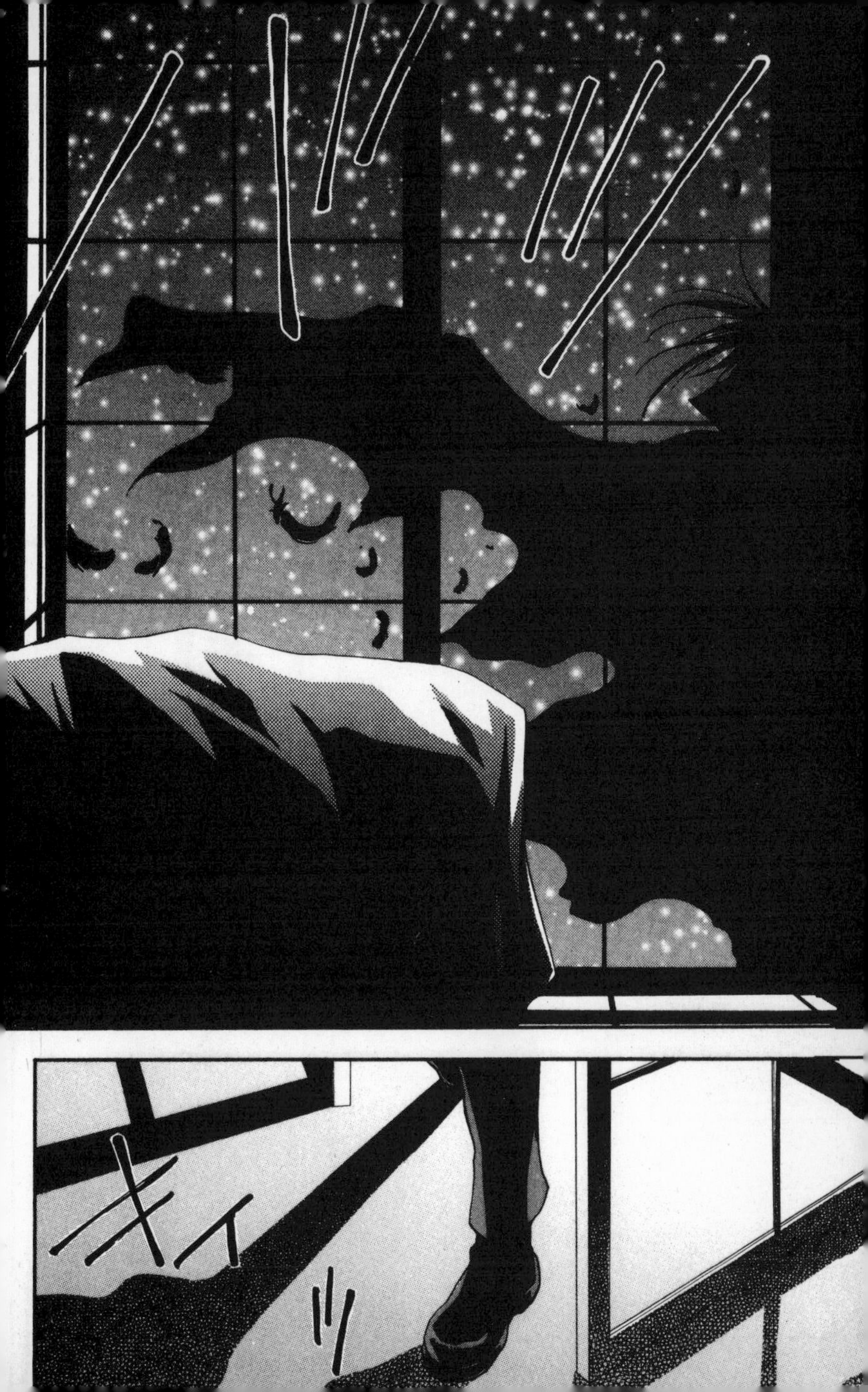
キイ
ッ

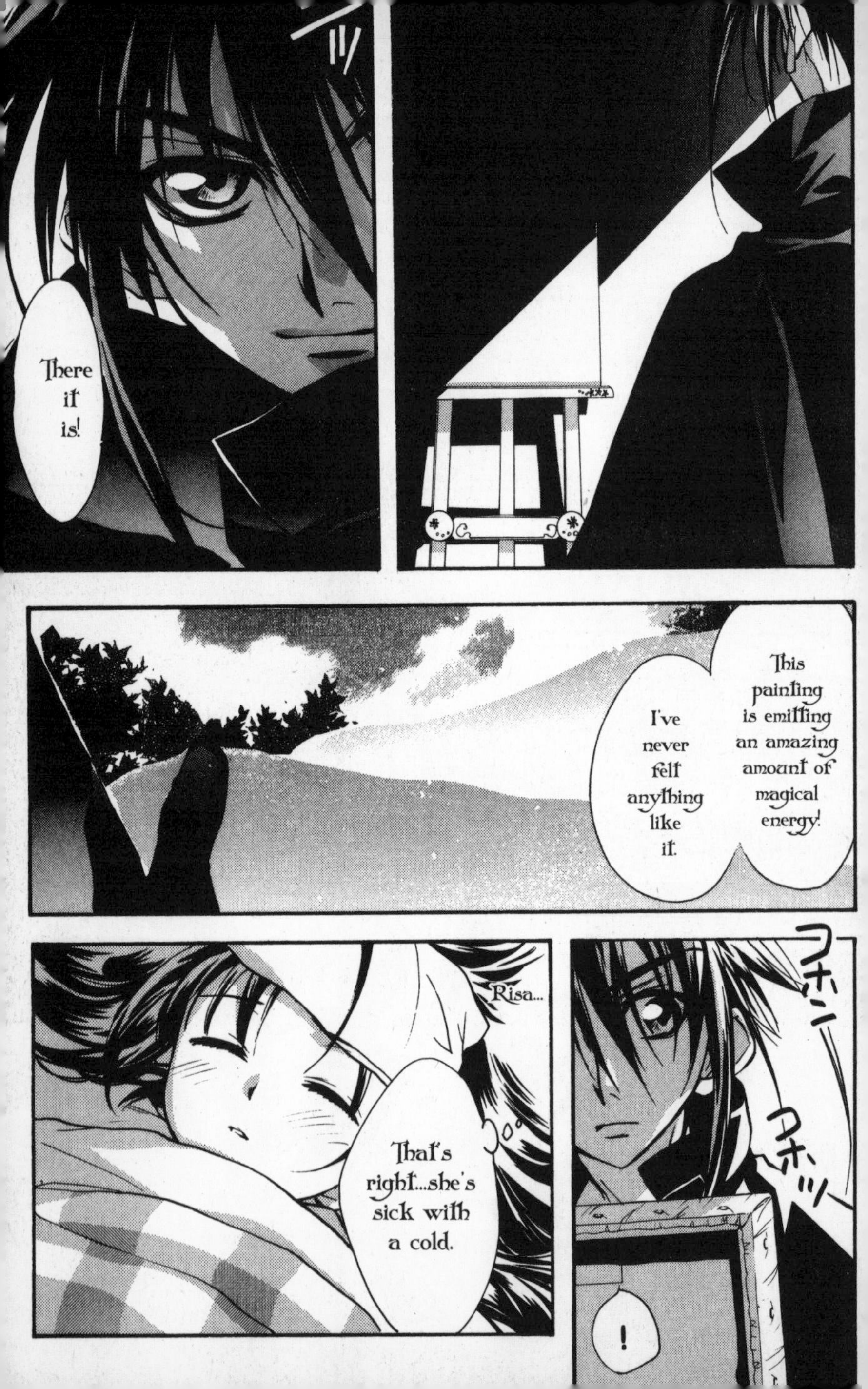
There it is!
This painting is emitting an amazing amount of magical energy!
I've never felt anything like it.
コホン
コホッ
!
Risa...
That's right...she's sick with a cold.

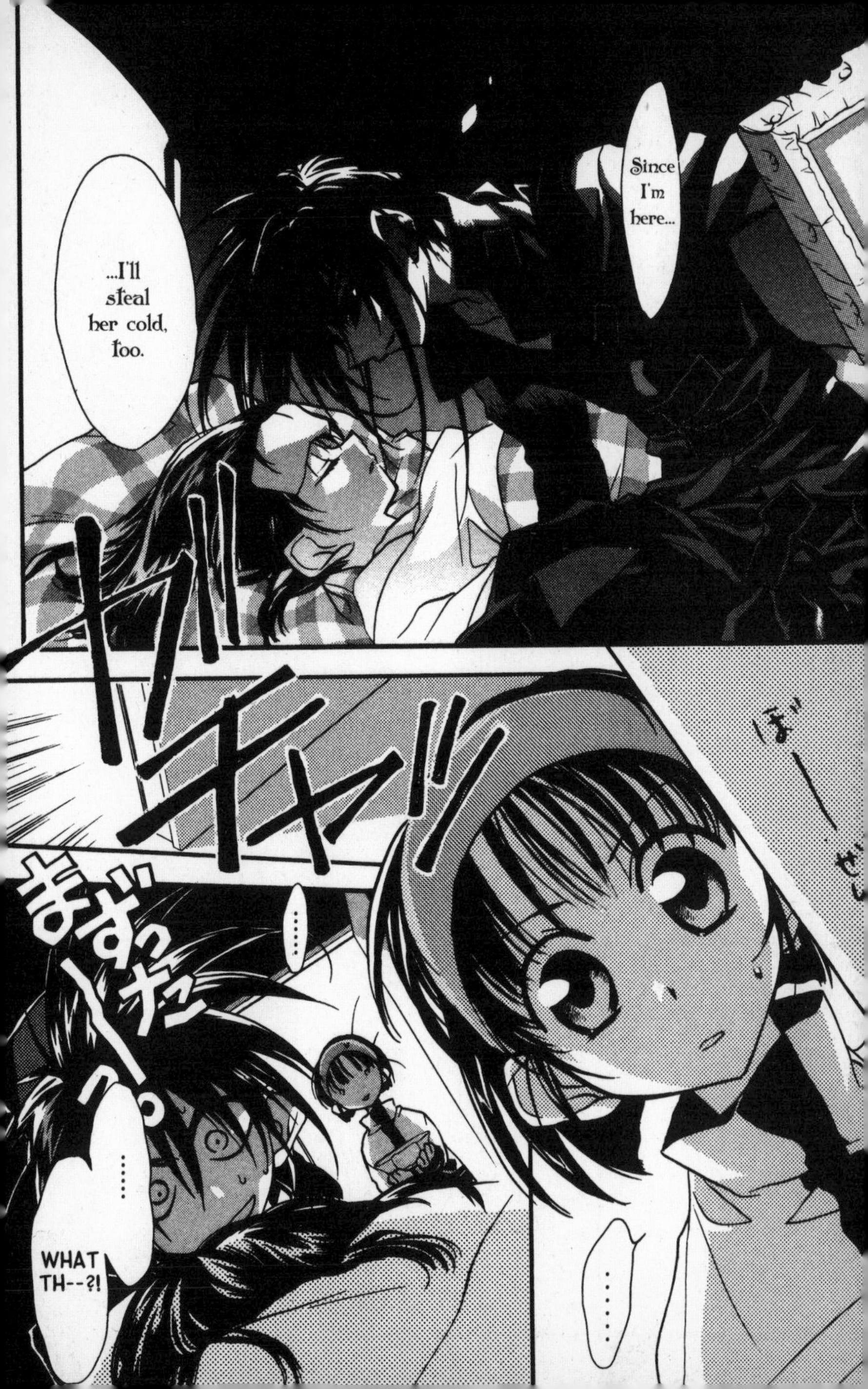

Since I'm here...
...I'll steal her cold, too.
ガチャ
ぼーーぜん
......
......
まずった〜っ
......
WHAT TH--?!

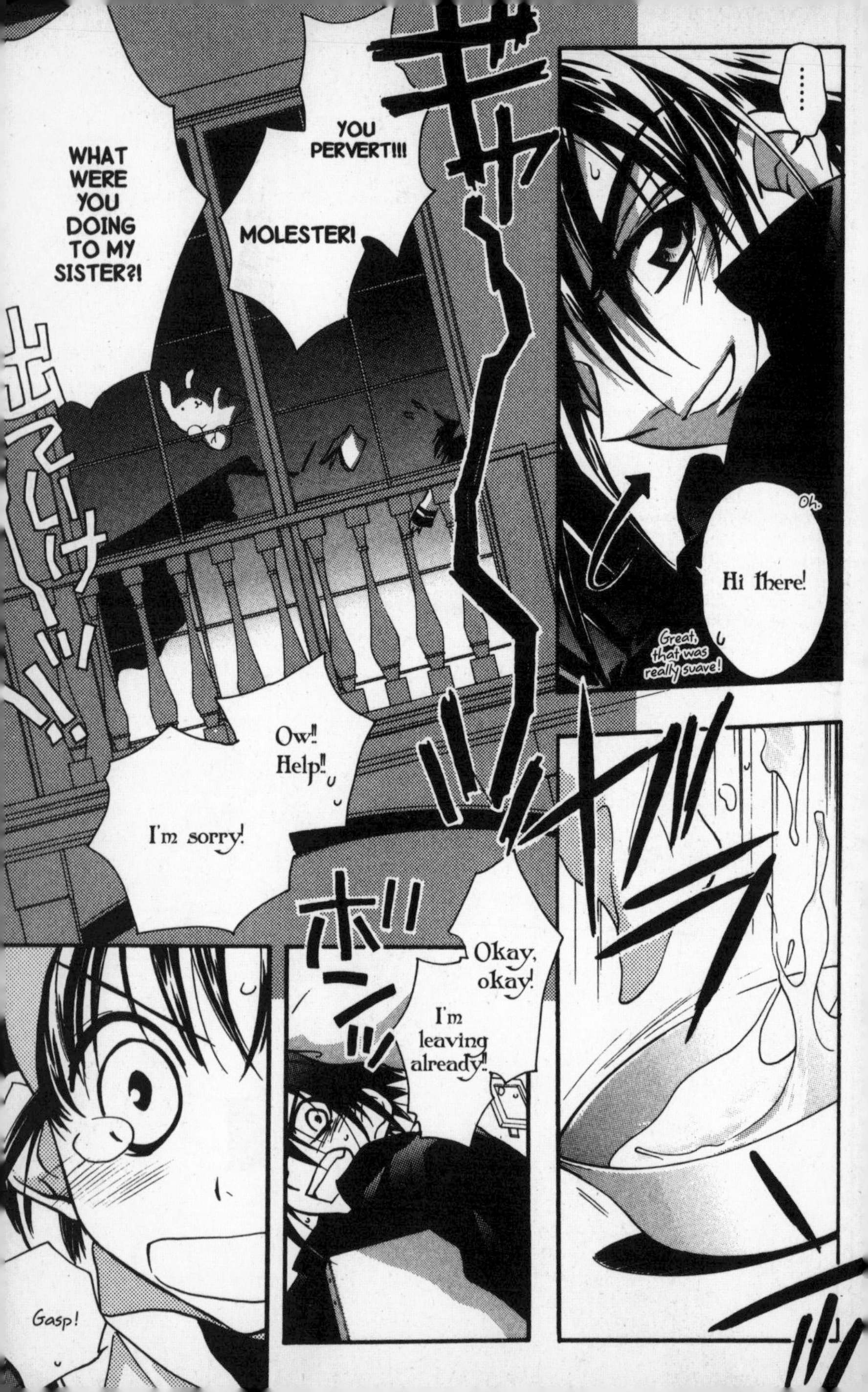
……
Oh.
Hi there!
Great, that was really suave!
YOU PERVERT!!!
MOLESTER!
WHAT WERE YOU DOING TO MY SISTER?!
Ow!! Help!!
I'm sorry!
Okay, okay!
I'm leaving already!!
Gasp!

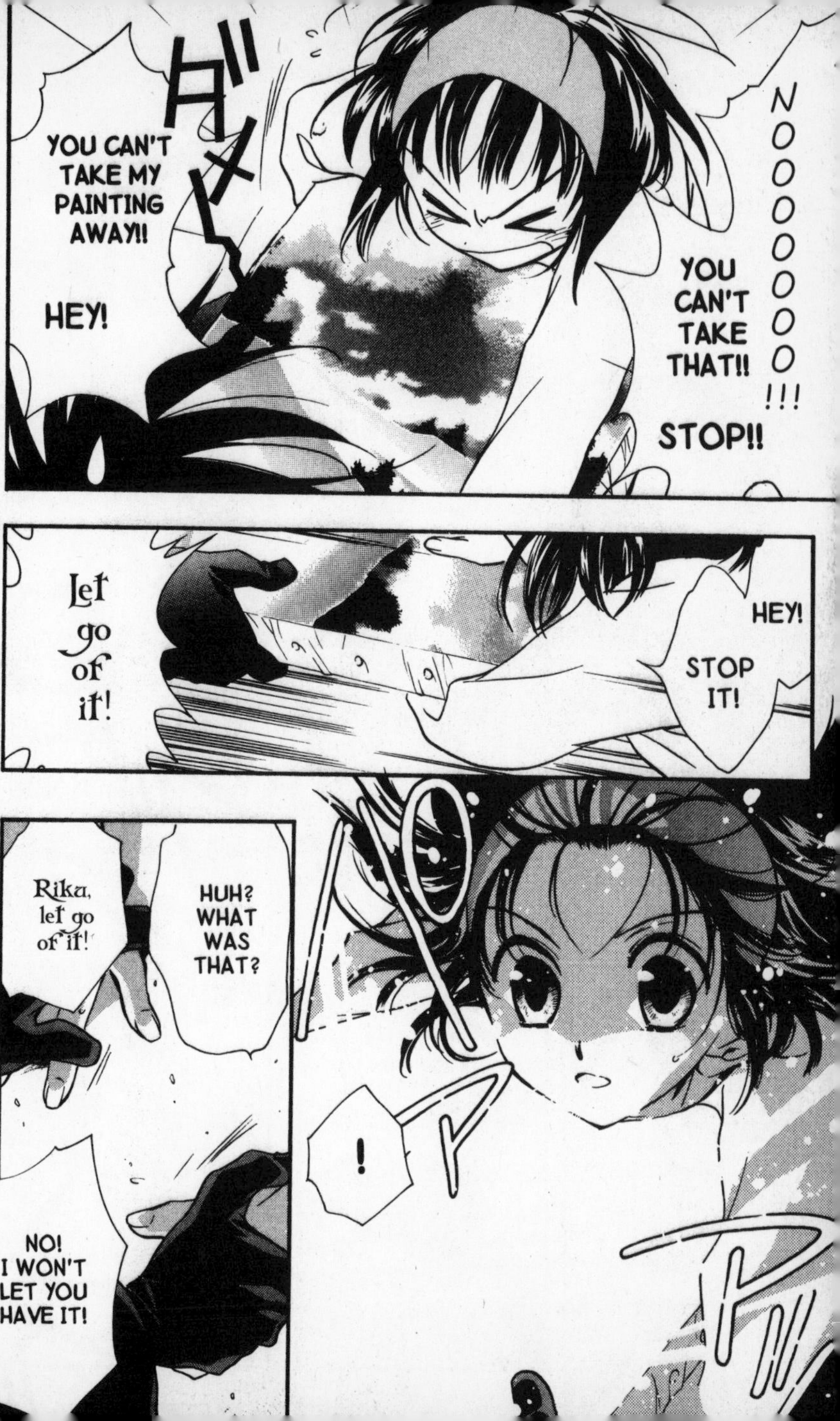
NOOOOOOOOO!!!
YOU CAN'T TAKE THAT!!
STOP!!
YOU CAN'T TAKE MY PAINTING AWAY!!
HEY!
HEY!
STOP IT!
Let go of it!
HUH? WHAT WAS THAT?
Riku, let go of it!
!
NO! I WON'T LET YOU HAVE IT!

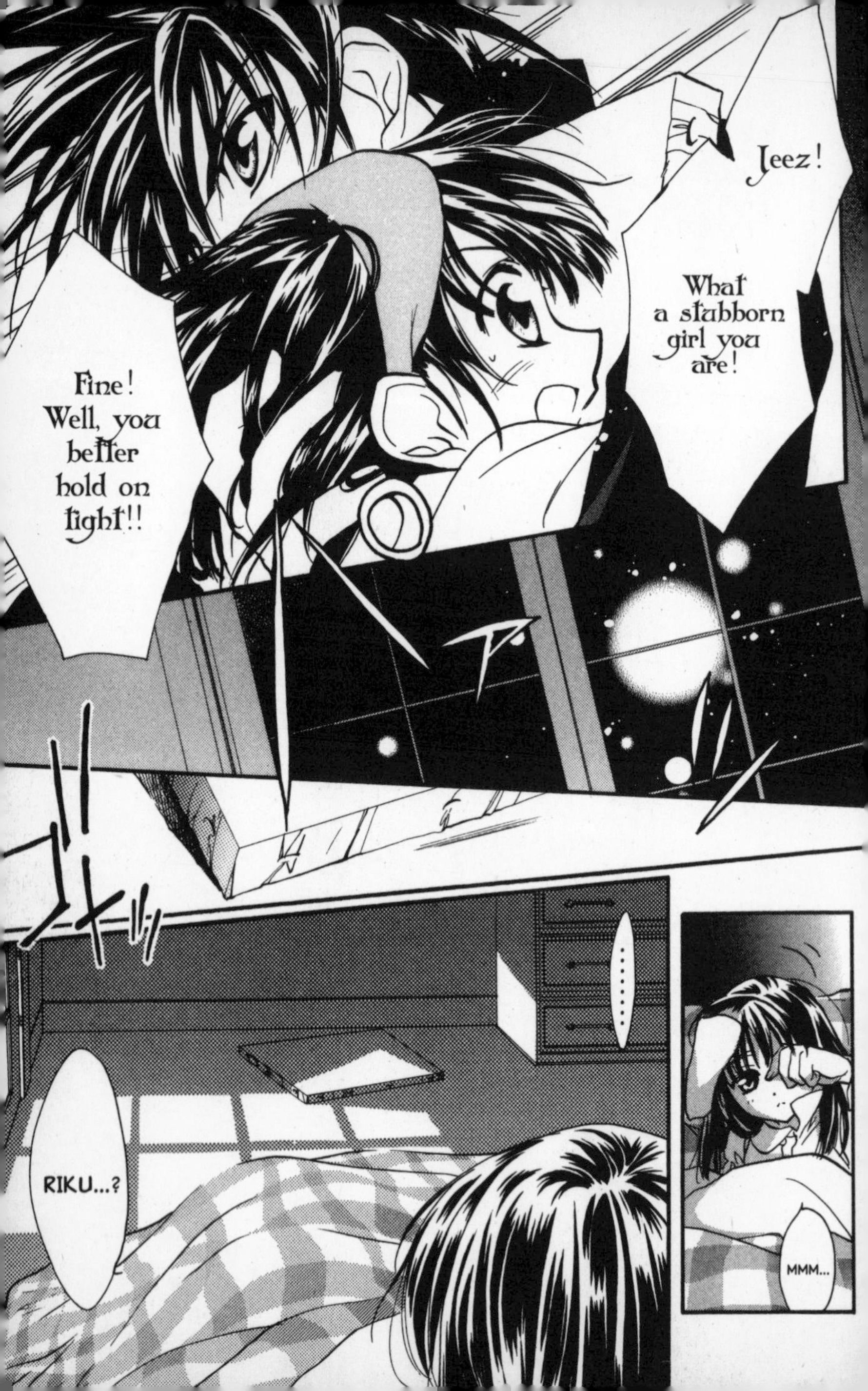
Jeez!
What a stubborn girl you are!
Fine! Well, you better hold on tight!!
MMM...
......
RIKU...?

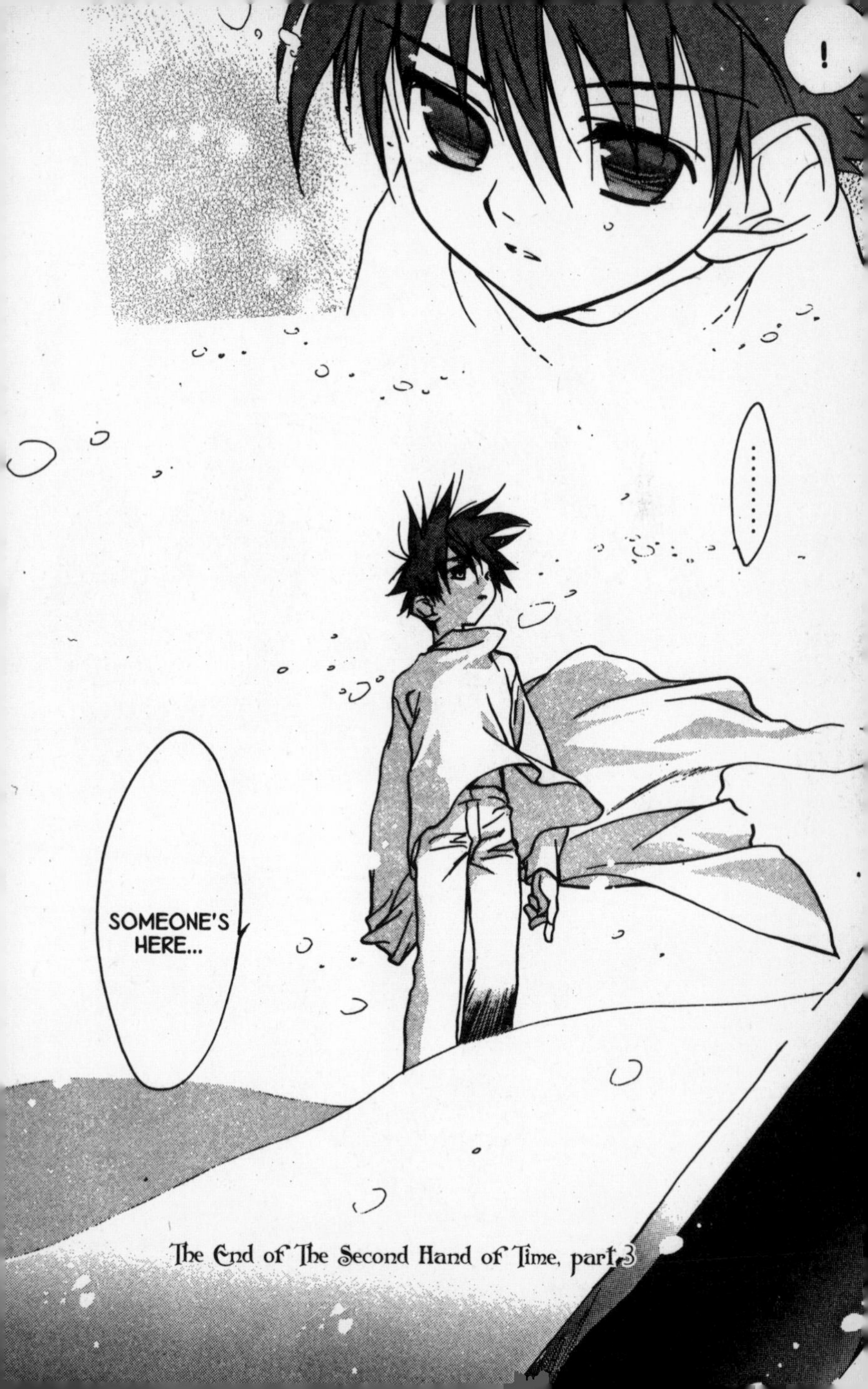
!
......
SOMEONE'S HERE...
The End of The Second Hand of Time, part 3

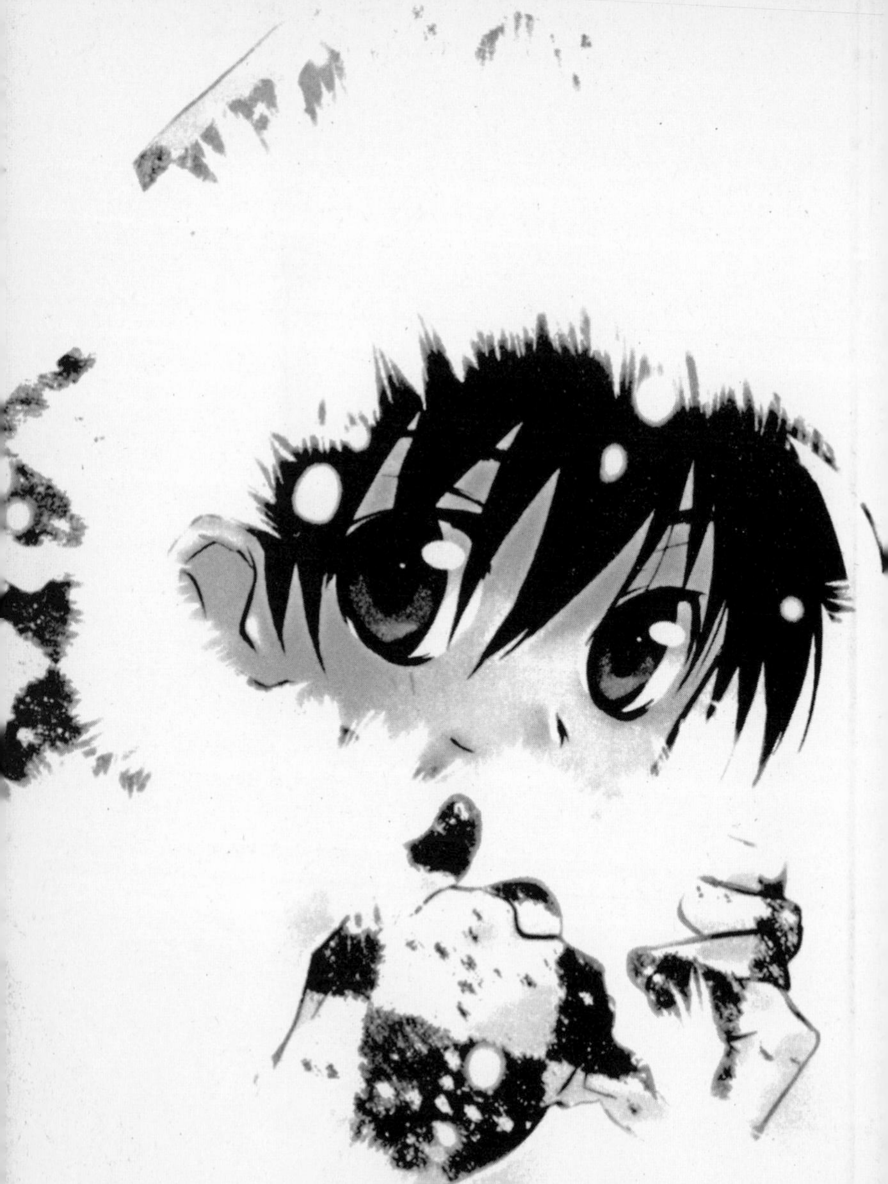

The Second Hand of Time, part 4

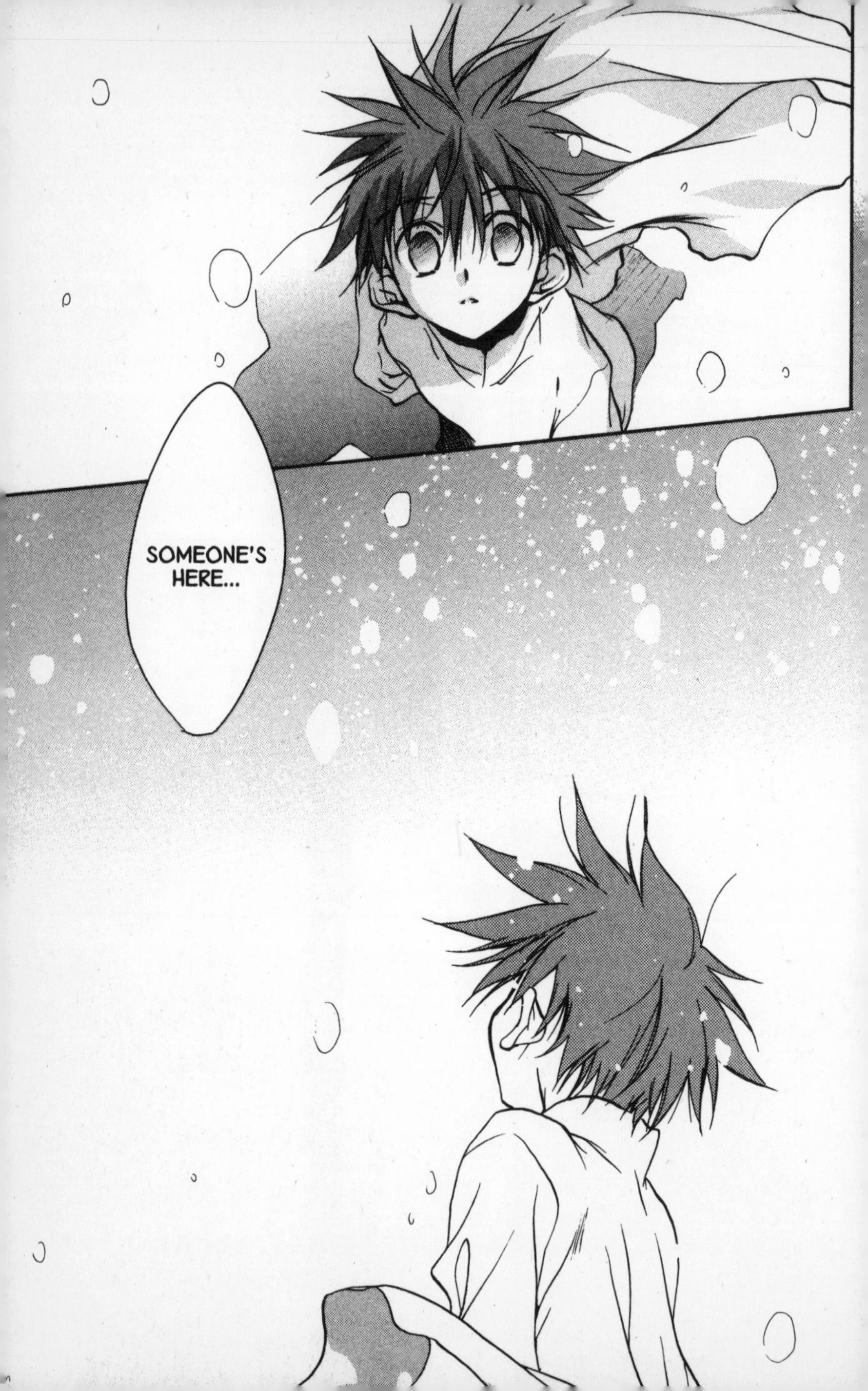
SOMEONE'S HERE...

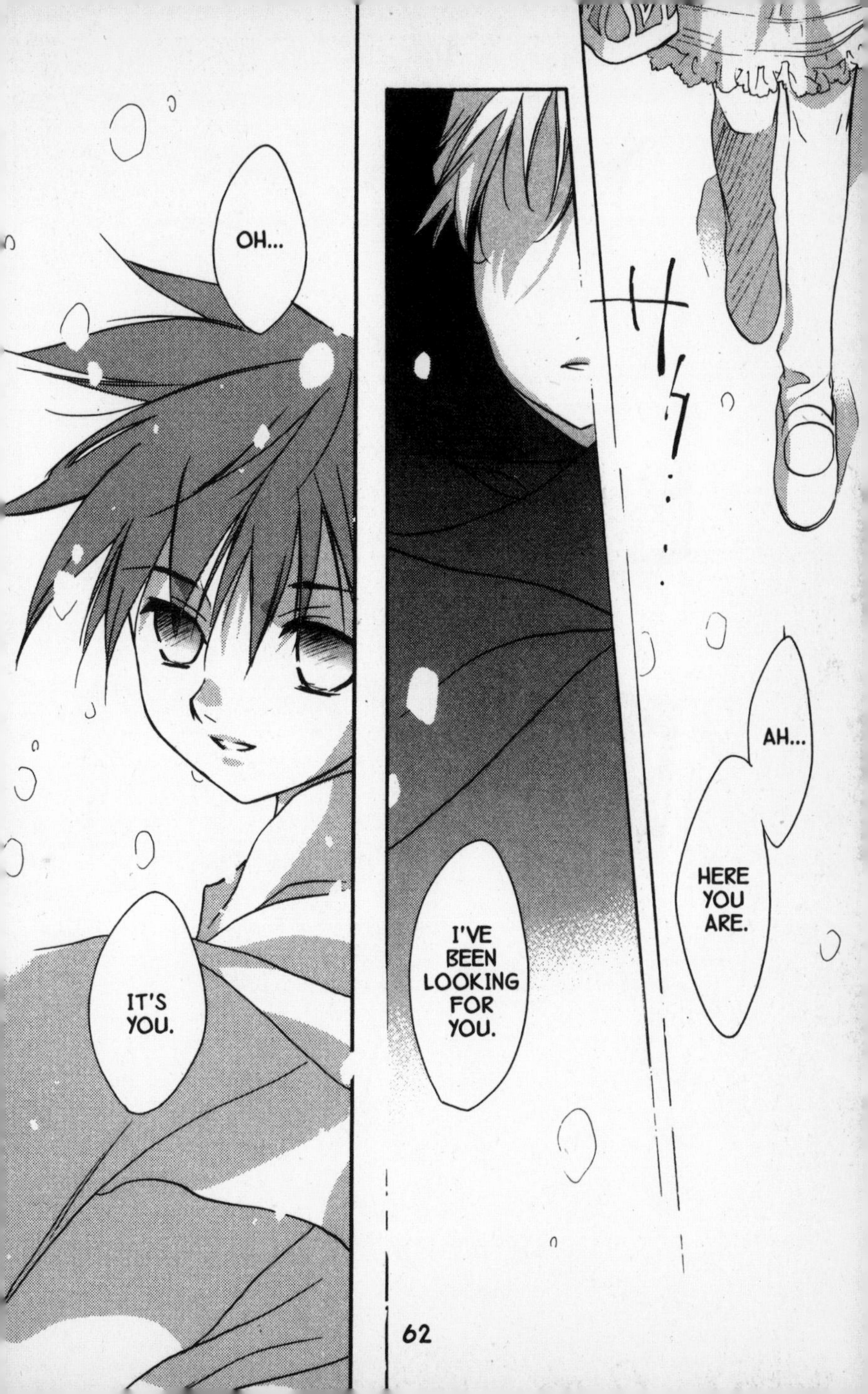
AH...
HERE YOU ARE.
I'VE BEEN LOOKING FOR YOU.
OH...
IT'S YOU.

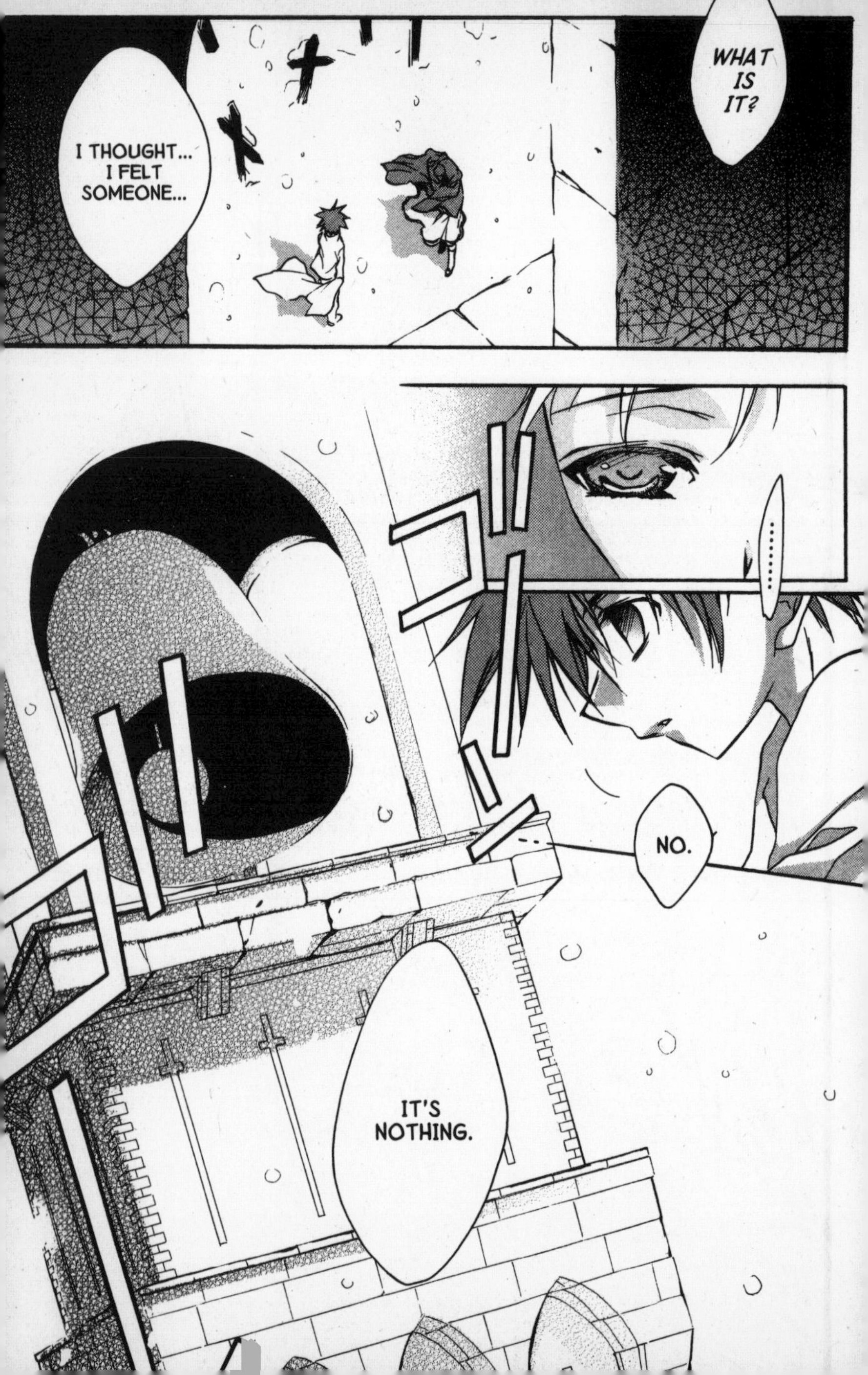
WHAT IS IT?
I THOUGHT... I FELT SOMEONE...
......
NO.
IT'S NOTHING.

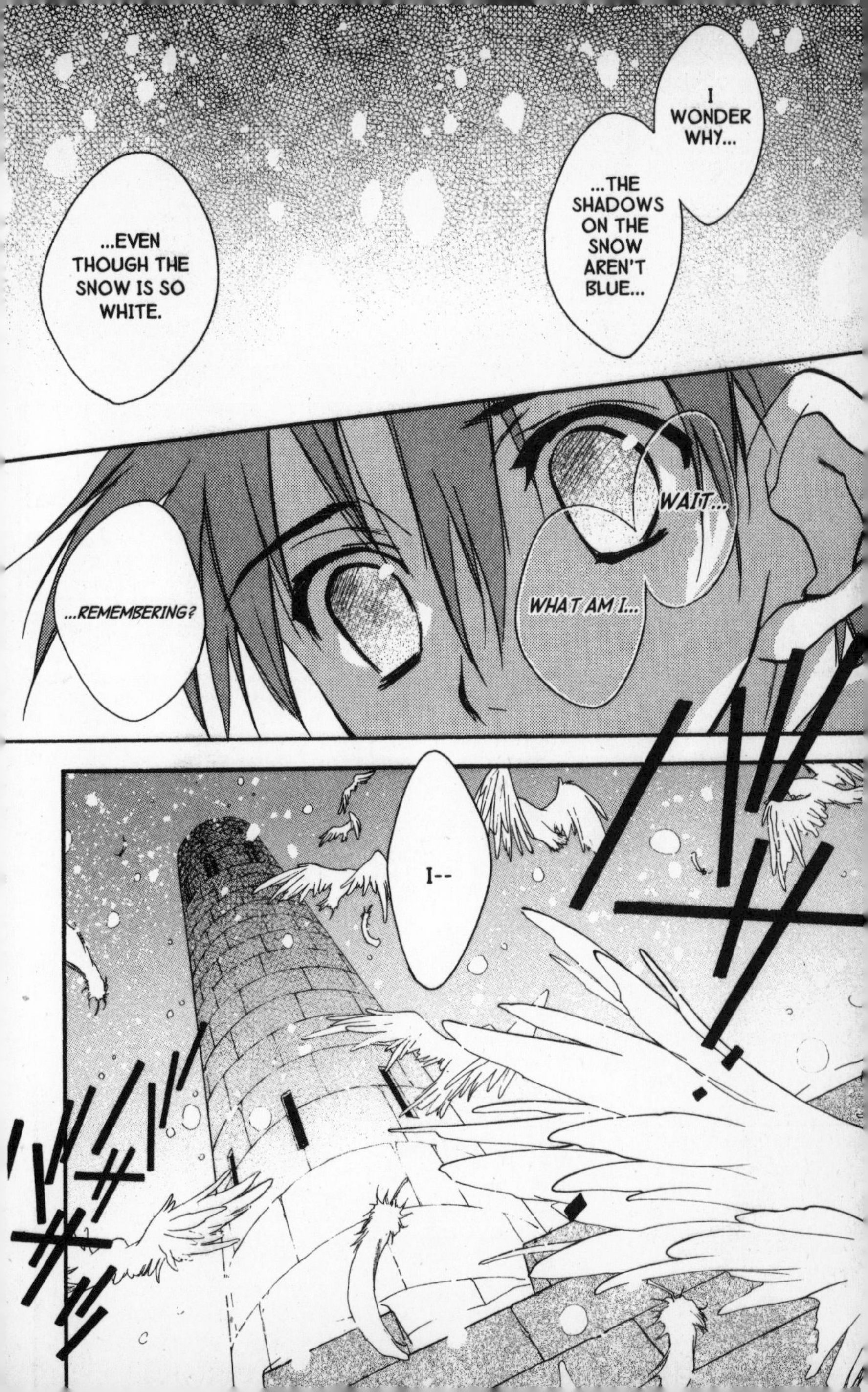
I WONDER WHY...
...THE SHADOWS ON THE SNOW AREN'T BLUE...
...EVEN THOUGH THE SNOW IS SO WHITE.
WAIT...
WHAT AM I...
...REMEMBERING?
I--

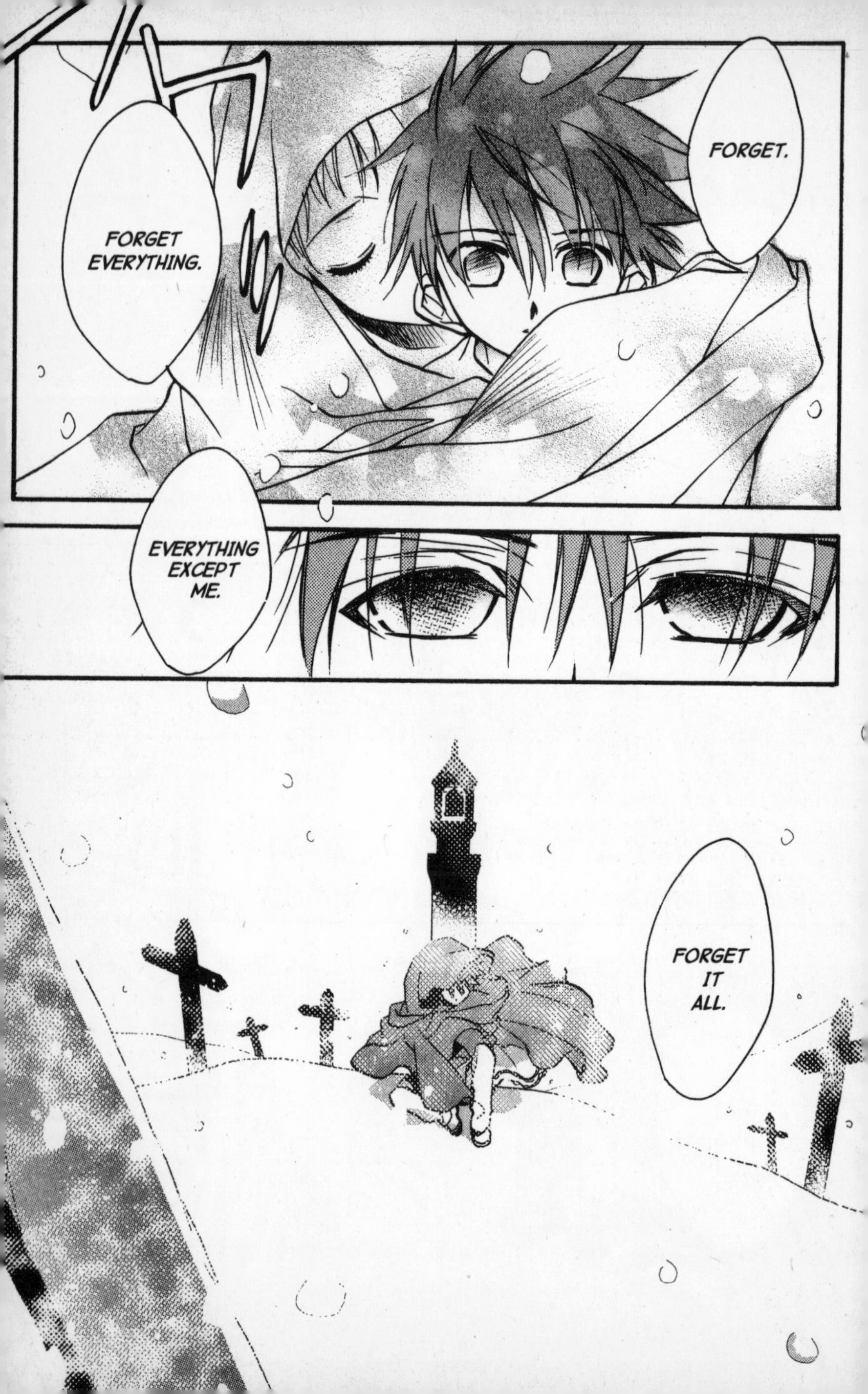
FORGET.
FORGET EVERYTHING.
EVERYTHING EXCEPT ME.
FORGET IT ALL.

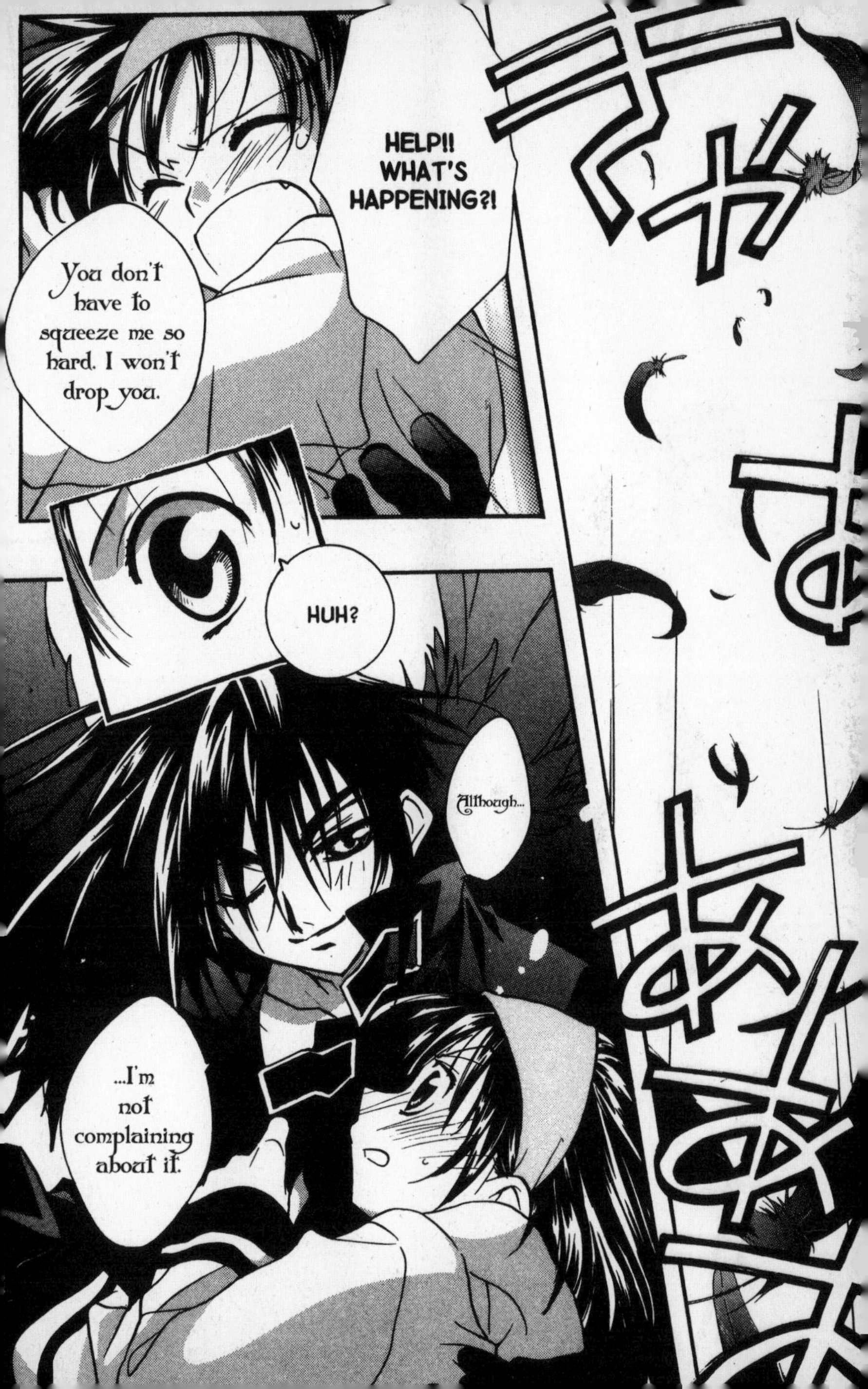
HELP!! WHAT'S HAPPENING?!
You don't have to squeeze me so hard. I won't drop you.
HUH?
Although...
...I'm not complaining about it.

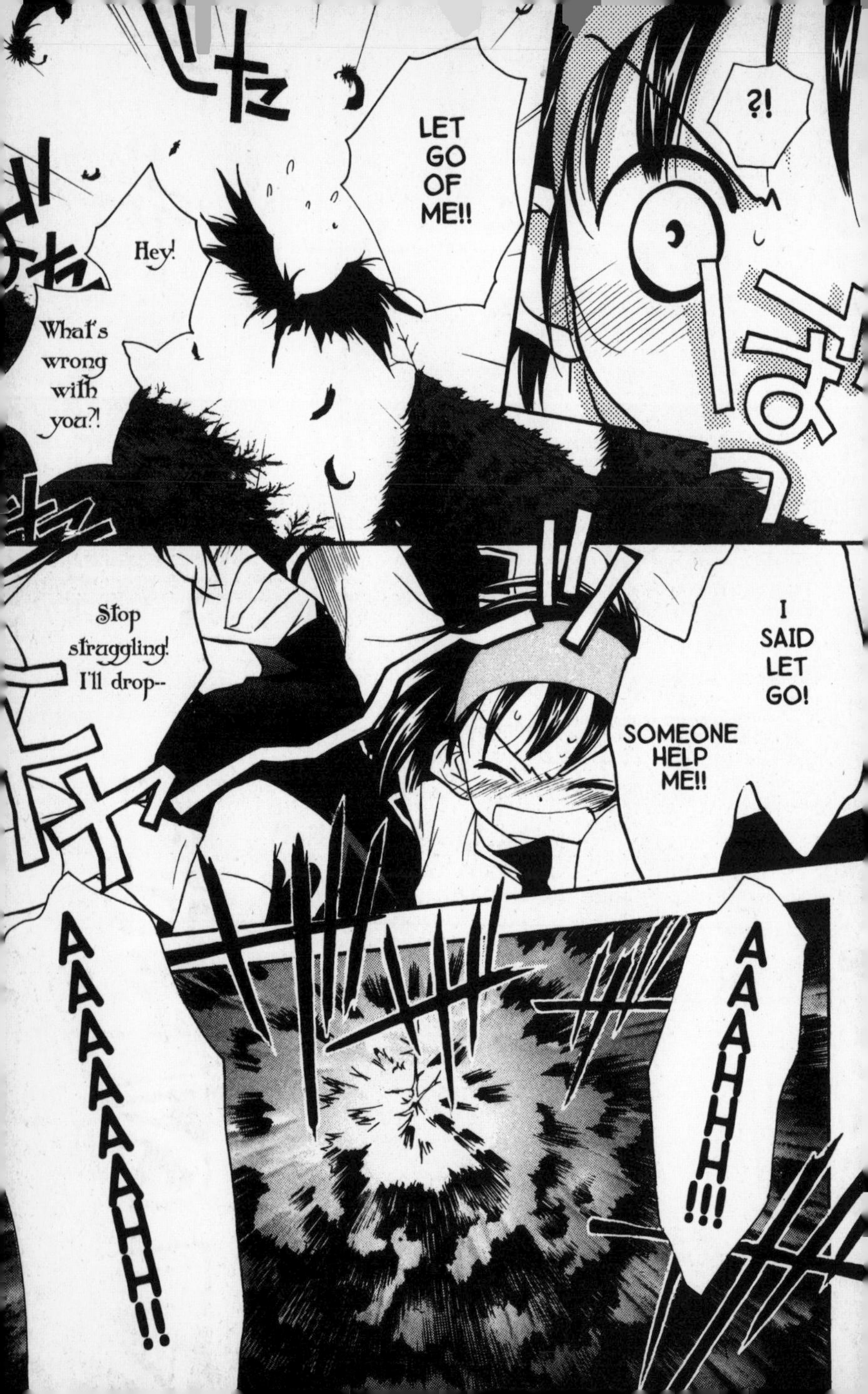

?!
LET GO OF ME!!
Hey!
What's wrong with you?!
I SAID LET GO!
SOMEONE HELP ME!!
Stop struggling! I'll drop--
AAAAHH!!!
AAAAAAAHH!!

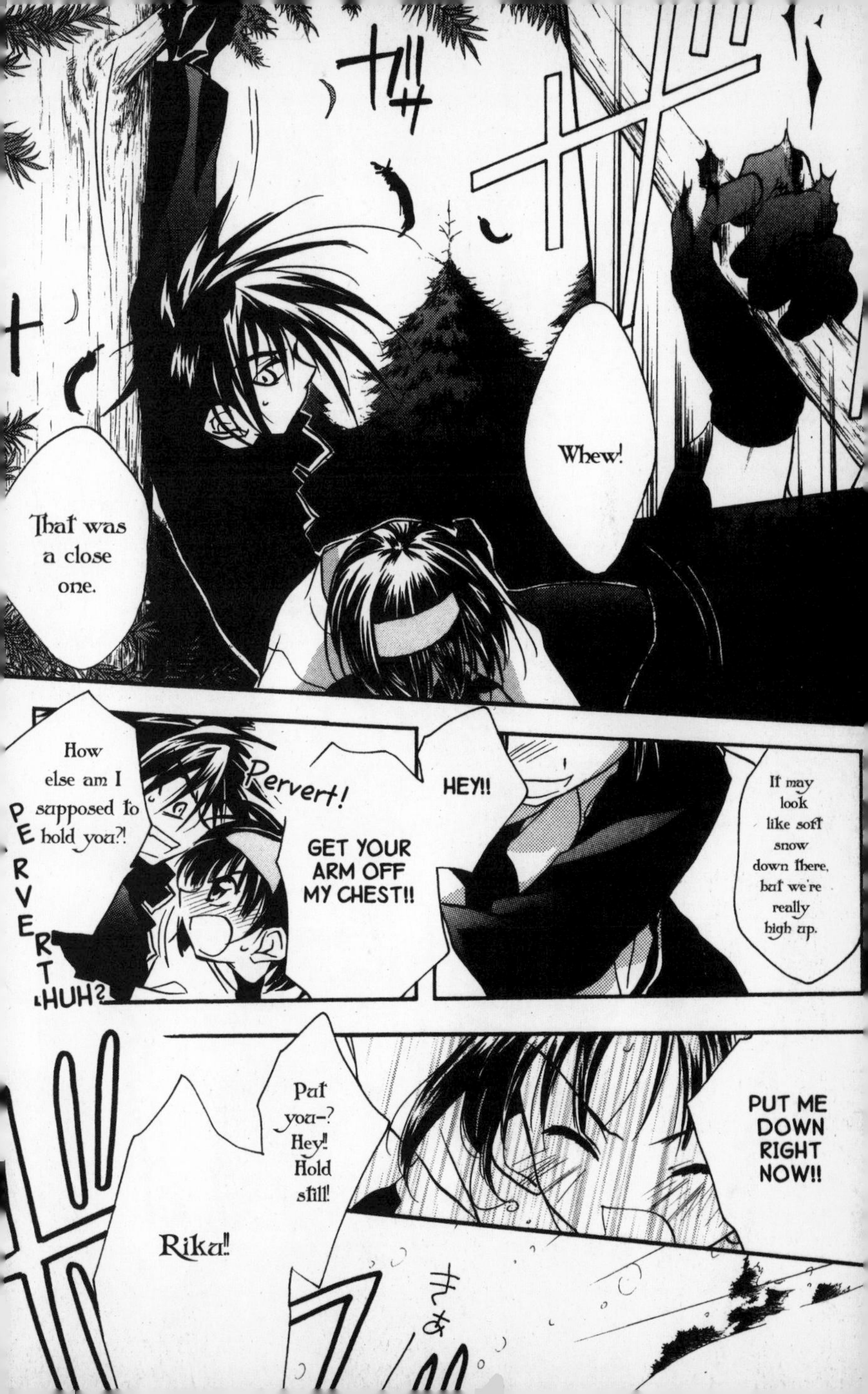
Whew!
That was a close one.
It may look like soft snow down there, but we're really high up.
HEY!!
GET YOUR ARM OFF MY CHEST!!
Pervert!
How else am I supposed to hold you?!
PERVERT
HUH?
PUT ME DOWN RIGHT NOW!!
Put you-? Hey!! Hold still!
Riku!!

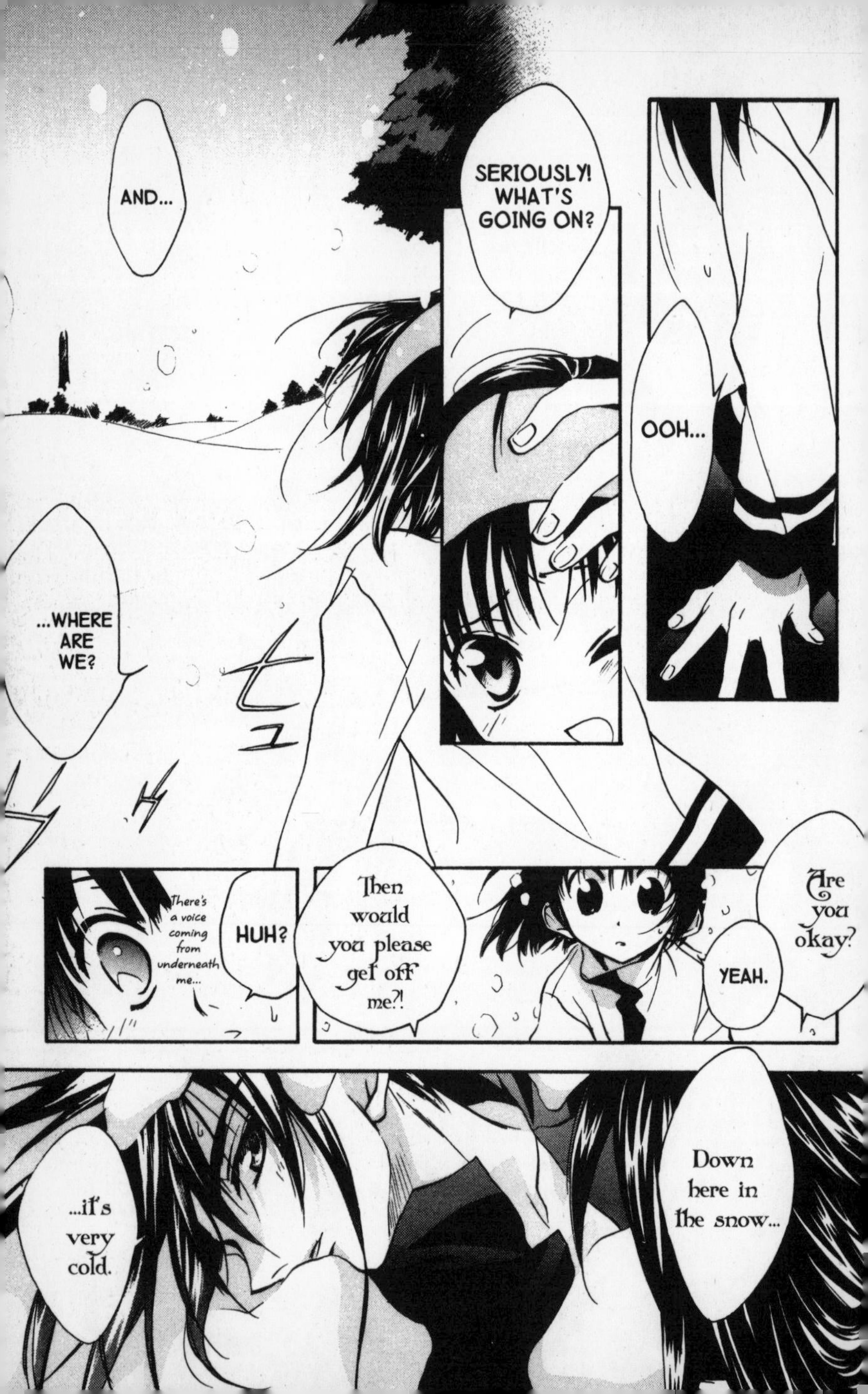
OOH...
SERIOUSLY! WHAT'S GOING ON?
AND...
...WHERE ARE WE?
Are you okay?
YEAH.
Then would you please get off me?!
HUH?
There's a voice coming from underneath me...
Down here in the snow...
...it's very cold.

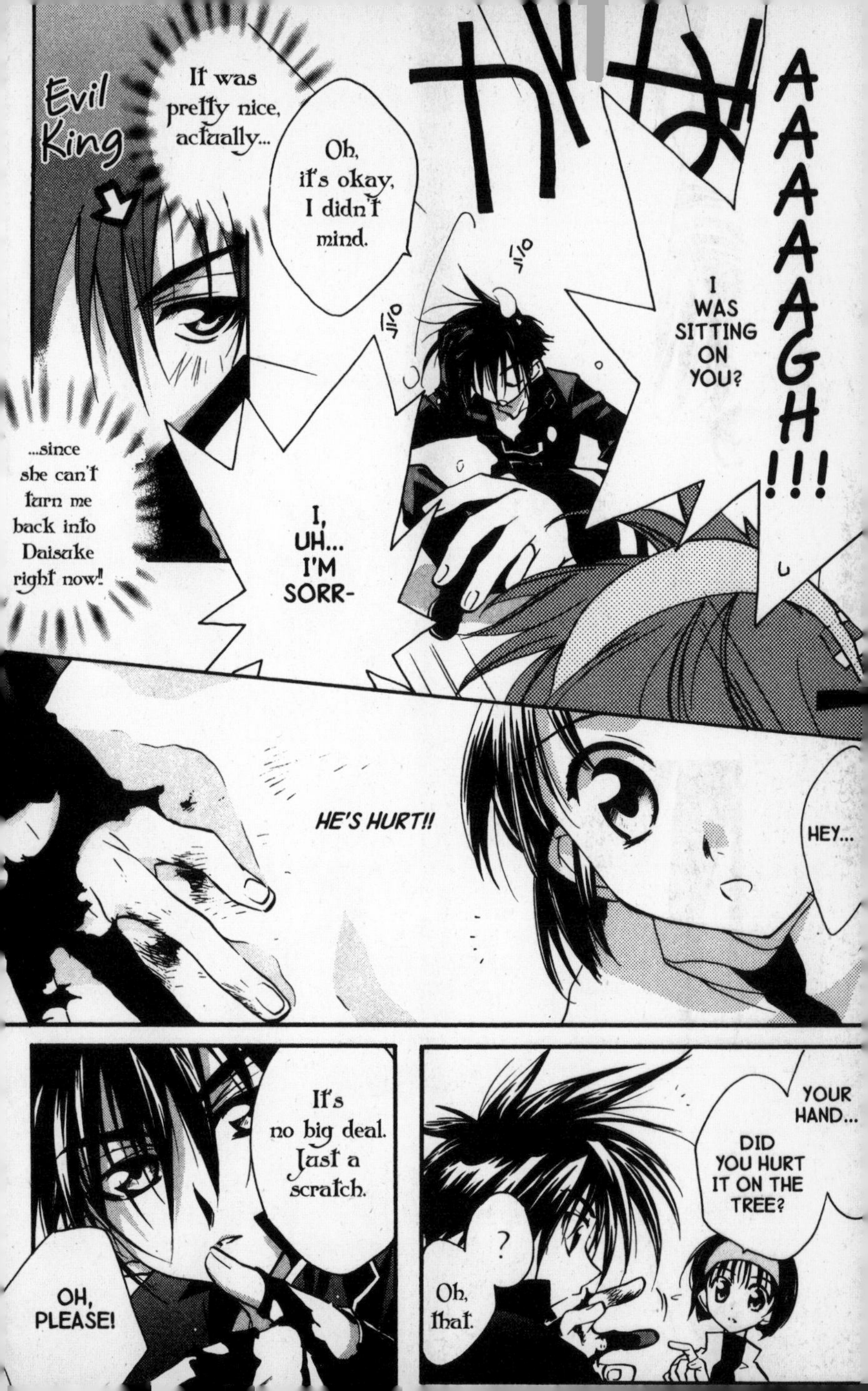
AAAAAAAGH!!!
I WAS SITTING ON YOU?
I, UH... I'M SORR-
Oh, it's okay, I didn't mind.
It was pretty nice, actually...
Evil King
...since she can't turn me back into Daisuke right now!!
HEY...
HE'S HURT!!
YOUR HAND...
DID YOU HURT IT ON THE TREE?
?
Oh, that.
It's no big deal. Just a scratch.
OH, PLEASE!

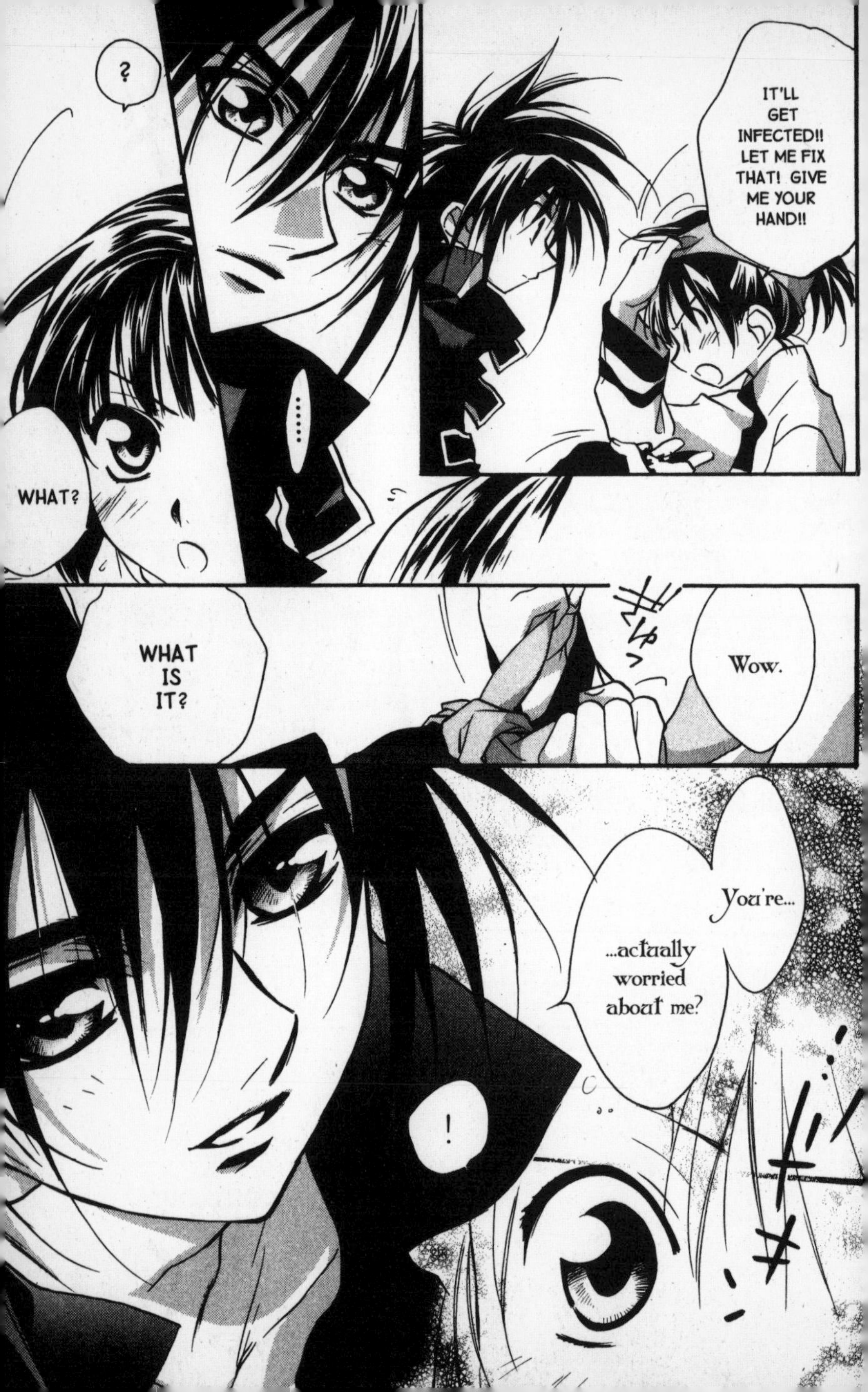
IT'LL GET INFECTED!! LET ME FIX THAT! GIVE ME YOUR HAND!!
?
......
WHAT?
ぎゅっ
Wow.
WHAT IS IT?
You're...
...actually worried about me?
!

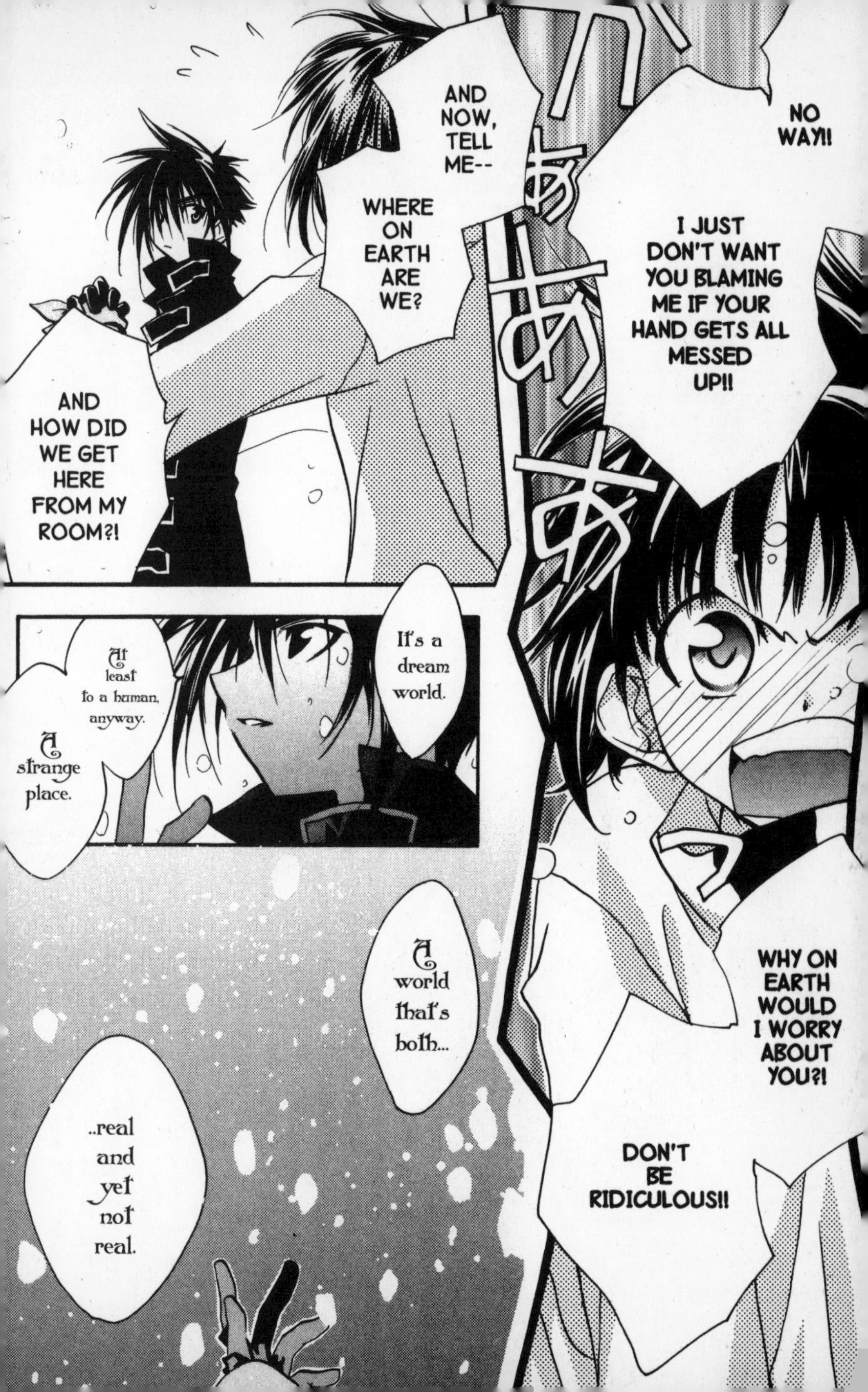
あああ
NO WAY!!
I JUST DON'T WANT YOU BLAMING ME IF YOUR HAND GETS ALL MESSED UP!!
WHY ON EARTH WOULD I WORRY ABOUT YOU?!
DON'T BE RIDICULOUS!!
AND NOW, TELL ME--
WHERE ON EARTH ARE WE?
AND HOW DID WE GET HERE FROM MY ROOM?!
It's a dream world.
At least to a human, anyway.
A strange place.
A world that's both...
..real and yet not real.

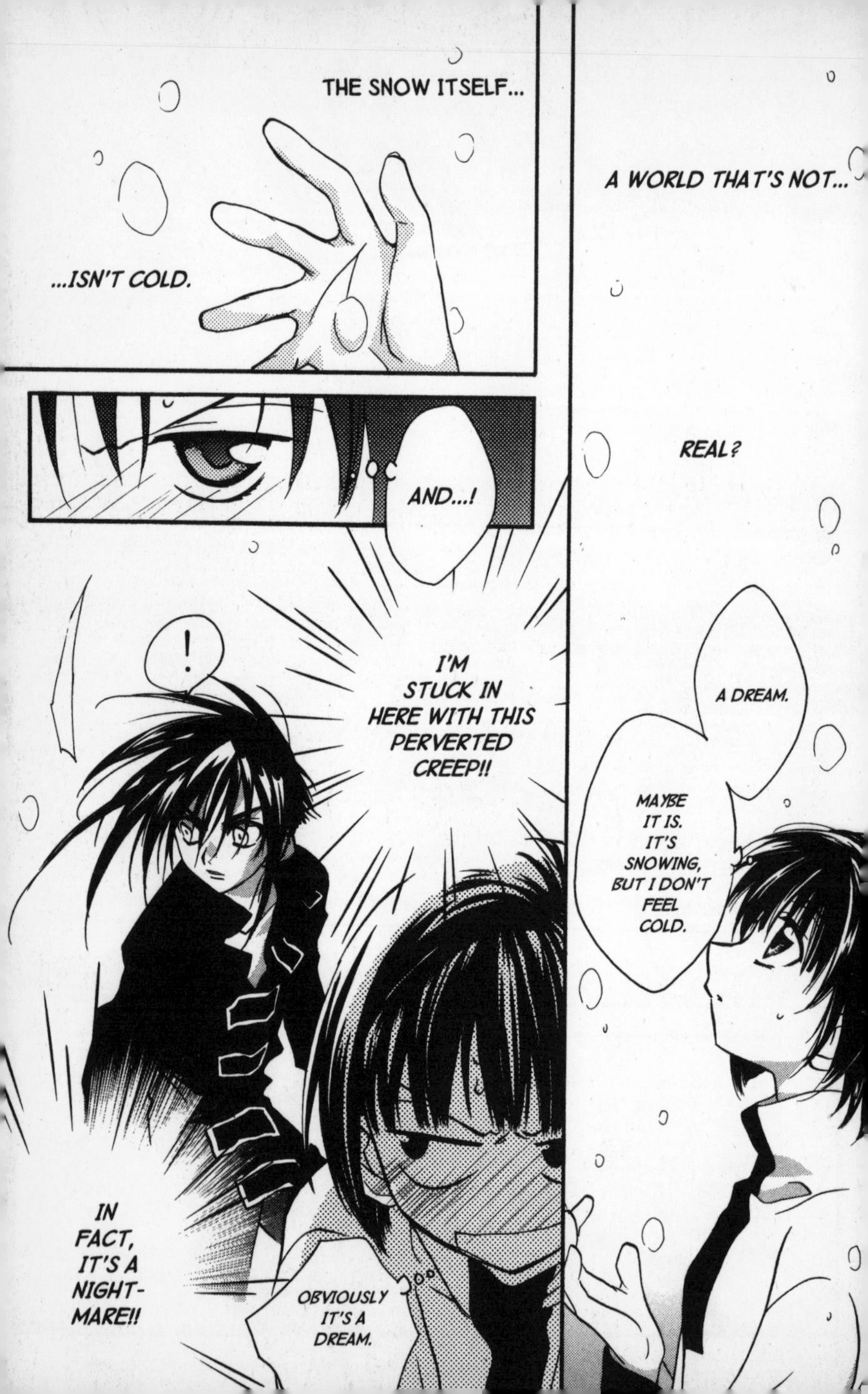
A WORLD THAT'S NOT...
REAL?
A DREAM.
MAYBE IT IS. IT'S SNOWING, BUT I DON'T FEEL COLD.
THE SNOW ITSELF...
...ISN'T COLD.
AND...!
!
I'M STUCK IN HERE WITH THIS PERVERTED CREEP!!
OBVIOUSLY IT'S A DREAM.
IN FACT, IT'S A NIGHTMARE!!

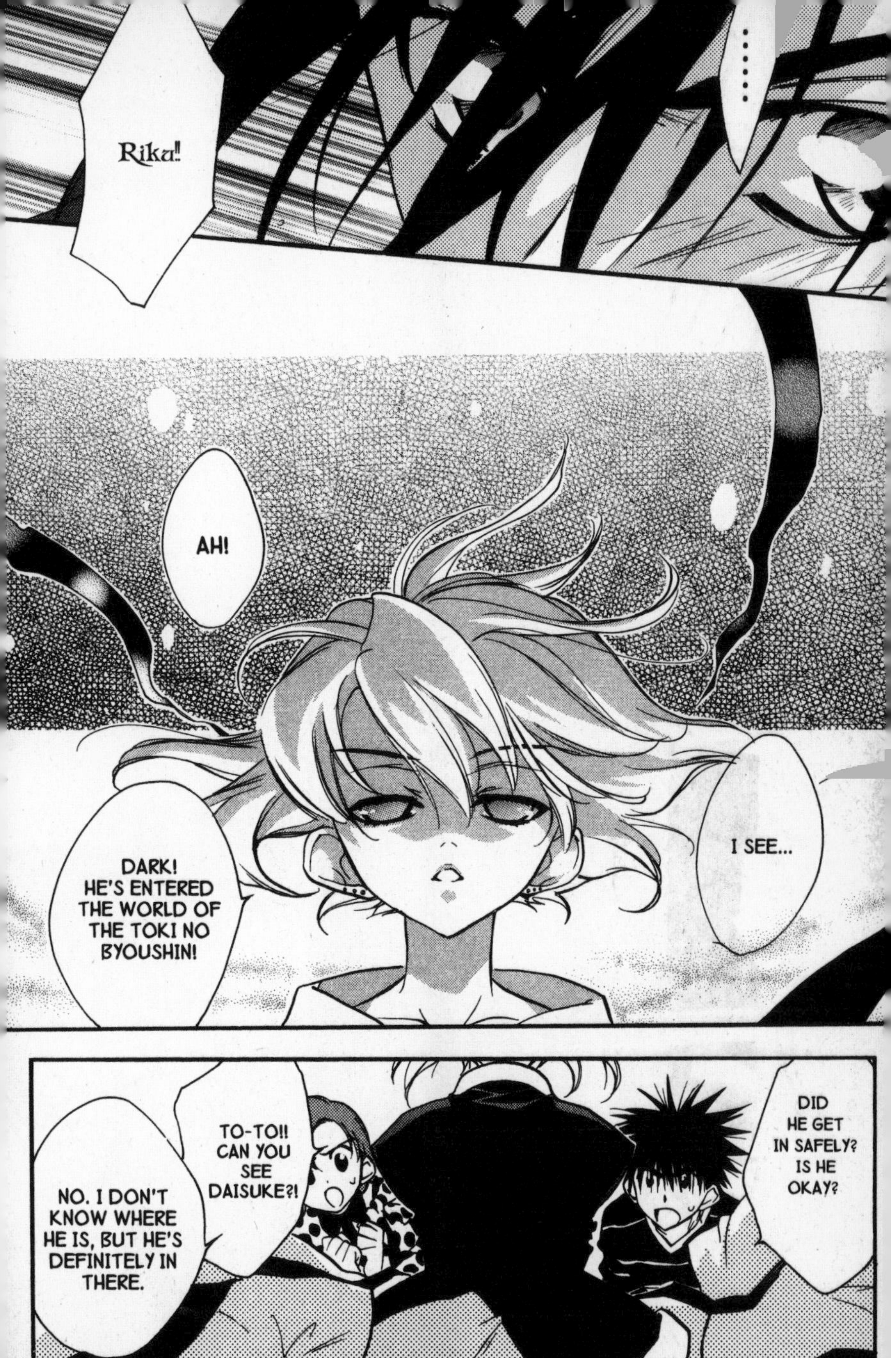
……
Riku!!
AH!
I SEE...
DARK! HE'S ENTERED THE WORLD OF THE TOKI NO BYOUSHIN!
DID HE GET IN SAFELY? IS HE OKAY?
TO-TO!! CAN YOU SEE DAISUKE?!
NO. I DON'T KNOW WHERE HE IS, BUT HE'S DEFINITELY IN THERE.

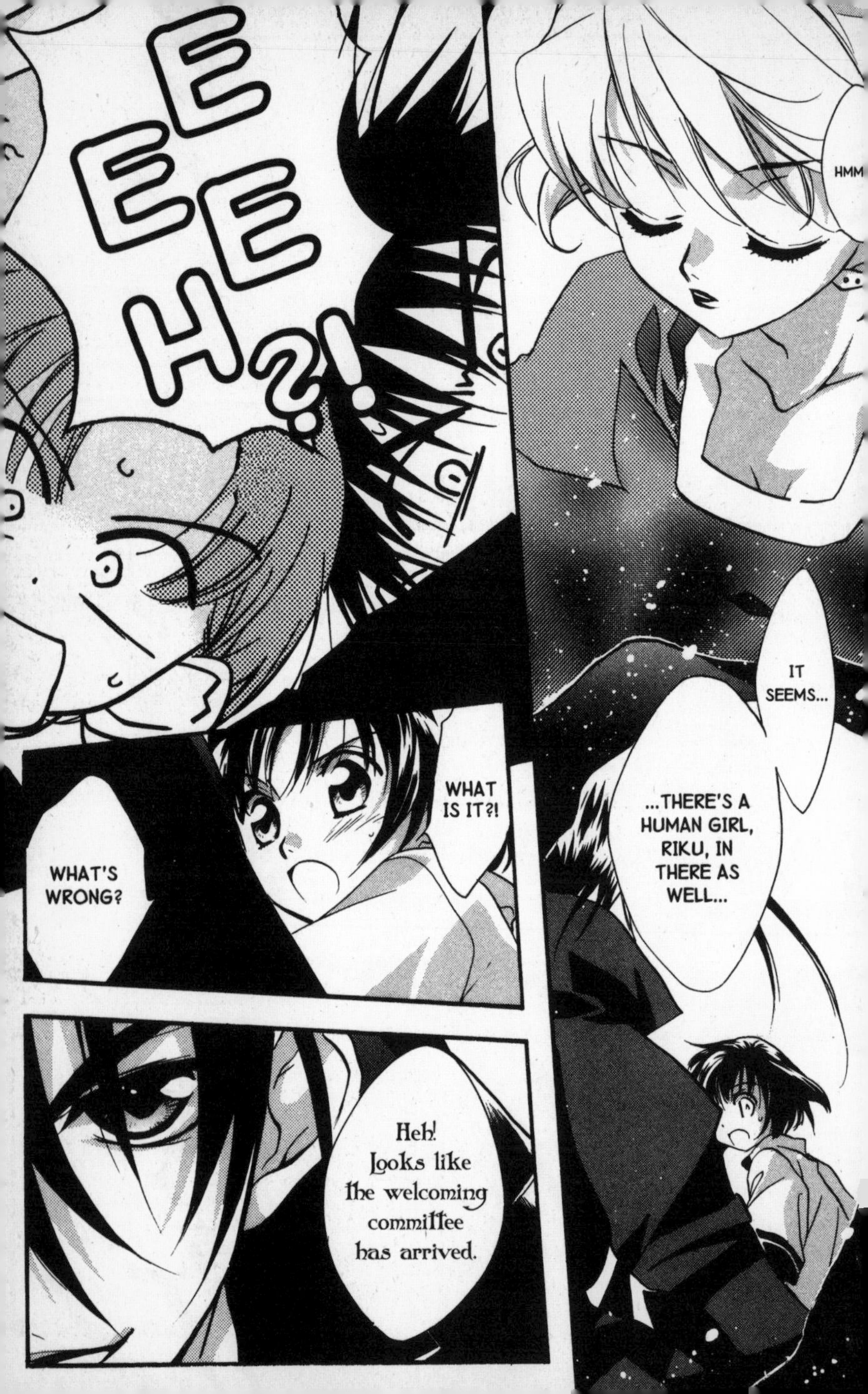
HMM
IT SEEMS...
...THERE'S A HUMAN GIRL, RIKU, IN THERE AS WELL...
EEEH?!
WHAT IS IT?!
WHAT'S WRONG?
Heh! Looks like the welcoming committee has arrived.

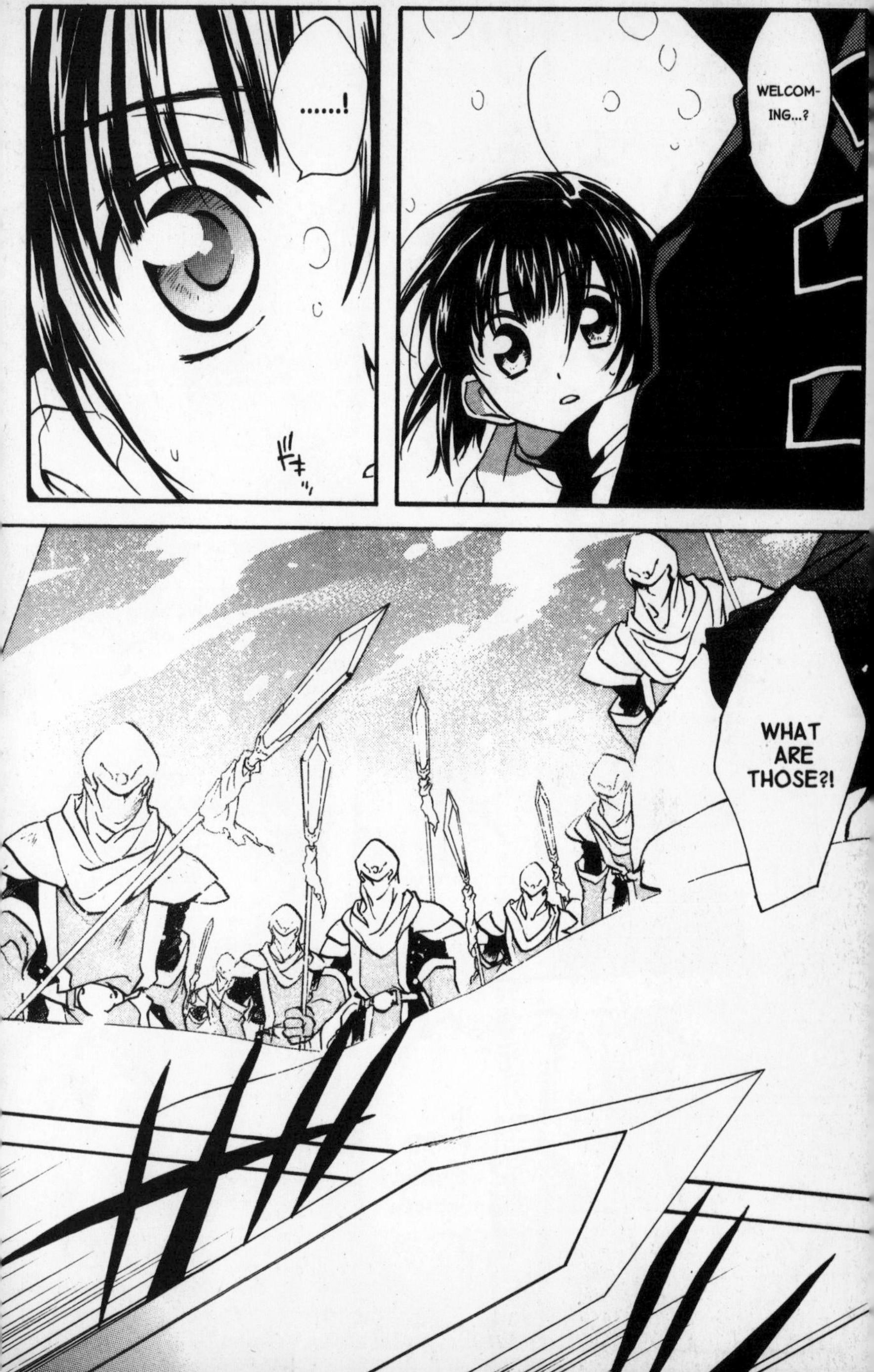
WELCOM-
ING...?
......!
ドキッ
WHAT ARE THOSE?!

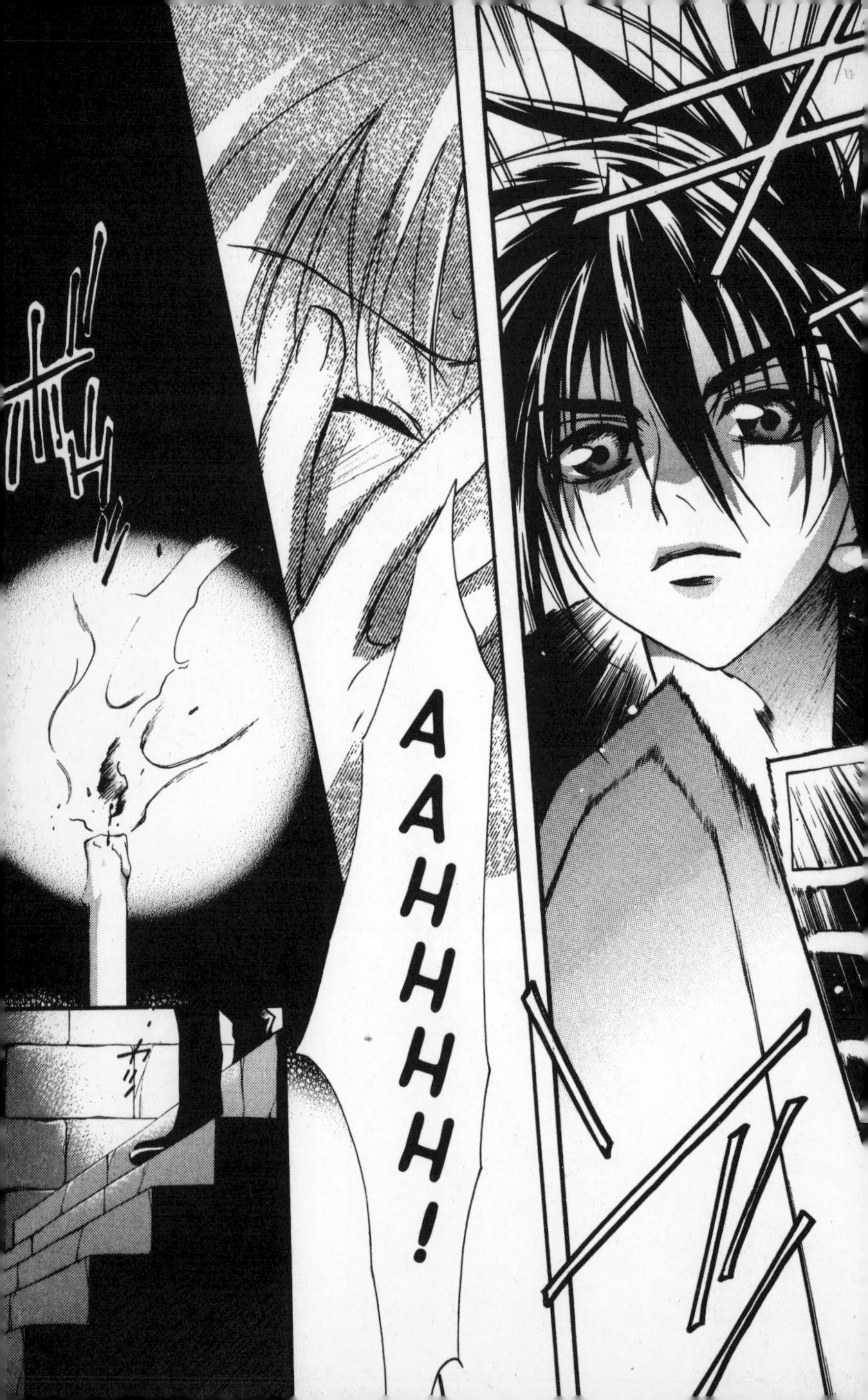
AAHHHH!

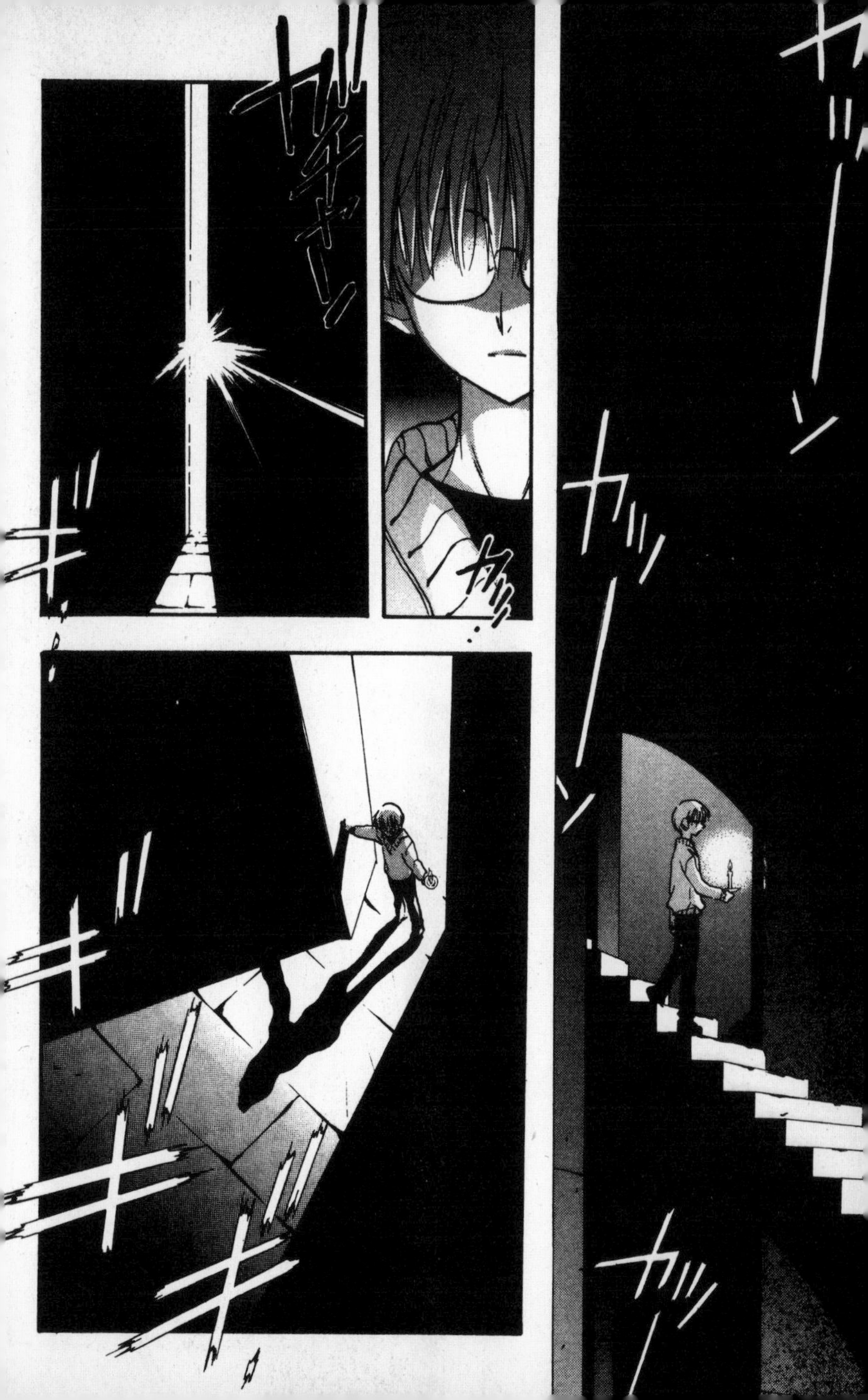

カッーーン
カッーーン
カッー
カッ
ガチャーン
ギィ
ギィィィ

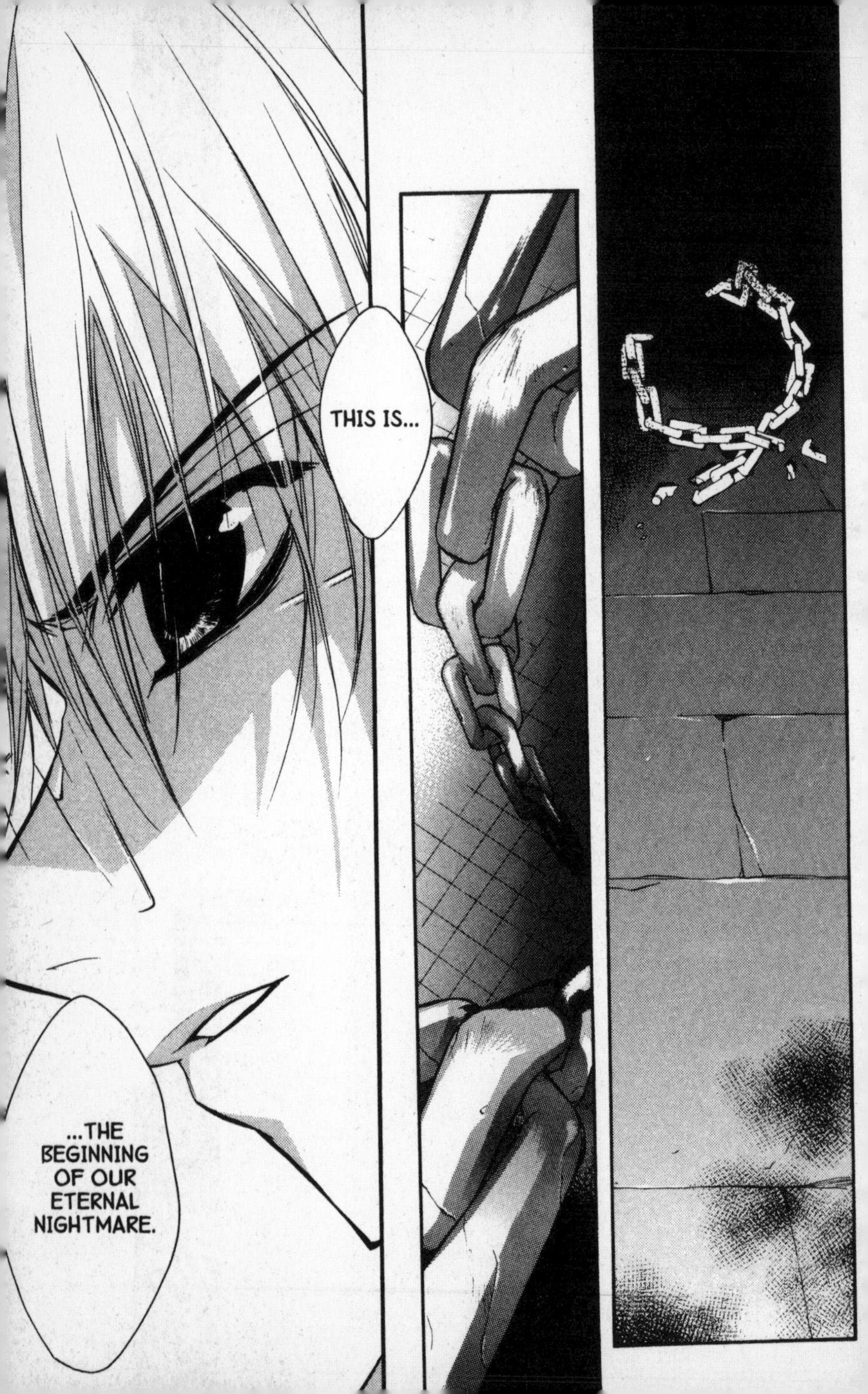
THIS IS...
...THE BEGINNING OF OUR ETERNAL NIGHTMARE.

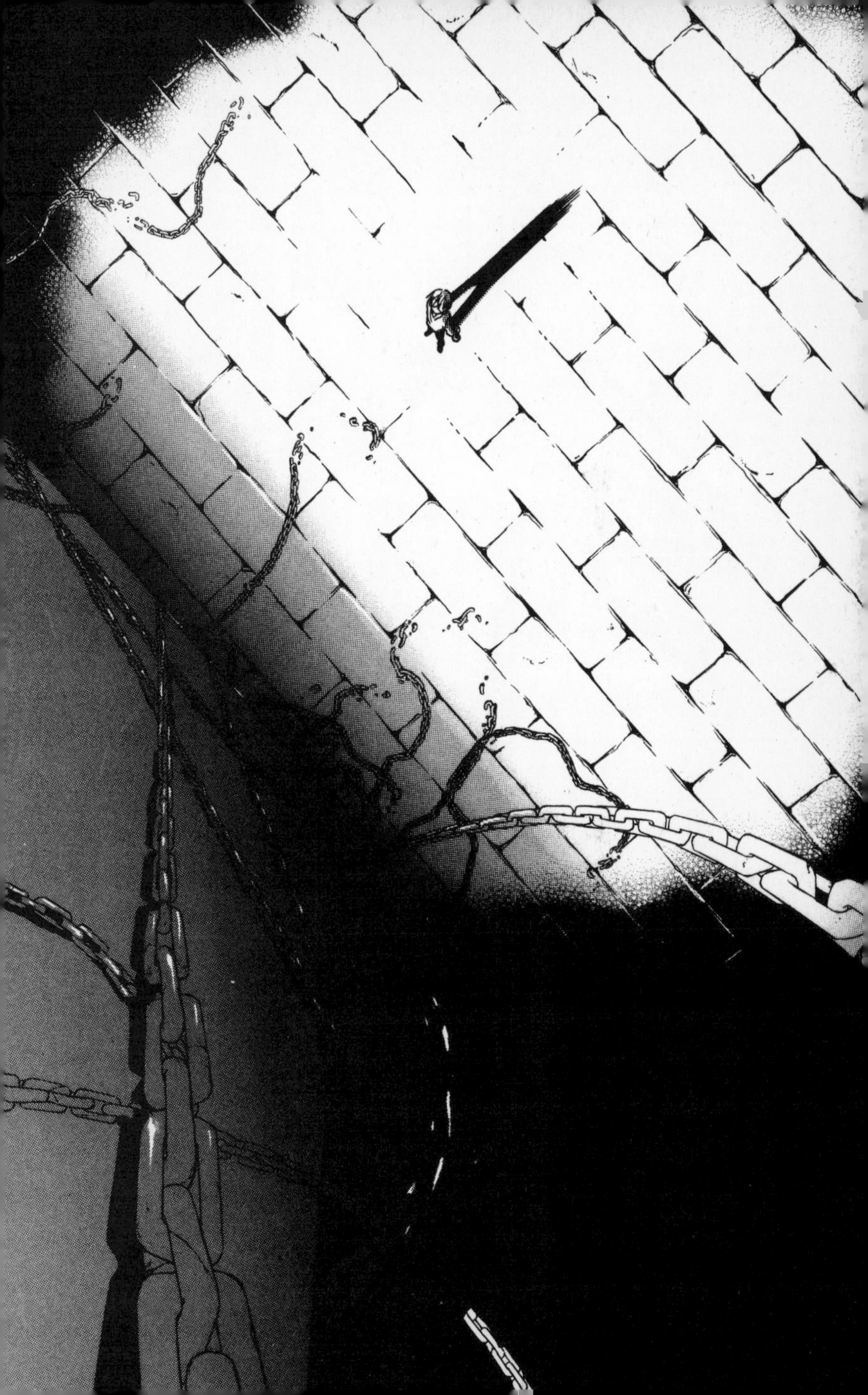

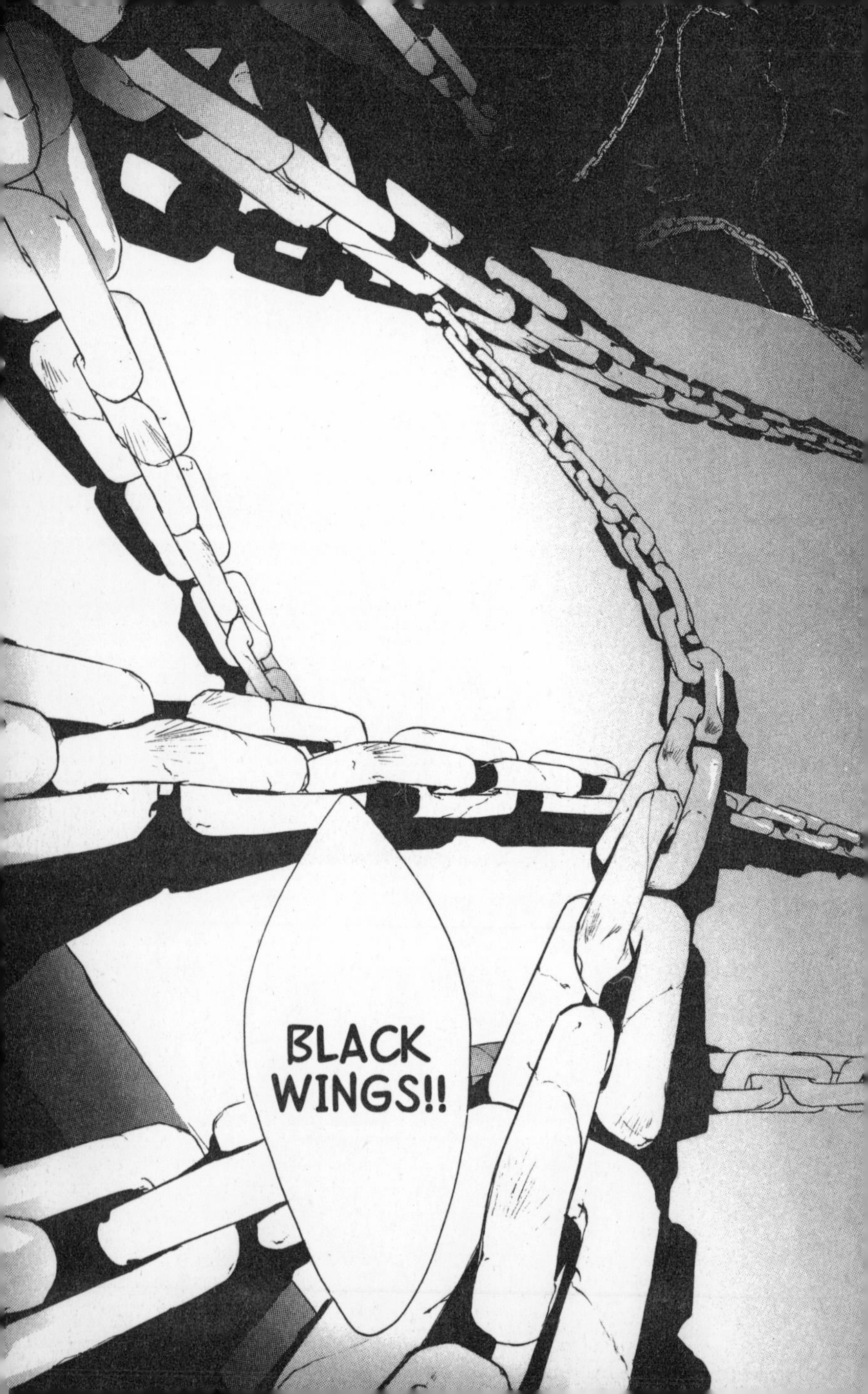
BLACK WINGS!!

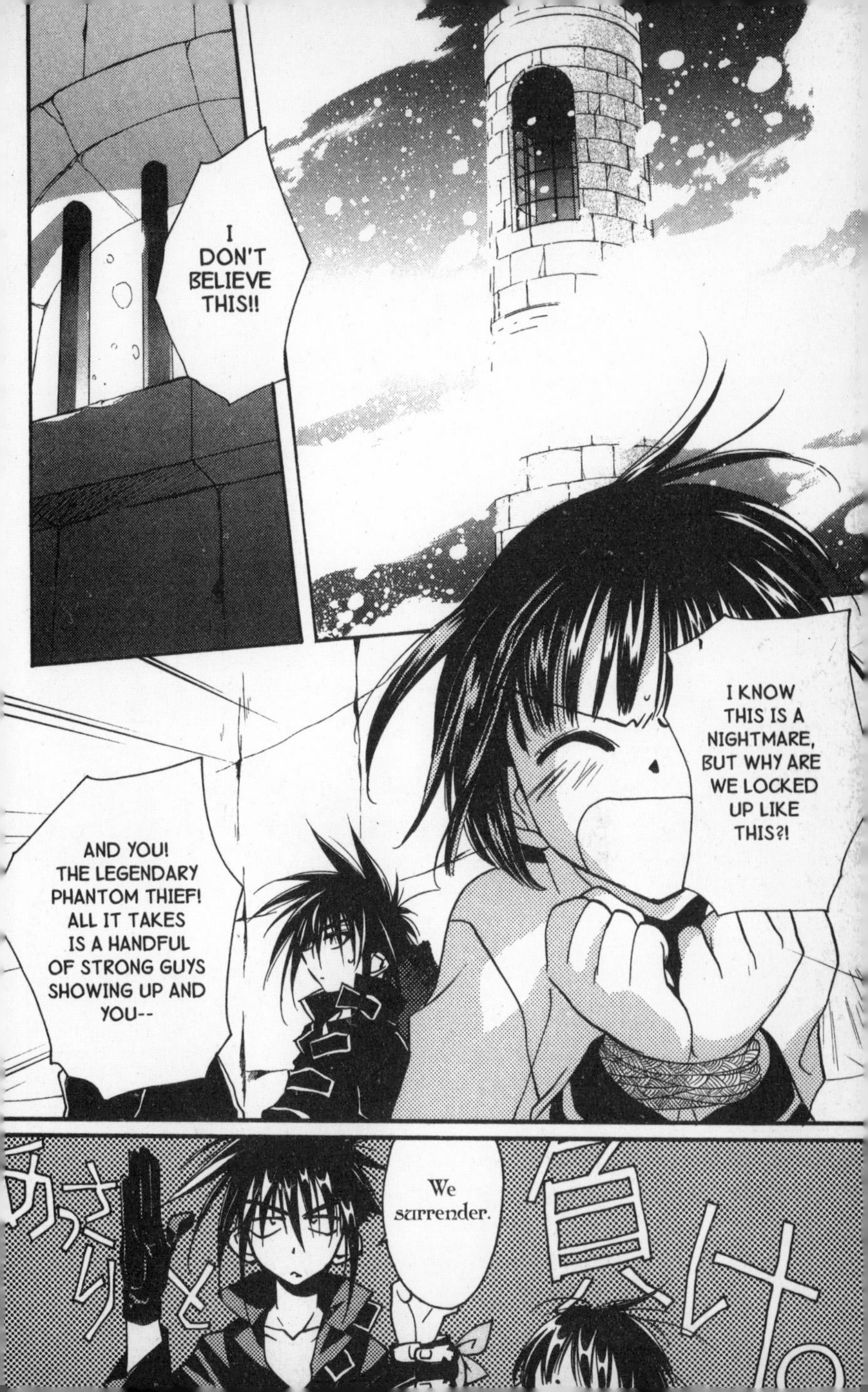
I DON'T BELIEVE THIS!!
I KNOW THIS IS A NIGHTMARE, BUT WHY ARE WE LOCKED UP LIKE THIS?!
AND YOU! THE LEGENDARY PHANTOM THIEF! ALL IT TAKES IS A HANDFUL OF STRONG GUYS SHOWING UP AND YOU--
あっさりと負けた。
We surrender.

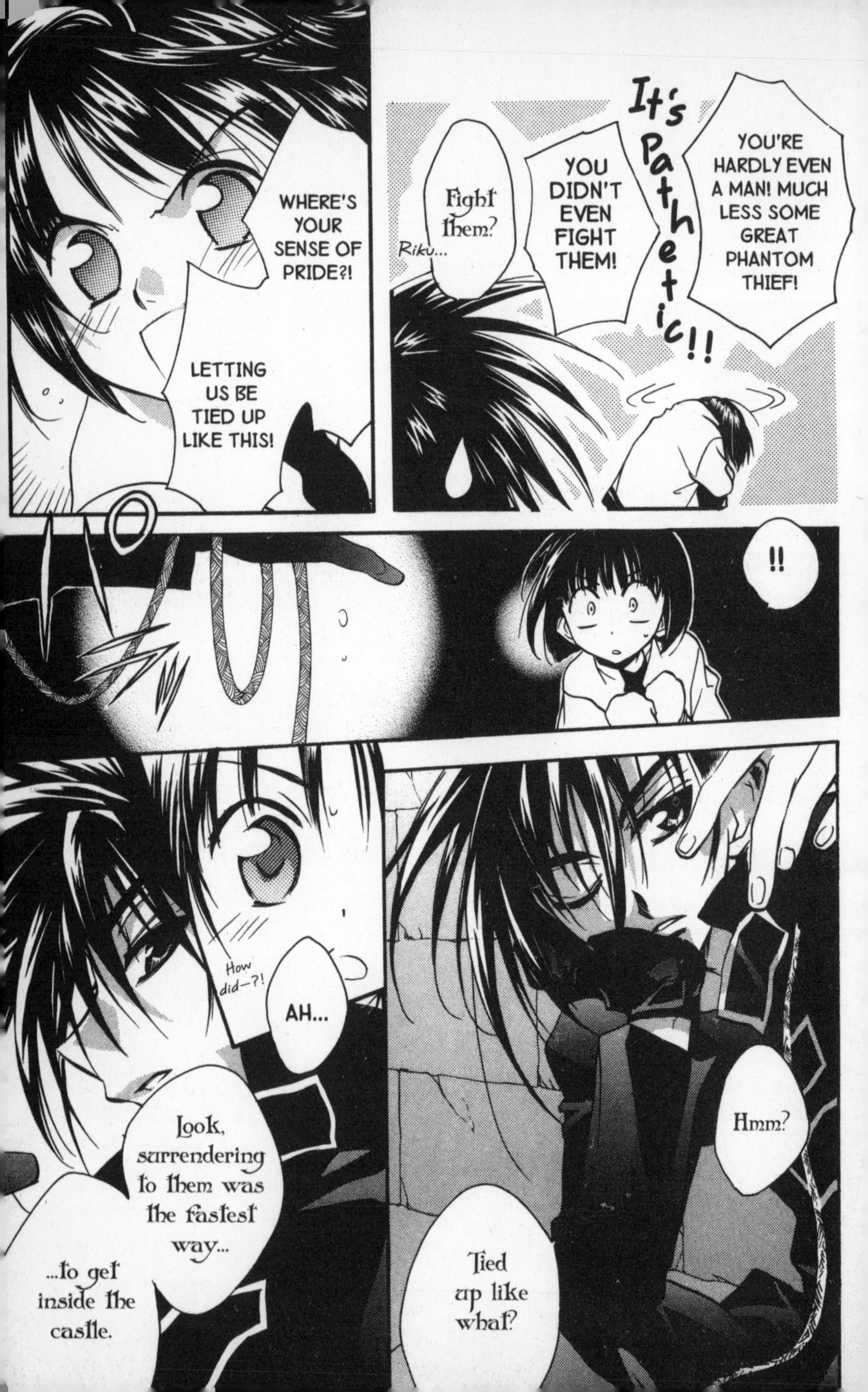
YOU'RE HARDLY EVEN A MAN! MUCH LESS SOME GREAT PHANTOM THIEF!
It's Pathetic!!
YOU DIDN'T EVEN FIGHT THEM!
Fight them?
Riku...
WHERE'S YOUR SENSE OF PRIDE?!
LETTING US BE TIED UP LIKE THIS!
!!
Hmm?
Tied up like what?
How did—?!
AH...
Look, surrendering to them was the fastest way...
...to get inside the castle.

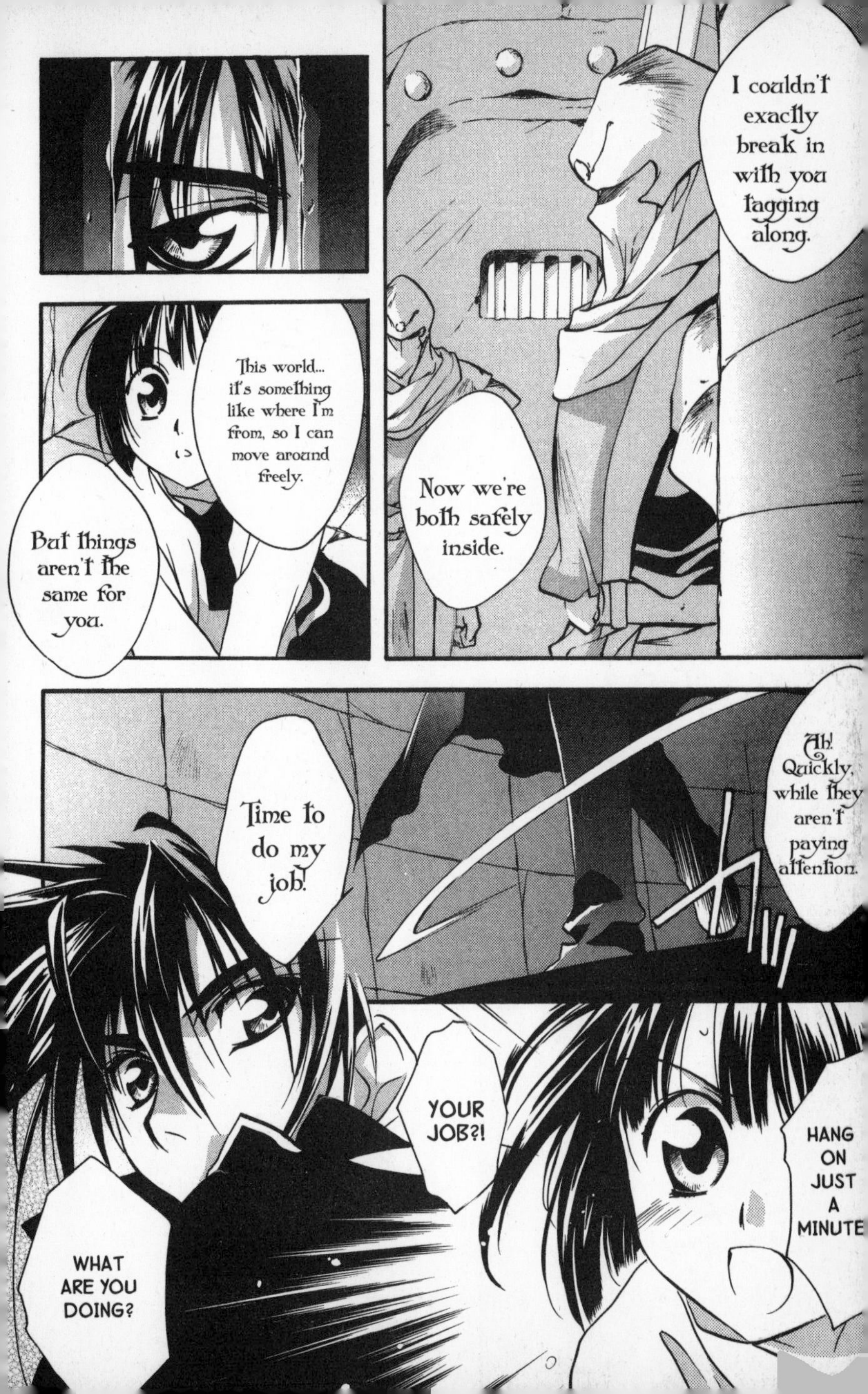

I couldn't exactly break in with you tagging along.
Now we're both safely inside.
This world... it's something like where I'm from, so I can move around freely.
But things aren't the same for you.
Ah! Quickly, while they aren't paying attention.
Time to do my job!
HANG ON JUST A MINUTE
YOUR JOB?!
WHAT ARE YOU DOING?

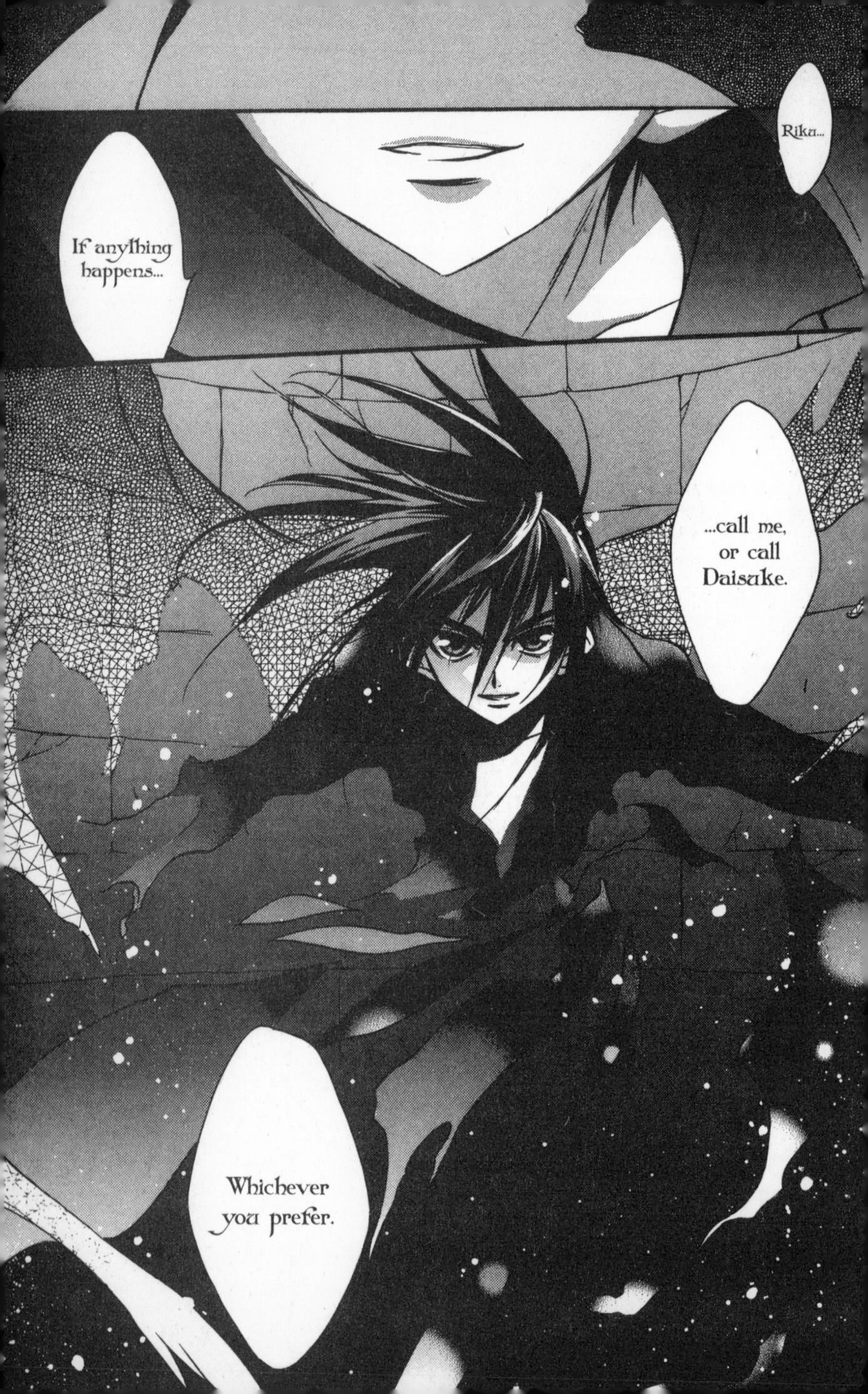
Riku...
If anything happens...
...call me, or call Daisuke.
Whichever you prefer.

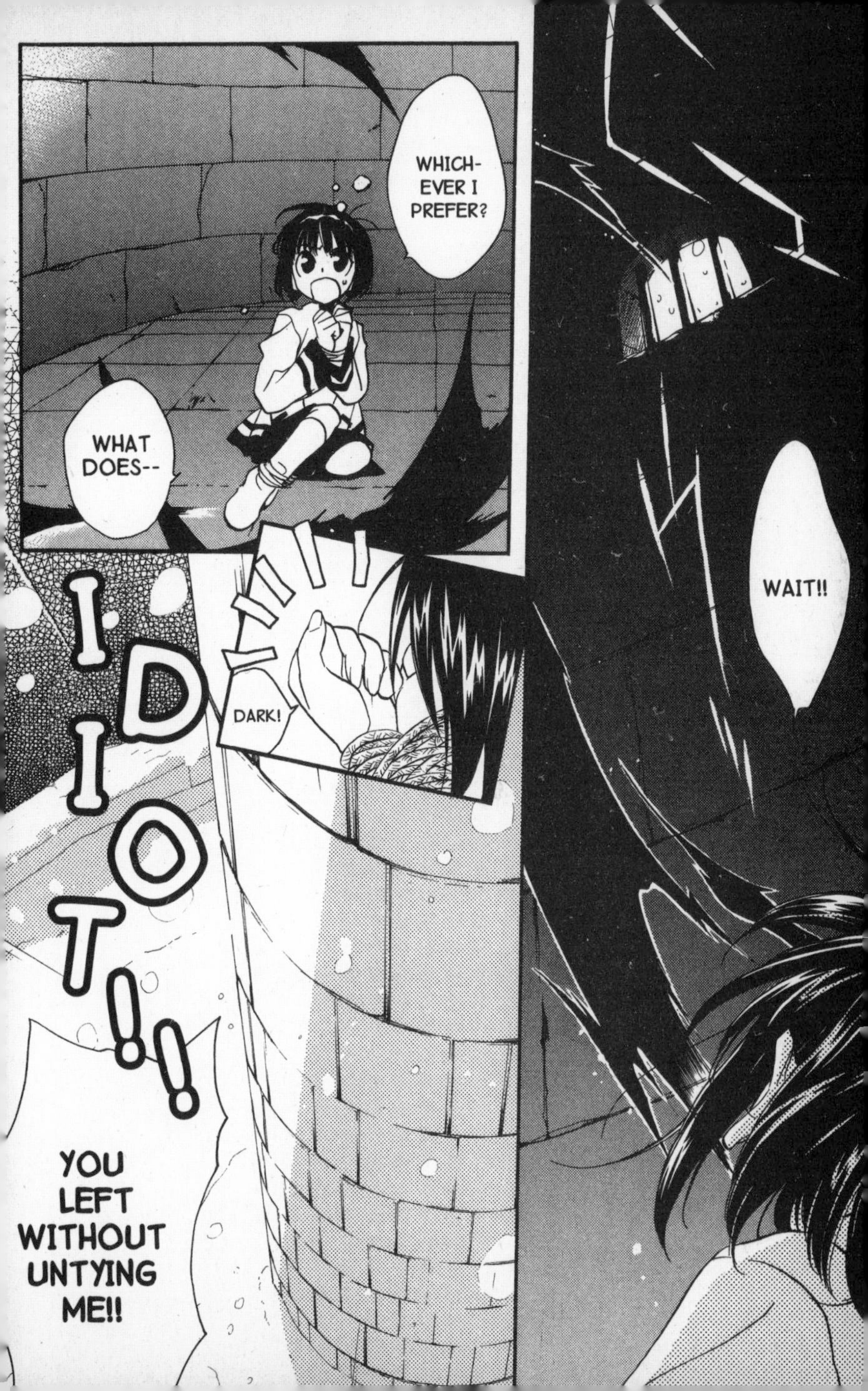
WAIT!!
WHICH-EVER I PREFER?
WHAT DOES--
DARK!
IDIOT!!!
YOU LEFT WITHOUT UNTYING ME!!

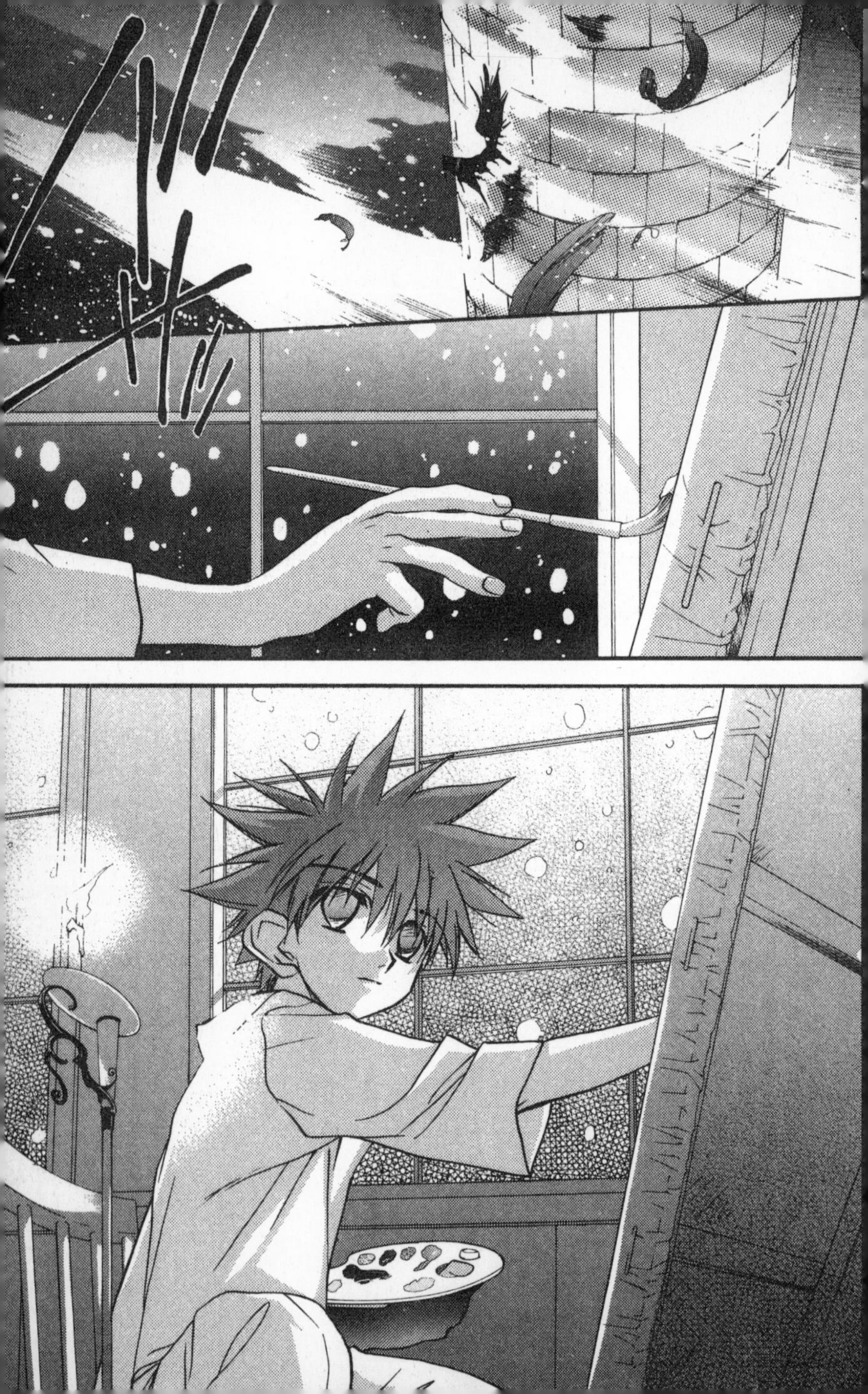

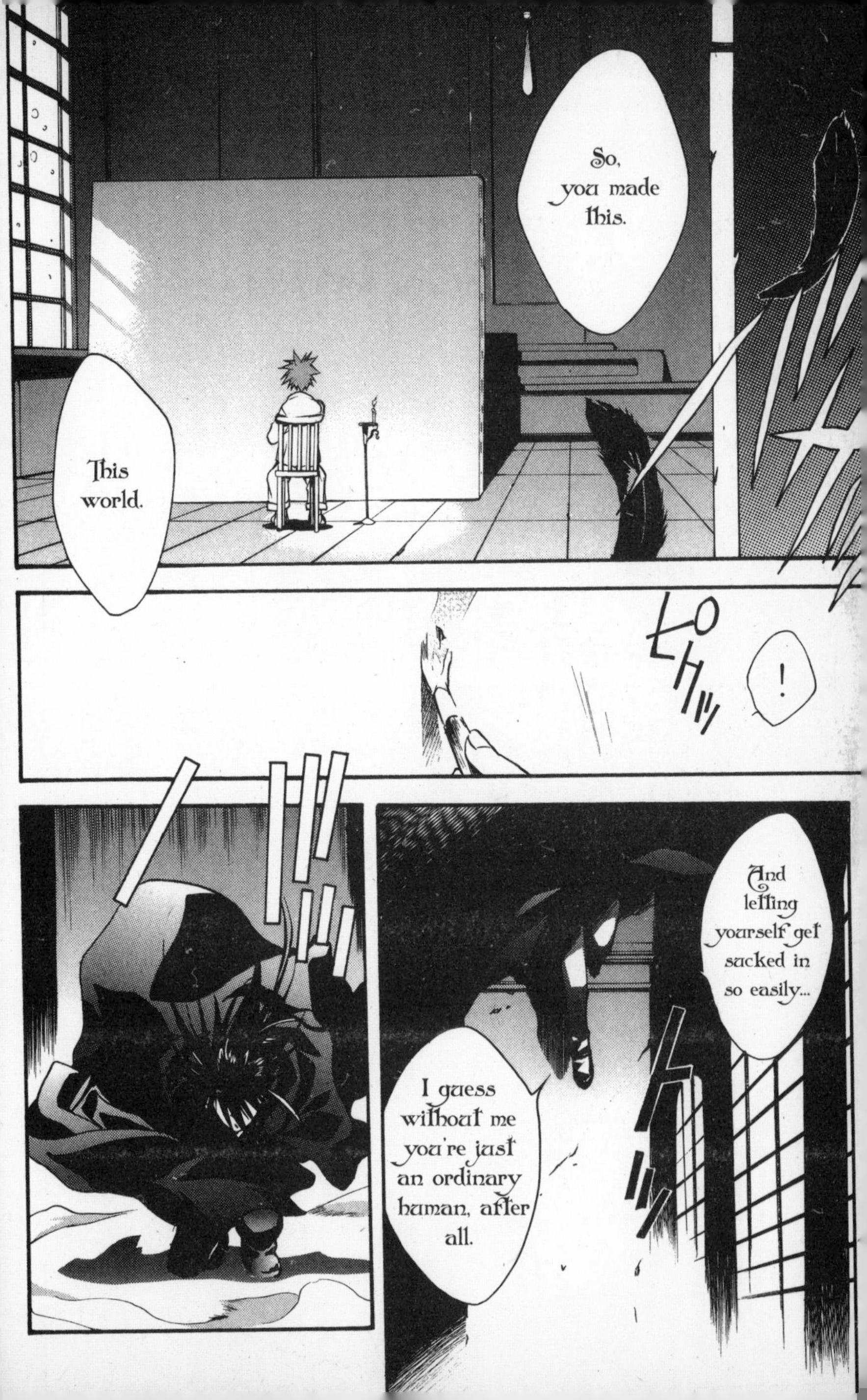
So, you made this.
This world.
!
And letting yourself get sucked in so easily...
I guess without me you're just an ordinary human, after all.

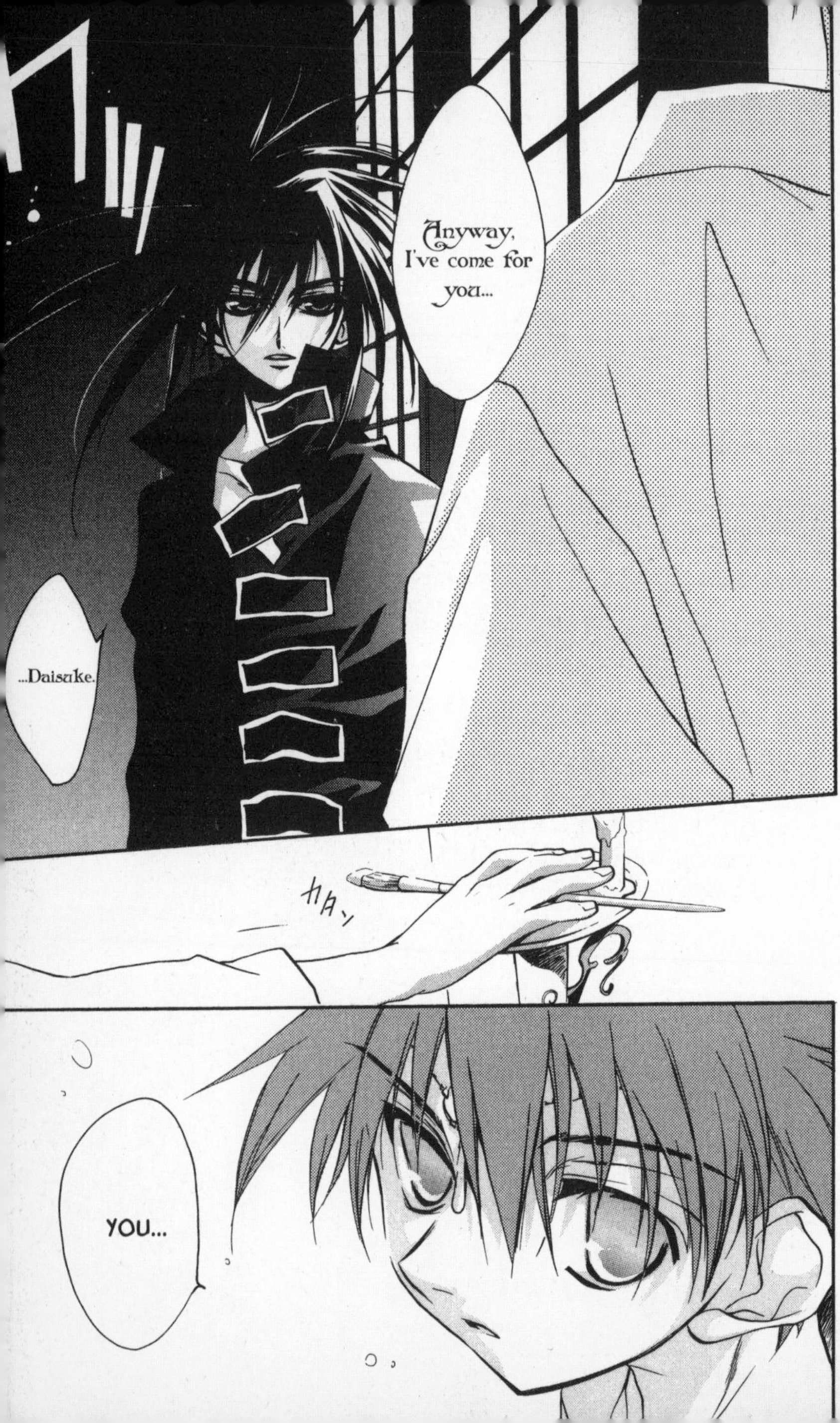
Anyway, I've come for you...
...Daisuke.
カタッ
YOU...

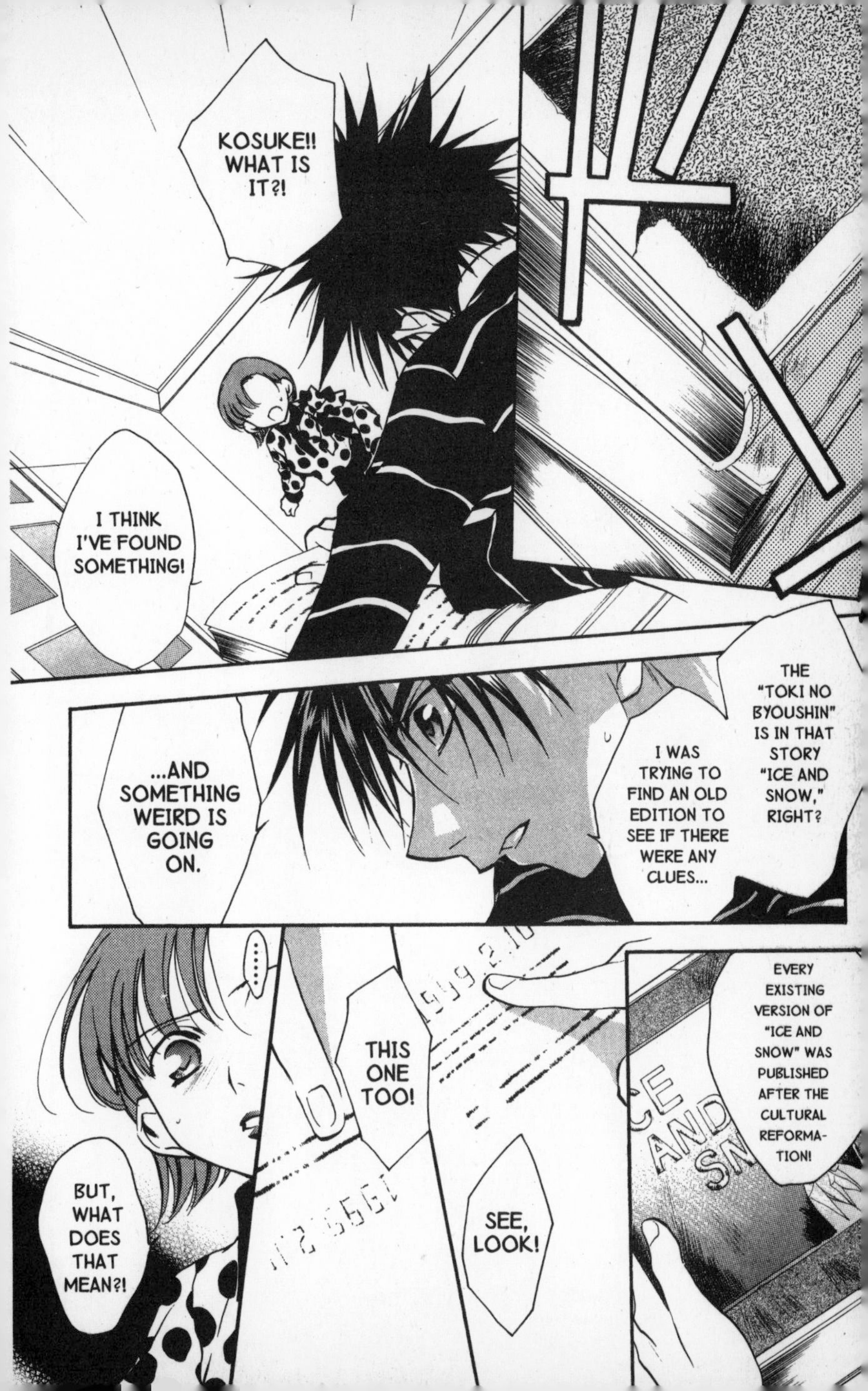
KOSUKE!! WHAT IS IT?!
I THINK I'VE FOUND SOMETHING!
THE "TOKI NO BYOUSHIN" IS IN THAT STORY "ICE AND SNOW," RIGHT?
I WAS TRYING TO FIND AN OLD EDITION TO SEE IF THERE WERE ANY CLUES...
...AND SOMETHING WEIRD IS GOING ON.
EVERY EXISTING VERSION OF "ICE AND SNOW" WAS PUBLISHED AFTER THE CULTURAL REFORMATION!
THIS ONE TOO!
SEE, LOOK!
......
BUT, WHAT DOES THAT MEAN?!

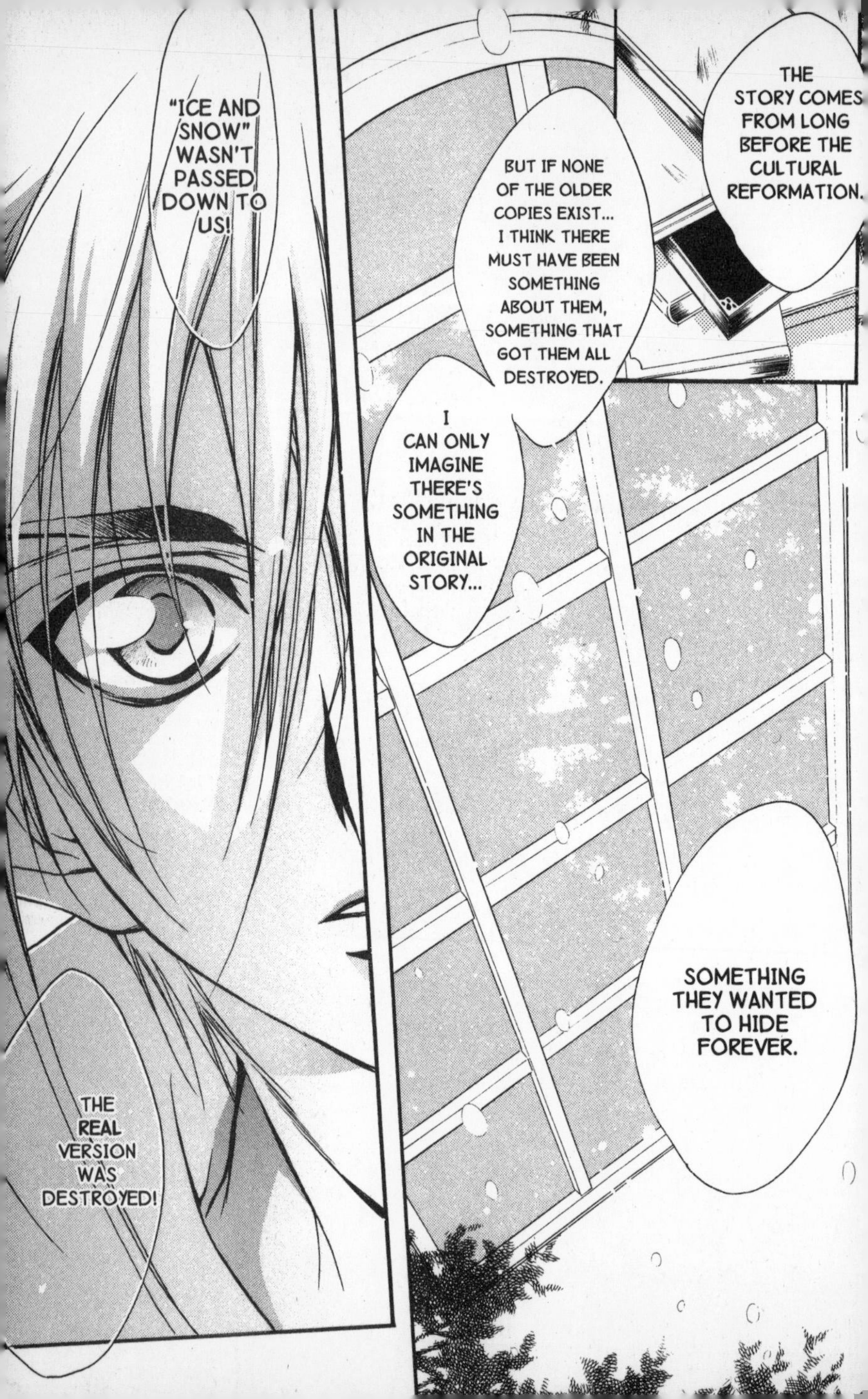
THE STORY COMES FROM LONG BEFORE THE CULTURAL REFORMATION.
BUT IF NONE OF THE OLDER COPIES EXIST... I THINK THERE MUST HAVE BEEN SOMETHING ABOUT THEM, SOMETHING THAT GOT THEM ALL DESTROYED.
I CAN ONLY IMAGINE THERE'S SOMETHING IN THE ORIGINAL STORY...
SOMETHING THEY WANTED TO HIDE FOREVER.
"ICE AND SNOW" WASN'T PASSED DOWN TO US!
THE REAL VERSION WAS DESTROYED!

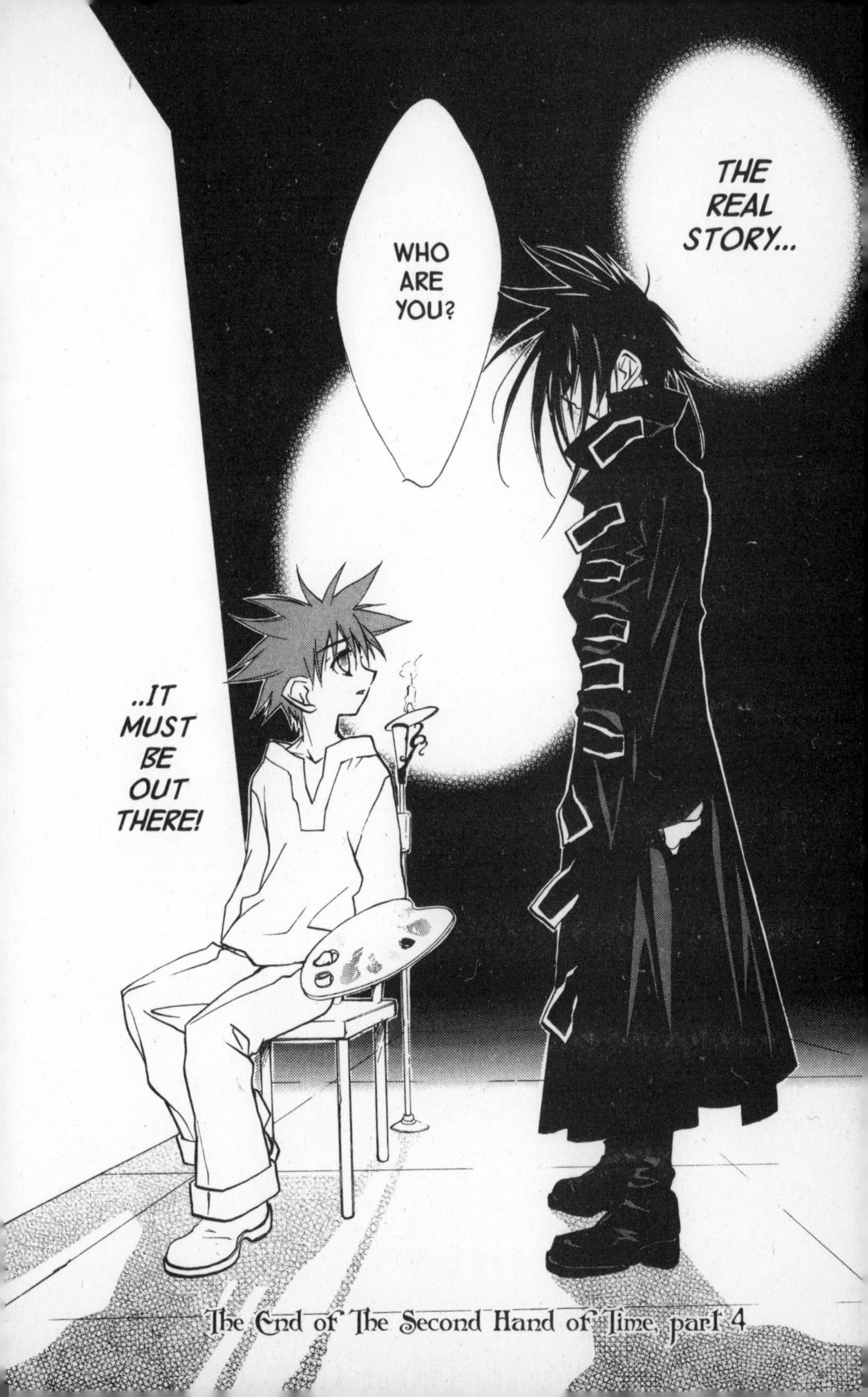
THE REAL STORY...
WHO ARE YOU?
..IT MUST BE OUT THERE!

The End of The Second Hand of Time, part 4

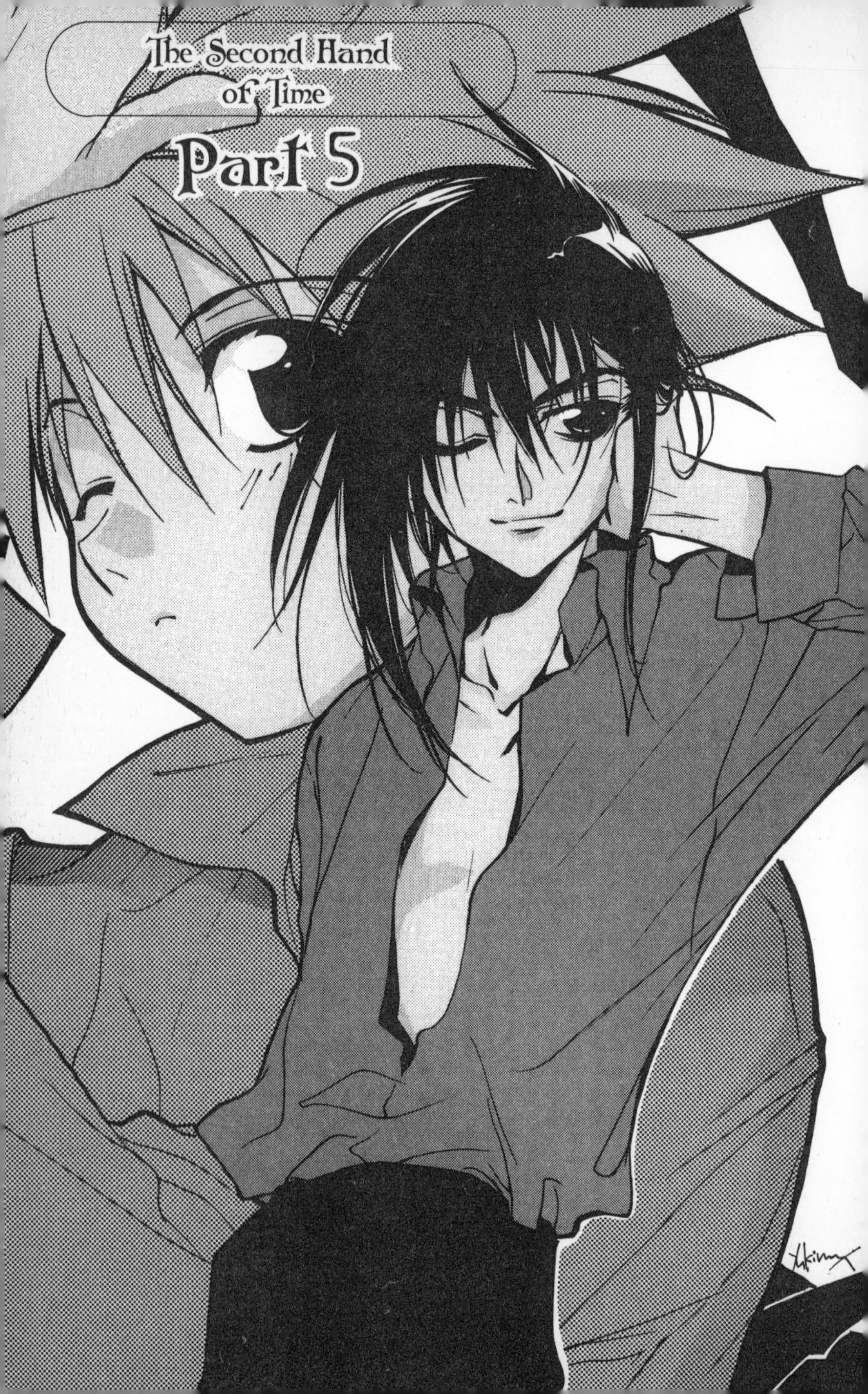
The Second Hand of Time
Part 5

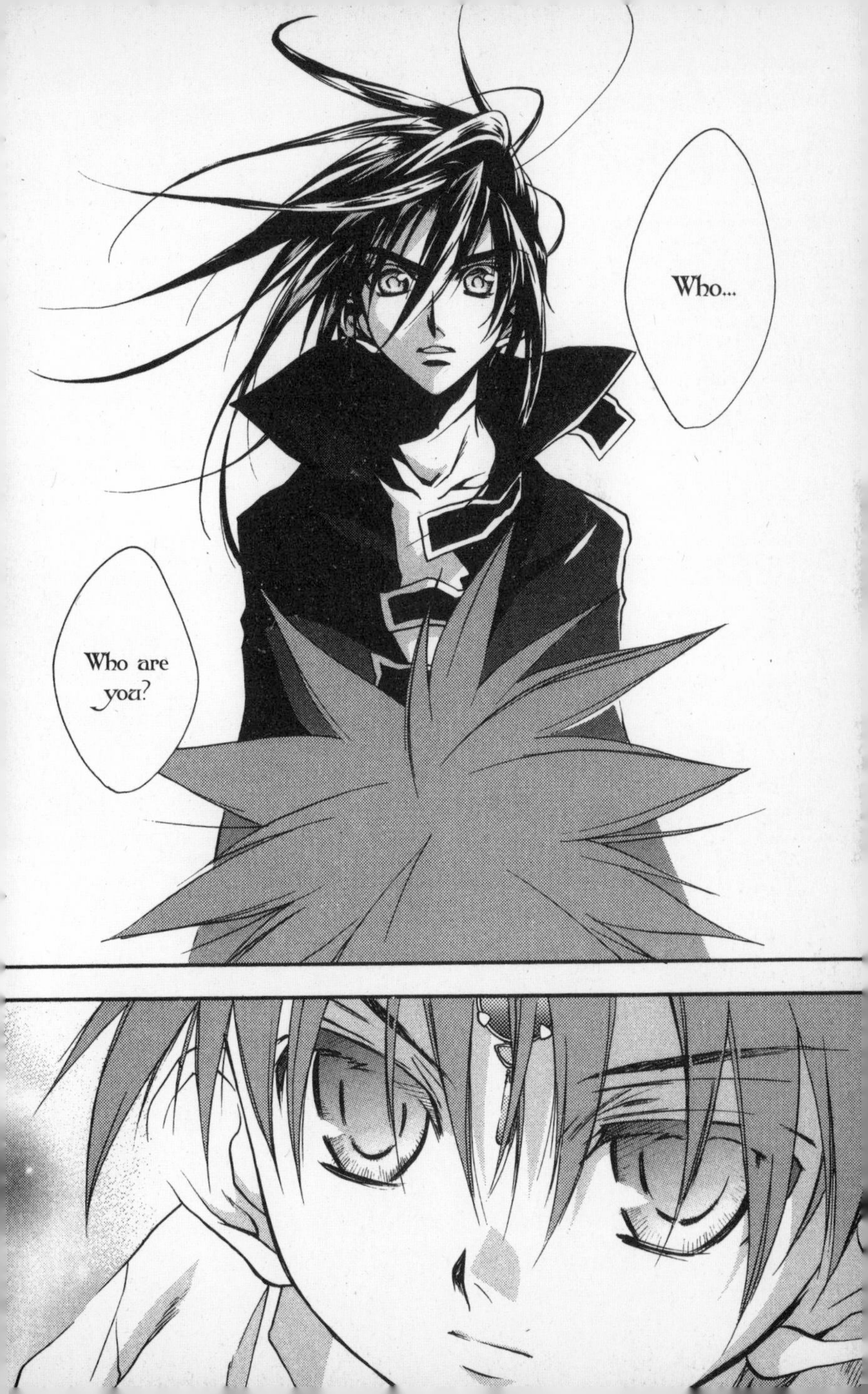
Who...
Who are you?

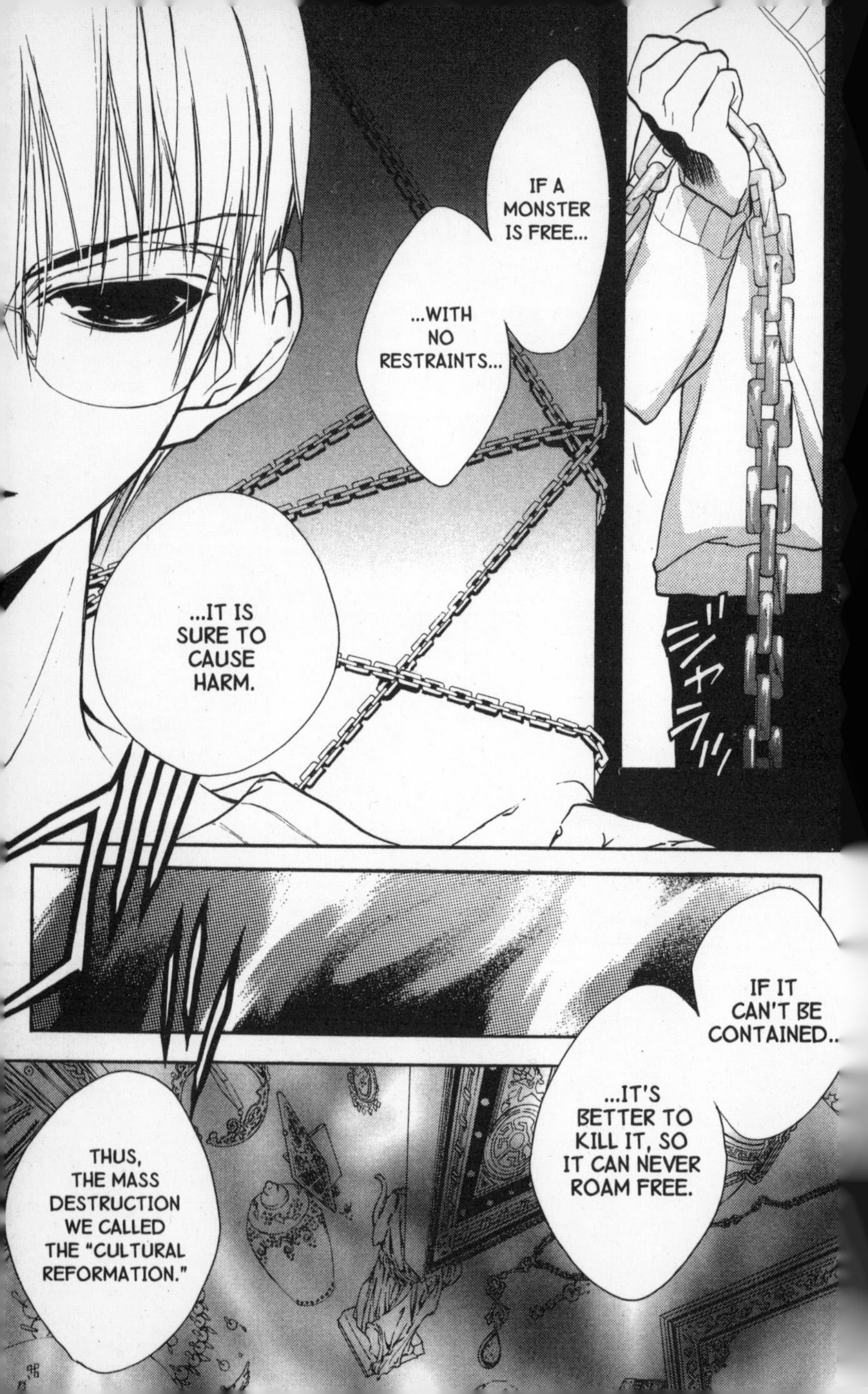
IF A MONSTER IS FREE...
...WITH NO RESTRAINTS...
...IT IS SURE TO CAUSE HARM.
IF IT CAN'T BE CONTAINED..
...IT'S BETTER TO KILL IT, SO IT CAN NEVER ROAM FREE.
THUS, THE MASS DESTRUCTION WE CALLED THE "CULTURAL REFORMATION."

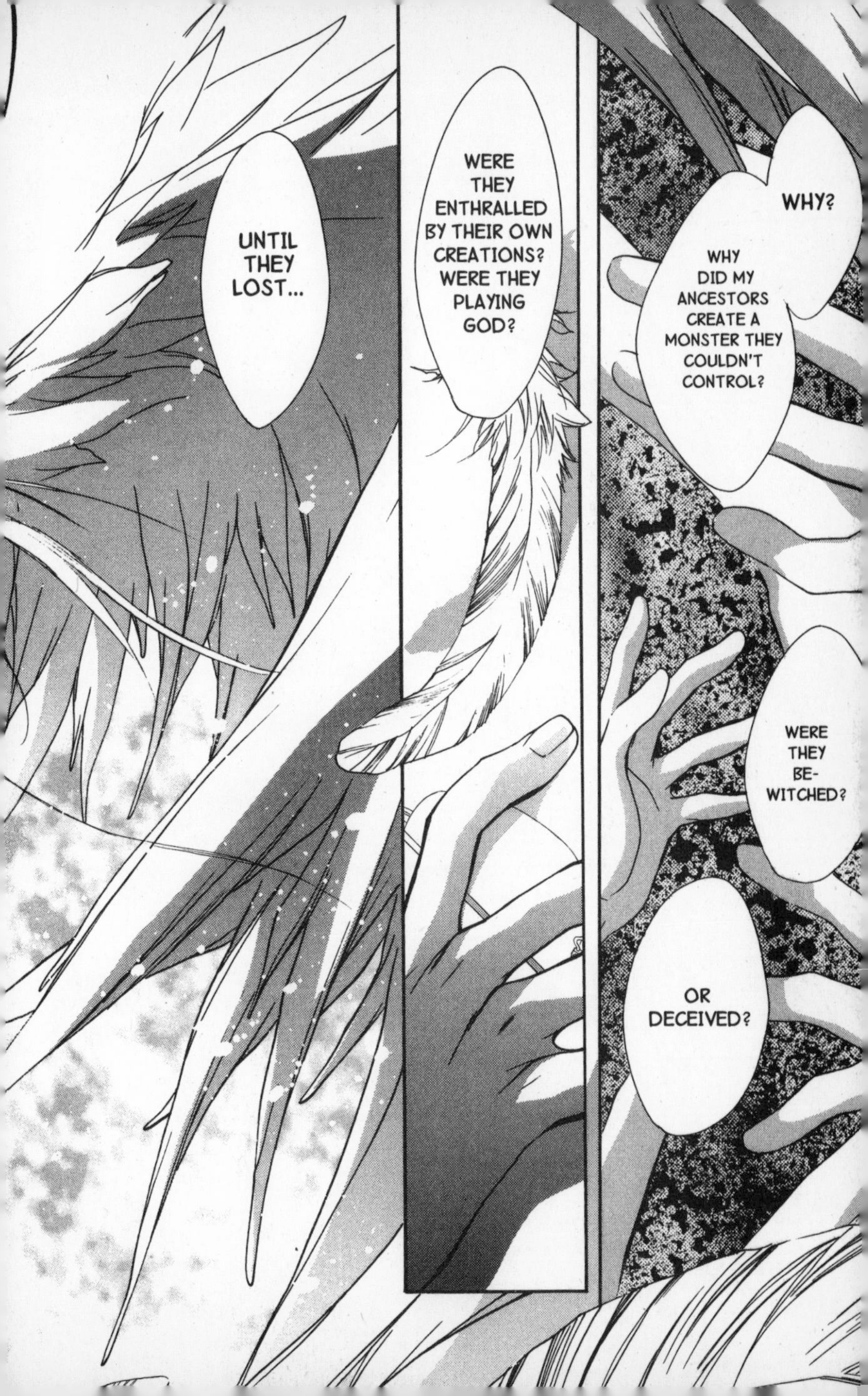
WHY?
WHY DID MY ANCESTORS CREATE A MONSTER THEY COULDN'T CONTROL?
WERE THEY BE-WITCHED?
OR DECEIVED?
WERE THEY ENTHRALLED BY THEIR OWN CREATIONS? WERE THEY PLAYING GOD?
UNTIL THEY LOST...

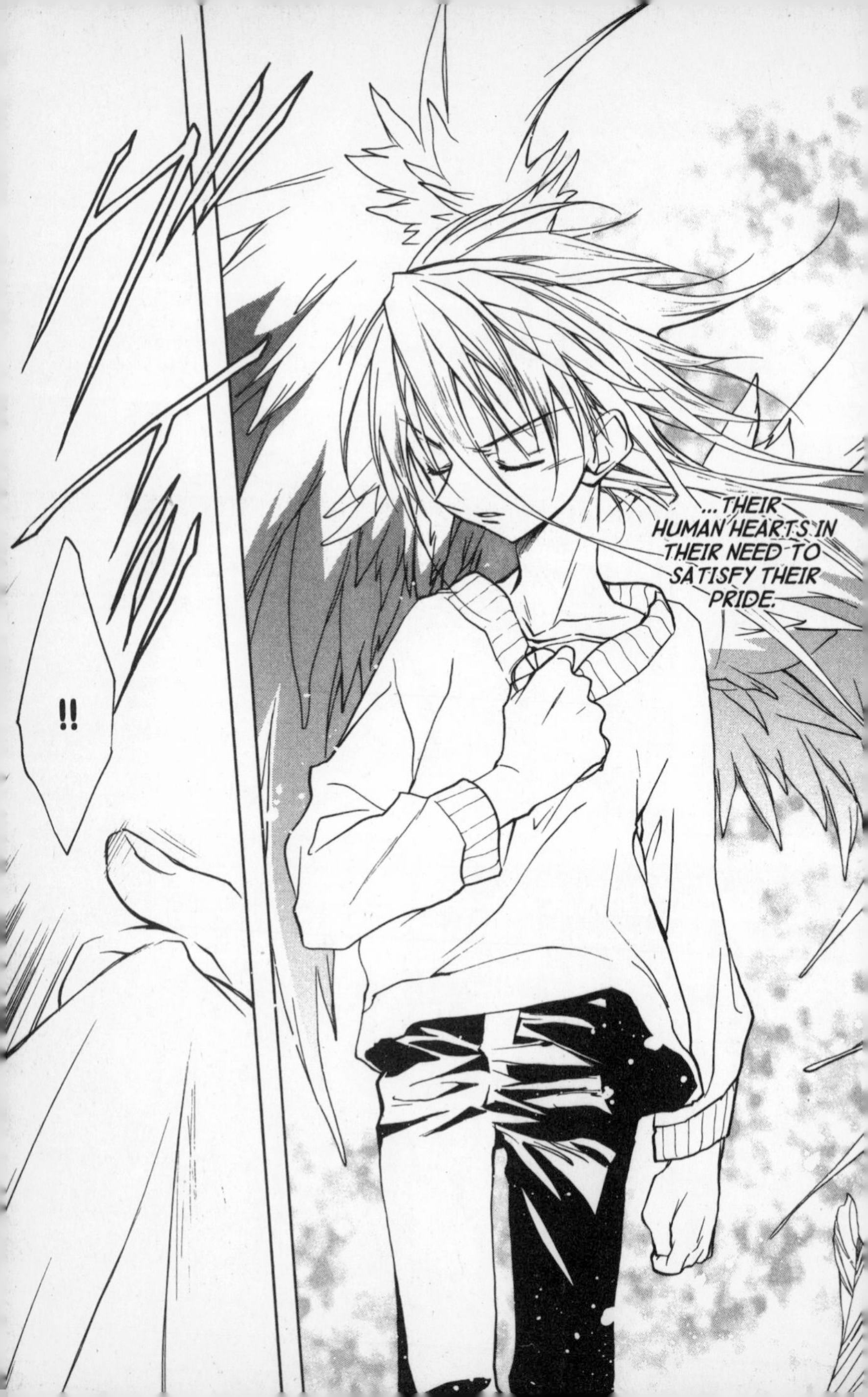
...THEIR HUMAN HEARTS IN THEIR NEED TO SATISFY THEIR PRIDE.
!!

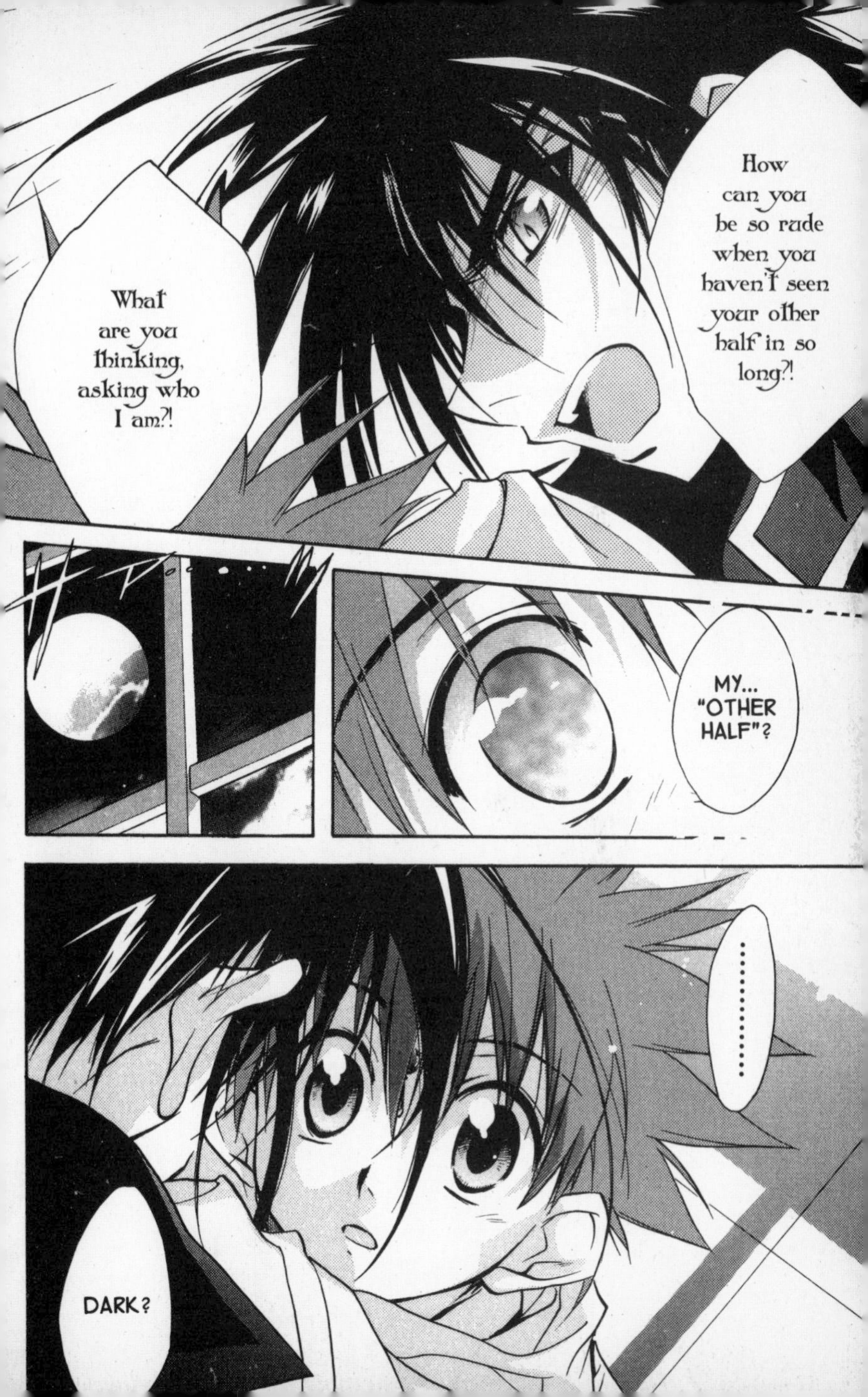
How can you be so rude when you haven't seen your other half in so long?!
What are you thinking, asking who I am?!
MY... "OTHER HALF"?
....
DARK?

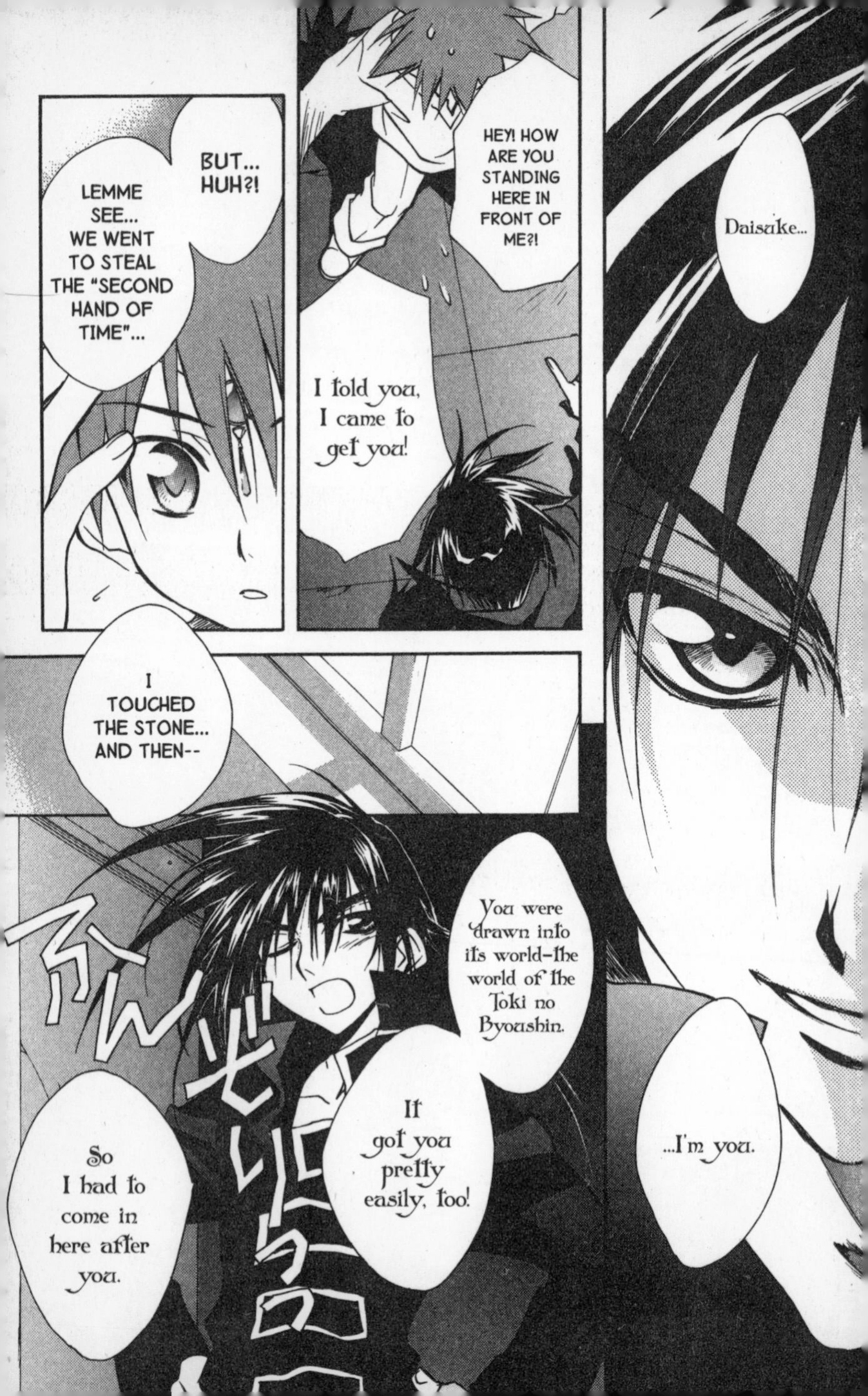
Daisuke...
...I'm you.
HEY! HOW ARE YOU STANDING HERE IN FRONT OF ME?!
I told you, I came to get you!
BUT... HUH?!
LEMME SEE... WE WENT TO STEAL THE "SECOND HAND OF TIME"...
I TOUCHED THE STONE... AND THEN--
You were drawn into its world-the world of the Toki no Byoushin.
It got you pretty easily, too!
So I had to come in here after you.

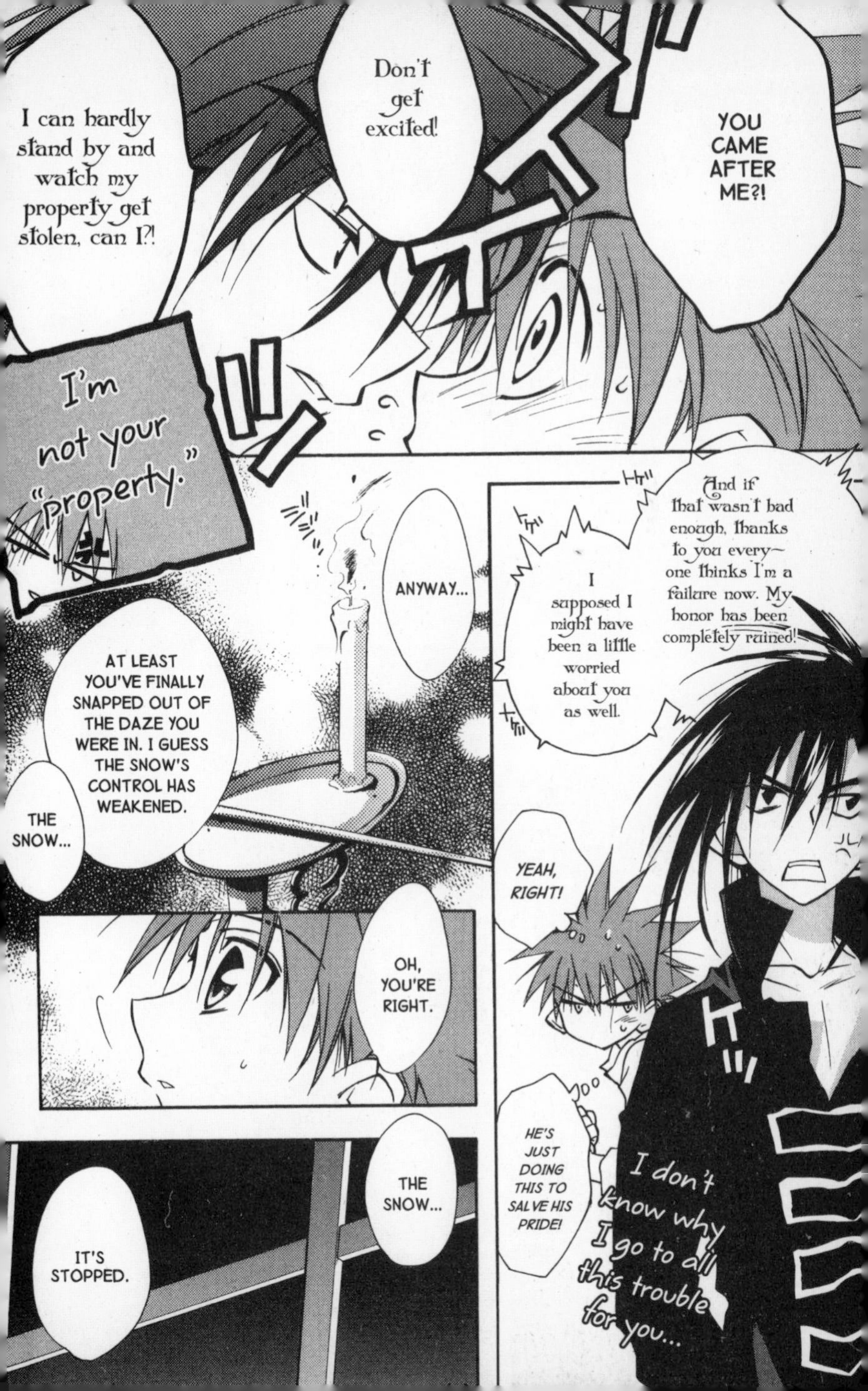
YOU CAME AFTER ME?!
Don't get excited!
I can hardly stand by and watch my property get stolen, can I?!
I'm not your "property."
And if that wasn't bad enough, thanks to you every~one thinks I'm a failure now. My honor has been completely ruined!
I supposed I might have been a little worried about you as well.
YEAH, RIGHT!
HE'S JUST DOING THIS TO SALVE HIS PRIDE!
I don't know why I go to all this trouble for you...
ANYWAY...
AT LEAST YOU'VE FINALLY SNAPPED OUT OF THE DAZE YOU WERE IN. I GUESS THE SNOW'S CONTROL HAS WEAKENED.
THE SNOW...
OH, YOU'RE RIGHT.
THE SNOW...
IT'S STOPPED.

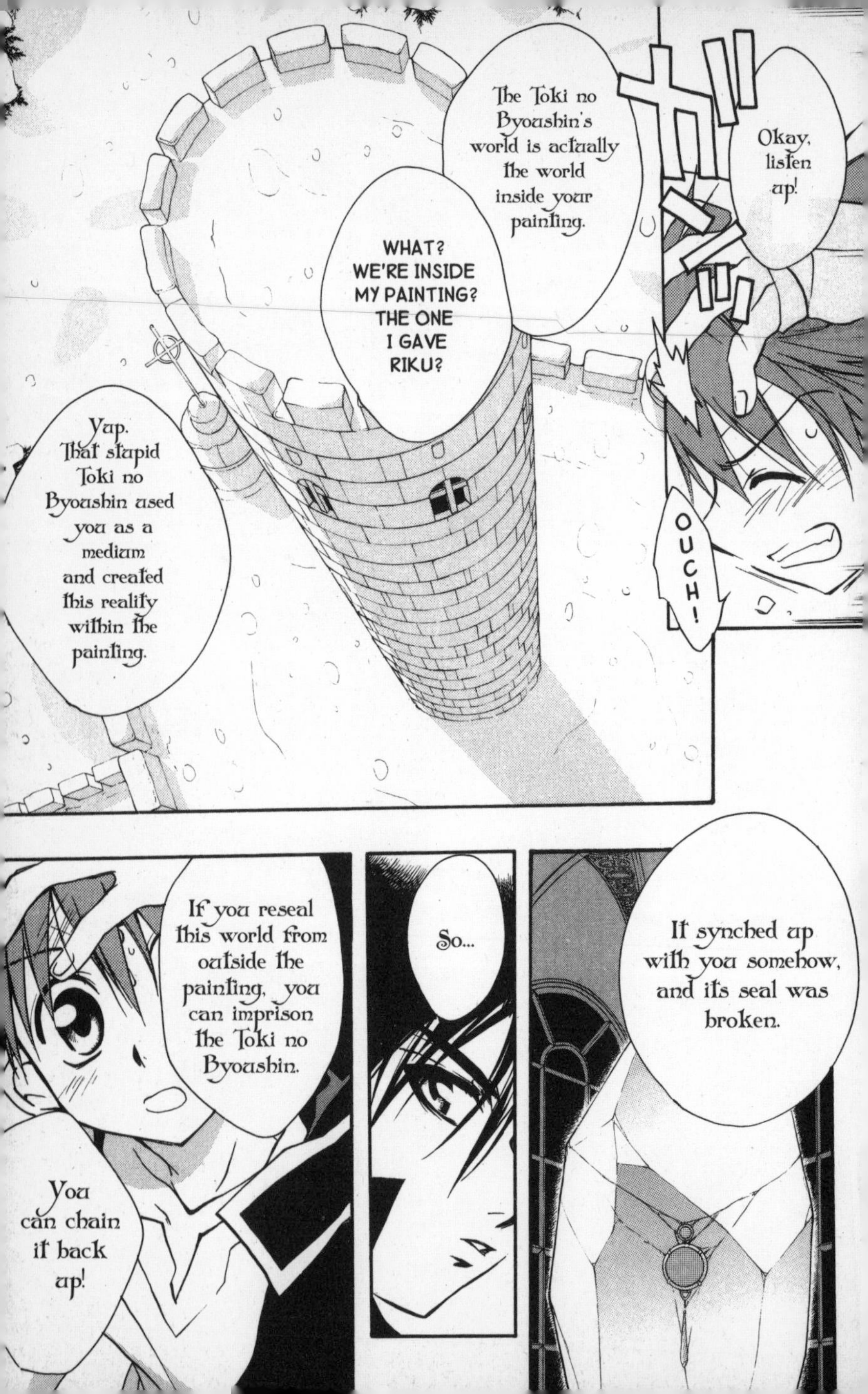
Okay, listen up!
OUCH!
The Toki no Byoushin's world is actually the world inside your painting.
WHAT? WE'RE INSIDE MY PAINTING? THE ONE I GAVE RIKU?
Yup. That stupid Toki no Byoushin used you as a medium and created this reality within the painting.
It synched up with you somehow, and its seal was broken.
So...
If you reseal this world from outside the painting, you can imprison the Toki no Byoushin.
You can chain it back up!

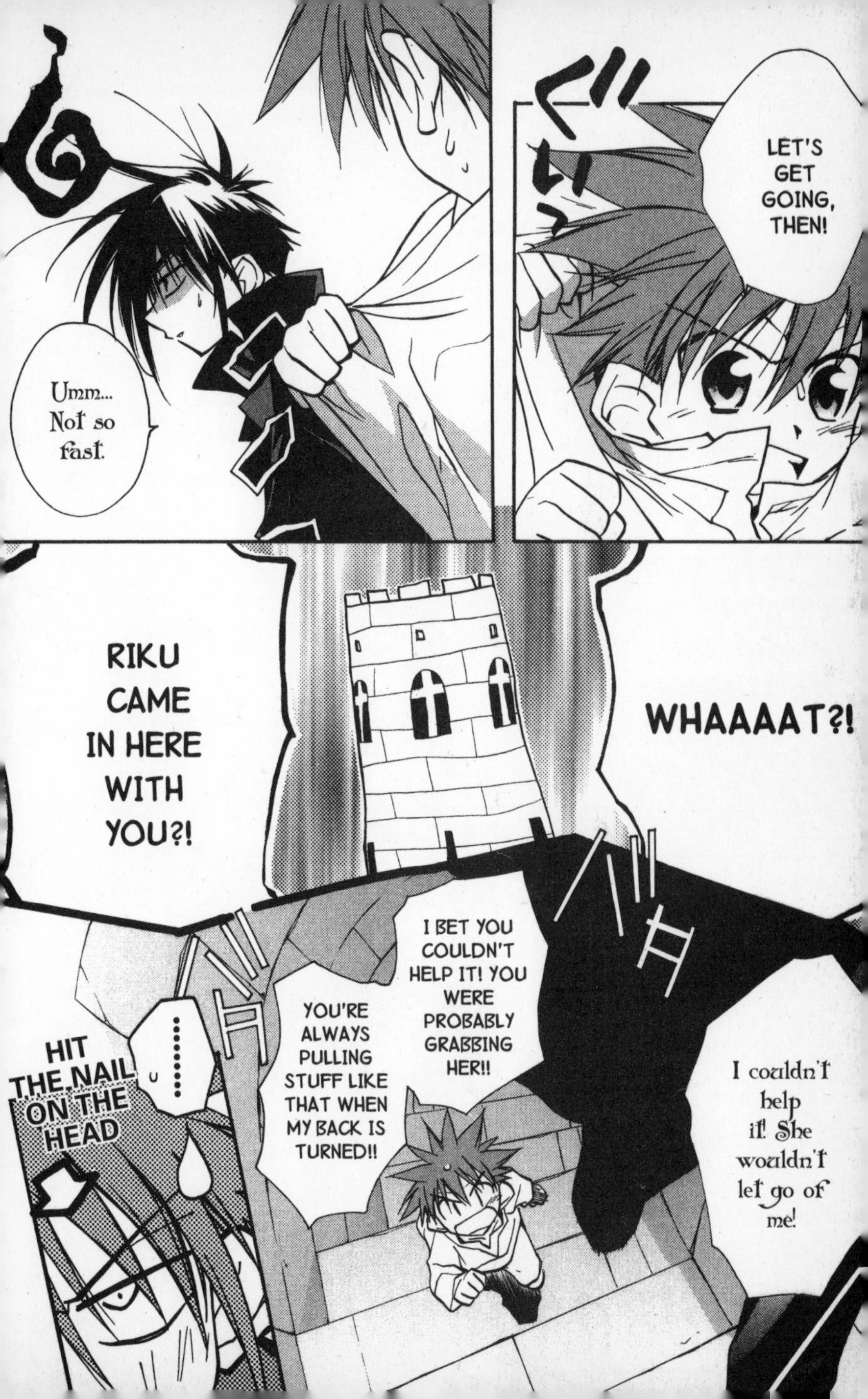
LET'S GET GOING, THEN!
Umm... Not so fast.
WHAAAAT?!
RIKU CAME IN HERE WITH YOU?!
I couldn't help it! She wouldn't let go of me!
I BET YOU COULDN'T HELP IT! YOU WERE PROBABLY GRABBING HER!!
YOU'RE ALWAYS PULLING STUFF LIKE THAT WHEN MY BACK IS TURNED!!
....
HIT THE NAIL ON THE HEAD

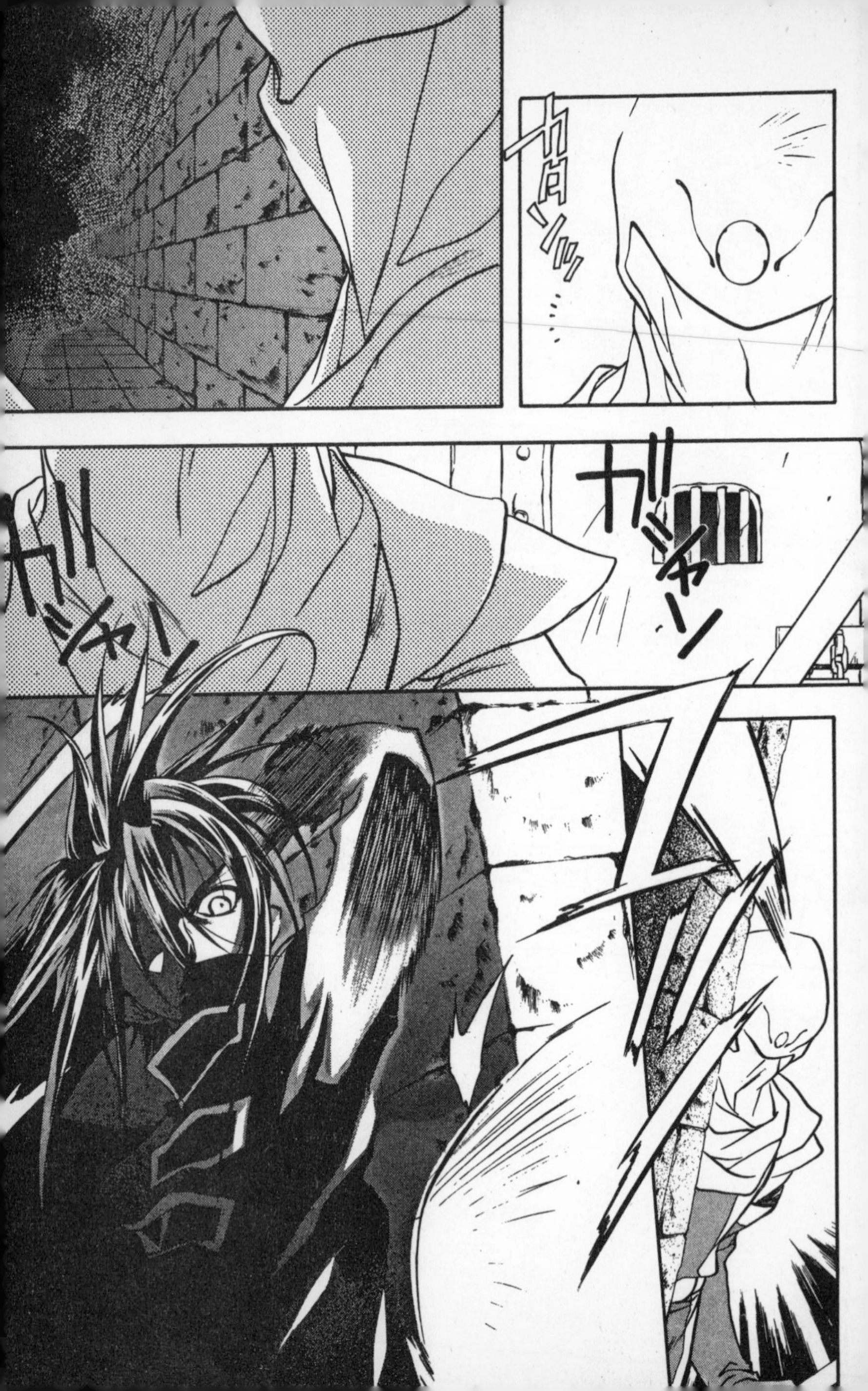
ガシャン
ガシャン

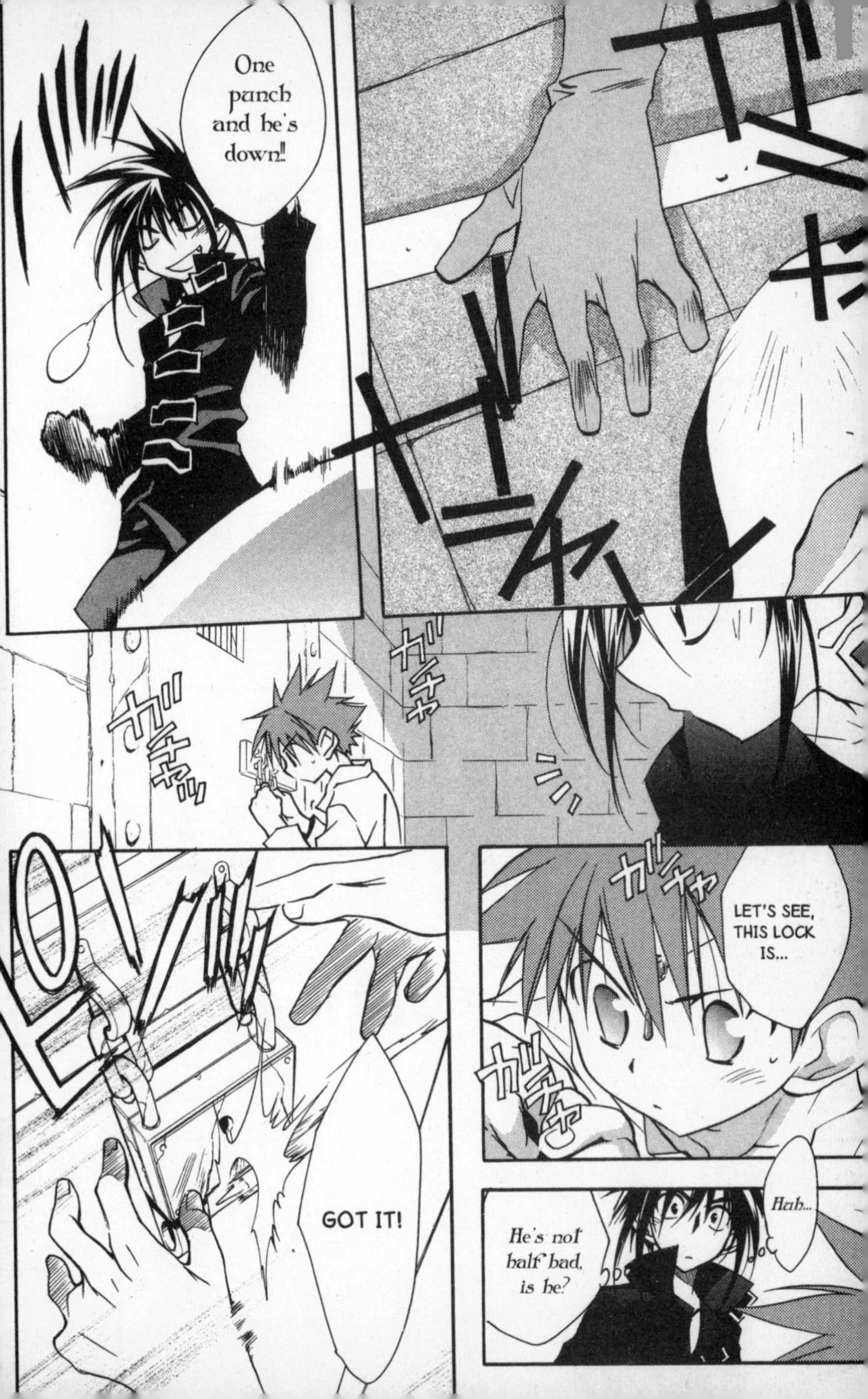
One punch and he's down!!
LET'S SEE, THIS LOCK IS...
Huh...
He's not half bad, is he?
GOT IT!

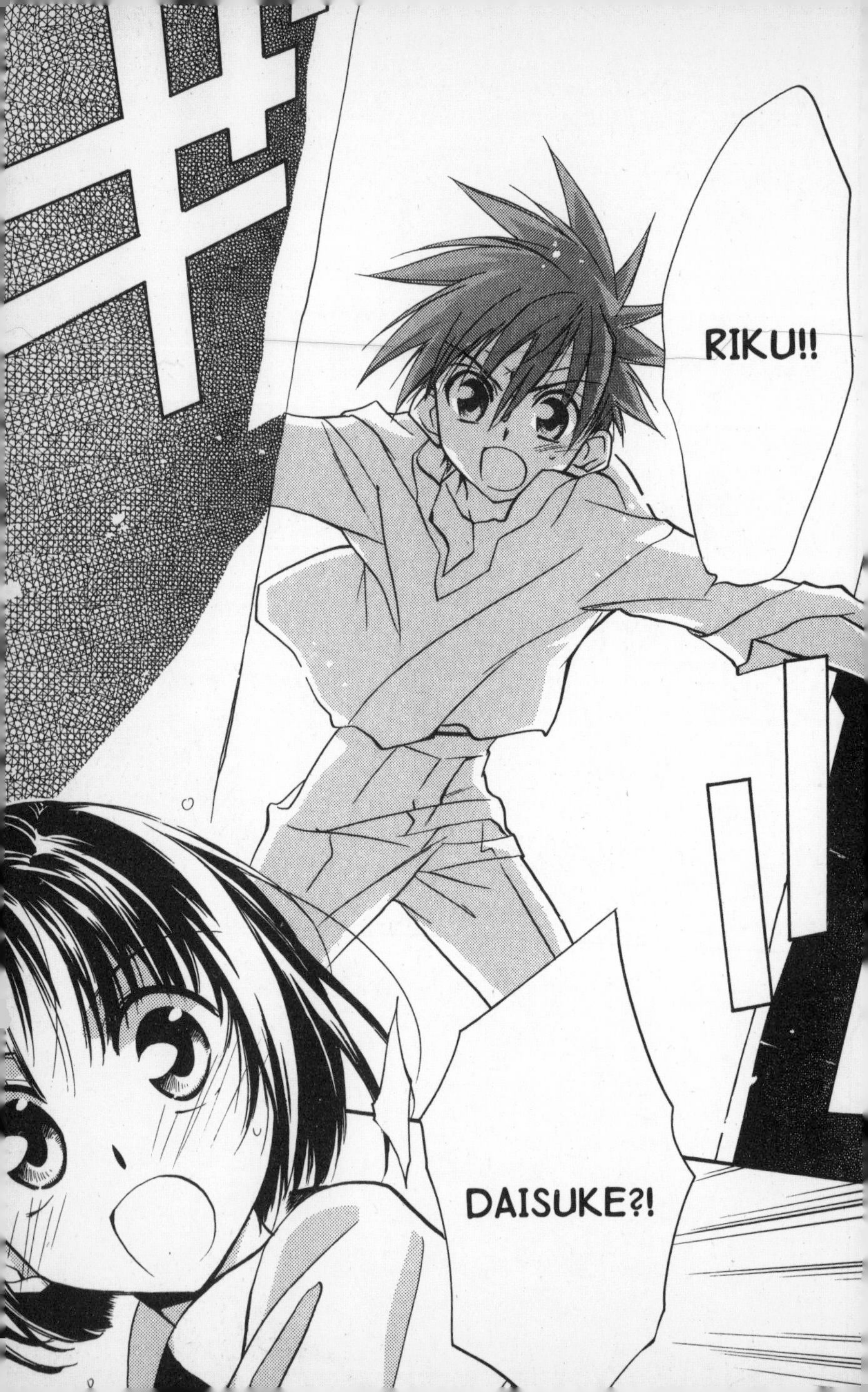
RIKU!!
DAISUKE?!

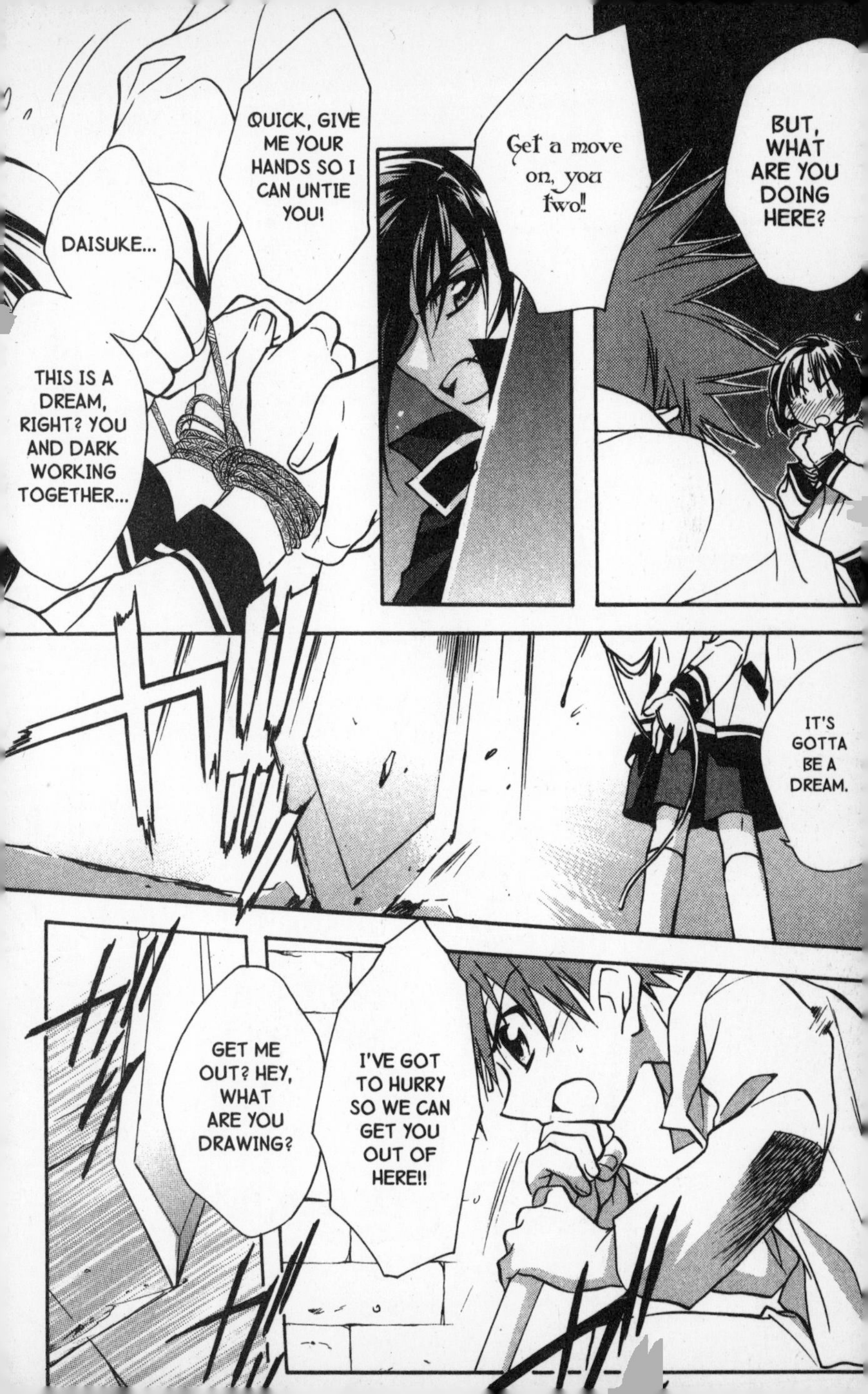
BUT, WHAT ARE YOU DOING HERE?
Get a move on, you two!!
QUICK, GIVE ME YOUR HANDS SO I CAN UNTIE YOU!
DAISUKE...
THIS IS A DREAM, RIGHT? YOU AND DARK WORKING TOGETHER...
IT'S GOTTA BE A DREAM.
I'VE GOT TO HURRY SO WE CAN GET YOU OUT OF HERE!!
GET ME OUT? HEY, WHAT ARE YOU DRAWING?

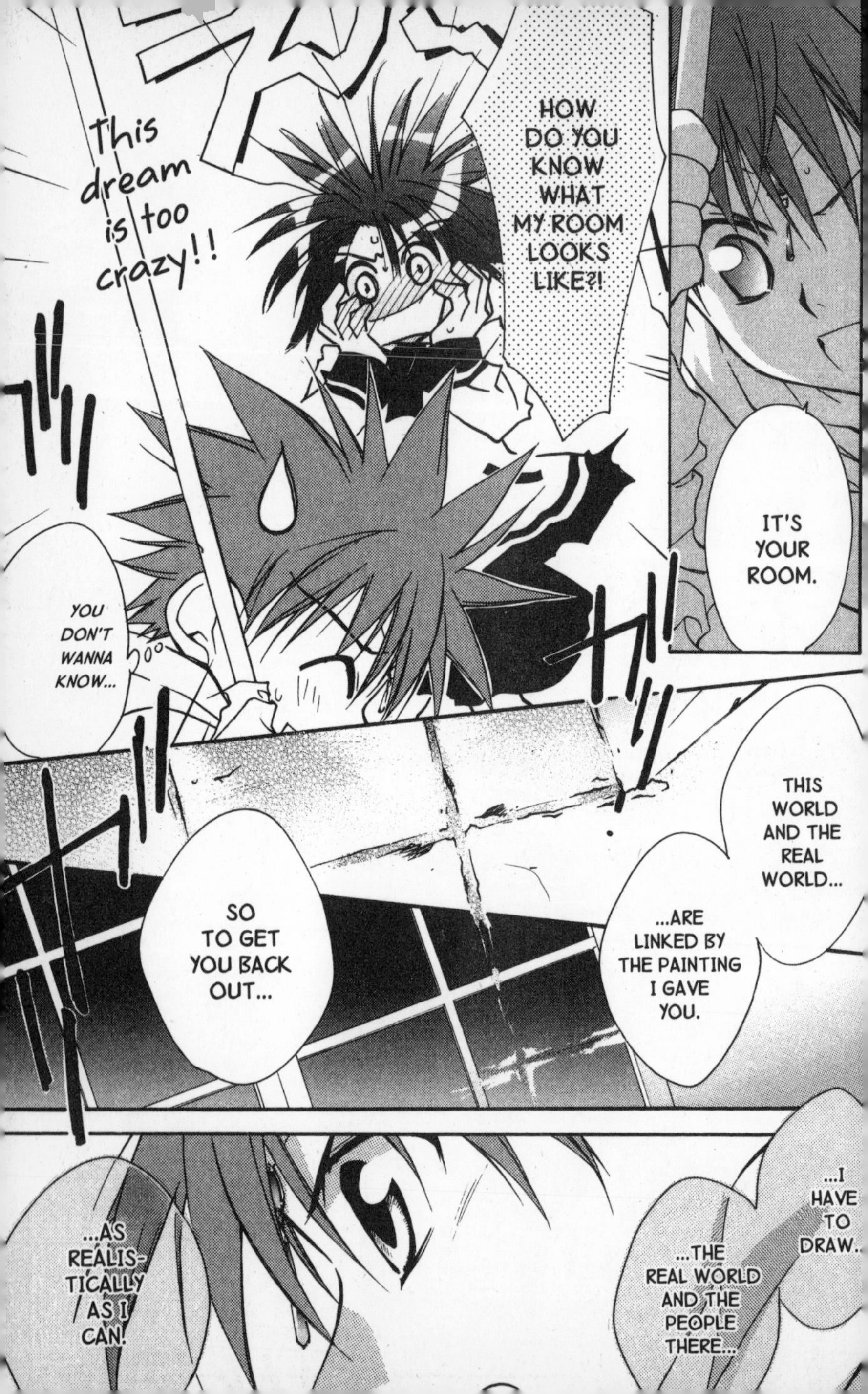
IT'S YOUR ROOM.
HOW DO YOU KNOW WHAT MY ROOM LOOKS LIKE?!
This dream is too crazy!!
YOU DON'T WANNA KNOW...
THIS WORLD AND THE REAL WORLD...
...ARE LINKED BY THE PAINTING I GAVE YOU.
SO TO GET YOU BACK OUT...
...I HAVE TO DRAW...
...THE REAL WORLD AND THE PEOPLE THERE...
...AS REALIS-TICALLY AS I CAN!

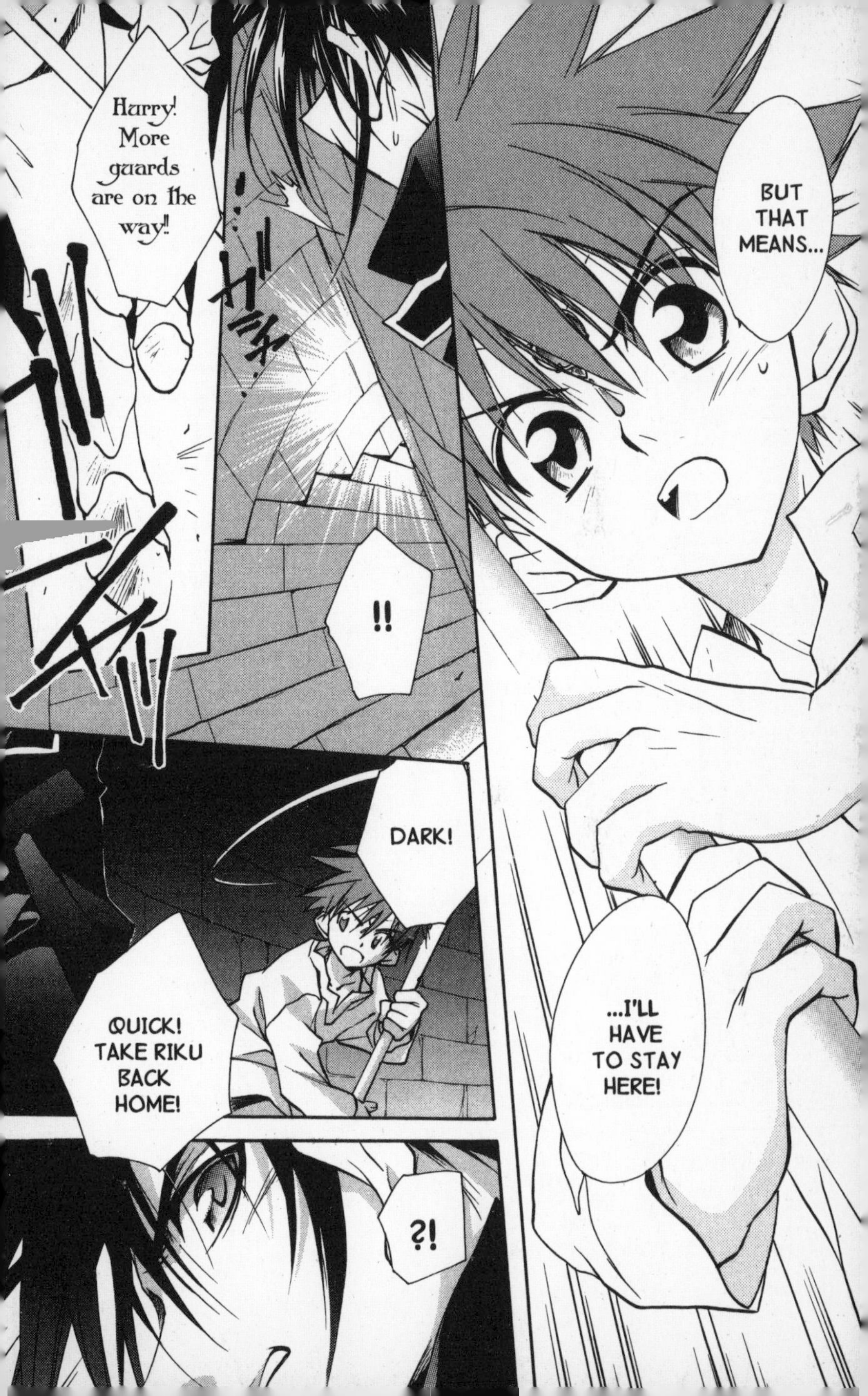

BUT THAT MEANS...
...I'LL HAVE TO STAY HERE!
!!
Hurry! More guards are on the way!!
DARK!
QUICK! TAKE RIKU BACK HOME!
?!

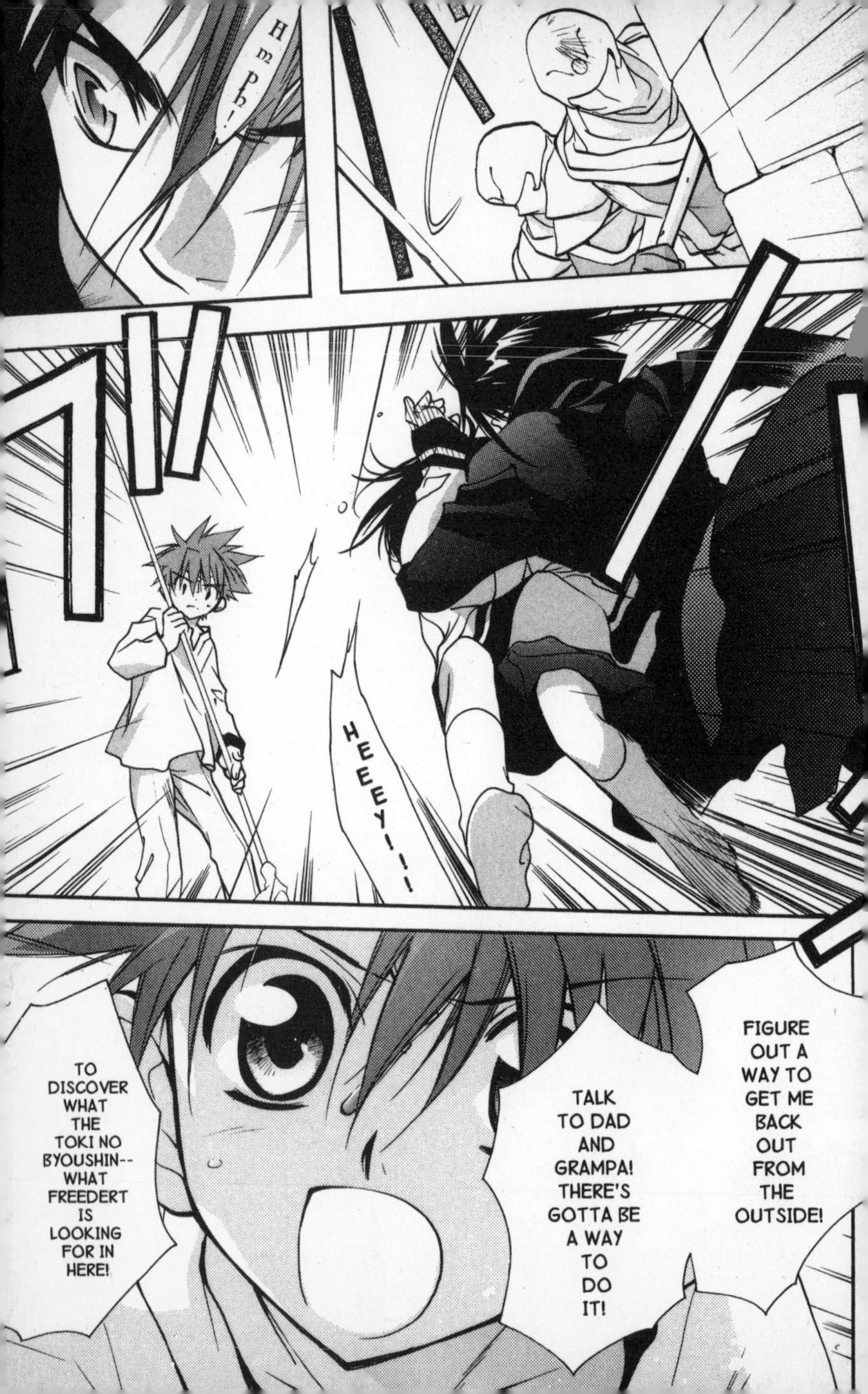
Hmph!
HEEEY!!!
FIGURE OUT A WAY TO GET ME BACK OUT FROM THE OUTSIDE!
TALK TO DAD AND GRAMPA! THERE'S GOTTA BE A WAY TO DO IT!
TO DISCOVER WHAT THE TOKI NO BYOUSHIN-- WHAT FREEDERT IS LOOKING FOR IN HERE!

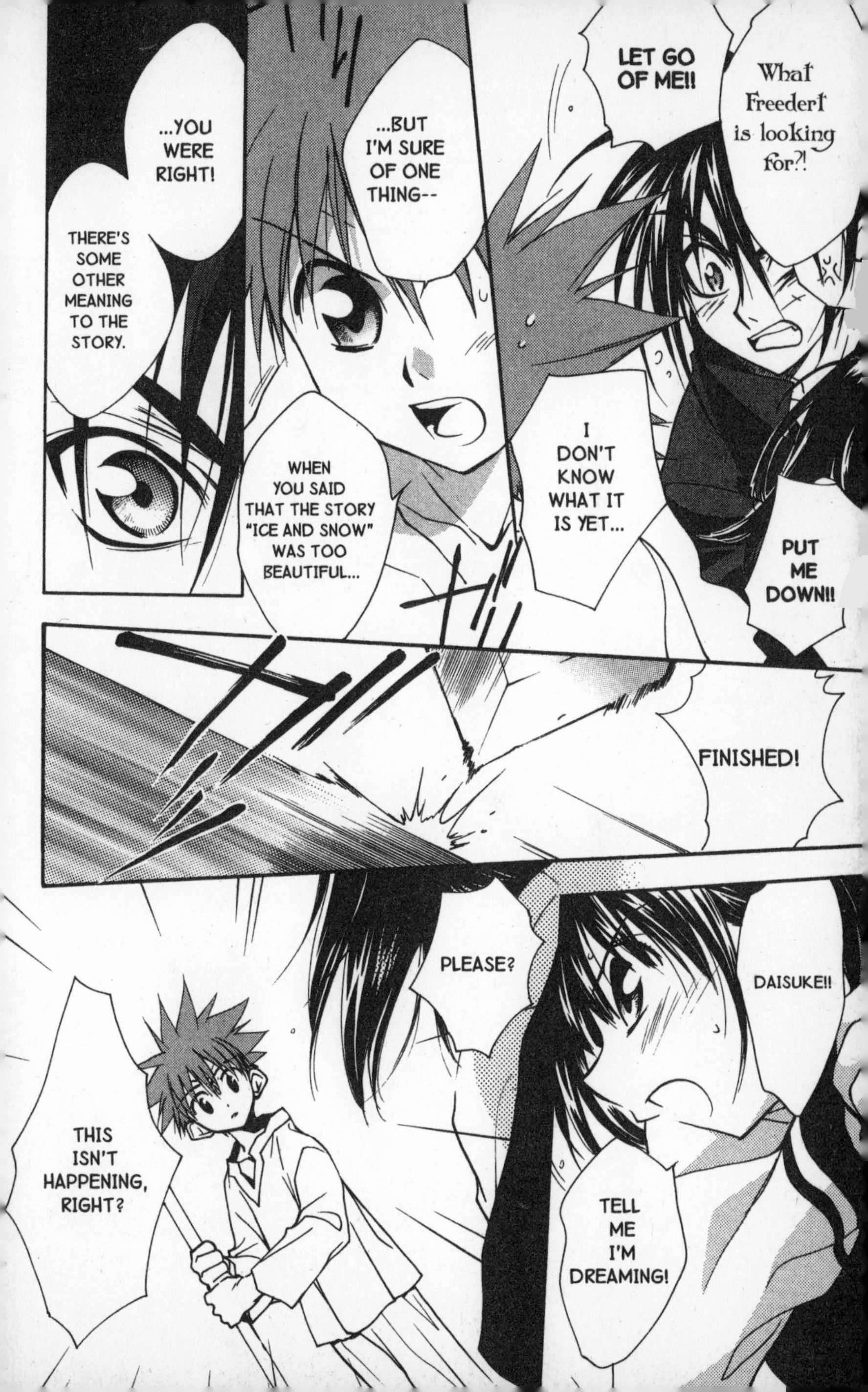
What Freedert is looking for?!
LET GO OF ME!!
PUT ME DOWN!!
...BUT I'M SURE OF ONE THING--
I DON'T KNOW WHAT IT IS YET...
WHEN YOU SAID THAT THE STORY "ICE AND SNOW" WAS TOO BEAUTIFUL...
...YOU WERE RIGHT!
THERE'S SOME OTHER MEANING TO THE STORY.
FINISHED!
DAISUKE!!
PLEASE?
TELL ME I'M DREAMING!
THIS ISN'T HAPPENING, RIGHT?

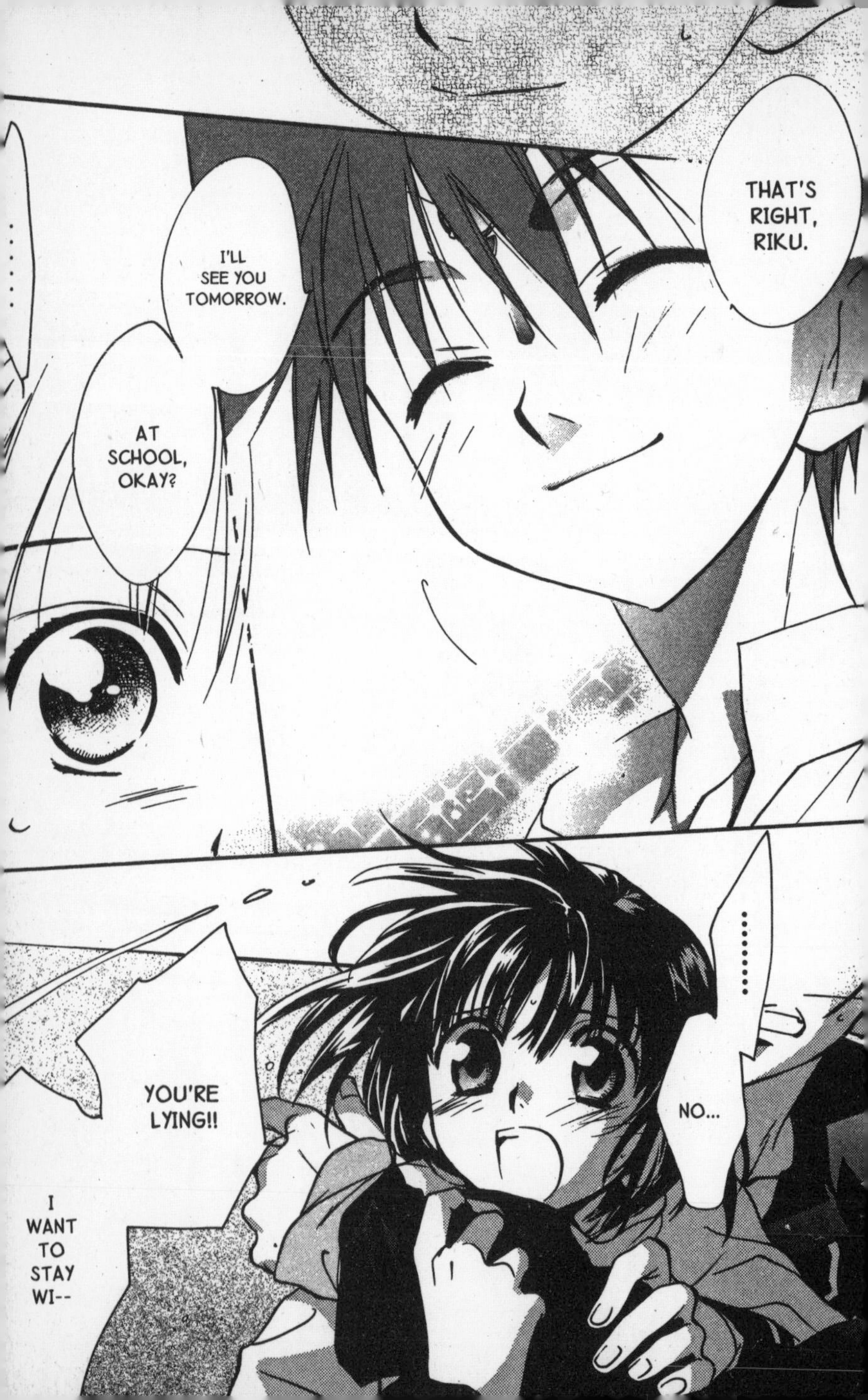
THAT'S RIGHT, RIKU.
I'LL SEE YOU TOMORROW.
AT SCHOOL, OKAY?
......
......
NO...
YOU'RE LYING!!
I WANT TO STAY WI--

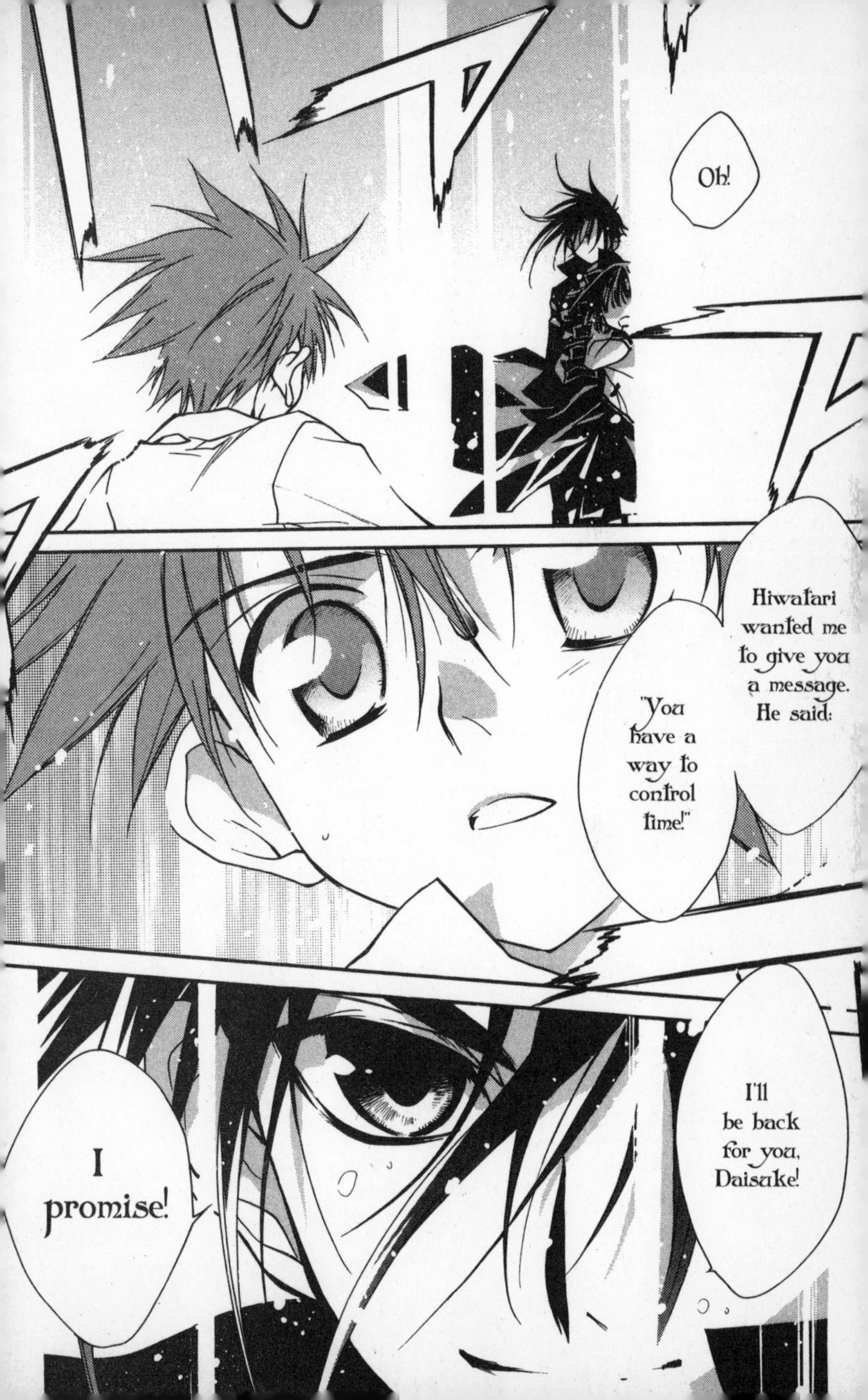
Oh!
Hiwatari wanted me to give you a message. He said:
"You have a way to control time!"
I'll be back for you, Daisuke!
I promise!

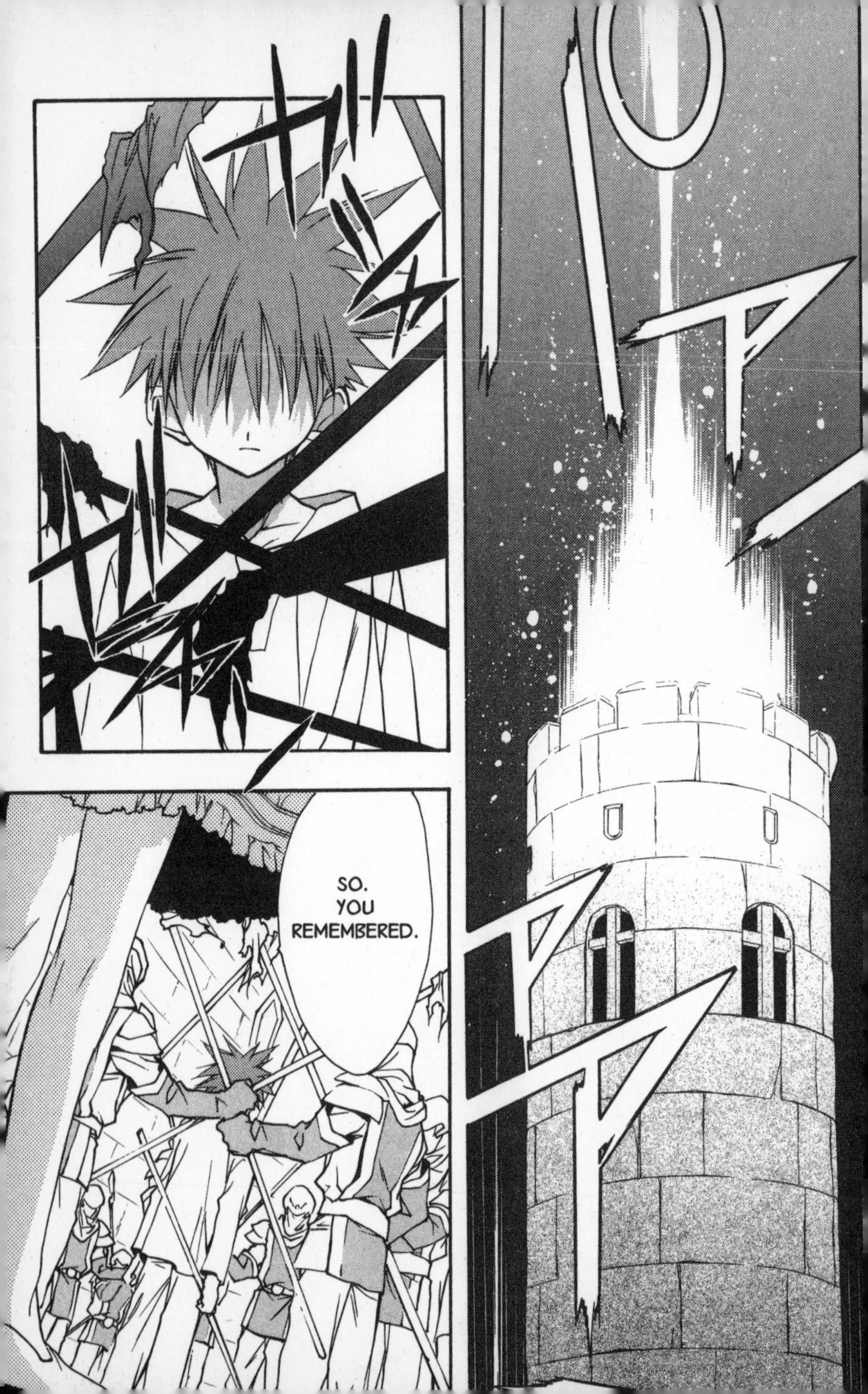
SO. YOU REMEMBERED.

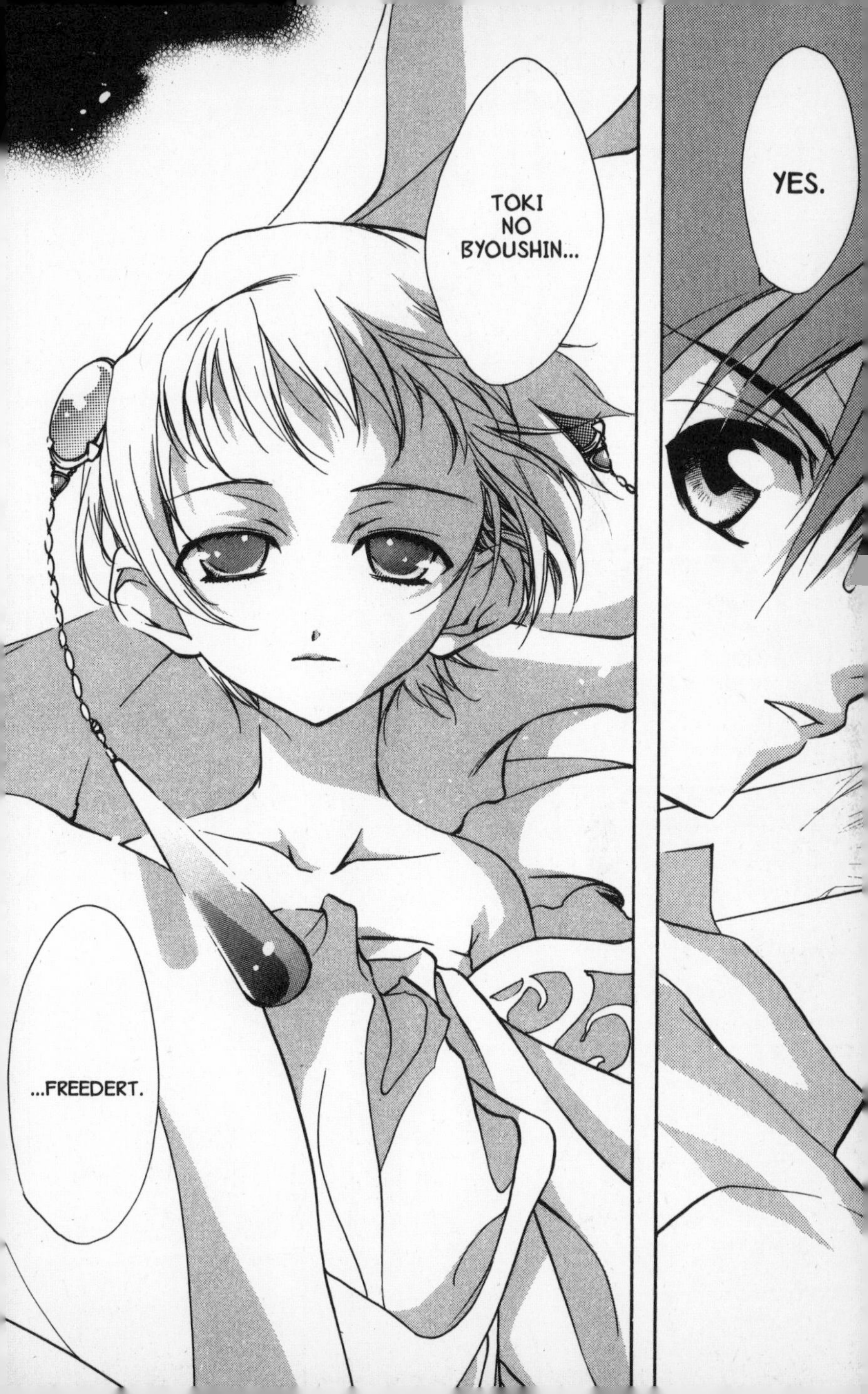
YES.
TOKI NO BYOUSHIN...
...FREEDERT.

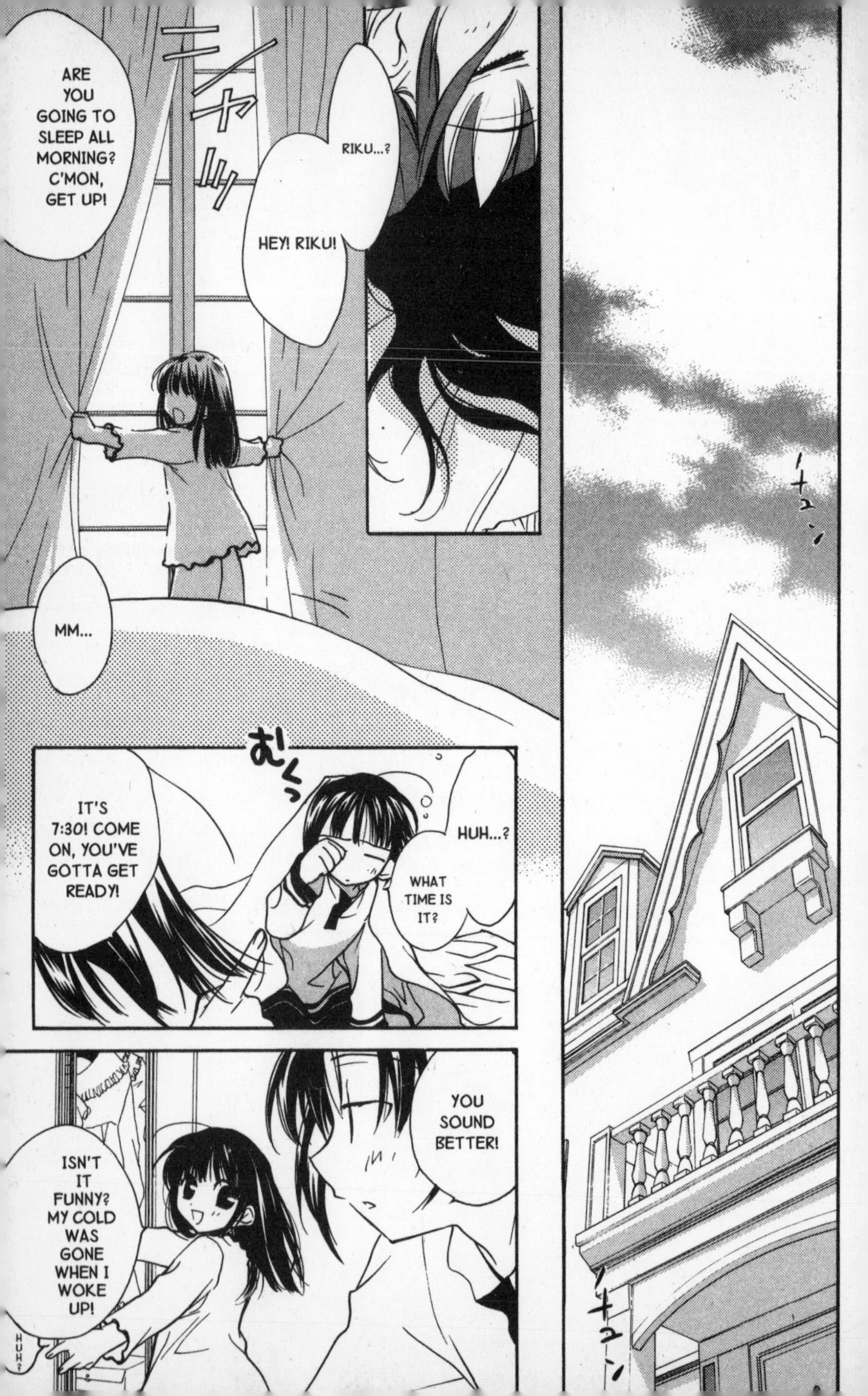
RIKU...?
HEY! RIKU!
ARE YOU GOING TO SLEEP ALL MORNING? C'MON, GET UP!
MM...
HUH...?
WHAT TIME IS IT?
むくっ
IT'S 7:30! COME ON, YOU'VE GOTTA GET READY!
YOU SOUND BETTER!
ISN'T IT FUNNY? MY COLD WAS GONE WHEN I WOKE UP!
HUH?

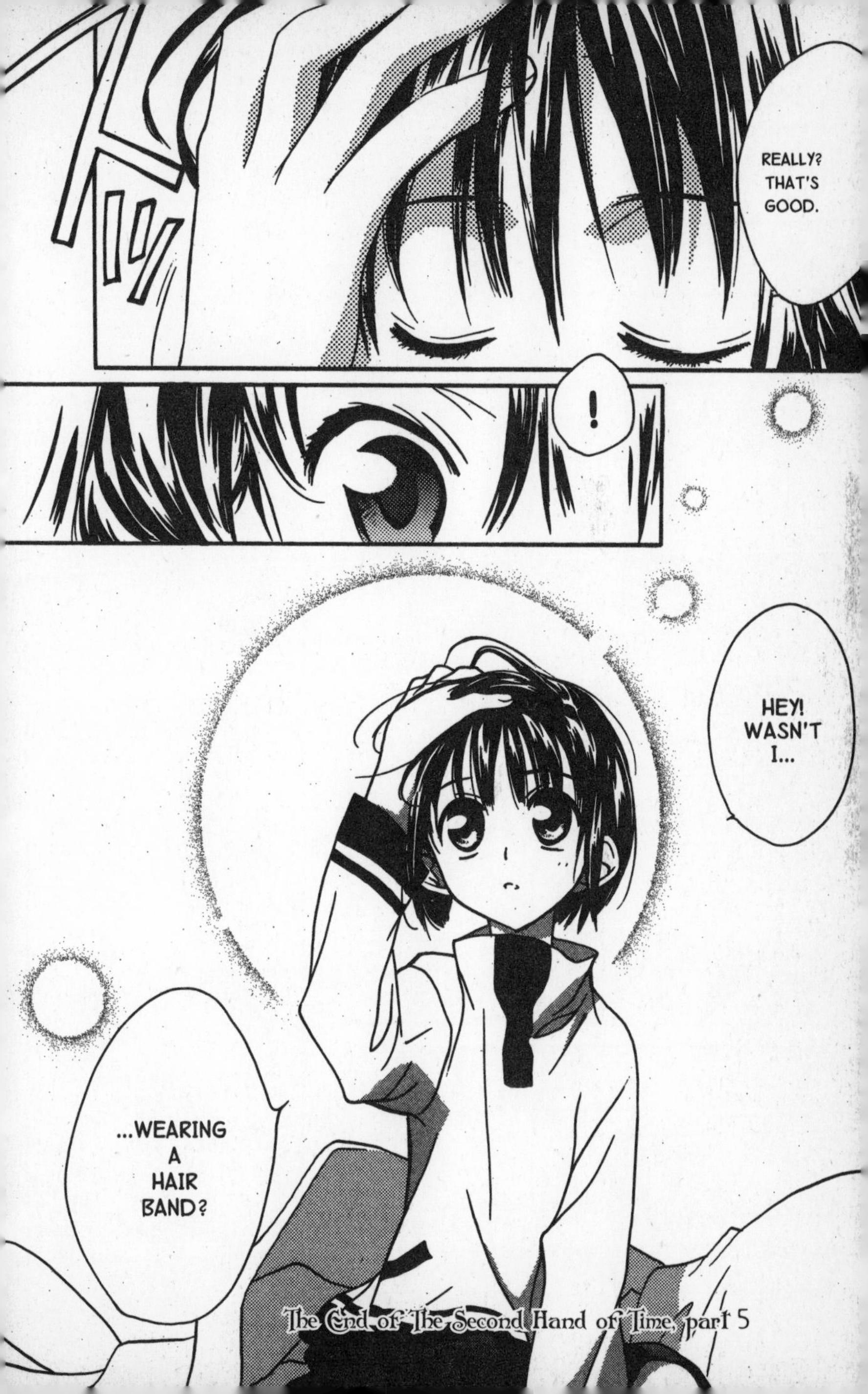
REALLY? THAT'S GOOD.
!
HEY! WASN'T I...
...WEARING A HAIR BAND?
The End of The Second Hand of Time, part 5

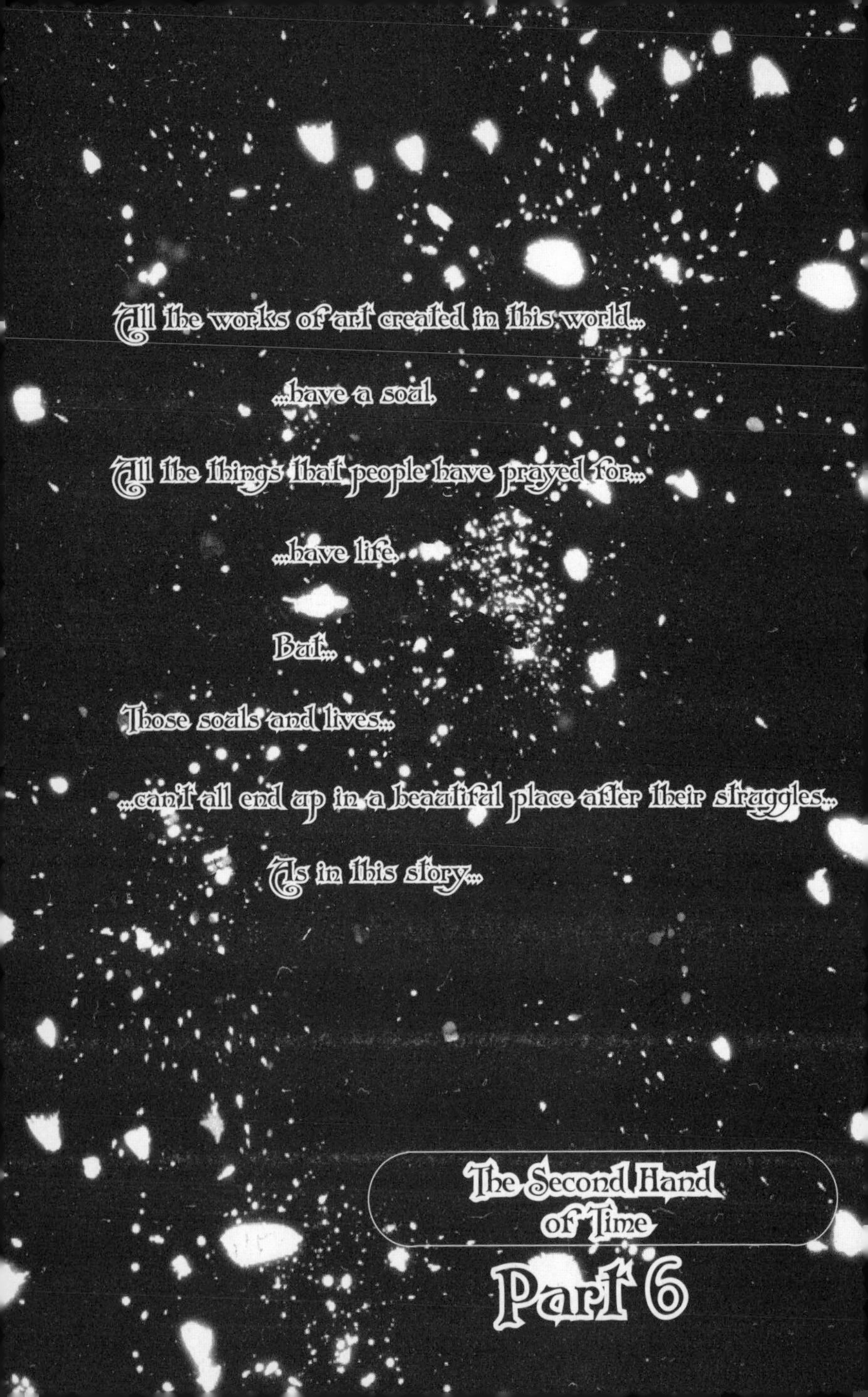
All the works of art created in this world...
...have a soul.
All the things that people have prayed for...
...have life.
But...
Those souls and lives...
...can't all end up in a beautiful place after their struggles...
As in this story...
The Second Hand of Time
Part 6

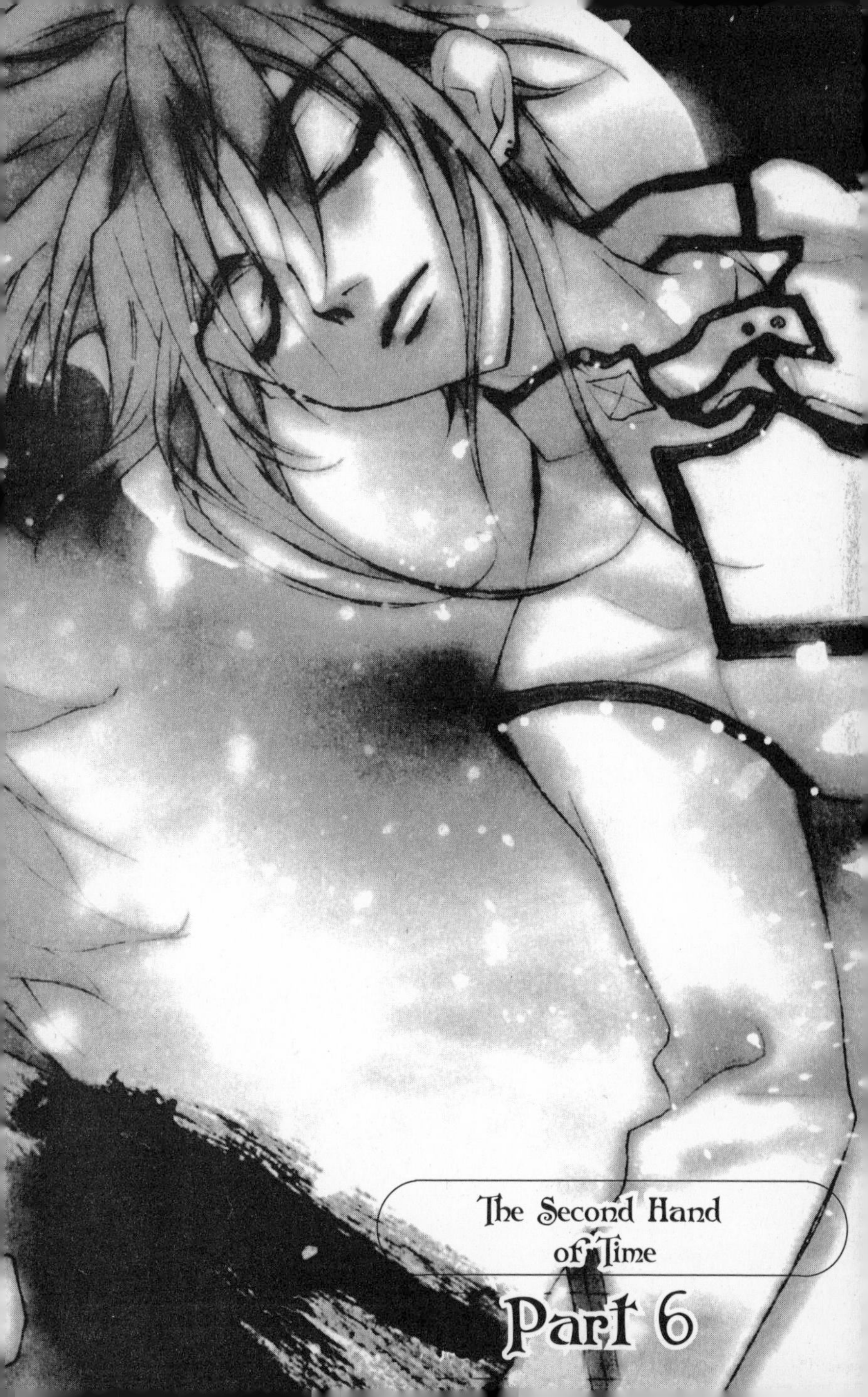
The Second Hand
of Time
Part 6

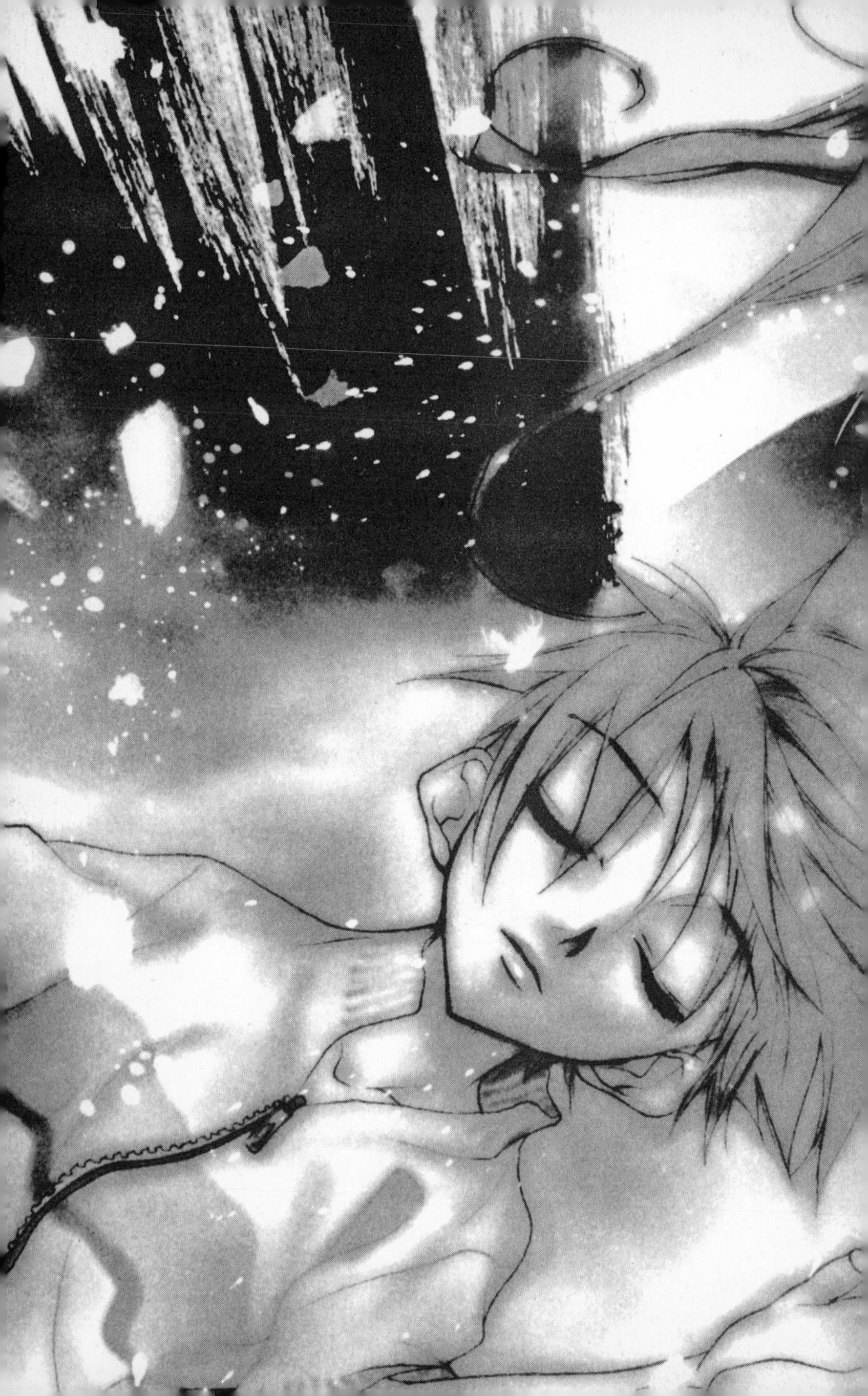

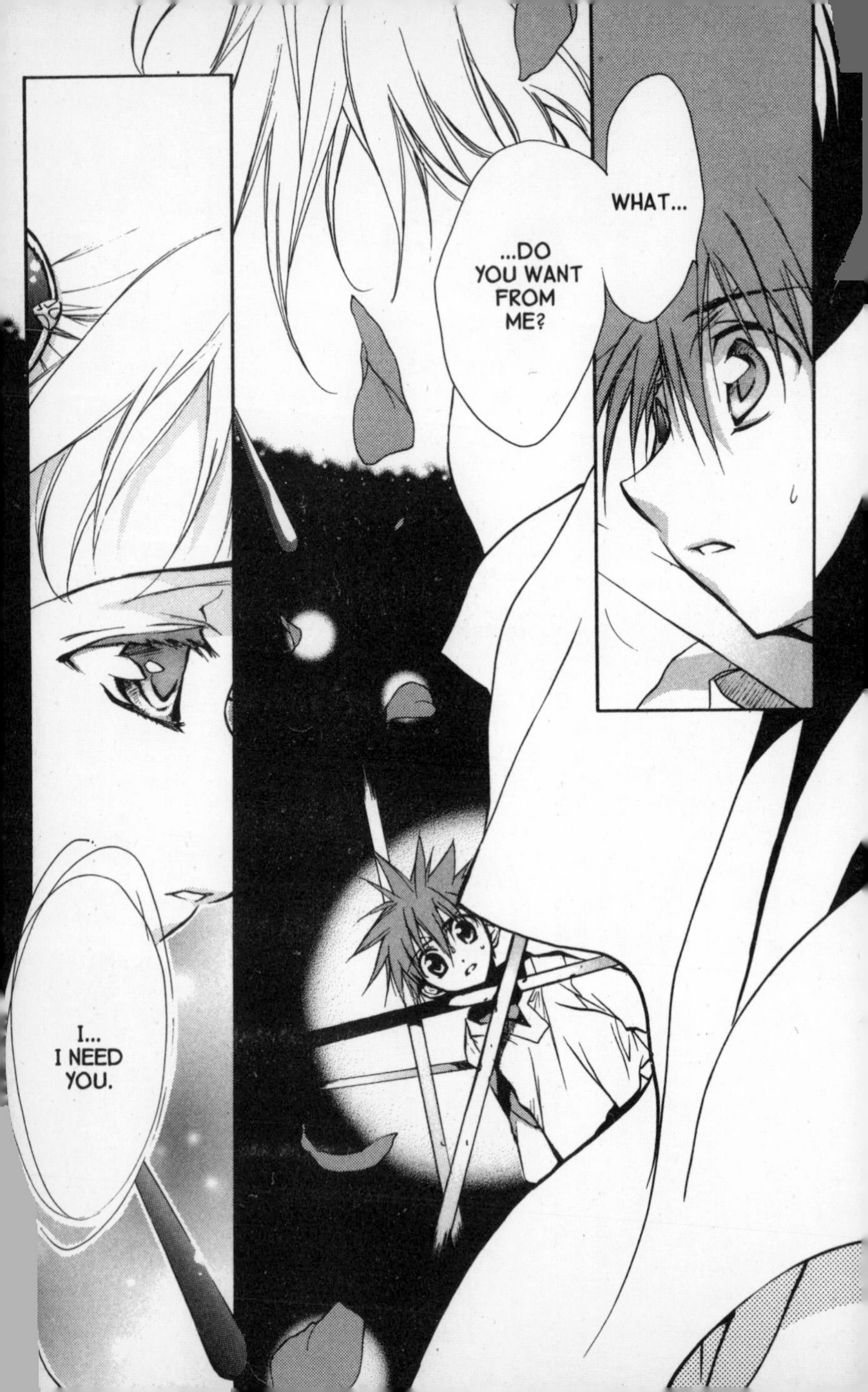
WHAT...
...DO YOU WANT FROM ME?
I... I NEED YOU.

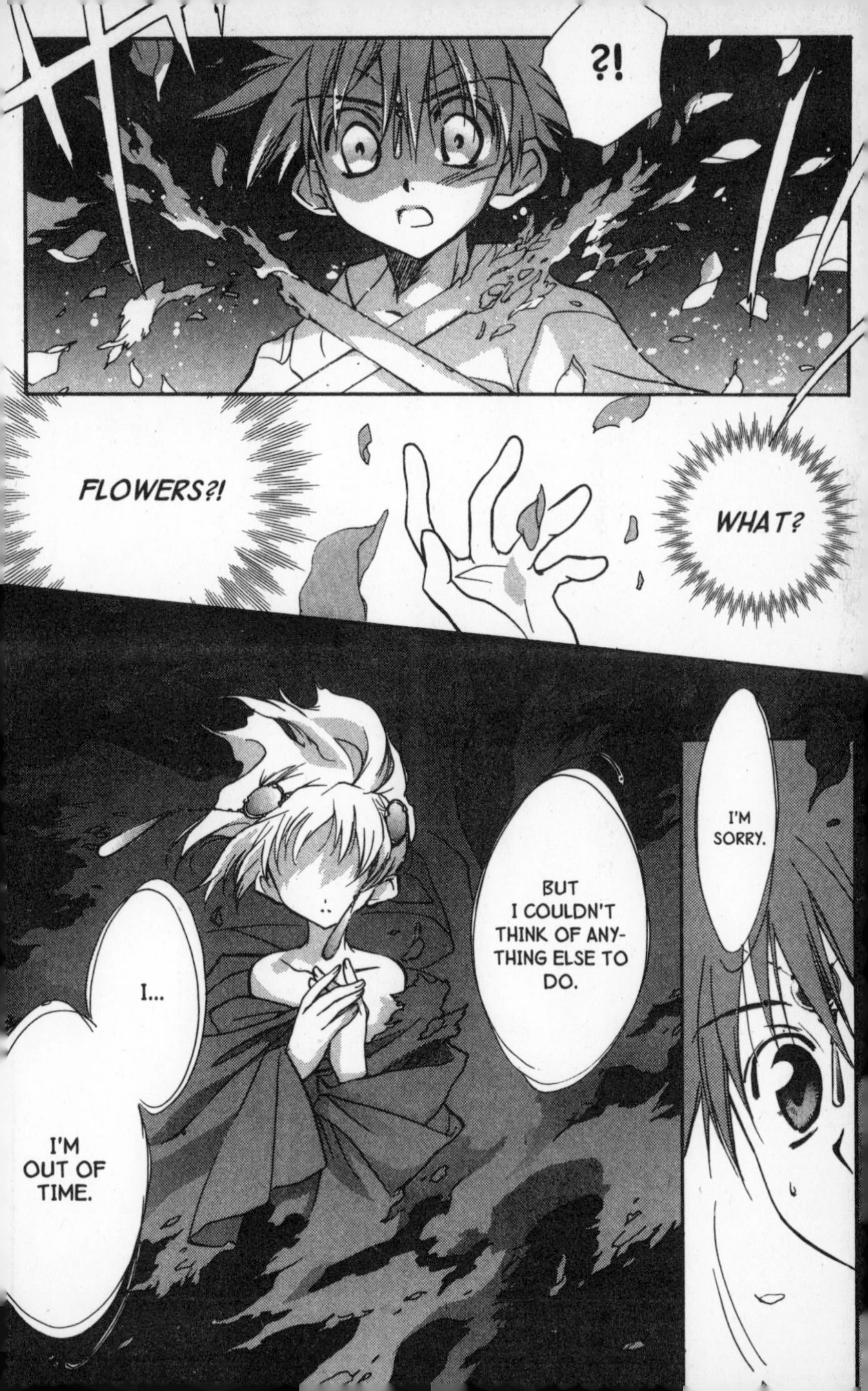
?!
WHAT?
FLOWERS?!
I'M SORRY.
BUT I COULDN'T THINK OF ANY-THING ELSE TO DO.
I...
I'M OUT OF TIME.

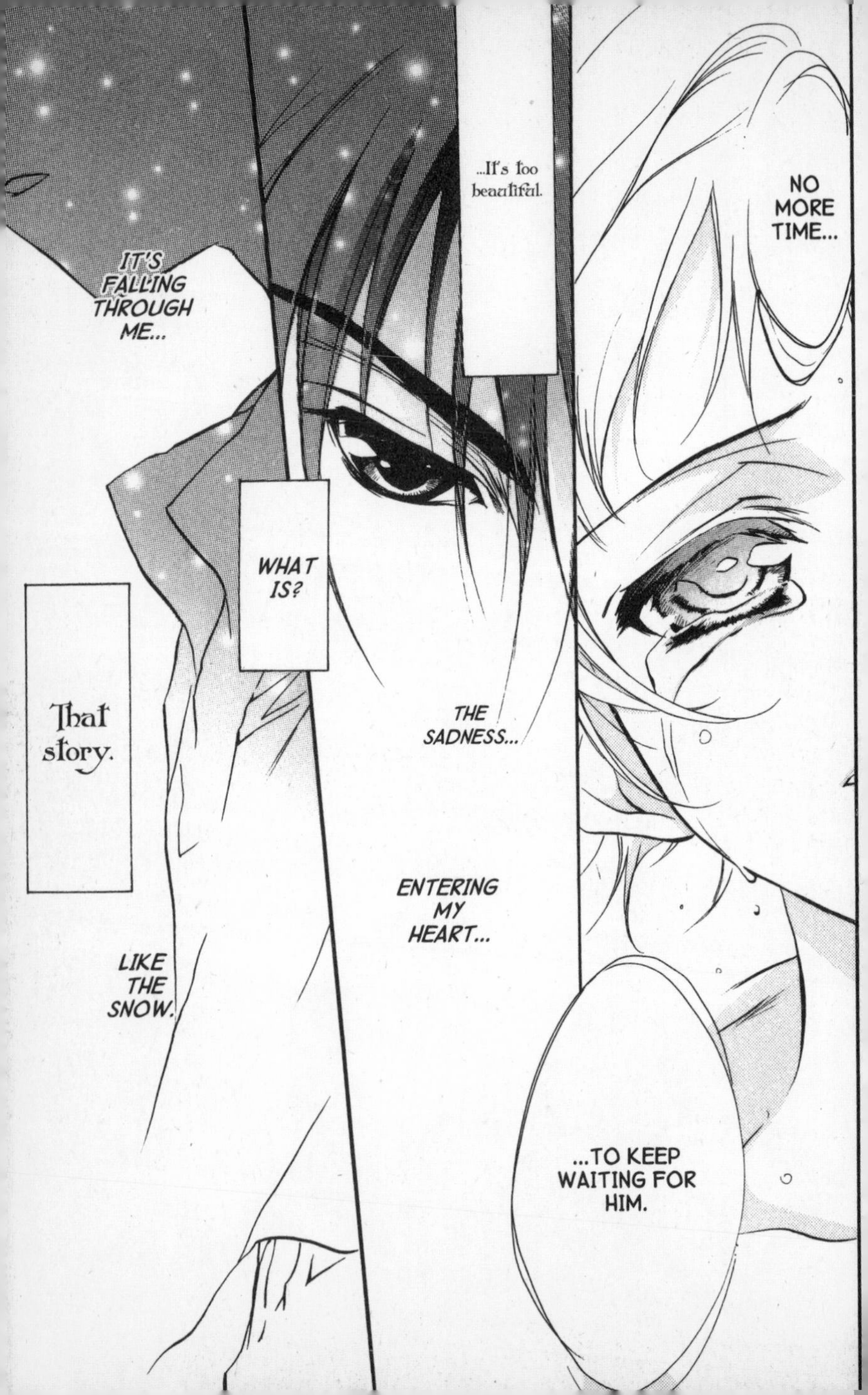

NO MORE TIME...
...TO KEEP WAITING FOR HIM.
...It's too beautiful.
THE SADNESS...
ENTERING MY HEART...
WHAT IS?
IT'S FALLING THROUGH ME...
That story.
LIKE THE SNOW.

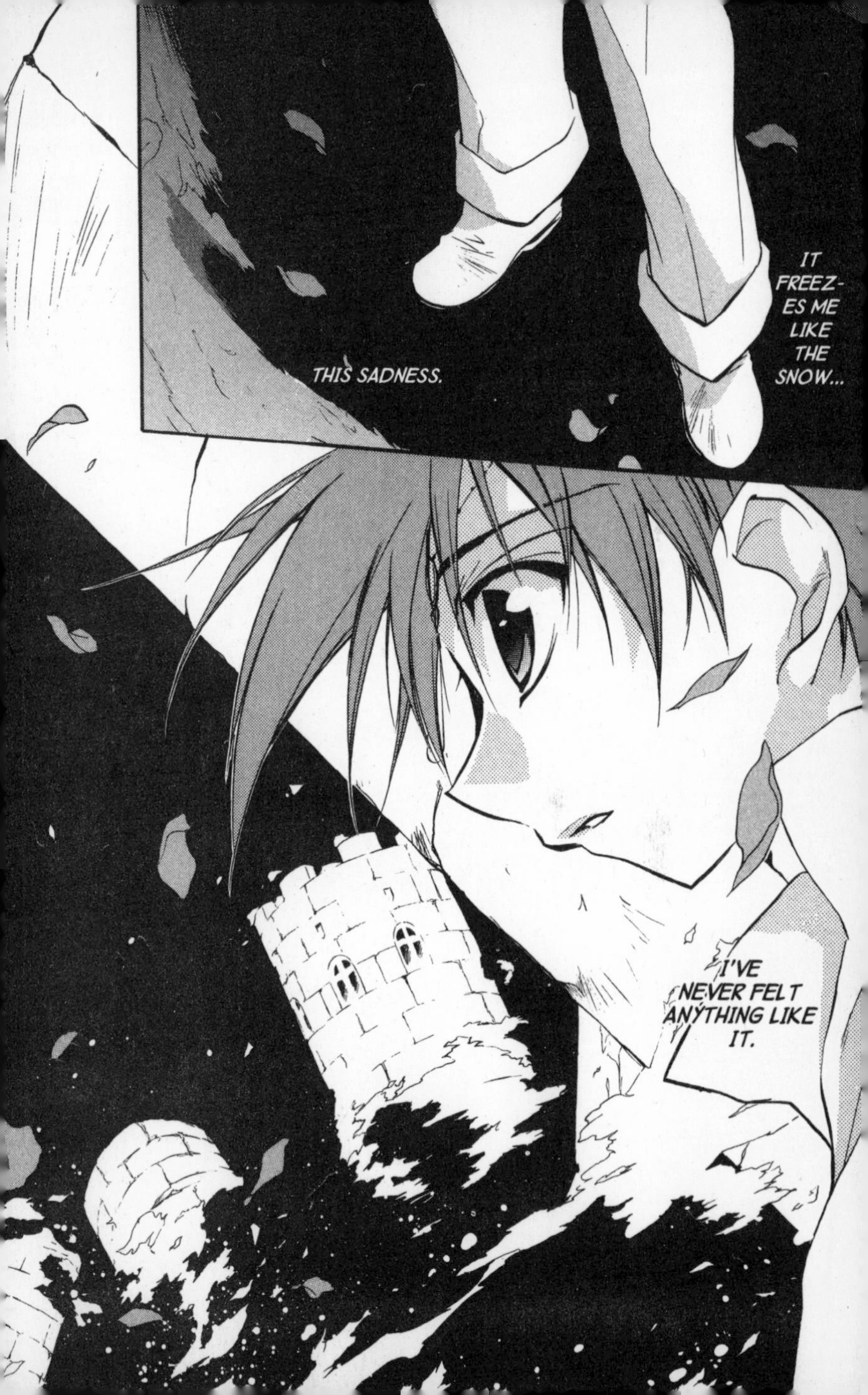
IT FREEZ-ES ME LIKE THE SNOW...
THIS SADNESS.
I'VE NEVER FELT ANYTHING LIKE IT.

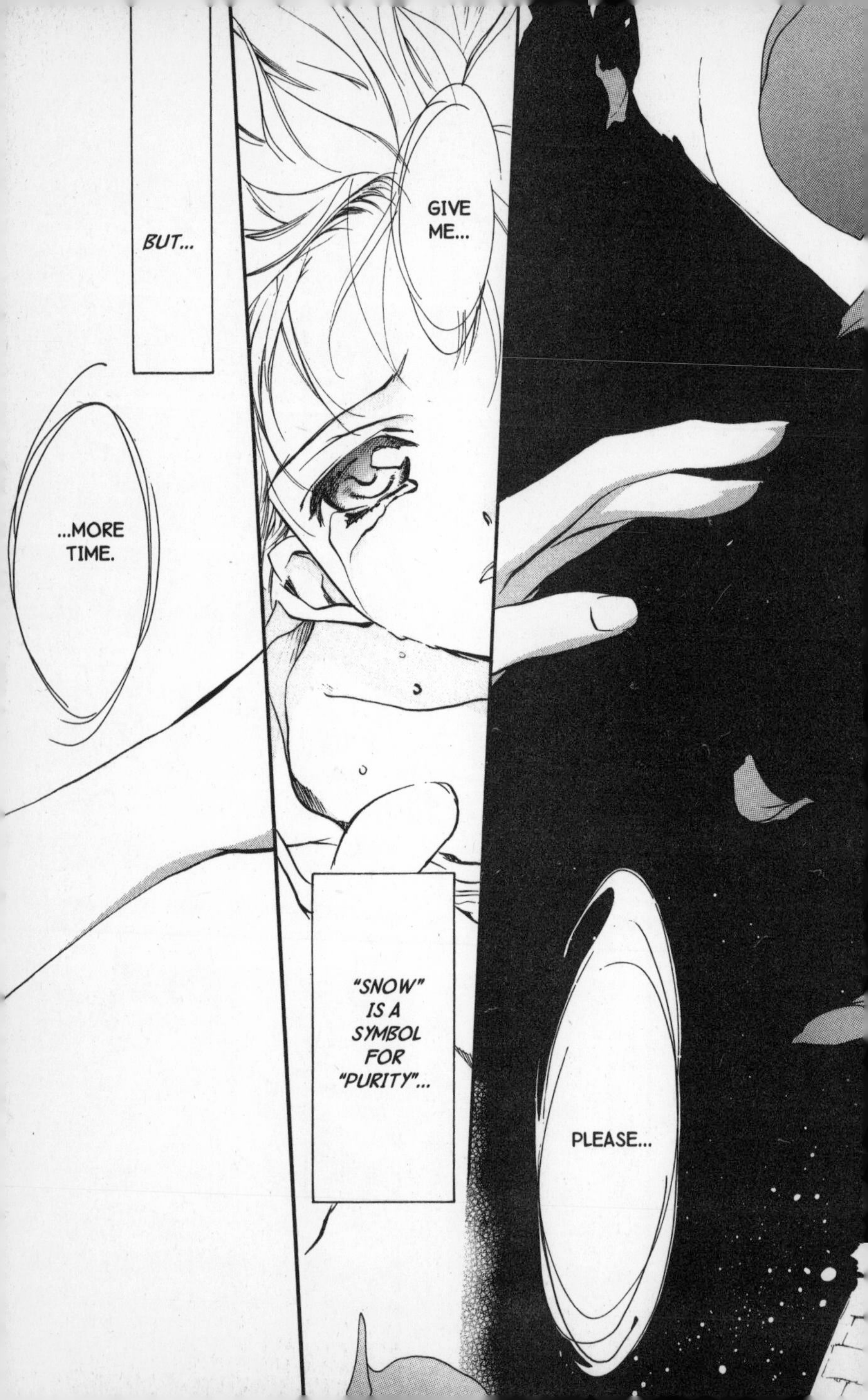
PLEASE...
GIVE ME...
"SNOW" IS A SYMBOL FOR "PURITY"...
BUT...
...MORE TIME.

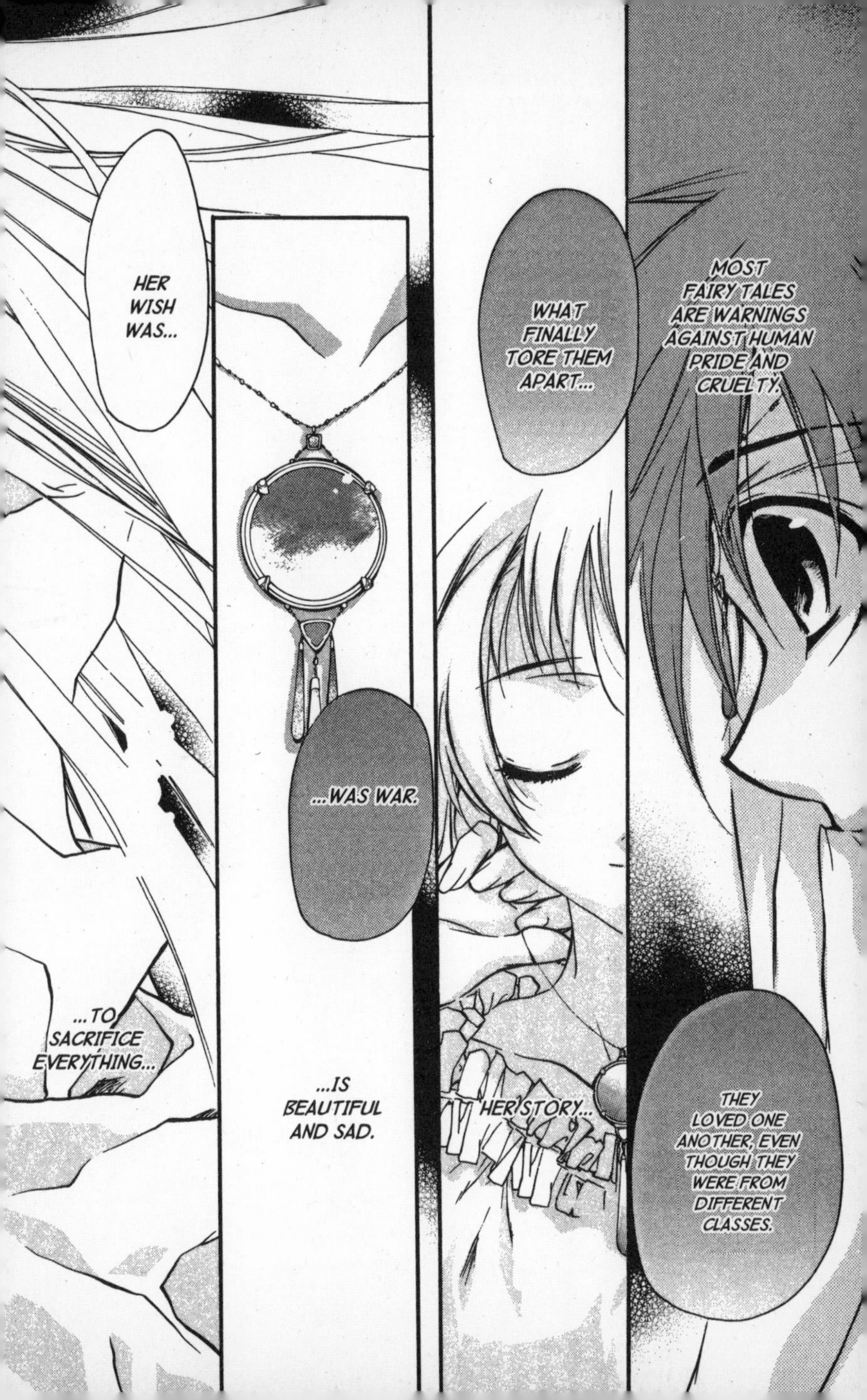
MOST FAIRY TALES ARE WARNINGS AGAINST HUMAN PRIDE AND CRUELTY.
THEY LOVED ONE ANOTHER, EVEN THOUGH THEY WERE FROM DIFFERENT CLASSES.
WHAT FINALLY TORE THEM APART...
...WAS WAR.
HER STORY...
...IS BEAUTIFUL AND SAD.
HER WISH WAS...
...TO SACRIFICE EVERYTHING...

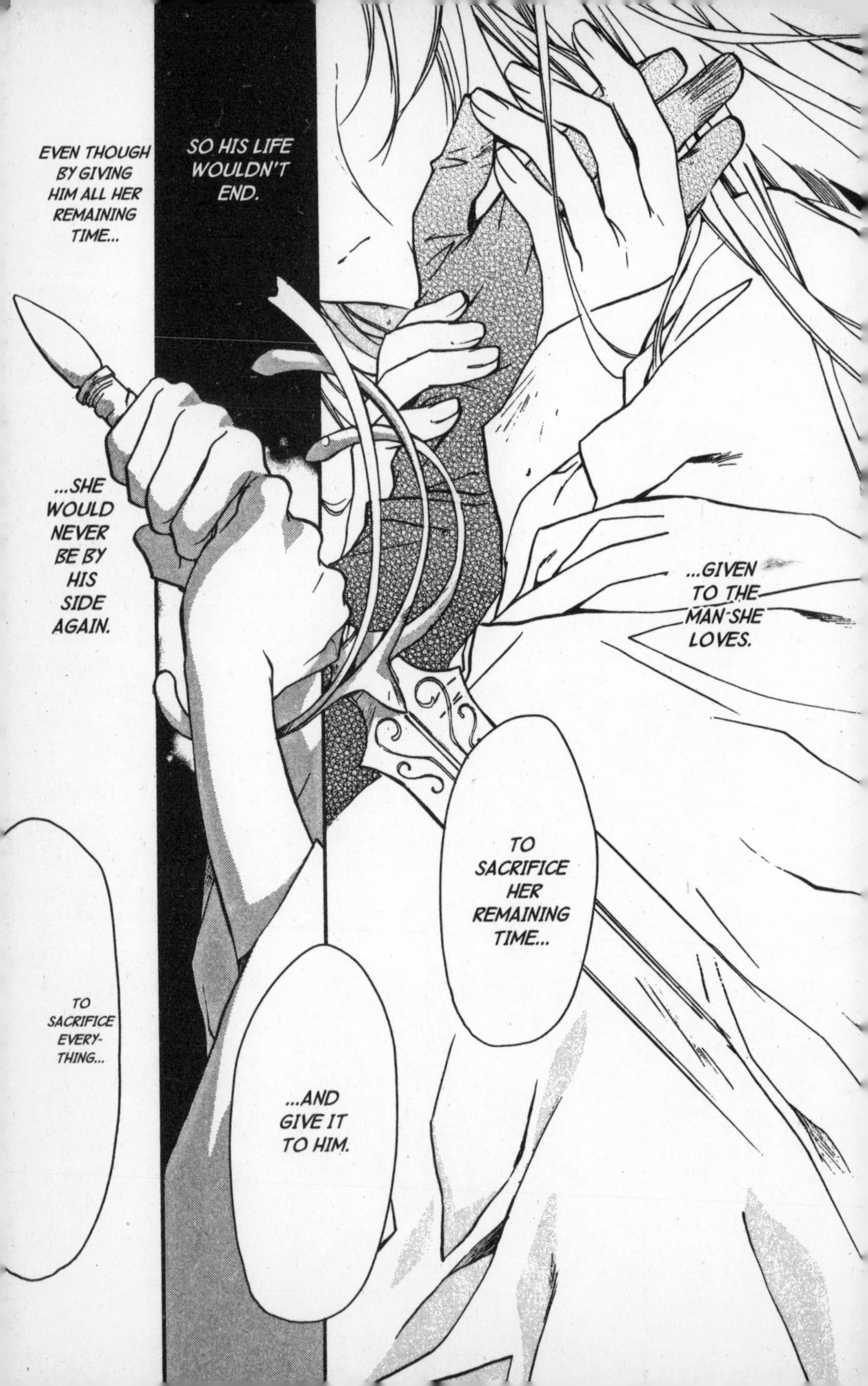
SO HIS LIFE WOULDN'T END.
EVEN THOUGH BY GIVING HIM ALL HER REMAINING TIME...
...GIVEN TO THE MAN SHE LOVES.
...SHE WOULD NEVER BE BY HIS SIDE AGAIN.
TO SACRIFICE HER REMAINING TIME...
...AND GIVE IT TO HIM.
TO SACRIFICE EVERY-THING...

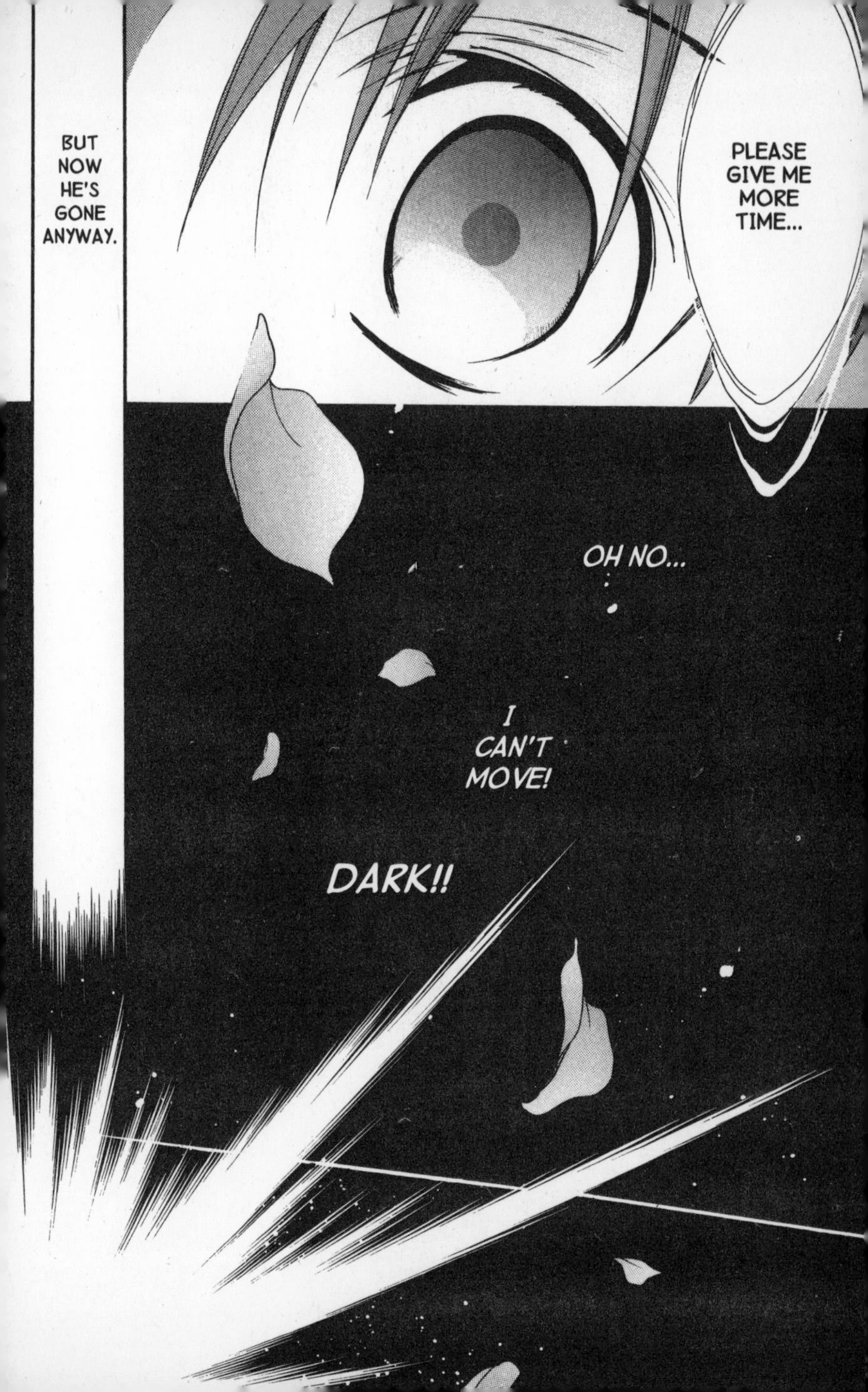
PLEASE GIVE ME MORE TIME...
BUT NOW HE'S GONE ANYWAY.
OH NO...
I CAN'T MOVE!
DARK!!

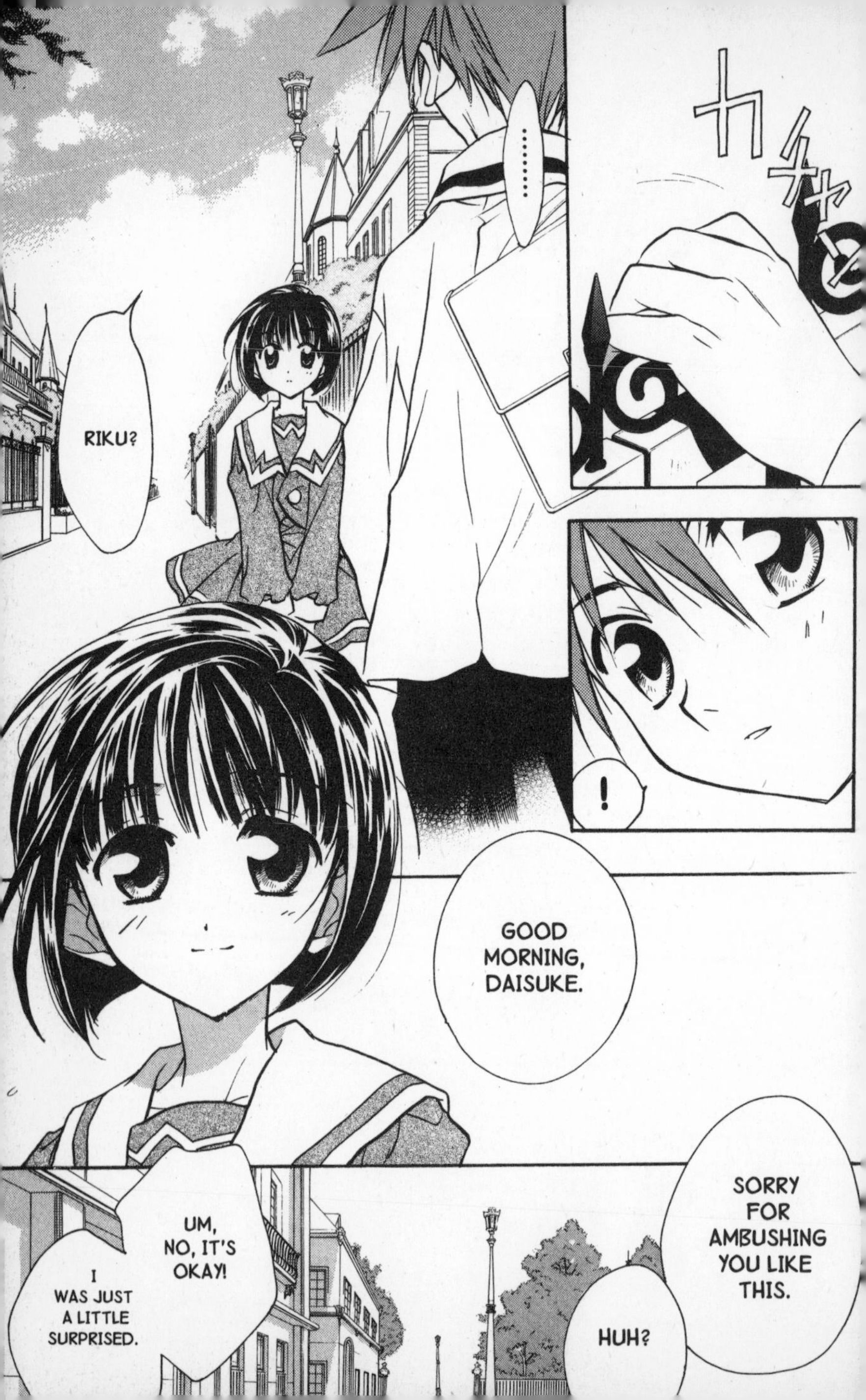

カチャ
!
......
RIKU?
GOOD MORNING, DAISUKE.
SORRY FOR AMBUSHING YOU LIKE THIS.
HUH?
UM, NO, IT'S OKAY!
I WAS JUST A LITTLE SURPRISED.

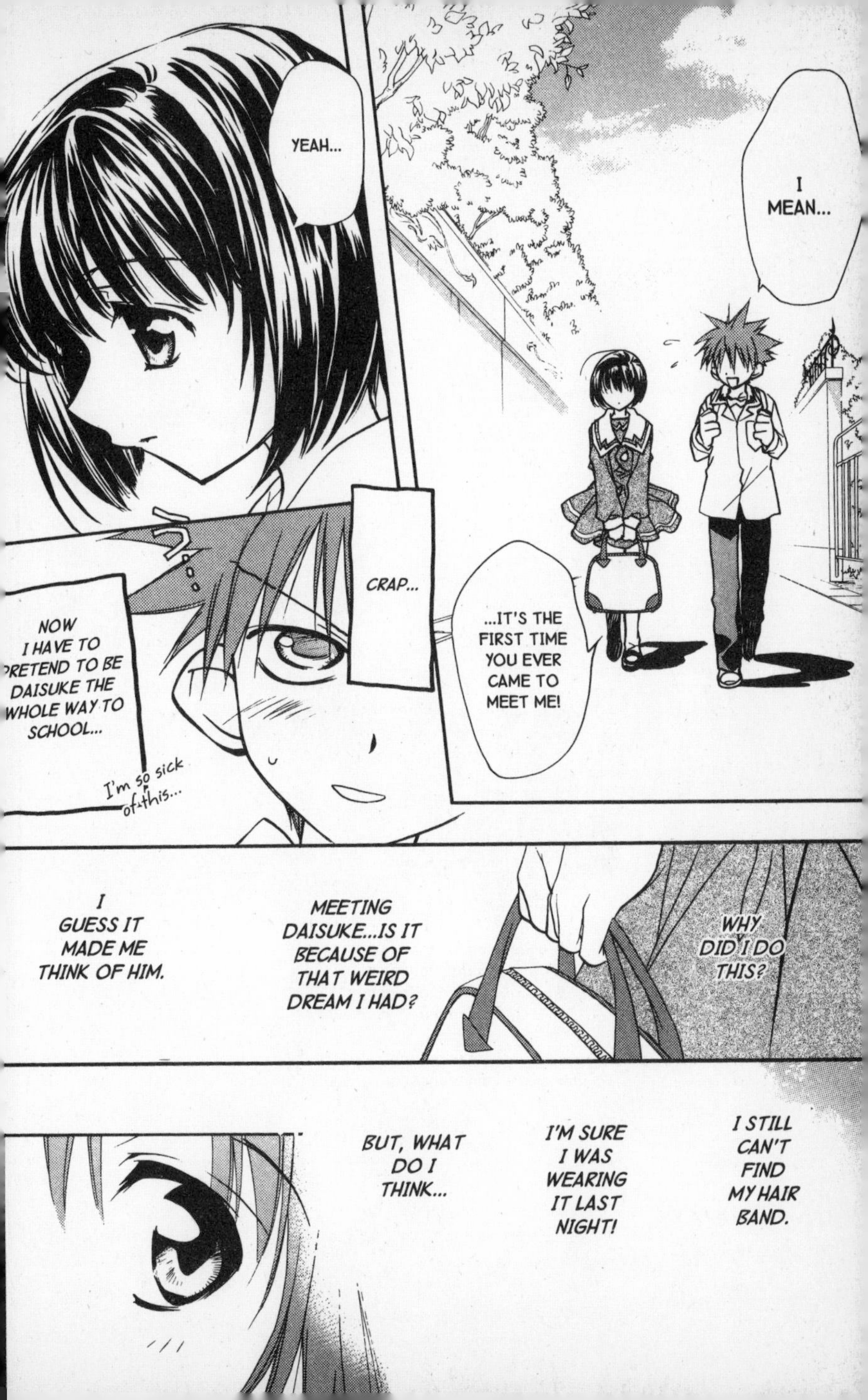
I MEAN...
...IT'S THE FIRST TIME YOU EVER CAME TO MEET ME!
YEAH...
CRAP...
NOW I HAVE TO PRETEND TO BE DAISUKE THE WHOLE WAY TO SCHOOL...
I'm so sick of this...
WHY DID I DO THIS?
MEETING DAISUKE...IS IT BECAUSE OF THAT WEIRD DREAM I HAD?
I GUESS IT MADE ME THINK OF HIM.
I STILL CAN'T FIND MY HAIR BAND.
I'M SURE I WAS WEARING IT LAST NIGHT!
BUT, WHAT DO I THINK...

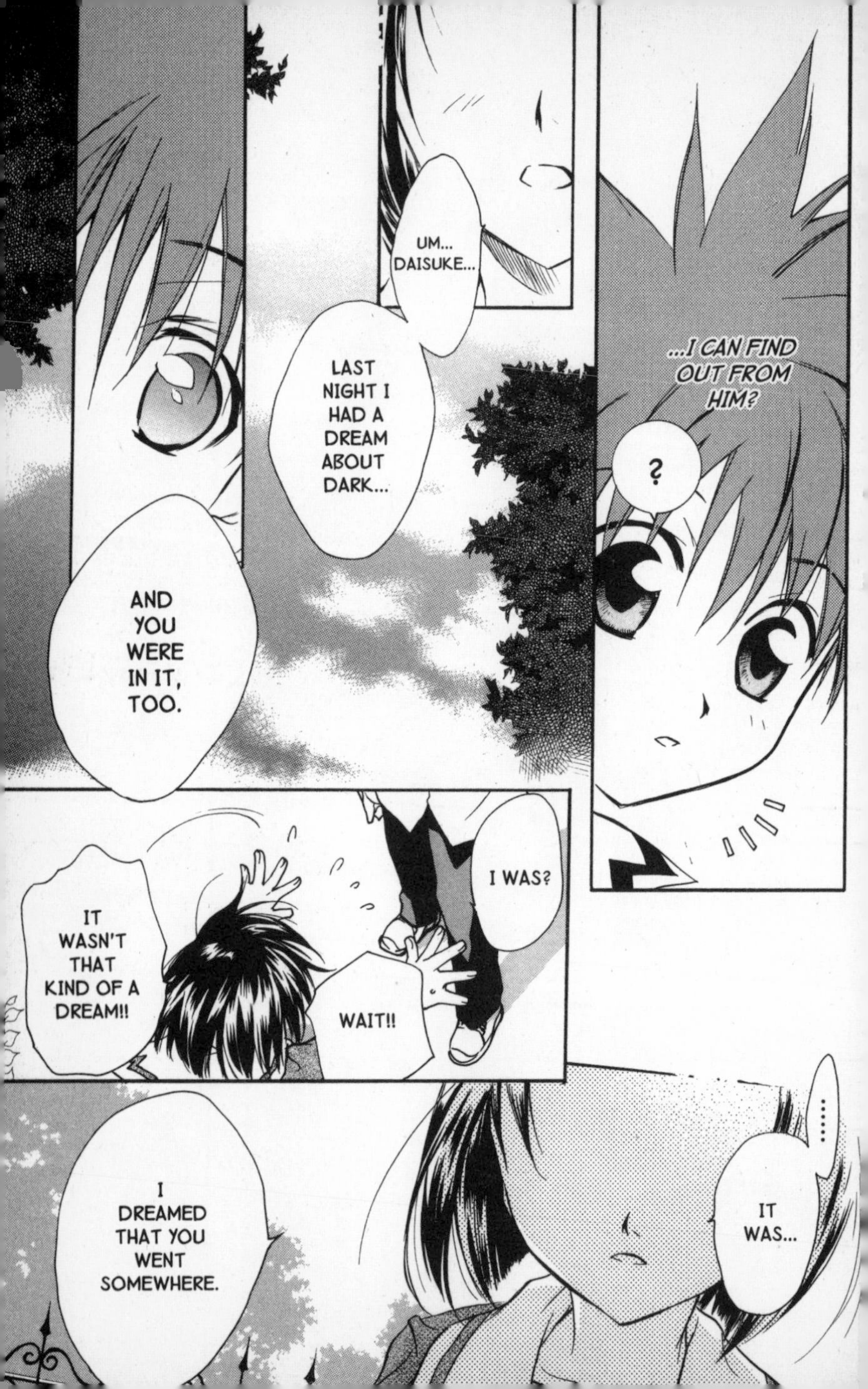
...I CAN FIND OUT FROM HIM?
?
UM... DAISUKE...
LAST NIGHT I HAD A DREAM ABOUT DARK...
AND YOU WERE IN IT, TOO.
I WAS?
WAIT!!
IT WASN'T THAT KIND OF A DREAM!!
......
IT WAS...
I DREAMED THAT YOU WENT SOMEWHERE.

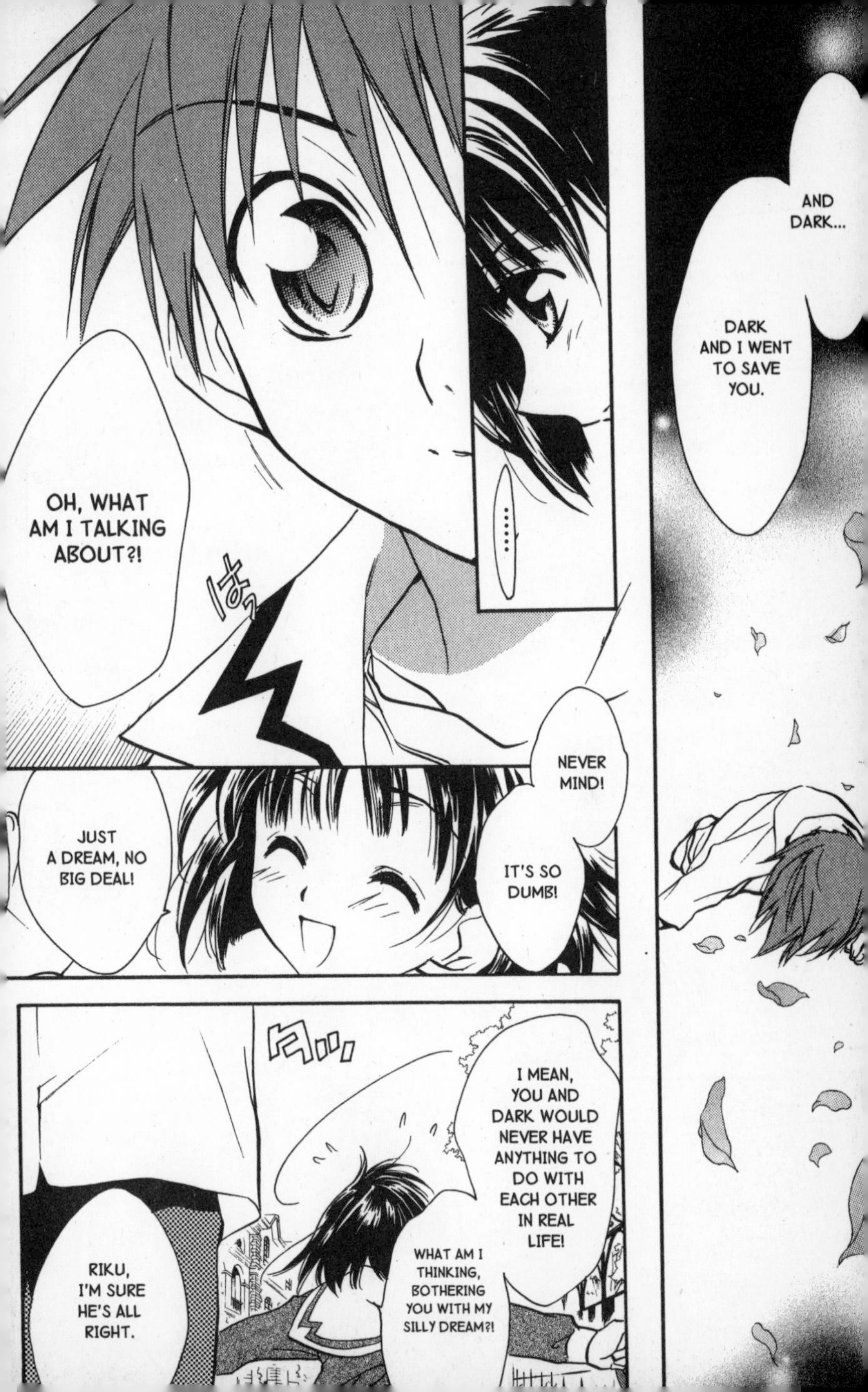
AND DARK...
DARK AND I WENT TO SAVE YOU.
......
はっ
OH, WHAT AM I TALKING ABOUT?!
NEVER MIND!
IT'S SO DUMB!
JUST A DREAM, NO BIG DEAL!
I MEAN, YOU AND DARK WOULD NEVER HAVE ANYTHING TO DO WITH EACH OTHER IN REAL LIFE!
WHAT AM I THINKING, BOTHERING YOU WITH MY SILLY DREAM?!
RIKU, I'M SURE HE'S ALL RIGHT.

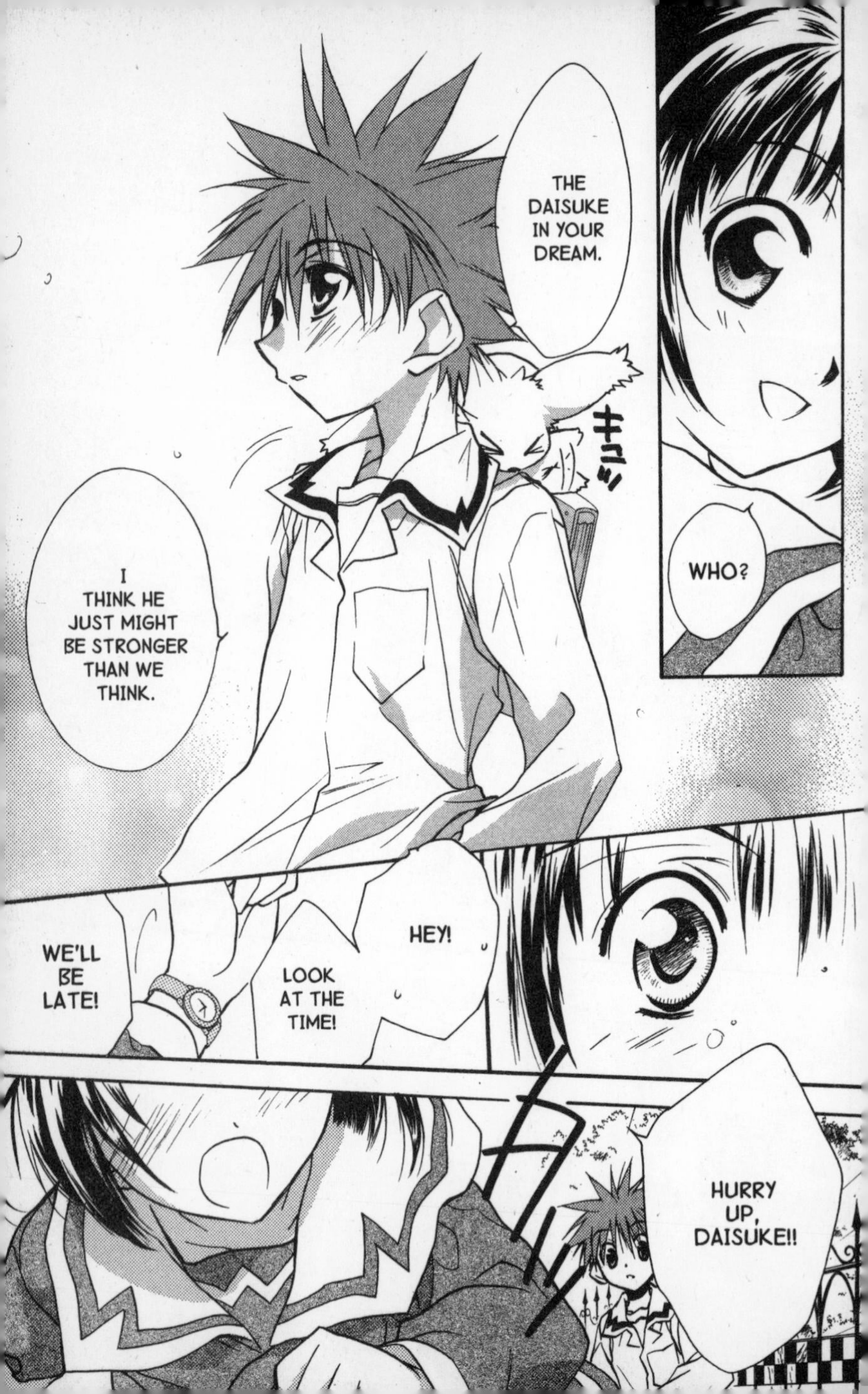
WHO?
THE DAISUKE IN YOUR DREAM.
キュッ
I THINK HE JUST MIGHT BE STRONGER THAN WE THINK.
HEY!
LOOK AT THE TIME!
WE'LL BE LATE!
HURRY UP, DAISUKE!!

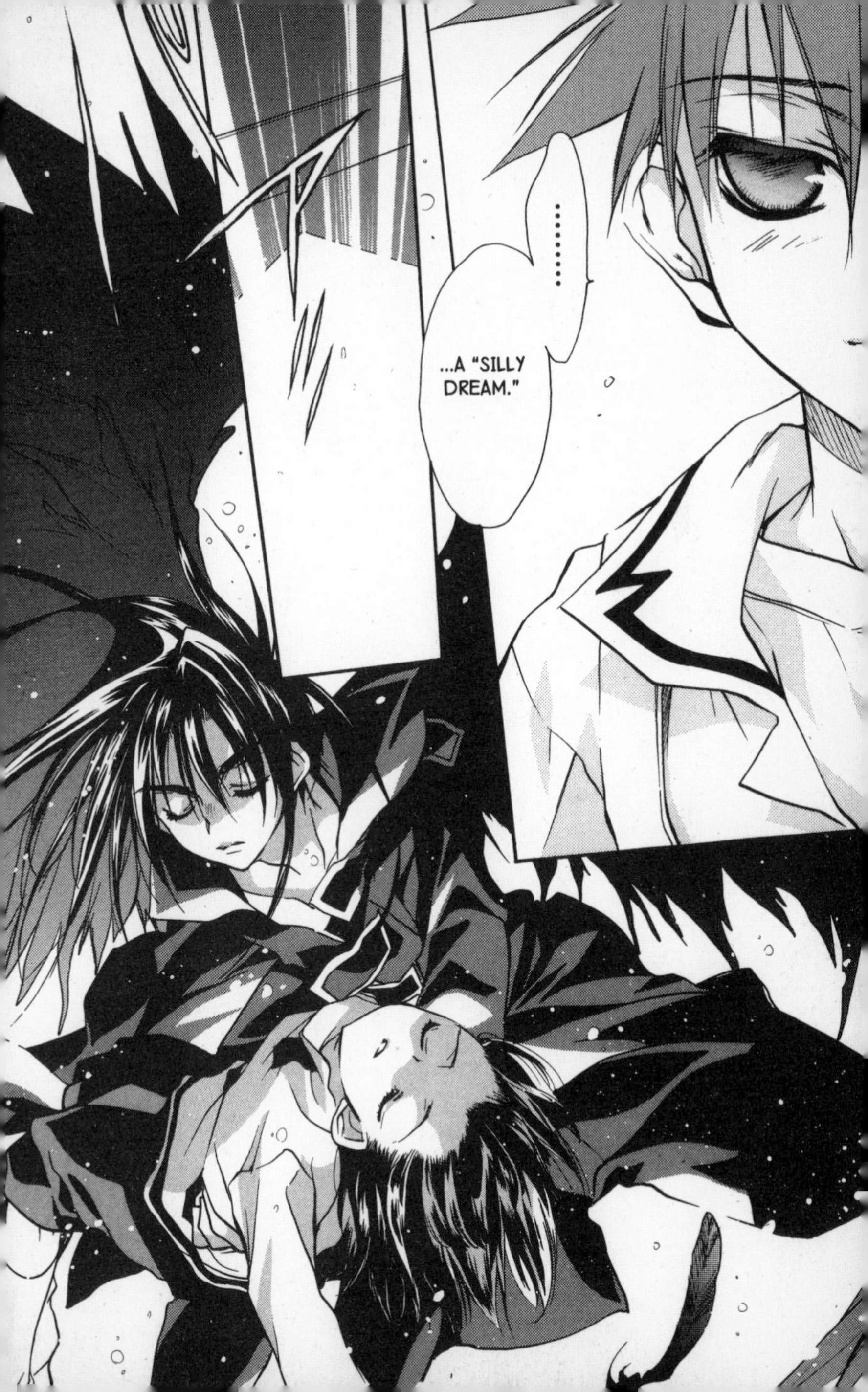
......
...A "SILLY DREAM."

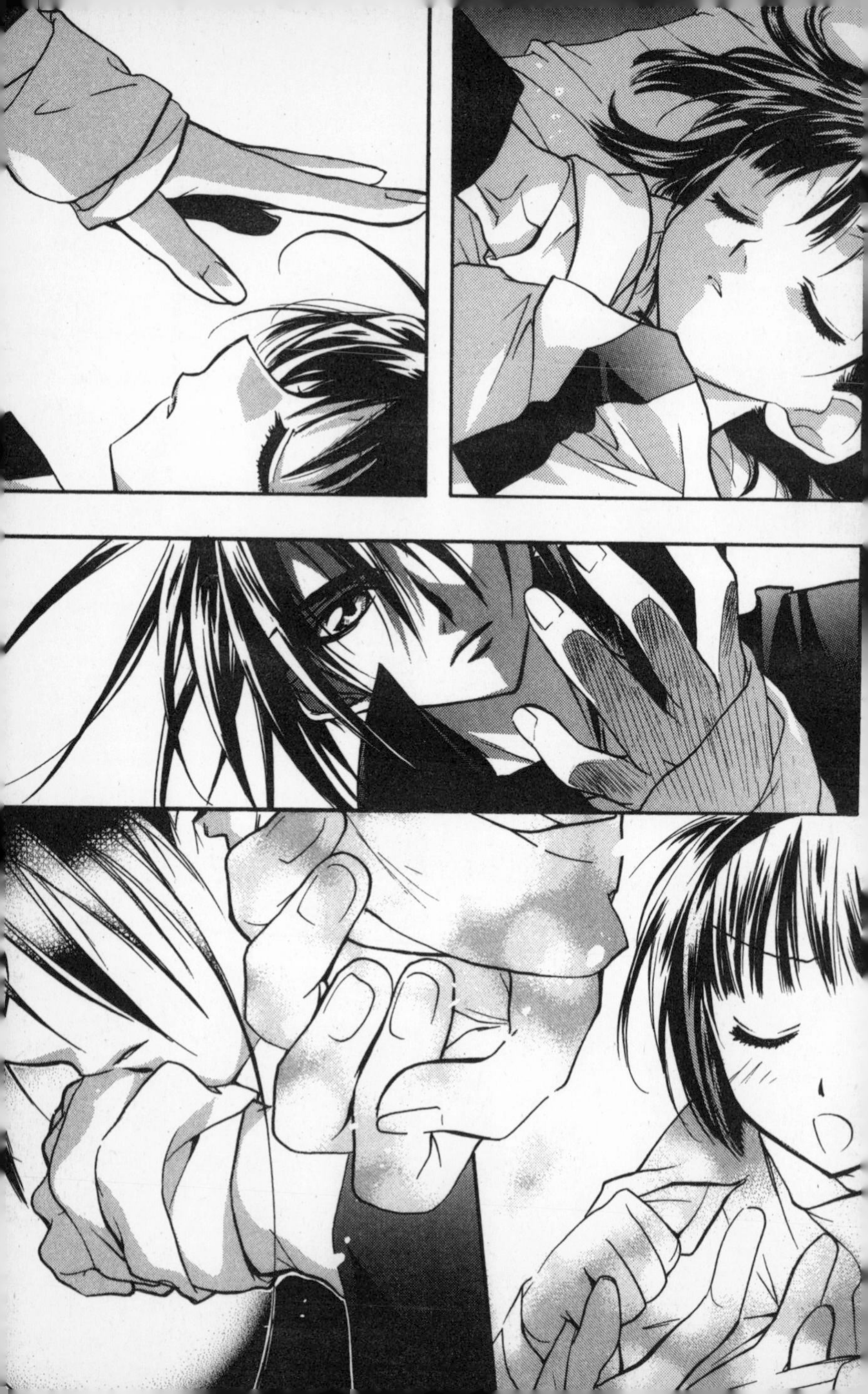

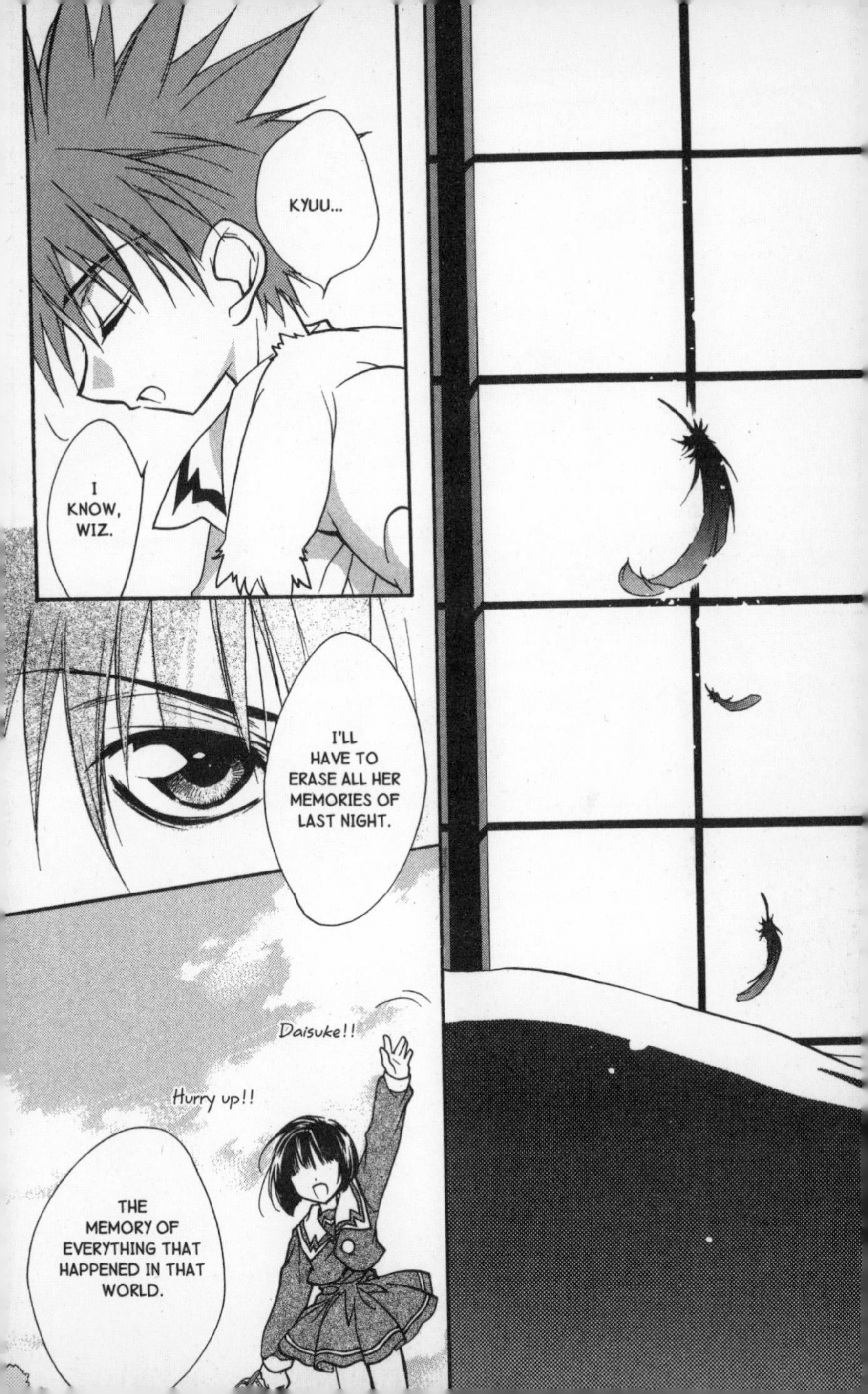
KYUU...
I KNOW, WIZ.
I'LL HAVE TO ERASE ALL HER MEMORIES OF LAST NIGHT.
Daisuke!!
Hurry up!!
THE MEMORY OF EVERYTHING THAT HAPPENED IN THAT WORLD.

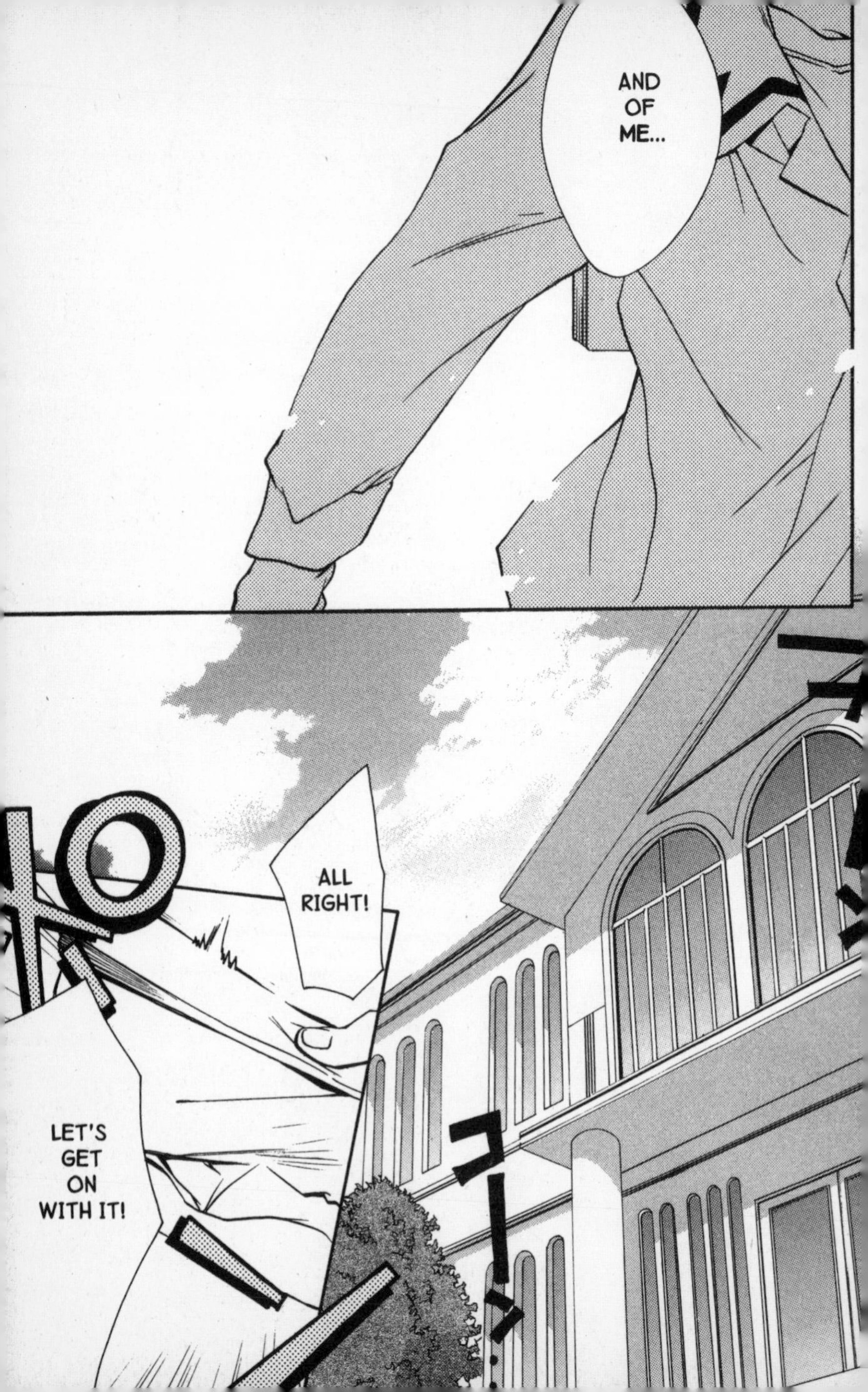
AND OF ME...
ALL RIGHT!
LET'S GET ON WITH IT!

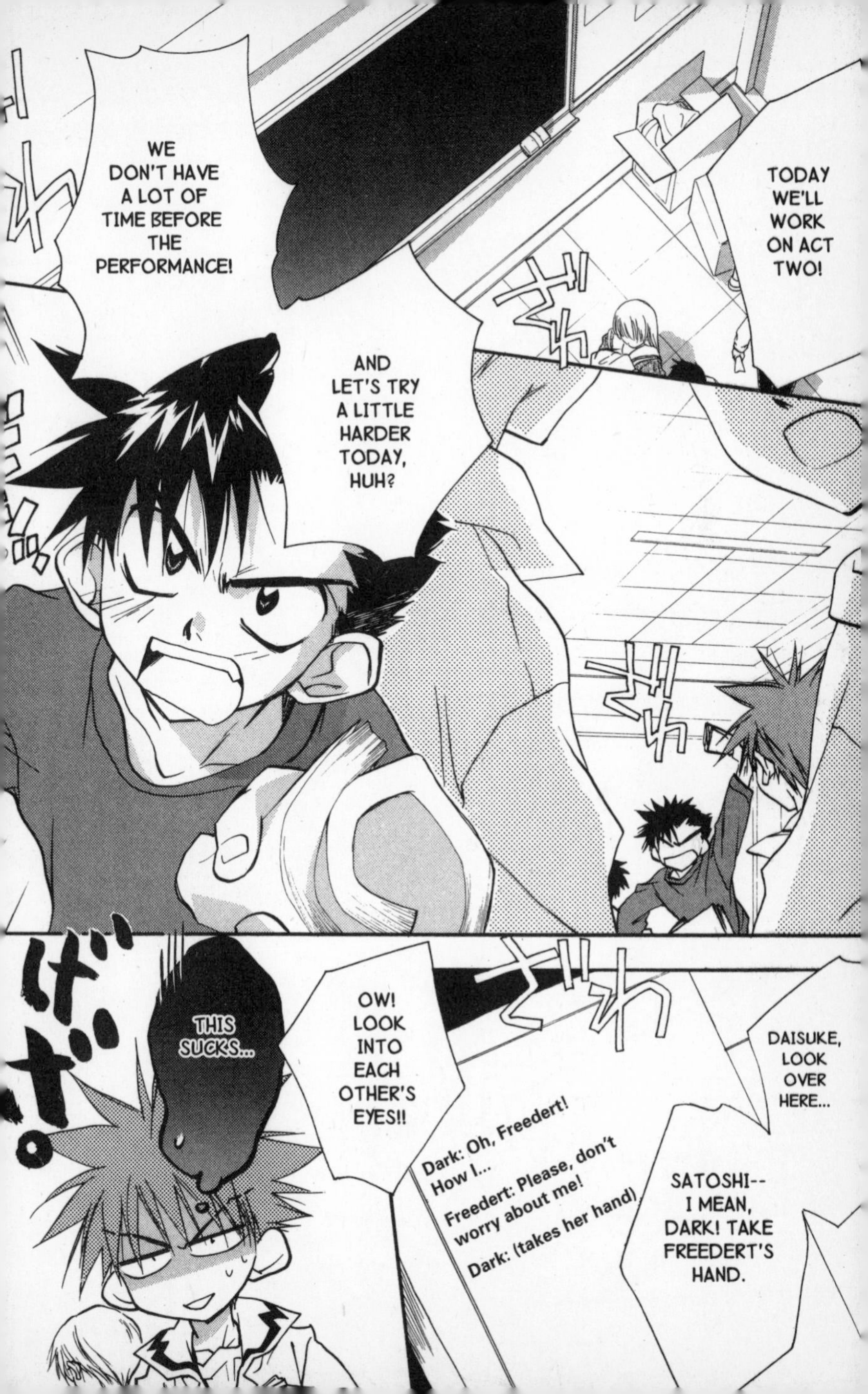
TODAY WE'LL WORK ON ACT TWO!
ざわ
WE DON'T HAVE A LOT OF TIME BEFORE THE PERFORMANCE!
AND LET'S TRY A LITTLE HARDER TODAY, HUH?
ざわ
DAISUKE, LOOK OVER HERE...
SATOSHI-- I MEAN, DARK! TAKE FREEDERT'S HAND.
Dark: Oh, Freedert! How I...
Freedert: Please, don't worry about me!
Dark: (takes her hand)
ざわ
OW! LOOK INTO EACH OTHER'S EYES!!
THIS SUCKS...
げっ。

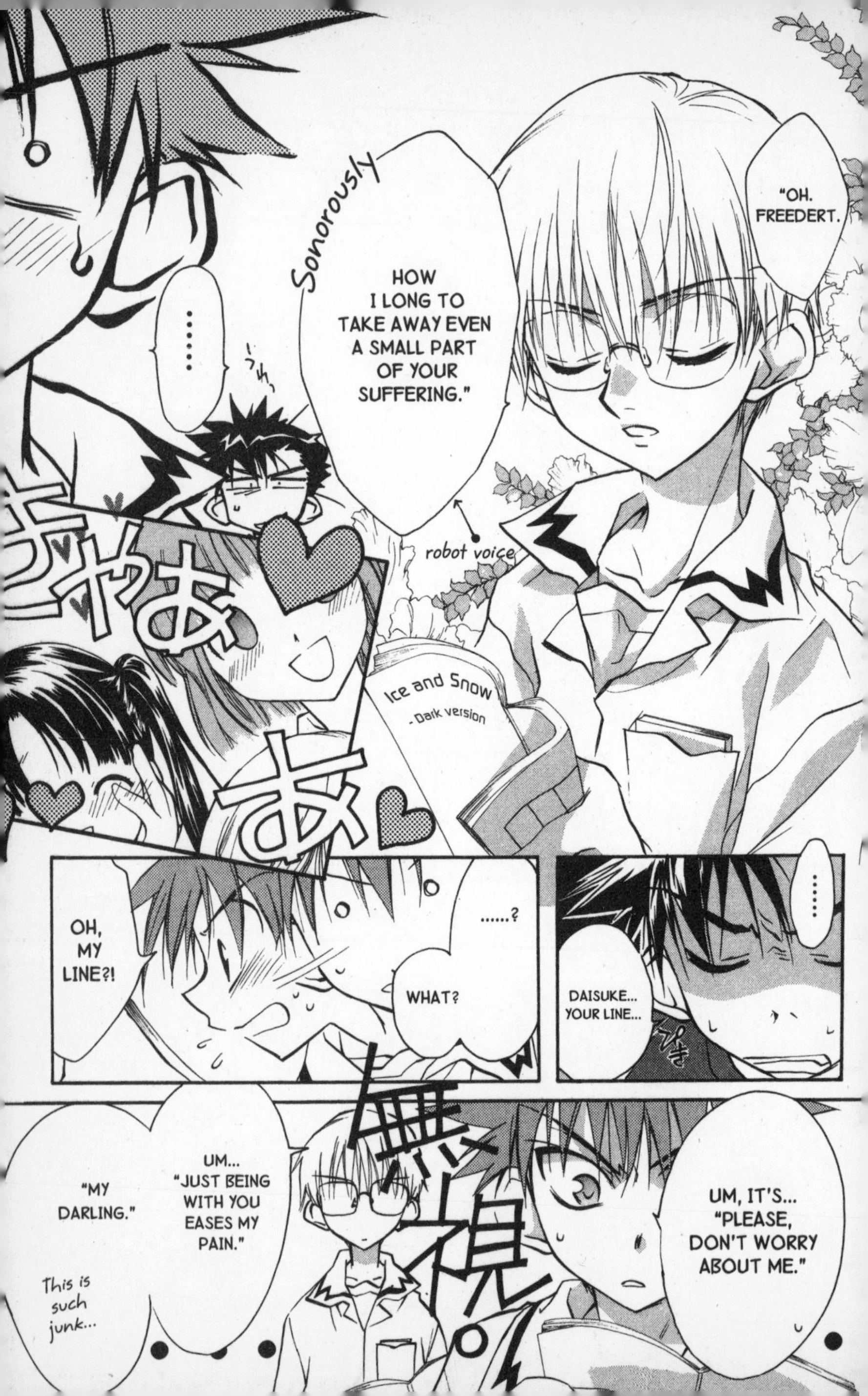
"OH. FREEDERT.
Sonorously
HOW I LONG TO TAKE AWAY EVEN A SMALL PART OF YOUR SUFFERING."
robot voice
Ice and Snow
- Dark version
......
きゃあ
あ
......
DAISUKE... YOUR LINE...
......?
WHAT?
OH, MY LINE?!
UM, IT'S... "PLEASE, DON'T WORRY ABOUT ME."
無視
UM... "JUST BEING WITH YOU EASES MY PAIN."
"MY DARLING."
This is such junk...

My pain.
(Takes Freedert's hand)
Dark: How can you be so wonderful?
......
OW!! OWOWOW!!
LET GO!!
"HOW CAN YOU BE SO WONDERFUL, MY PRECIOUS FREEDERT?"
Ice and Snow
- Dark version
ARE YOU TRYING TO START SOMETHING, YOU CREEP?

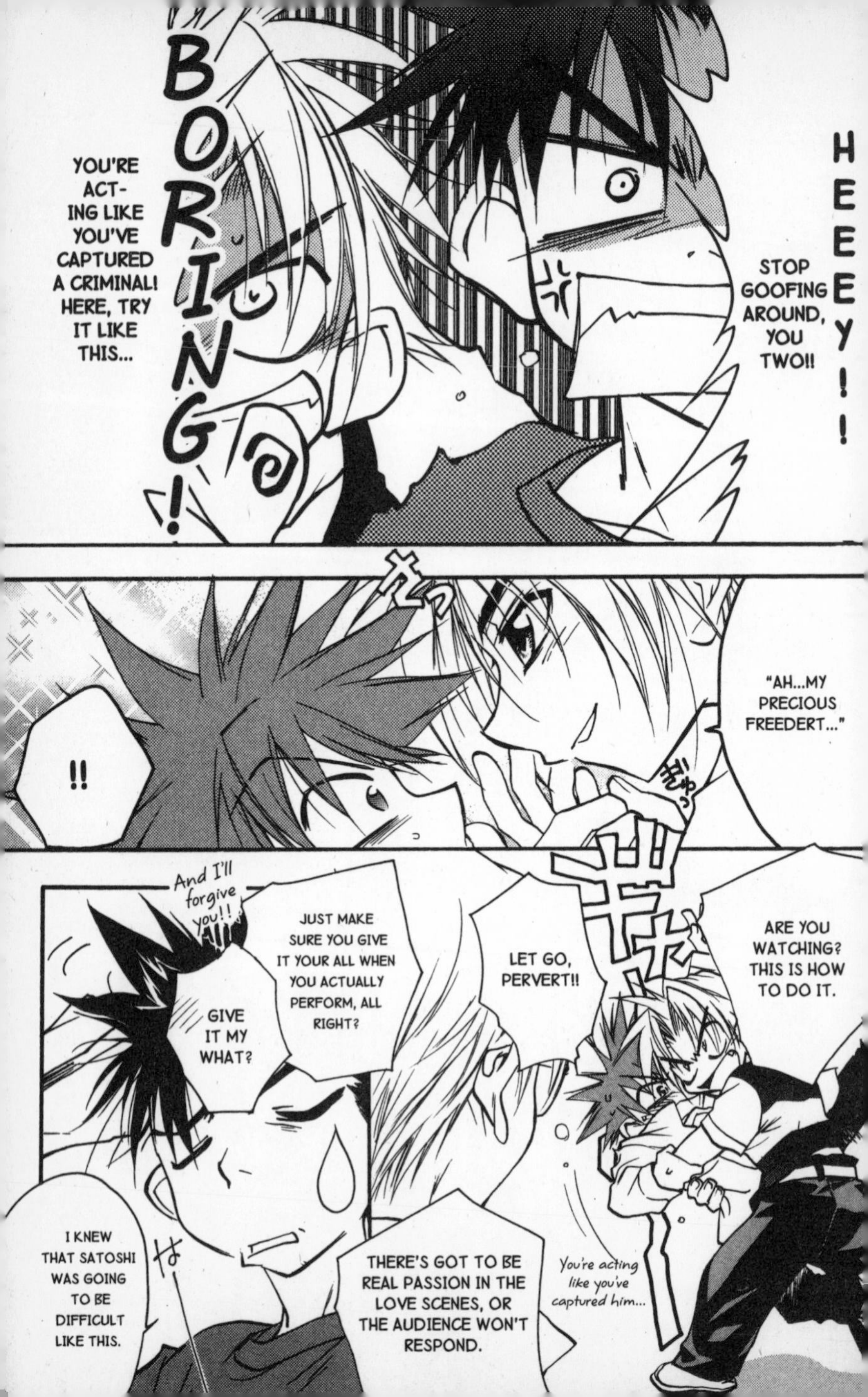
HEEEY!!
STOP GOOFING AROUND, YOU TWO!!
BORING!
YOU'RE ACT-ING LIKE YOU'VE CAPTURED A CRIMINAL! HERE, TRY IT LIKE THIS...
"AH...MY PRECIOUS FREEDERT..."
!!
ARE YOU WATCHING? THIS IS HOW TO DO IT.
LET GO, PERVERT!!
You're acting like you've captured him...
JUST MAKE SURE YOU GIVE IT YOUR ALL WHEN YOU ACTUALLY PERFORM, ALL RIGHT?
And I'll forgive you!!
GIVE IT MY WHAT?
THERE'S GOT TO BE REAL PASSION IN THE LOVE SCENES, OR THE AUDIENCE WON'T RESPOND.
I KNEW THAT SATOSHI WAS GOING TO BE DIFFICULT LIKE THIS.

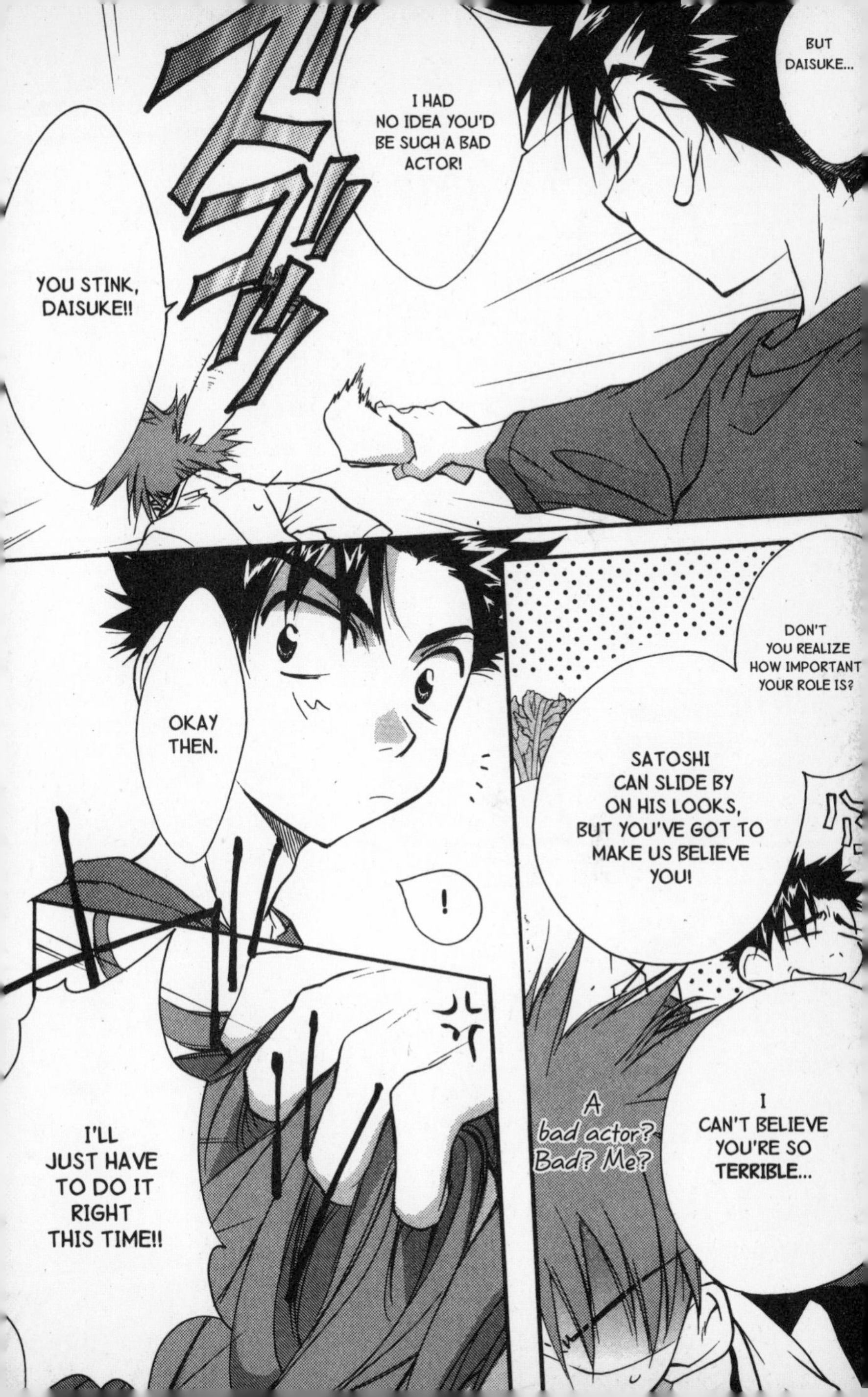
BUT DAISUKE...
I HAD NO IDEA YOU'D BE SUCH A BAD ACTOR!
YOU STINK, DAISUKE!!
DON'T YOU REALIZE HOW IMPORTANT YOUR ROLE IS?
SATOSHI CAN SLIDE BY ON HIS LOOKS, BUT YOU'VE GOT TO MAKE US BELIEVE YOU!
I CAN'T BELIEVE YOU'RE SO **TERRIBLE**...
A bad actor? Bad? Me?
OKAY THEN.
!
I'LL JUST HAVE TO DO IT RIGHT THIS TIME!!

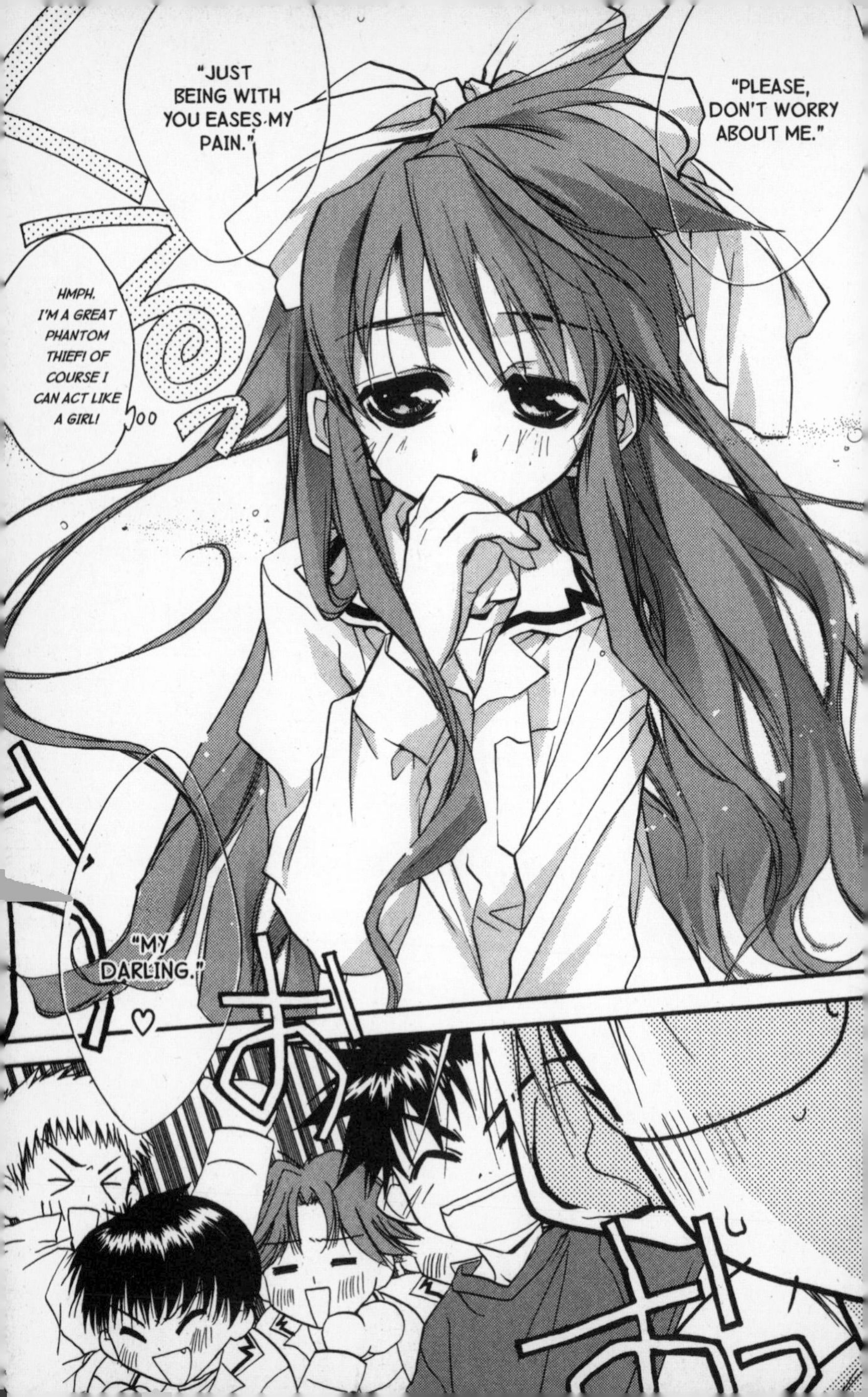
"PLEASE, DON'T WORRY ABOUT ME."
"JUST BEING WITH YOU EASES MY PAIN."
HMPH. I'M A GREAT PHANTOM THIEF! OF COURSE I CAN ACT LIKE A GIRL!
"MY DARLING."

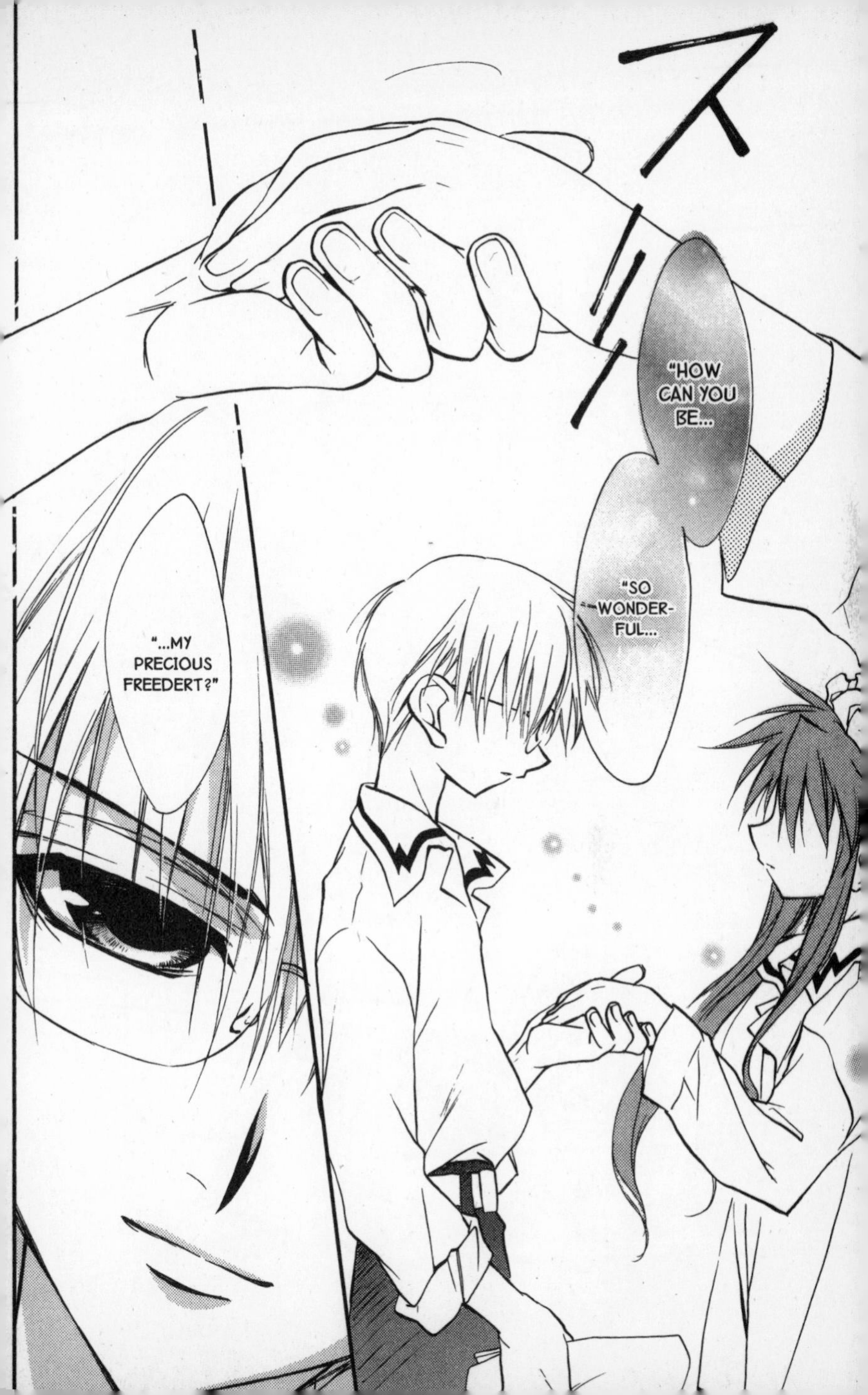
"HOW CAN YOU BE...
"SO WONDER-FUL...
"...MY PRECIOUS FREEDERT?"

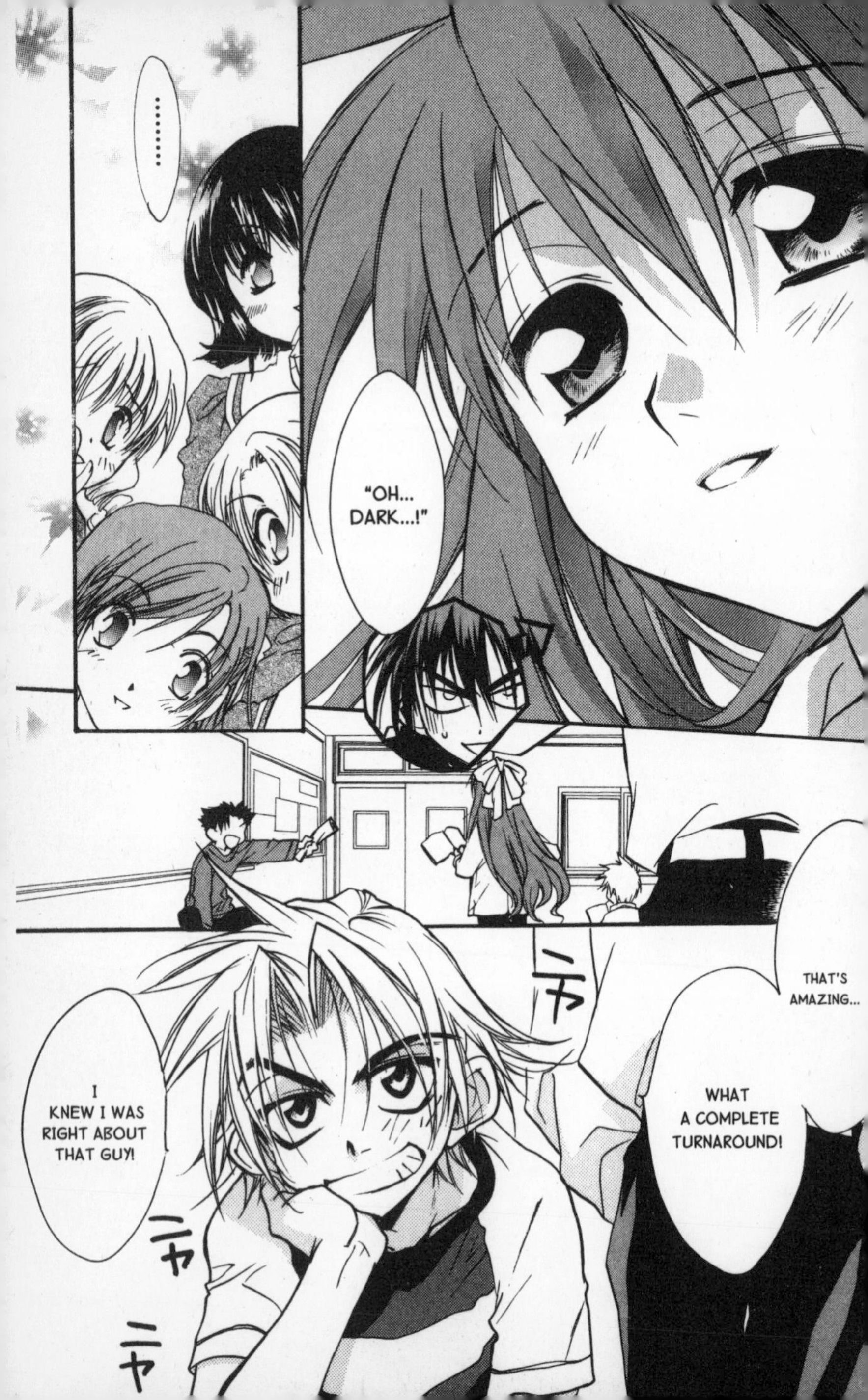
"OH... DARK...!"
......
ニヤ
THAT'S AMAZING...
WHAT A COMPLETE TURNAROUND!
ニヤ
ニヤ
I KNEW I WAS RIGHT ABOUT THAT GUY!

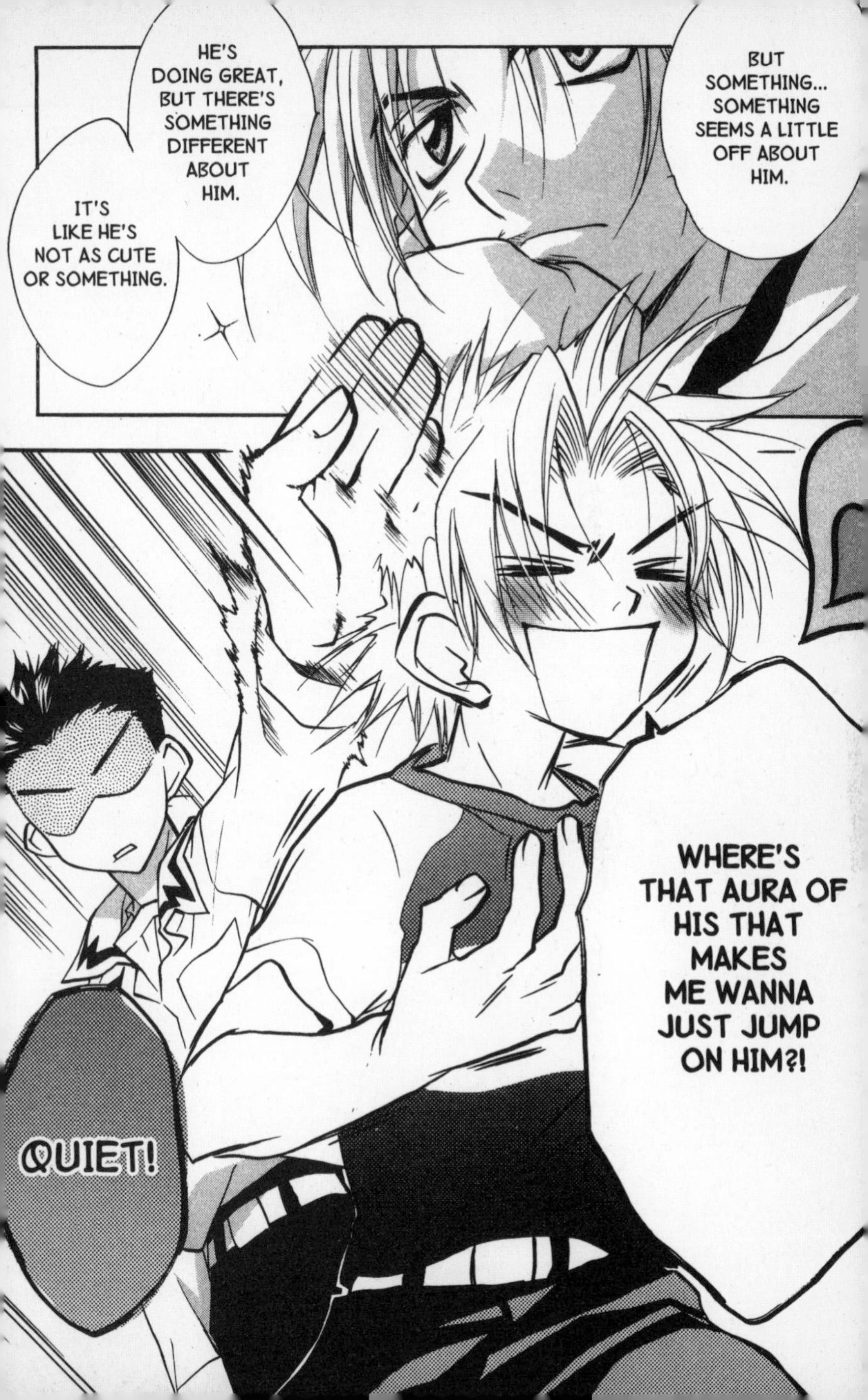
BUT SOMETHING... SOMETHING SEEMS A LITTLE OFF ABOUT HIM.
HE'S DOING GREAT, BUT THERE'S SOMETHING DIFFERENT ABOUT HIM.
IT'S LIKE HE'S NOT AS CUTE OR SOMETHING.
WHERE'S THAT AURA OF HIS THAT MAKES ME WANNA JUST JUMP ON HIM?!
QUIET!

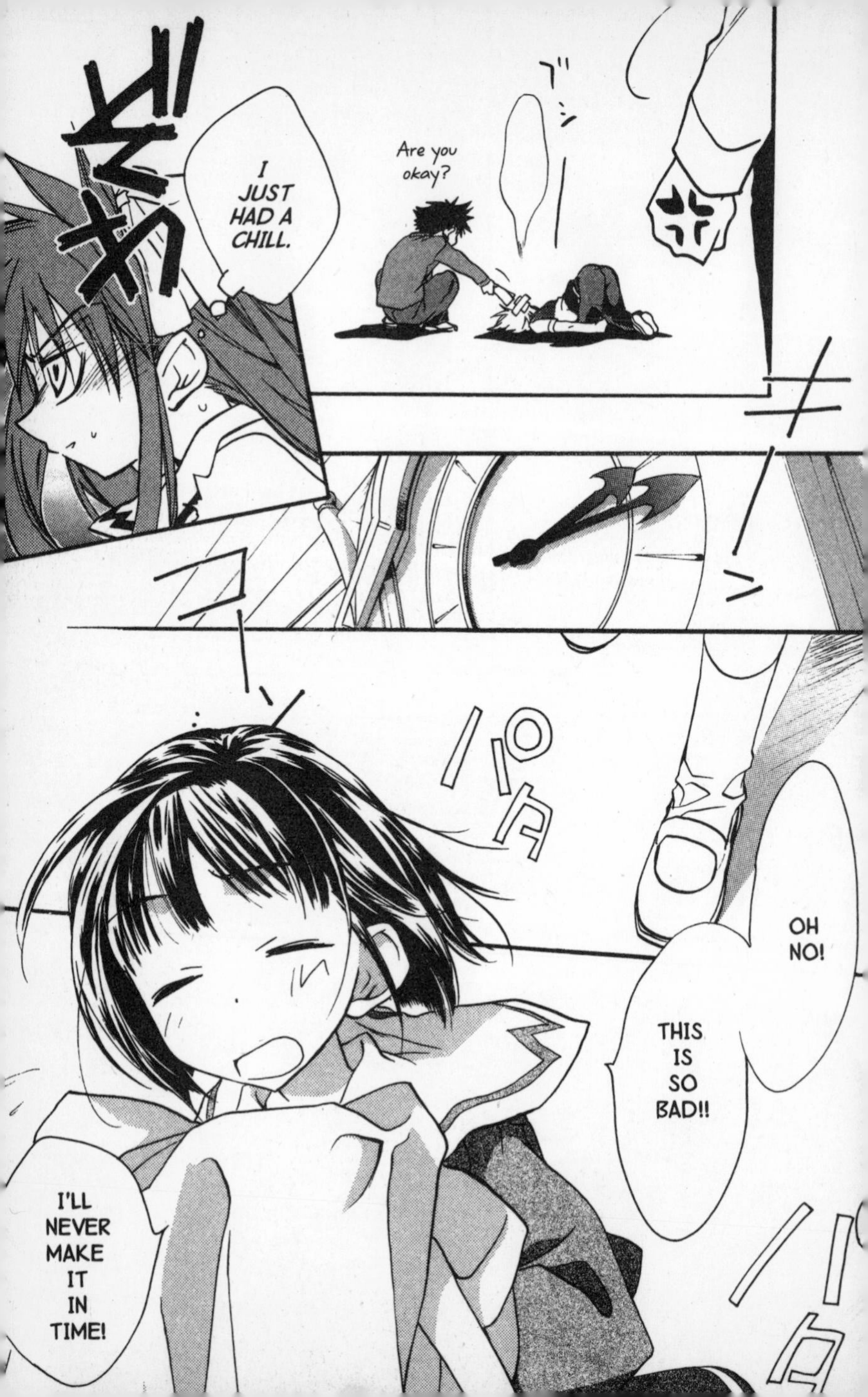
Are you okay?
I JUST HAD A CHILL.
OH NO!
THIS IS SO BAD!!
I'LL NEVER MAKE IT IN TIME!

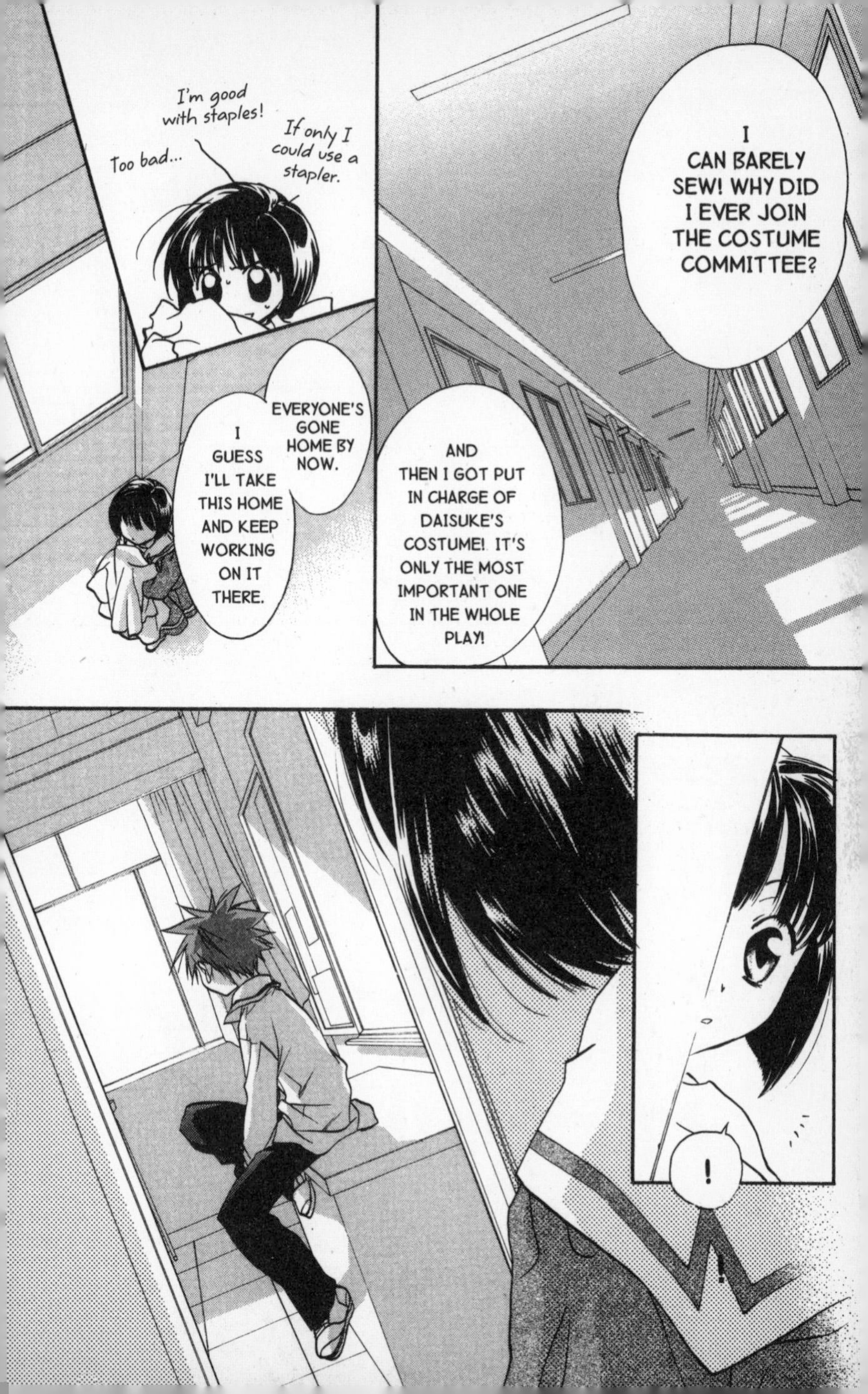
I CAN BARELY SEW! WHY DID I EVER JOIN THE COSTUME COMMITTEE?
AND THEN I GOT PUT IN CHARGE OF DAISUKE'S COSTUME! IT'S ONLY THE MOST IMPORTANT ONE IN THE WHOLE PLAY!
If only I could use a stapler.
I'm good with staples!
Too bad...
EVERYONE'S GONE HOME BY NOW.
I GUESS I'LL TAKE THIS HOME AND KEEP WORKING ON IT THERE.
!
!

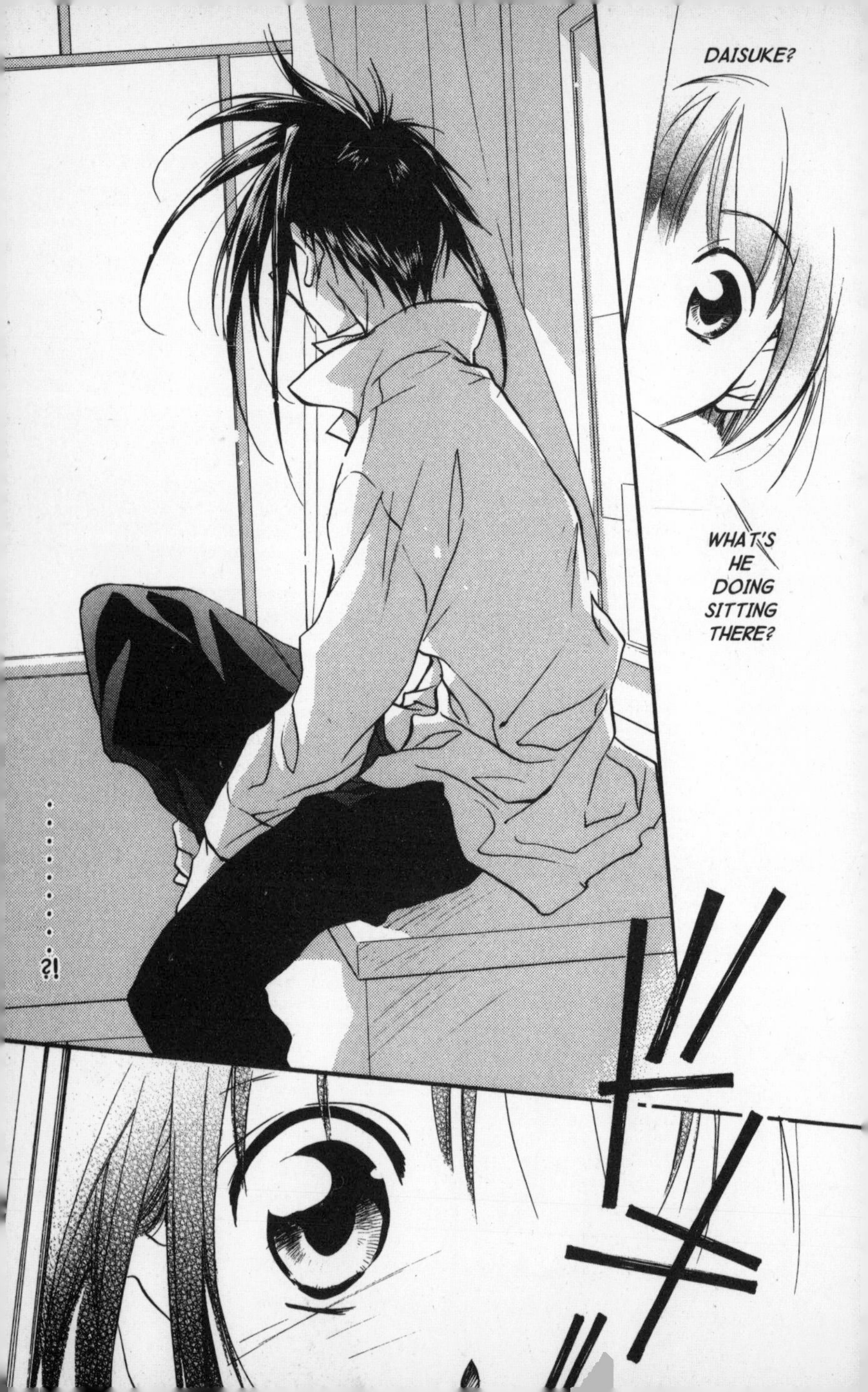

DAISUKE?
WHAT'S HE DOING SITTING THERE?
..........?!

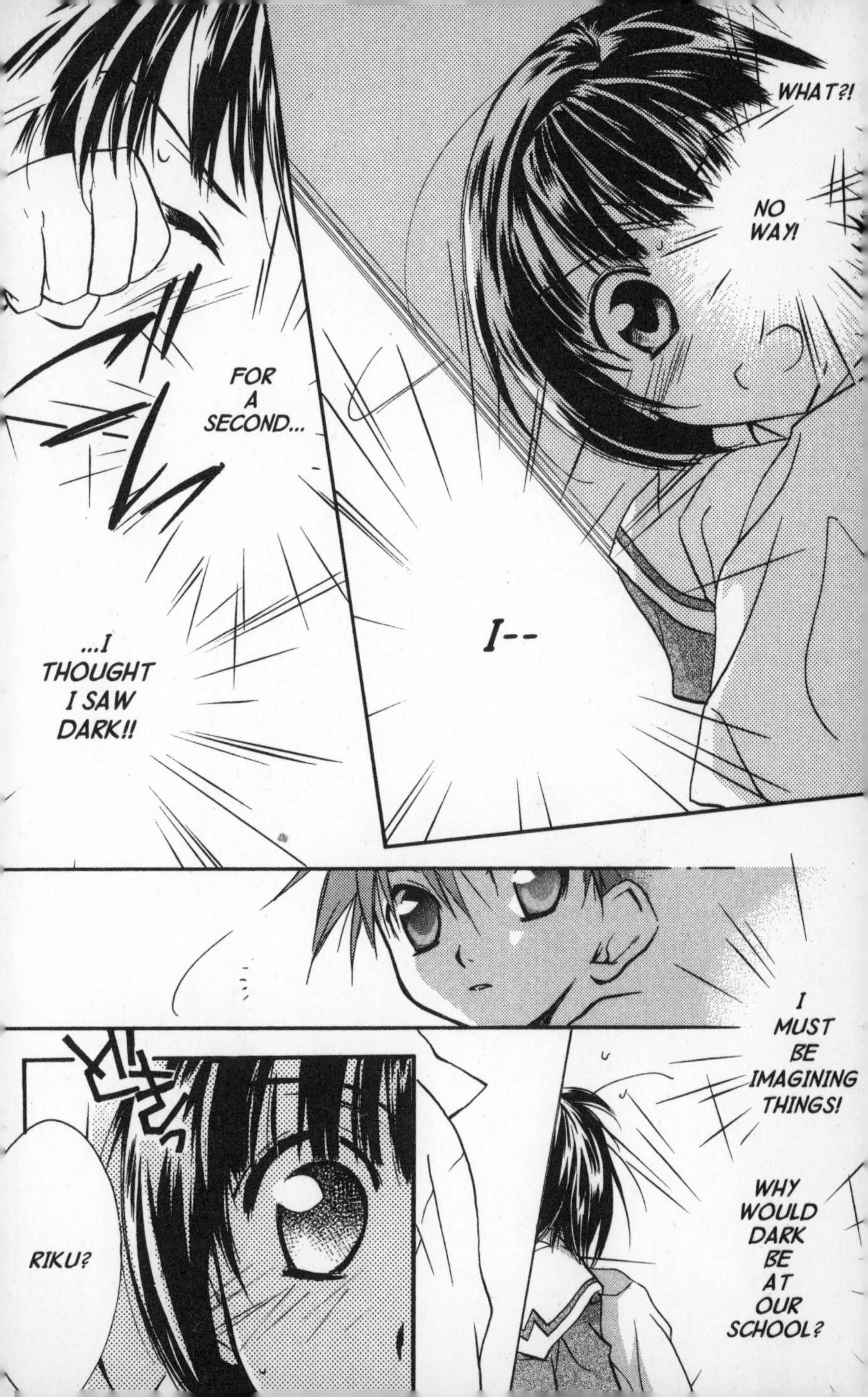
WHAT?!
NO WAY!
I--
FOR A SECOND...
...I THOUGHT I SAW DARK!!
I MUST BE IMAGINING THINGS!
WHY WOULD DARK BE AT OUR SCHOOL?
RIKU?

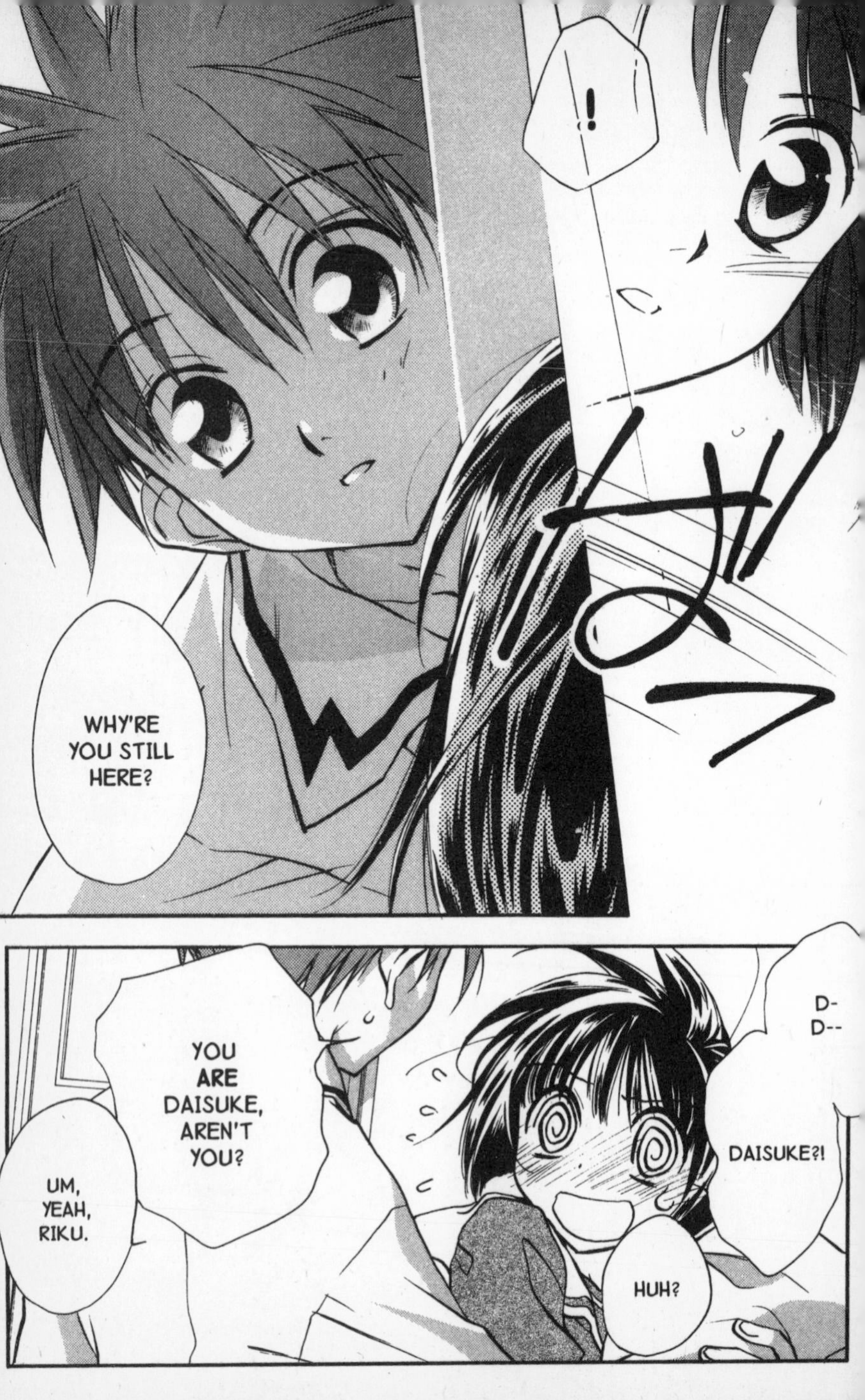
!
WHY'RE YOU STILL HERE?
D- D-- DAISUKE?!
HUH?
YOU **ARE** DAISUKE, AREN'T YOU?
UM, YEAH, RIKU.

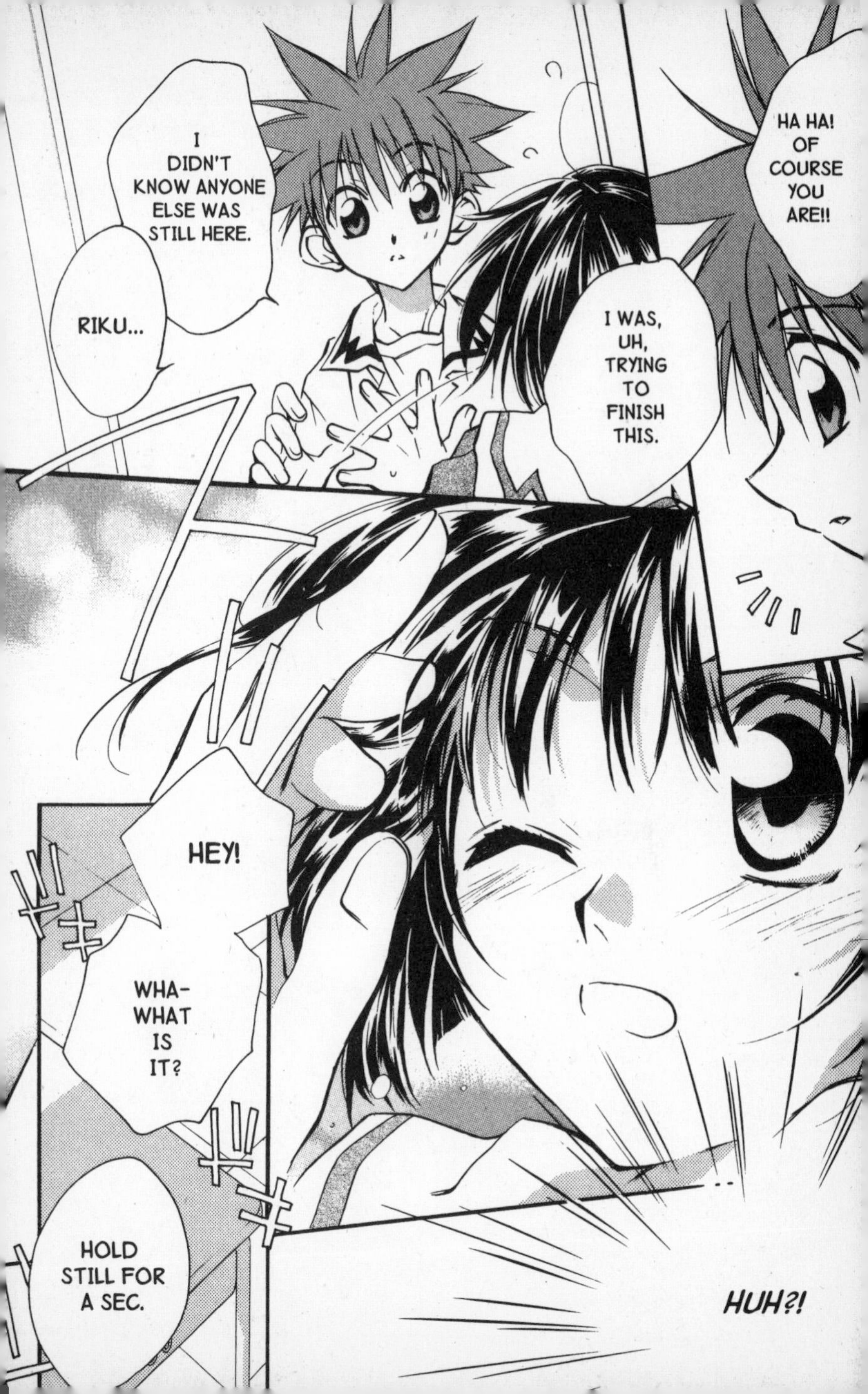
RIKU...
I DIDN'T KNOW ANYONE ELSE WAS STILL HERE.
I WAS, UH, TRYING TO FINISH THIS.
HA HA! OF COURSE YOU ARE!!
HEY!
WHA-WHAT IS IT?
HOLD STILL FOR A SEC.
HUH?!

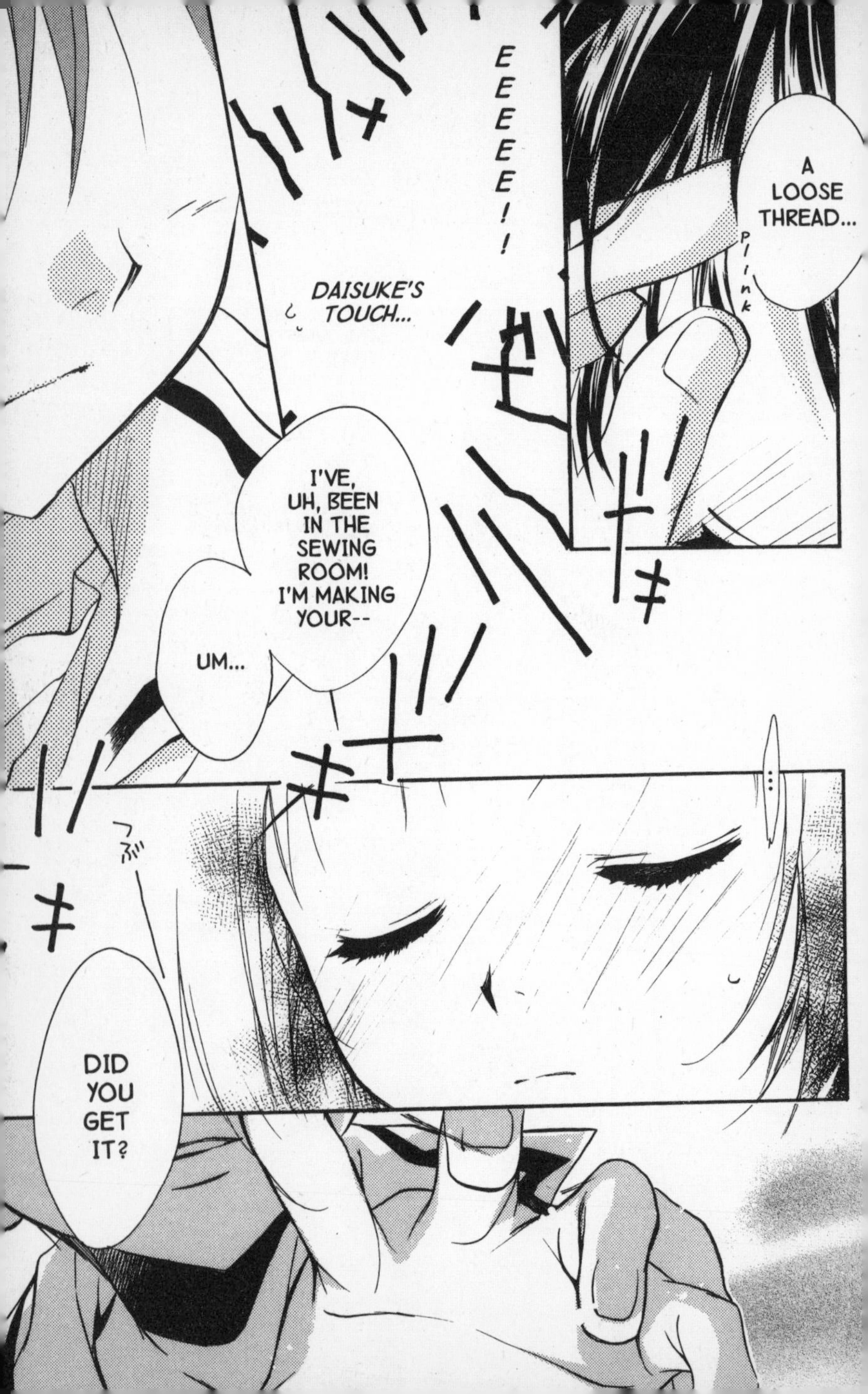
A LOOSE THREAD...
Plink
EEEEEE!!
DAISUKE'S TOUCH...
I'VE, UH, BEEN IN THE SEWING ROOM! I'M MAKING YOUR--
UM...
DID YOU GET IT?

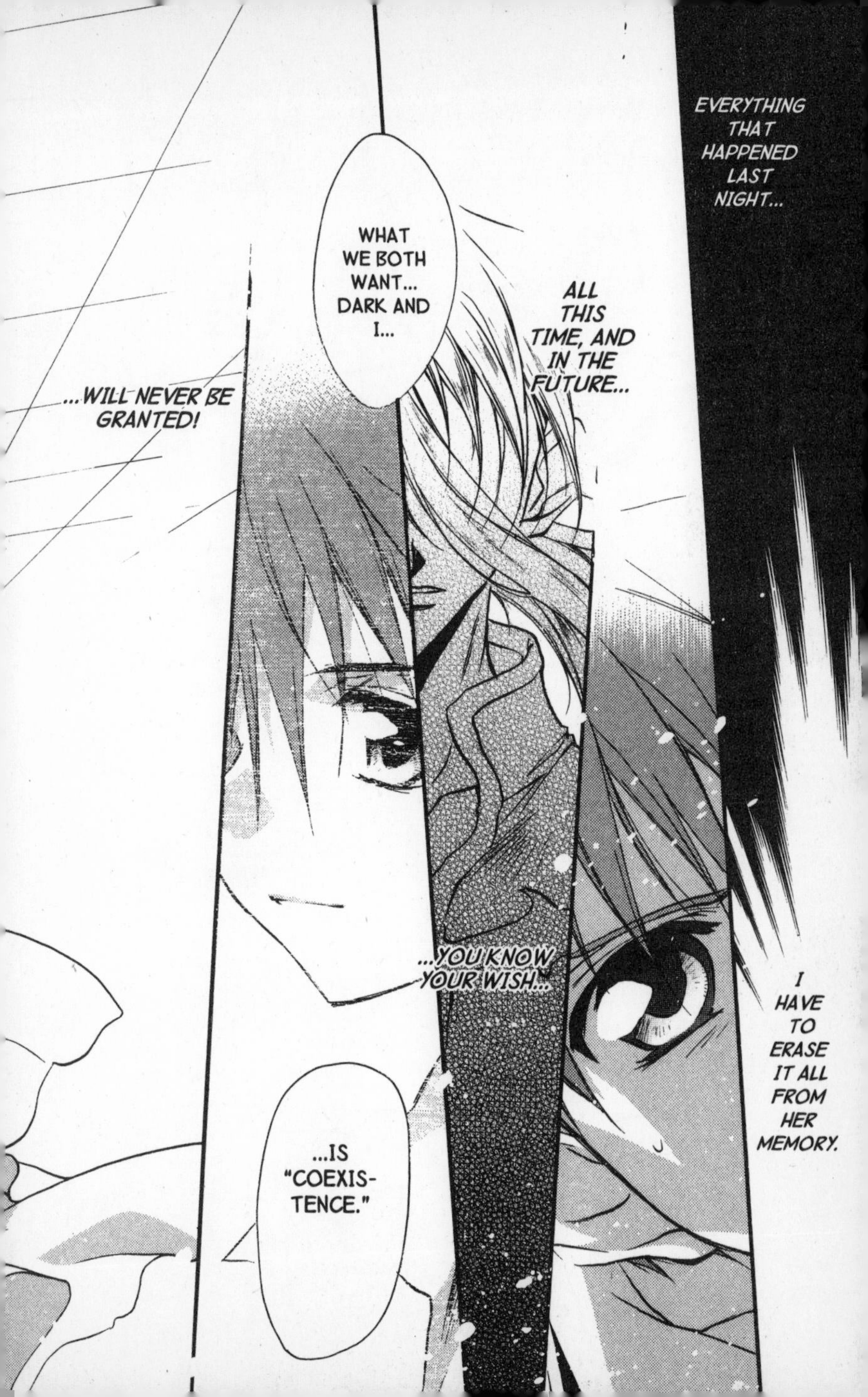
EVERYTHING THAT HAPPENED LAST NIGHT...
I HAVE TO ERASE IT ALL FROM HER MEMORY.
ALL THIS TIME, AND IN THE FUTURE...
...YOU KNOW YOUR WISH...
WHAT WE BOTH WANT... DARK AND I...
...IS "COEXISTENCE."
...WILL NEVER BE GRANTED!

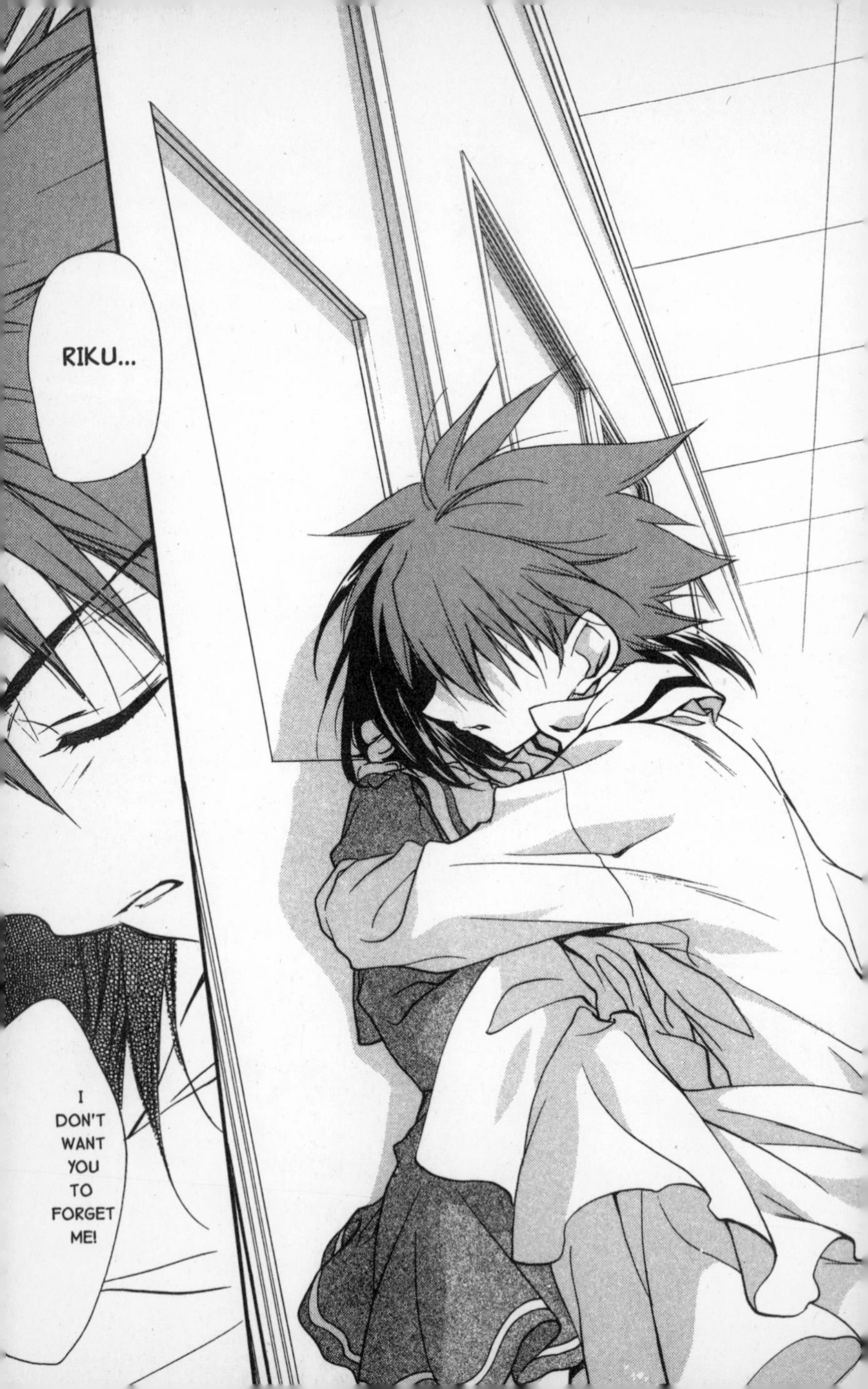
RIKU...
I DON'T WANT YOU TO FORGET ME!

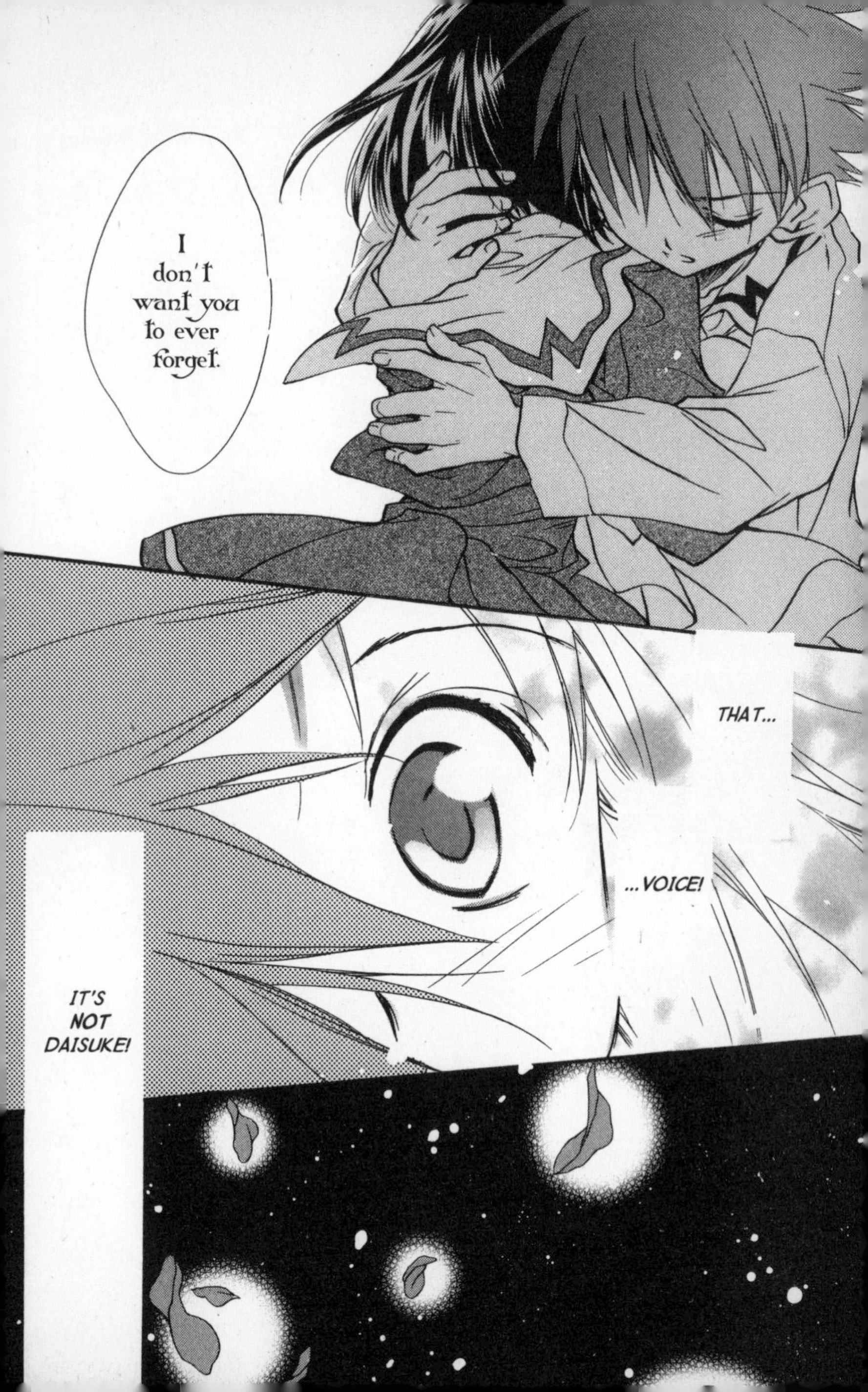
I don't want you to ever forget.
THAT...
...VOICE!
IT'S NOT DAISUKE!

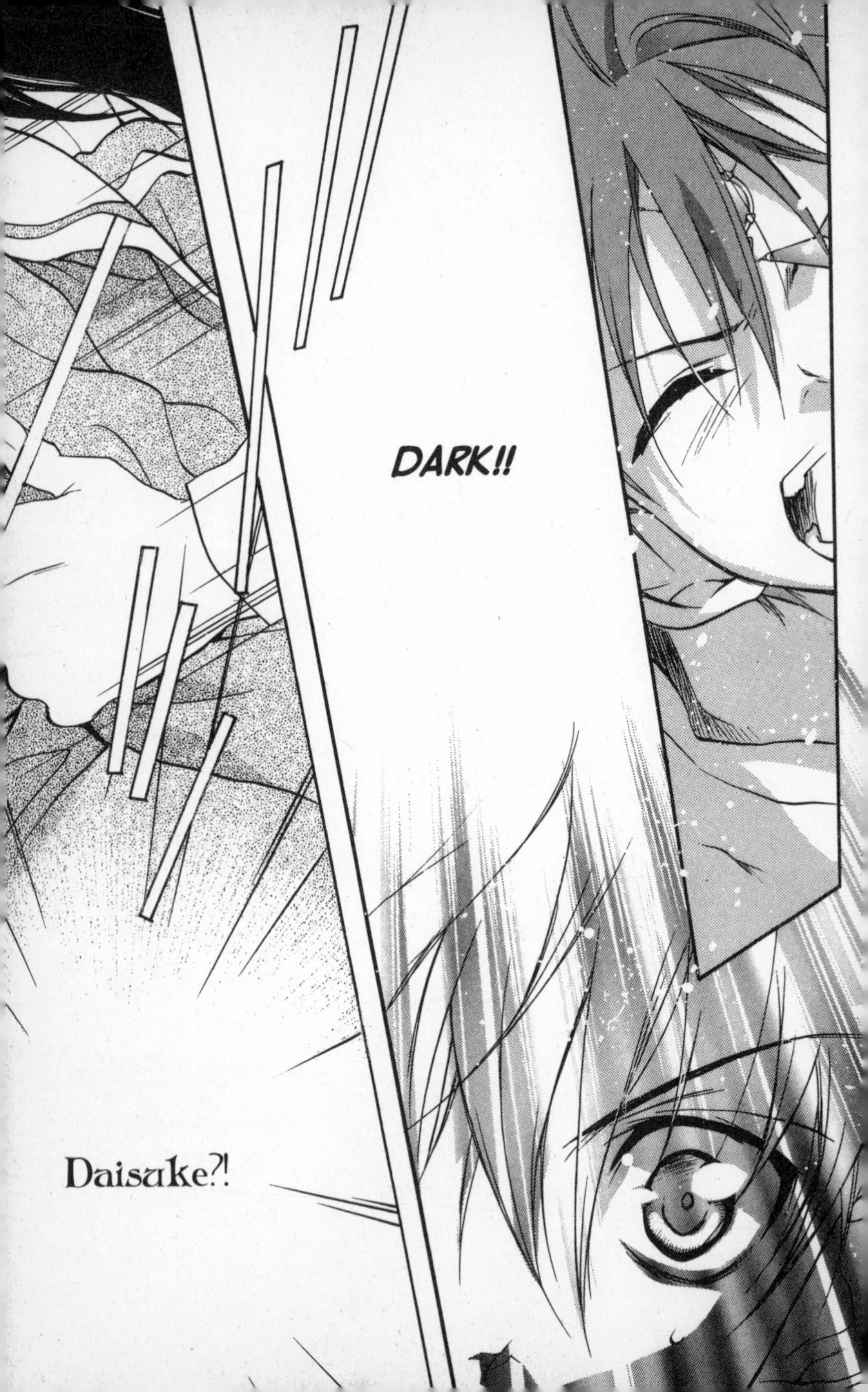
DARK!!
Daisuke?!

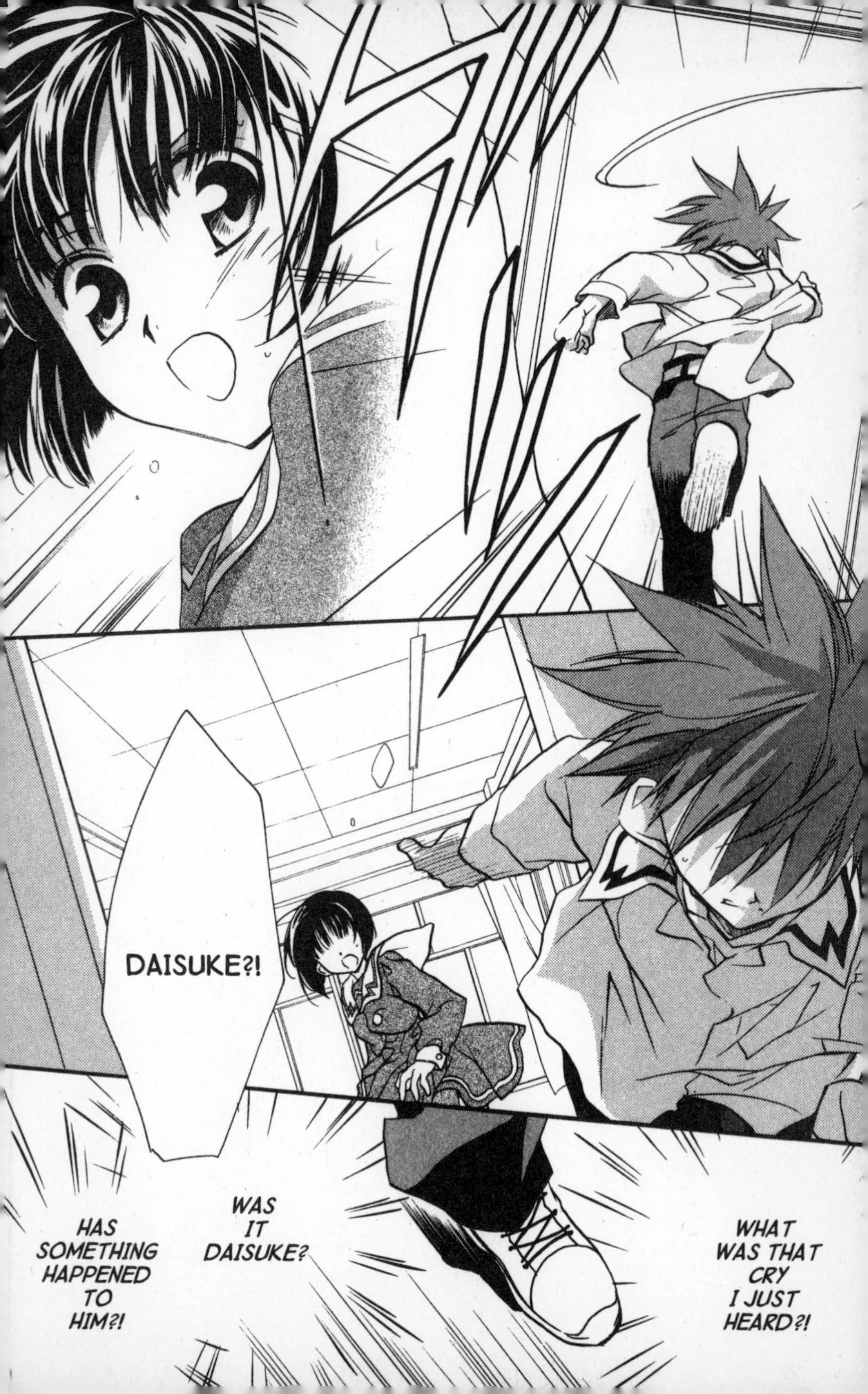
DAISUKE?!
WHAT WAS THAT CRY I JUST HEARD?!
WAS IT DAISUKE?
HAS SOMETHING HAPPENED TO HIM?!

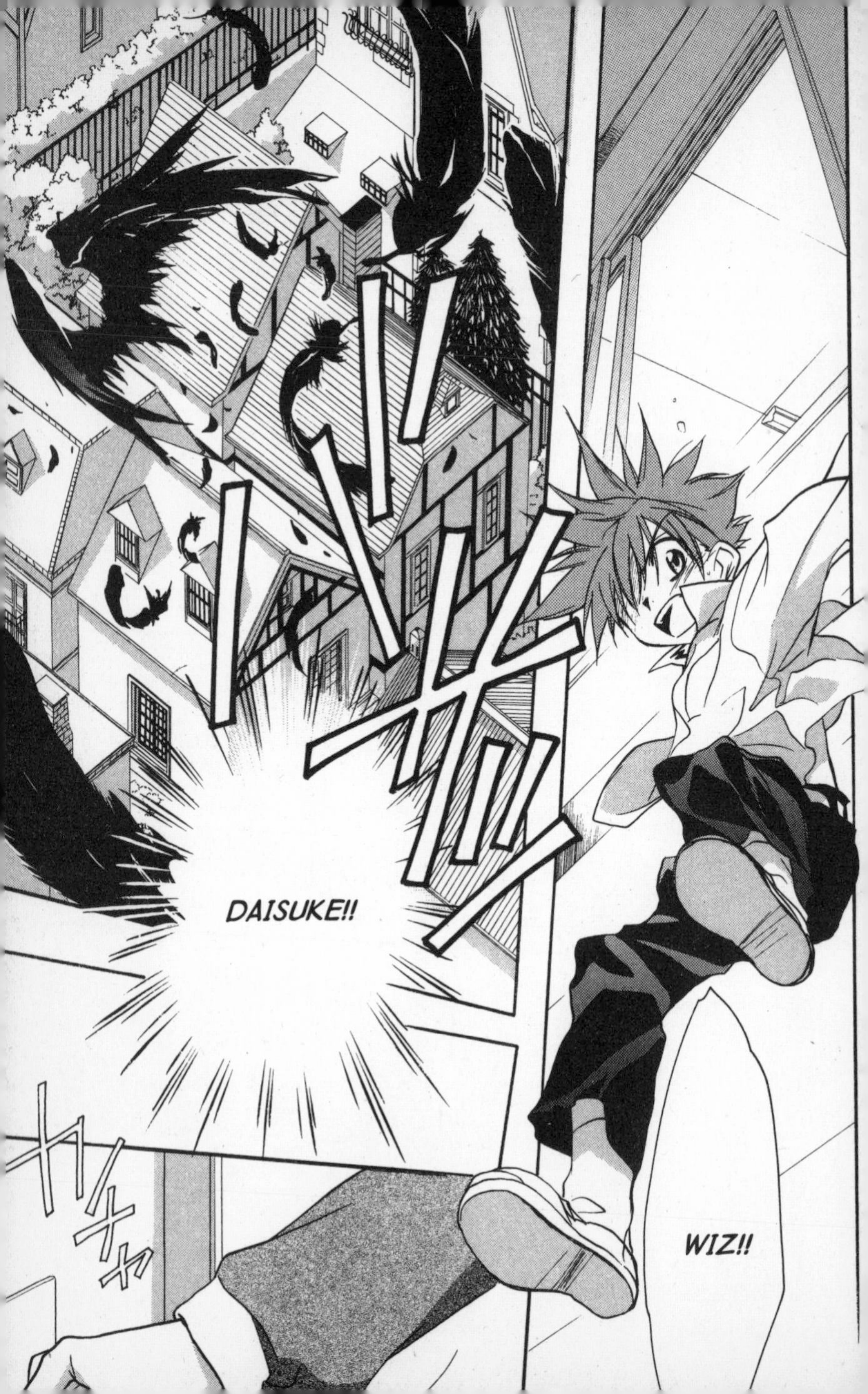
DAISUKE!!
WIZ!!

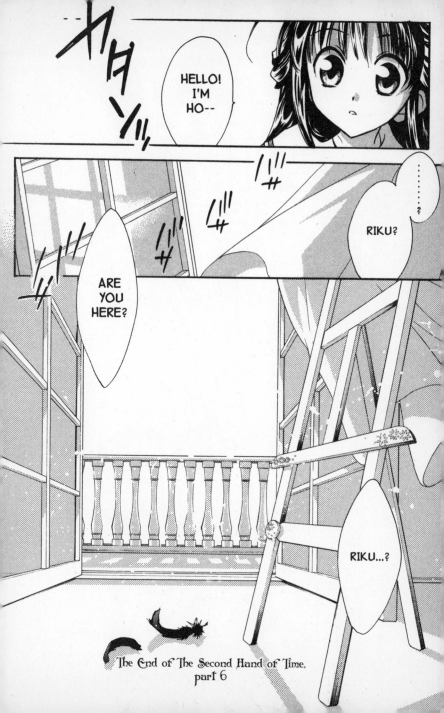

HELLO! I'M HO--

RIKU?

ARE YOU HERE?

RIKU...?

The End of The Second Hand of Time, part 6

Messed up from struggling

T-shirt showing
through

Dark's Complaint

So...
I've been wanting to say this...
When we turn into my body, my clothes...
Here.
Here.
And here...
They get way too small and tight.
'Cause they're yours!
WELL, SORRY I'M SO MUCH SMALLER THAN YOU!
But the tightest part of all is right-
AAAGH!!!
DON'T BE DISGUSTING!!
Don't look at him!!
...ooh...sorry!

BOYS' mini-manga

HANDSOME BOYS

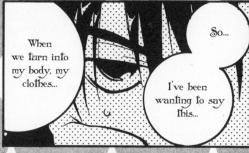

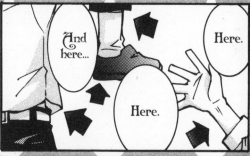

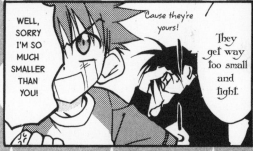

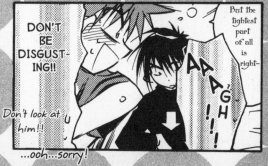

Girls' mini-manga

Riku and Risa

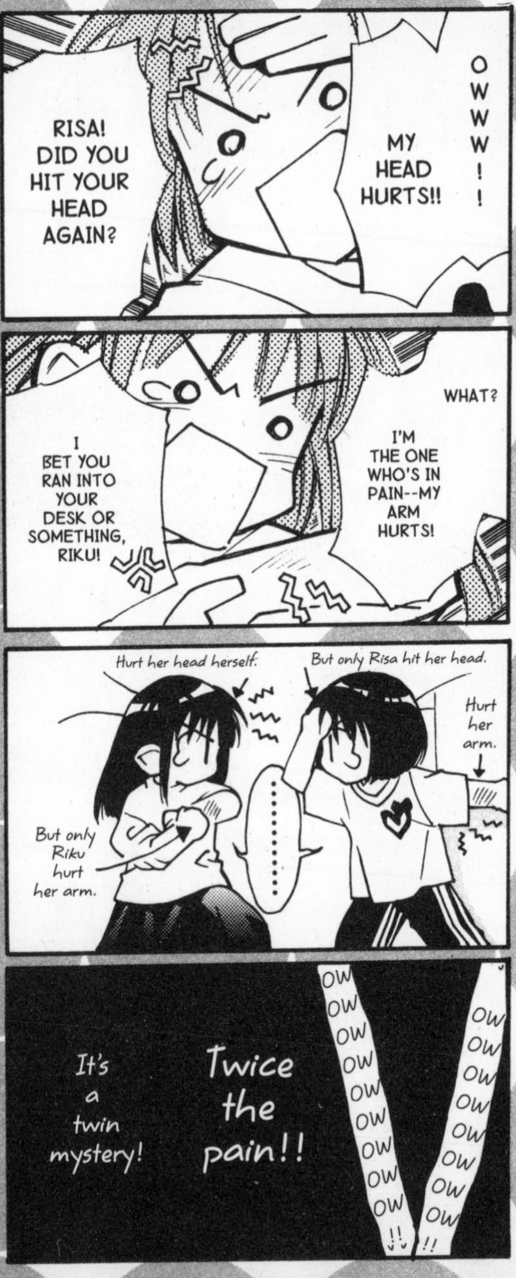
OWWW!!
MY HEAD HURTS!!
RISA! DID YOU HIT YOUR HEAD AGAIN?
WHAT?
I'M THE ONE WHO'S IN PAIN--MY ARM HURTS!
I BET YOU RAN INTO YOUR DESK OR SOMETHING, RIKU!
But only Risa hit her head.
Hurt her arm.
Hurt her head herself.
......
But only Riku hurt her arm.
OW OW OW OW OW OW OW OW !!
OW OW OW OW OW OW OW OW OW !!
Twice the pain!!
It's a twin mystery!

GIRLS CUTE

One Magic Night

Fan Art Gallery

Thanks for all the fun postcards you've sent me!! Here are some of my favorite drawings of yours in this fan art gallery!

Mika Hiromatsu Fukuoka Prefecture

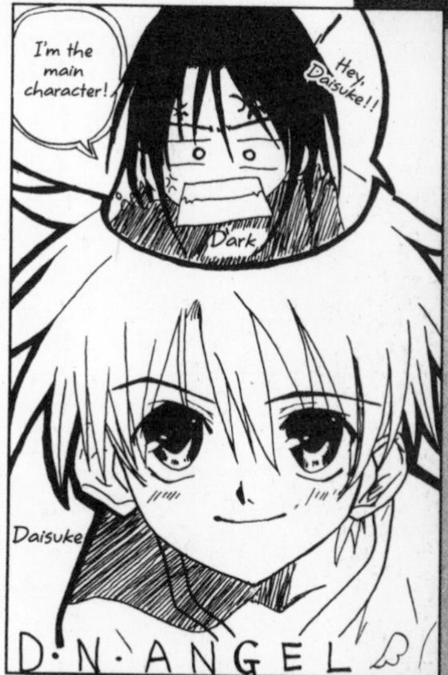
I'm the main character!
Hey, Daisuke!!
Dark
Daisuke
D·N·ANGEL

Kiri Futaba Miyazaki Prefecture

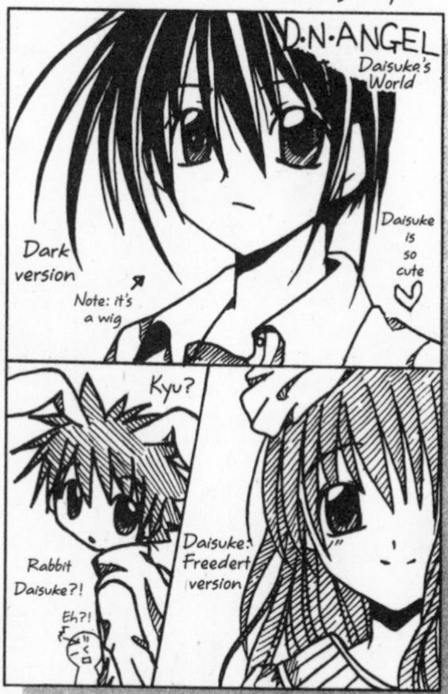
D·N·ANGEL
Daisuke's World
Dark version
Note: it's a wig
Daisuke is so cute
Kyu?
Rabbit Daisuke?!
Eh?!
Daisuke: Freedert version

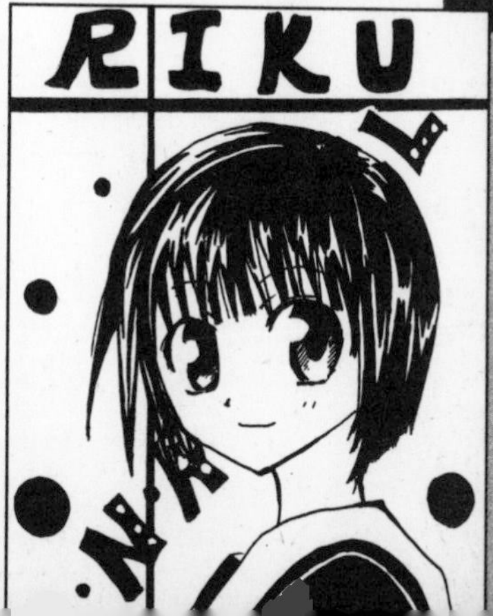
RIKU

Yukie Akagawa Niigata Prefecture

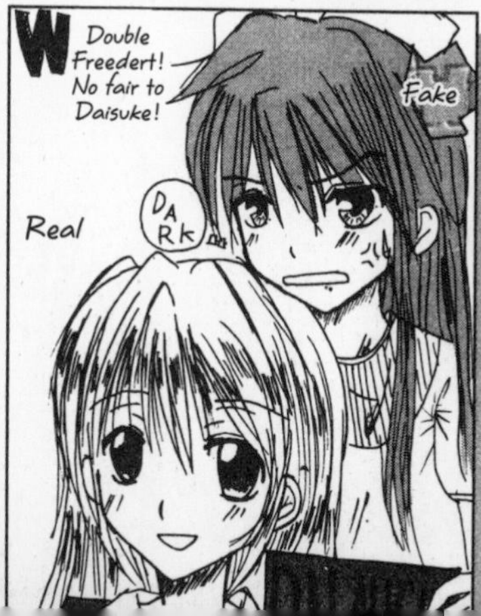
W
Double Freedert! No fair to Daisuke!
Fake
DARK
Real

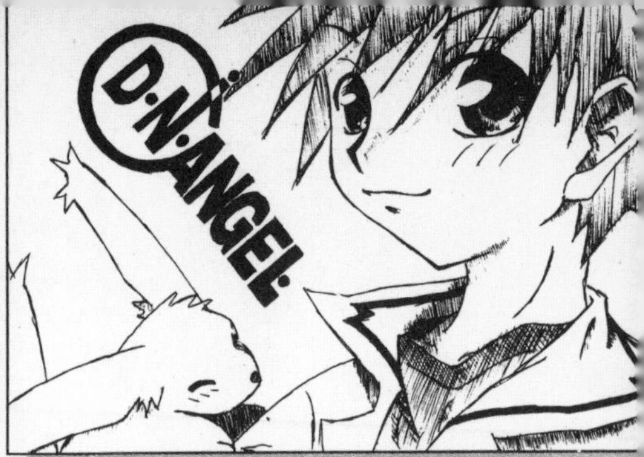
D.N.ANGEL

▲ "Krad" - Shizuoka Prefecture

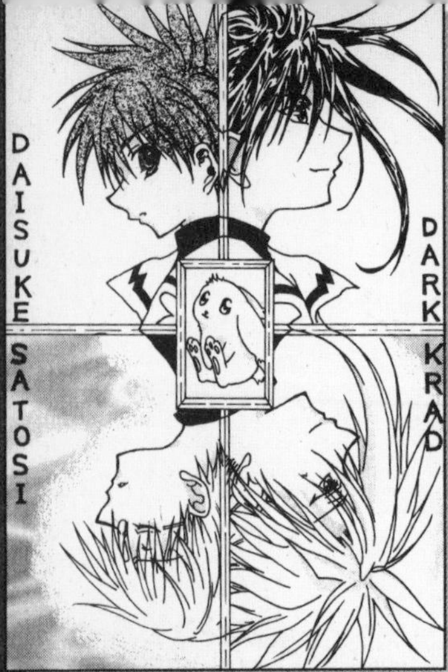
DAISUKE SATOSI
DARK KRAD

▲Ichigo Sawamura - Ibaraki Prefecture

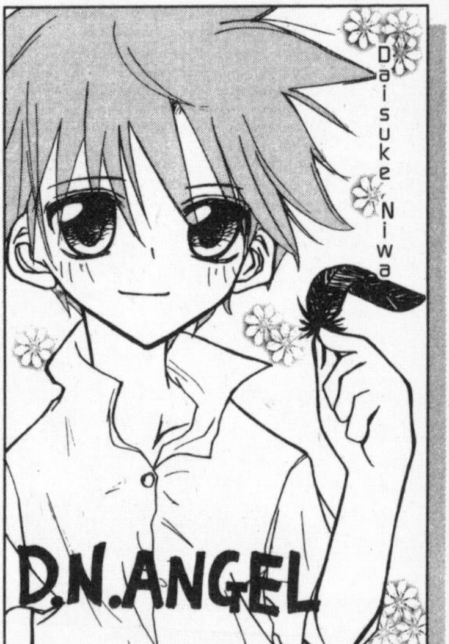
Daisuke Niwa
D.N.ANGEL

▶ Izumiko Katori Tochigi Prefecture

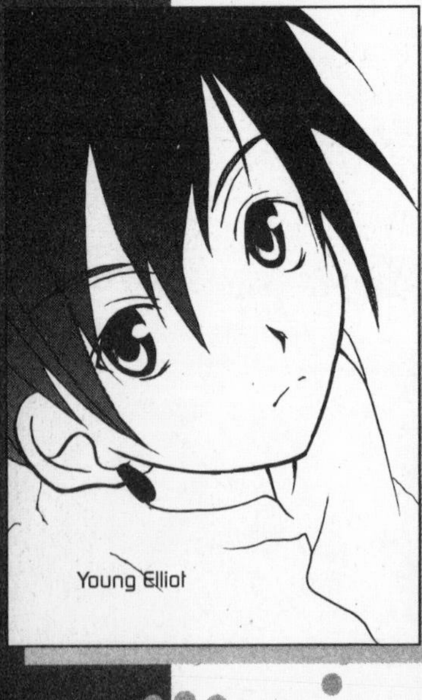
Young Elliot

◀ "Uchu" Niigata Prefecture

▼ "Aa-chin" - Wakayama Prefecture

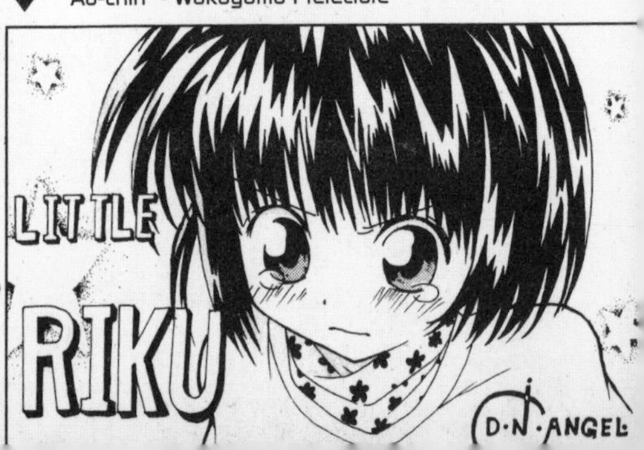
LITTLE
RIKU
D·N·ANGEL

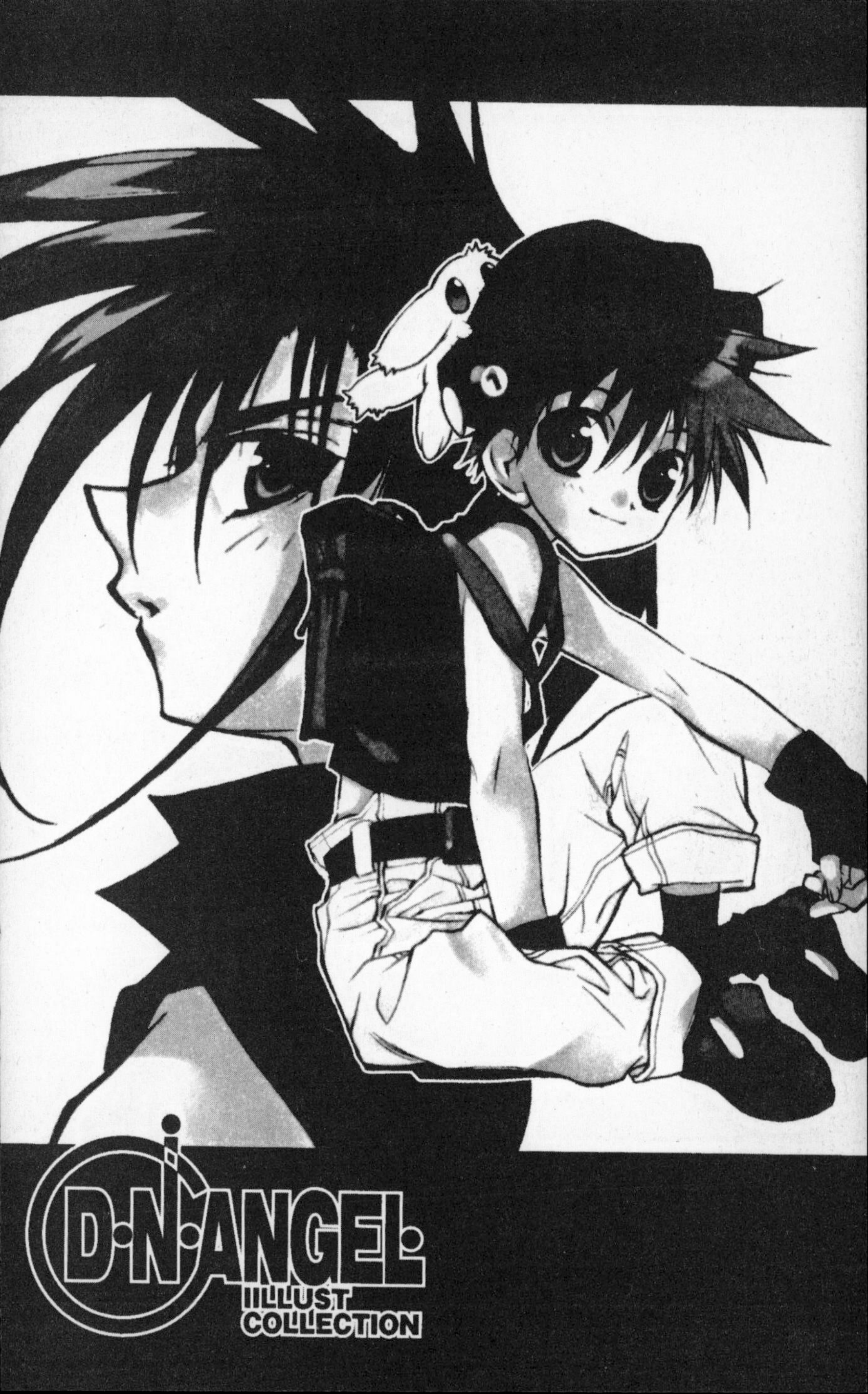
D·N·ANGEL
ILLUST
COLLECTION

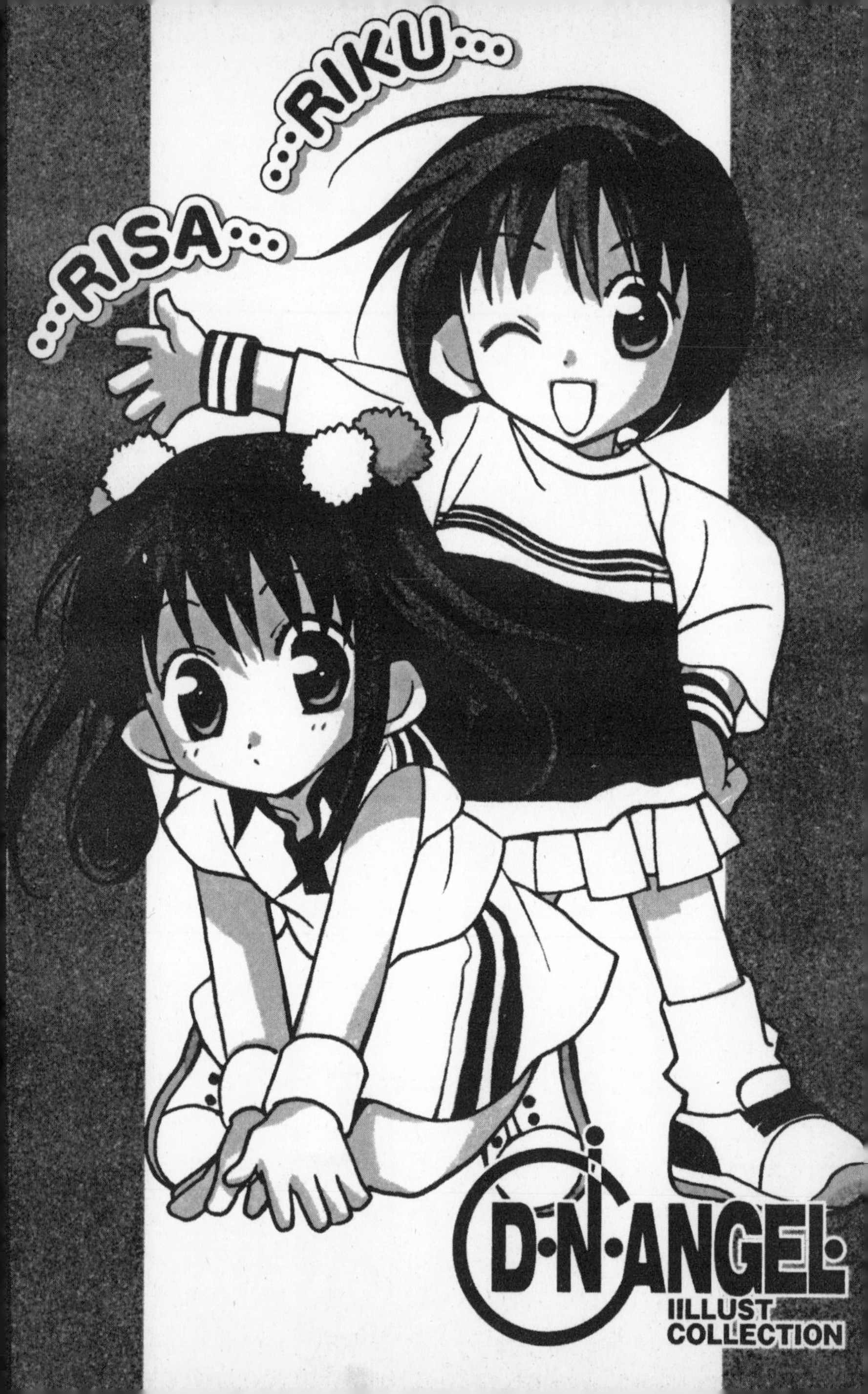

...RISA...
...RIKU...
D·N·ANGEL
ILLUST COLLECTION

D·N·AN〔
IILLU
COLL

D•N•ANGEL
THINGS TO COME...

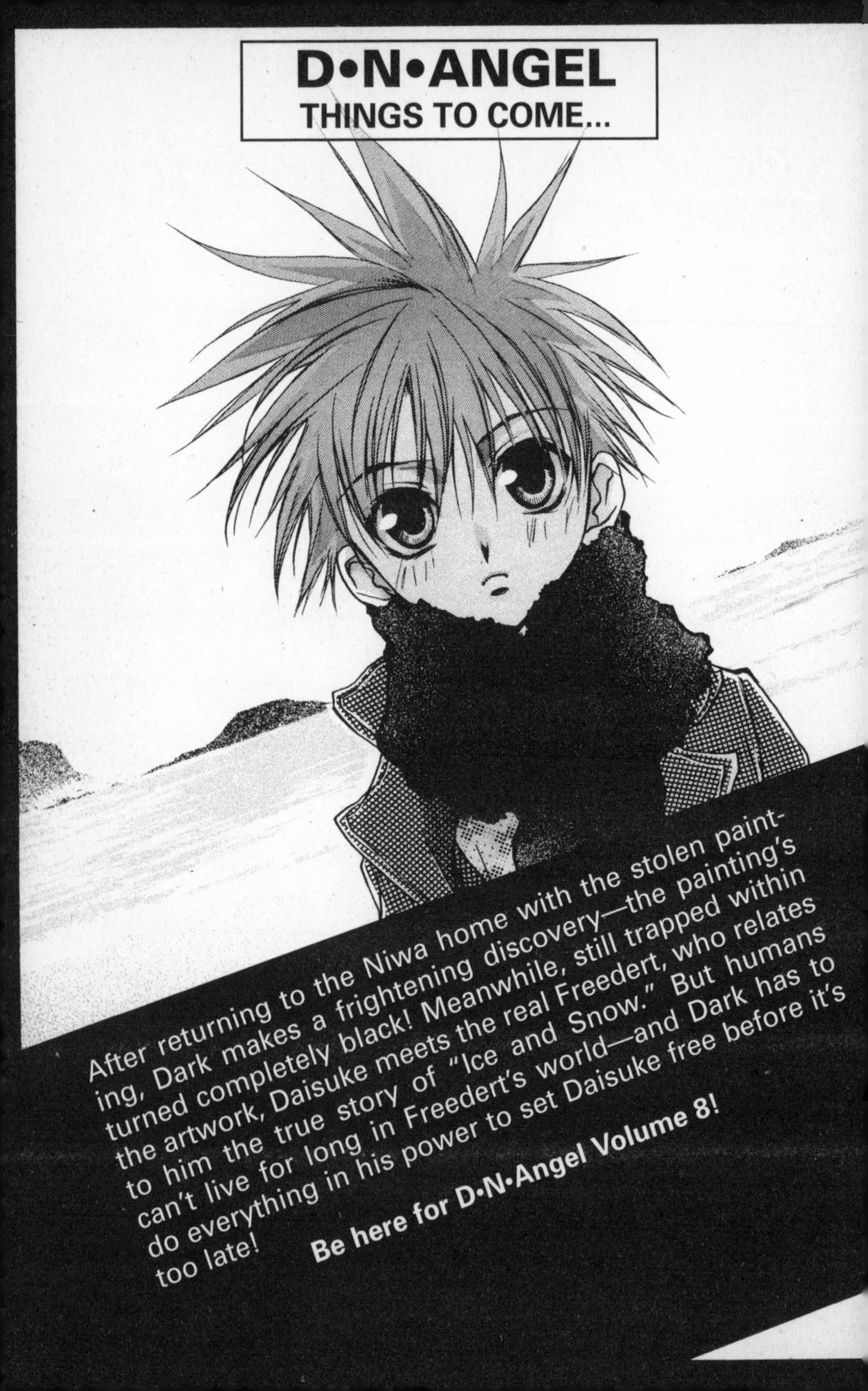

After returning to the Niwa home with the stolen painting, Dark makes a frightening discovery—the painting's turned completely black! Meanwhile, still trapped within the artwork, Daisuke meets the real Freedert, who relates to him the true story of "Ice and Snow." But humans can't live for long in Freedert's world—and Dark has to do everything in his power to set Daisuke free before it's too late!

Be here for D•N•Angel Volume 8!

TOKYOPOP SHOP

WWW.TOKYOPOP.COM/SHOP

HOT NEWS!
Check out
TOKYOPOP.COM/SHOP
The world's best
collection of manga in
English is now available
online in one place!

SOKORA REFUGEES

PLANET BLOOD

THE TAROT CAFÉ

WWW.TOKYOPOP.COM/SHOP

0 00000 00000 0

- LOOK FOR SPECIAL OFFERS
- PRE-ORDER UPCOMING RELEASES!
- COMPLETE YOUR COLLECTIONS